ELEGY OF THE FALLEN SWORDS

SONG OF THE FALLEN SWORDS
BOOK 5

RYAN KIRK

WATERSTONE
MEDIA

RYAN KIRK

ELEGY OF THE FALLEN SWORDS

To Paul,

One of the two best-looking redheaded men found across the land

PROLOGUE

The knowledge that Nightkeep's Singers gladly ferried him toward their doom never ceased to bring the ghost of a smile to the Seer's lips. That they performed the deed with such precision only sweetened the secret hatred he held deep in his heart. Though they flew over the forbidden zone, pursued by the unforeseen consequences of the Seer's actions, Nightkeep's experienced Singers still brought the enormous floating city to a halt so gently a glass filled to the brim with water wouldn't have spilled a single drop. They might be shortsighted, destructive fools, but they knew their work.

He stood at the fence that marked the safe border of Nightkeep's expansive surface. Belzrak, leader of one of the shadow tribes, stood beside him, silent and thoughtful. Together, they stared at the surface below, a mountainous land of jagged granite, snow-capped peaks that blinded the eye when the sun broke through the clouds, and dark forests that marched up the sides of the mountains like a relentless army, desperate to reach the inhospitable summits. Belzrak, who guarded his words tighter than the clans guarded their precious secrets, said nothing of the sight.

"I can sense its presence clearly from here," the Seer said, attempting to bait the quiet leader into a revealing conversation.

Belzrak only grunted and nodded, as though the Seer were a child stating the obvious and attempting to pass it off as wisdom.

The Seer didn't give in to the frustration Belzrak so readily inspired. "How many warriors will we need, do you think?"

Faced with a direct question, Belzrak's sense of honor compelled him to respond. "None. We descend alone."

The Seer wasn't given a chance to express his disbelief.

"If you two think I'll let you go down there alone, you're even greater fools than I thought."

The Seer startled at the proximity of the voice, but Belzrak didn't so much as blink. The leader of the surface tribe was old enough to have gray streaks in his hair, but his senses remained as sharp as the blades of shadow he effortlessly formed.

Lynae, the Blade of Nightkeep, stepped between them. The force of her presence loomed over them, though she was shorter and smaller than either man. She was much younger than her unlikely companions, and it would have been easy to underestimate her, but such a mistake would have been the Seer's last. Besides being one of the most skilled and dangerous Manirah in the world, she possessed a quick and discerning mind that the Seer respected even as he conspired against it.

It was the clan warriors who always gave him trouble. Singers, who so easily lost themselves in theories and ideas, bent more easily to his manipulations, but those Manirah who lived and died by their maniblades were harder to persuade. Like the Singers, they perceived the Song in their spirits, but their survival hinged upon their ability to perceive reality accurately. They weren't so easily swayed by ideas that contradicted their experience.

The Seer addressed his question to Belzrak. "In this, I agree with the Blade. Wouldn't it be prudent to bring more warriors? Defeating the guardians of the last shrine was a bloody affair."

Belzrak pointed to the mountains, in the general direction the Seer sensed the shrine to be. "Even if I agreed, we don't field enough warriors. This is the oldest of the shrines, and the tribe that guards it possesses numbers all other wandering tribes tremble before. These peaks are riddled with caves and tunnels that would drive any cartographer mad. Any attempt to capture the shrine would cost many lives and end in failure."

The tribal leader interrupted Lynae's objection before she voiced it. "I mean no disrespect, Blade. It is not a judgment of the quality of your warriors, but of the enormity of the task."

Lynae was mollified, and Belzrak continued. "More to the point, there is no need to draw our weapons against one another. The situation has changed. You, my friend, have made your abilities known. The tribe will recognize your right to the shrine. You sing with the shadow like none since she who first gifted us the ability to control it."

Praise rarely dripped from Belzrak's lips, and his words were sweeter than honey.

Lynae wasn't so easily persuaded. "That's no reason not to bring a protective force. Even a squad or two of Swords might make a difference."

"Any show of force, especially from you, will be construed as hostility," Belzrak said.

Lynae remained unmoved, so Belzrak added, "Besides,

if we descend alone into a trap, you're not losing anyone but me and him."

The Blade, who considered the Seer more a wound in her side than an ally, readily saw the wisdom in that argument. After a moment's deliberation, she said, "Fine, but I'm joining you, too. Someone needs to protect Nightkeep's interests."

So their party was set at three, and they prepared for their journey to the surface.

Semuel, Nightkeep's Elder, met them at the Nest as Lynae connected to a dragon that would deliver them to the surface. "The nuddu isn't much more than a day behind us. The Engines, thankfully, remain stable."

"Did the scouts spot any signs of habitation?" Lynae asked.

"They reported none," Semuel answered, and Lynae's face fell.

It was pride alone that led Lynae to believe that her scouts would somehow discover a people who'd learned to live in the forbidden zone, a people for whom silence and camouflage were the basic ingredients of survival. The surface tribes lived like ghosts, for such a life was the only way to avoid becoming one.

The nuddu's continued pursuit, too, came as no surprise, though its initial arrival had been.

The Seer had mistakenly believed all the nuddu had fled the forbidden zone after he'd torn the bars of their cage down, but at least one had remained, and it had caught Nightkeep's scent. Without a shrine, the Seer could do nothing to deter it, and so its sudden arrival had only bolstered Semuel's resolve to deliver the Seer to a new shrine as quickly as possible.

As he often did, the Seer sensed the work of the shadow song. What else explained the extraordinarily convenient timing of the nuddu's arrival? Instead of endless debates with Nightkeep's council, the nuddu encouraged Semuel to order the Singers on their current path.

Lynae climbed onto the dragon first, followed by the Seer and Belzrak. Semuel wished them luck as the dragon walked to the edge of Nightkeep and jumped off. The Seer's heart stuck in his throat and his stomach performed somersaults as they fell, and he silently cursed Lynae, who knew he no longer liked flying. There was no need for such a vigorous descent.

The dragon spread its wings and leveled off, but the Seer's heart and stomach continued to dance to a beat over which he had no control. Belzrak, unbothered by the flight though he'd spent almost his entire life on the surface, pointed Lynae in the direction they should go.

The Seer's heart didn't return to its normal pace until they had landed and he was off the dragon's back. Belzrak's directions had brought them to a flat outcropping of rock. A close examination of their surroundings left the Seer confused, for he saw no trace of a trail, nor a cave opening that would lead him to the shrine. He sensed its dark presence within the mountain, but short of tunneling through countless tons of rock, he had no idea how to reach it.

Lynae's dragon returned to Nightkeep to wait for further instructions. It leaped into the sky and left them alone on the barren mountainside. Belzrak looked pleased with the situation, and he led them higher up the mountainside.

If the tribal leader followed a trail, the Seer could discern no sign of it. They scrambled up slopes steep enough to require the use of their hands, then followed a route so narrow the Seer shuffled sideways to prevent dropping into a crevice from which there would be no rescue. The Seer huffed and groaned as they gained elevation. His knees complained and his thighs burned. Sweat dripped into his eyes and his tongue stuck to the roof of his mouth.

His companions didn't even have the decency to break a sweat. They would climb for a bit, then wait for him to catch up, admiring the vistas the elevation unlocked. Once he rejoined them, they'd leave again, giving him no chance to catch his breath.

Let them enjoy their views. His imagination filled with thoughts of revenge, and those visions gave him the strength to carry on.

So lost in the visions was he that he didn't immediately notice they weren't alone. Lynae and Belzrak had stopped at a boulder, and there was a lean, silver-haired woman there. The sharp angles of her face reminded the Seer of the jagged peaks that surrounded them, and her gray eyes were hard as the granite underfoot. When those eyes turned toward him, it felt like she judged him more a full meal for her tribe than their most powerful ally.

She and Belzrak spoke in the language of the tribes, familiar enough to the Seer's ears that he believed he should be able to follow the conversation, but it had drifted far enough from the language of the cities that his efforts were as doomed to failure as the cities' attempts at survival.

The discussion between the tribal leaders was brief and nearly emotionless. They could have been discussing the weather or exchanging recipes for roasted Seer. In time, Belzrak said, "She would like proof of who you are."

The Seer shot Belzrak an irritated glare. "She doesn't trust your word? We don't have time for this."

"I can no more shift her opinion than I can raise one of these mountains," Belzrak replied.

It occurred to the Seer that the new arrival wasn't the only believer in need of another sign. Belzrak's own daughter had been killed by Radyn in his unexpected raid upon Nightkeep. He still believed in the Seer, but his faith was a fragile construct, liable to collapse if its foundation wasn't repaired.

Most of the displays the Seer knew would fail to impress the surface tribes. They'd been manipulating the shadow song long before he'd grown the first hair on his chin. Alone, there was little he could do that they couldn't. He called upon the shrine buried somewhere in the mountain, hoping his song was strong enough to reach it.

The shadow in his spirit stretched until it brushed against the cube, then took hold of the shrine's power like a lover who feared separation from his beloved. The Seer's grip was weak. He'd originally imagined shaking the mountain, but his control over the shrine's power was too tenuous. He was just as likely to send a boulder crashing down upon them as he was to impress his allies. Instead, he focused the strength of his master and thrust it like a needle into the eye of the heavens.

A lance of shadow exploded from the top of the mountain, drawing every eye upward. It punched a hole through the clouds and into the mysteries beyond, into the darkness between the stars the Seer now knew his distant ancestors had traveled.

He kept the display brief out of necessity. When their hard-nosed guest turned from the fading darkness to the Seer, he swore he glimpsed hope behind the bitter mask she kept locked across her face.

The surface tribes' hatred of the clans was written in their blood and bone. Upon the surface, they spoke of the cowards who deserted the world, who left those upon the surface to die. Their continued survival was a way of spitting in the face of history. Generations had been born, lived, and died without a meaningful chance of revenge. Their hatred had become a bitter poison under the shadow's influence, preparing the way for the Seer. The tribal leader opened her arms out wide and embraced the Seer as a long-lost son.

Without another word, she led them higher up the mountain. Fortunately, it wasn't far before they reached a crack wide enough for the Seer to shuffle through sideways. The crack squeezed the Seer as he pulled in his stomach, the mountain judging him for neglecting his body for so long. He popped out the other side of the crack and stepped into a tunnel large enough for three to walk abreast.

The tunnel shared its design with the ones beneath the bog where the Seer had found the first shrine. Its builders eschewed straight lines and right angles, and in that decision, the Seer understood the surface clan's ancestors better. Abandoned for dead by those who had taken to the sky, but still possessing much of the same knowledge, their architecture was a rebellion against those who had left. The tunnel bent and curved, rose and fell, each twist and turn a silent condemnation of the cities' creators.

Their guide led them through the tunnels, navigating their complexity with the ease of long familiarity. They stopped outside a door inscribed with the symbols of the shadow song. The Makers' steel thrummed with the awakened power of the shrine, the symbols on the door ringing with sympathetic echoes of the shrine's song.

Their guide spoke briefly, and Belzrak translated. "She

will go no farther, but you are welcome within if you can unlock the door."

"Thank her for me," the Seer said.

As Belzrak obliged, the Seer stepped up to the door and put his hand next to the lock. The shadow song reached out from the lock and brushed against his spirit, seeking a companion, which it found residing within the Seer's soul. Satisfied, the lock in the door disengaged with a metallic *thunk*, and the Seer pulled the door open.

The shrine was a twin to the one he'd found beneath the bog. It sat upon a pedestal, a perfect cube of inky darkness with edges sharp enough to draw blood. Shadow song filled the room even as light snuck through the hole the Seer had drilled to the surface, the first sunlight this room had ever seen.

He glanced back to ensure his guide hadn't changed her mind. She and Belzrak stood side by side at the door, blocking Lynae from entering, though the Blade of Nightkeep made no effort to push her way in.

The Seer approached the shrine, his eagerness restrained by the need to show respect for his audience's benefit. He stopped a pace away, bowed, then took the final step that connected him to his destiny. The cube was cool to the touch. He closed his eyes and connected his spirit to the shrine.

A world of shadow spread out before him, and he was like a blind man given sight. Eight days had passed since Kaya had destroyed the first shrine and died for her transgression, eight days since his sight had extended so far, and the world had shifted. The nuddu, freed from their equatorial cage after generations of patient waiting, hunted the cities, which fled like deer before a hungry dragon.

So far, none of the cities had fallen, for the nuddu were powerful but mindless. They pursued the Song of the

Engines, but the cities were designed to fly faster. Without tactics, the nuddu were a manageable danger.

So he gave them tactics.

The Seer danced between his choices. All were in play. Firestone, of course, was the jewel of them all, and he'd see the city burn before his soul traveled to the gate. Not today, though. Its Engine burned like a second sun, wrapped in a mystery he didn't dare poke at until he was better prepared.

No, Firestone's day would come soon enough. Once he had complete control of the situation, once Radyn and Jyn and all their friends knew there was nothing they could do to save themselves from their doom, then he would strike.

Before he forgot, he commanded the nuddu following Nightkeep to seek other cities. He needed the transportation, and the nuddu's departure would strengthen his tenuous alliance with the council. But if not Nightkeep, where should he send them?

The answer came quickly enough. There was another failure that demanded retribution. A mercy that had resulted in the destruction of a shrine.

A sneer cut across the Seer's face, and he issued his commands to the nuddu.

Today marked the beginning of humanity's final stand.

1

Radyn kneeled in the dirt and let the sharp blades of memory cut his heart to shreds. His hand trembled as he pressed his palm against the freshly turned soil. He listened for her familiar Song, knowing that her voice was gone from the world for good. Truthfully, he didn't know what had pulled him out here. What did he expect? Some sudden warmth in the soil? A single note of her Song? Some sign that her death had meaning?

He knew better, but it was only here, before Kaya's grave, that he felt any sense of peace and hope.

Firestone and Underhill lived, saved by Kaya's selfless courage, only the life they'd been given was more a stay of execution than a rebirth. Both cities, one buried underneath the soil and the other using the clouds for cover, kneeled before the headsman, whose mighty axe remained upraised, waiting only for the perfect moment to bring the sharpened edge down and end their suffering.

Radyn closed his open hand, the loose soil still damp from the freezing rain that had passed through yesterday afternoon. The child in him who had grown up as a farmer welcomed the rain, knowing the moisture would get locked in the soil as winter froze the land. Their fields would welcome the seed come spring, if they lasted that long.

A soft growl escaped the back of his throat at the unfairness of it all.

Father. Elora. Jelrik. Kaya. Spirits that now existed only as scars across his heart, and still fate's headsman demanded more blood. He laid claim to Firestone and Underhill, to Jyn and Miranda, to Nikki and Magni, to Aria and their unborn child, no more than a few weeks away from entering this wounded world.

Radyn's spirit tended toward hope, but finding hope in a world so dark felt like closing his eyes to reality.

Soft footsteps approached behind him. He raised his clenched fist, which still trembled. The tremor hadn't stopped since he'd killed that girl on Nightkeep. He opened his fist, let the soil drop to the grave, then stood and stuffed his hands in his pockets. His gaze lingered a moment longer on Kaya's grave, and then he turned to face the new arrival.

Nikki ignored him as she paid her respects to Kaya's memory. Only after she rose from her bow did she face him. "What's so important that you wanted us to meet out here?"

Radyn arched an eyebrow. "It's good to see you, too, and how have you been?"

The Shield wrapped her arms around herself and shivered. "Everyone in Firestone and Underhill knows what you and Kaya did, and everyone knows you and the Blade have barely had a civil conversation since, so I know how you've been. What I don't know is why you sent a messenger to ask me to come out here when I have a perfectly warm apartment we could have met within."

"I didn't want to risk meeting anywhere within Underhill."

Nikki cast her eyes across the barren surroundings. "Fair enough. What warrants the secrecy?"

"I'd like you to work for me."

Nikki's eyes narrowed. "I report only to the Blade. Beyond that, I only investigate what I wish."

"I'm well aware. My request isn't anything Jyn would disapprove of. If he wasn't being pulled in a dozen different directions, he might even ask you to do it himself."

"I'm listening."

"I want you to locate the source of the shadow song."

Nikki snorted. "And how exactly am I supposed to do that? What you're asking for requires a Singer, and if you haven't noticed, that's not the uniform I wear."

"The Singers couldn't sense the source. I'm not asking you to look at this as a Manirah, but as an investigator. Before she died, Kaya told me to find it. She said it was near the center of the continent."

"If you think I'm about to head out on some sort of one-woman expedition into the forbidden zone, I'm afraid you've completely misjudged me."

"I want you to search the archives."

"You think the secret to our survival has been sitting in Firestone's archives the entire time?"

"I think you'll find clues there. We didn't know what we were looking for before."

"And what are we looking for?"

Like a fish attracted to a worm wriggling on a hook, Nikki couldn't help but be drawn in by the mystery. She was asking the same question that had been running through his mind whenever grief and anger had given his spirit a reprieve.

"We now know that humans on the surface survived the fall of the Makers' civilization. Given the numbers we've encountered, it seems safe to assume there was some degree of preparation that allowed them to survive the exodus, and that they're connected to the shadow song. There have to be traces in the old journals, a detail that would have been meaningless to an archivist convinced no one on the surface survived. A clue that will speed my search."

Nikki tapped her fingers against her arm. "Can't you just close your eyes and focus really hard?"

Radyn offered a rueful smile. "I very much wish that I could. In time, Kaya might have, but it's far beyond me."

He let the words hang in the air, Kaya's gravestone silently punctuating his claim.

"Why me? Why not speak to an archivist?"

"Mostly because I trust you, but also because you're a natural investigator. I don't know any more than I already told you. It's a mystery, which means it's more your territory than mine. But also, and this is the real kicker, the Seer has already found another Shrine. I just came from informing Jyn."

Nikki swore. "And how do you know that?"

"I closed my eyes and focused really hard."

Nikki snorted again and shook her head, unable to resist a mystery with such high stakes. "Fine. I'll look."

Radyn bowed deeply. "Thank you, and please hurry. Now that the Seer has a second shrine, I don't know how much time we have."

He waited until Nikki had long since returned to the warmth of Underhill before making his way back. He spent the time in silent grief, mourning Kaya and the future she would never have. When his tears were spent and his heart grew empty, he walked around the mound to the main gate, which opened to admit him. A maze of hallways, warm thanks to the efforts of Underhill's Engine, led him to his apartment.

He stopped with his hand on the door. A familiar Song hummed from within, and Radyn almost turned around to seek sanctuary elsewhere.

His time with Aria grew short, though, and so he let himself in. She sat at a table, engrossed in a set of diagrams for an irrigation system powered by the Engine. Orenil sat on their couch, half-heartedly flipping through one of Aria's books. He was standing and halfway to Radyn before the Sword had taken off his first boot.

Aria apologized with her eyes. She'd no doubt asked the desperate Singer to return later, but was too kind-hearted to force the point when he insisted he stay. It wasn't the first time he'd visited their apartment in the past week.

Even the most callous and cynical of spirits wouldn't deny the depth of Orenil's grief. The young Singer's hair was badly in need of a wash and a comb, and his red-rimmed eyes spoke of some potent mix of exhaustion and sorrow. The white robes that marked him as a Singer carried dust and stains from hem to hem. He walked with a manic, uneven energy that carried him across the room in a heartbeat, then froze him in place as he confusedly looked around, like he wasn't sure how he'd gotten to where he stood.

Orenil didn't bother with a greeting. "Have you felt the most recent changes to the Song?"

The knot of snakes in Radyn's stomach tightened. "No. I haven't connected much with my shards."

The Singer's face fell, but only for a moment. He reached for Radyn's arm, then looked surprised when Radyn quickly pulled away. "Come with me. We need to visit the Engine and Sing to it."

"I'm not a Singer, Orenil."

Orenil waved the concern away. "Nonsense. We both know what you're capable of. She took you through the Engine. You possess the skill to Sing, even if you haven't been trained." He grabbed again at Radyn's wrist.

Radyn gently slapped the attempt away. "I only lived through that because Kaya's gifts protected me."

The mention of Kaya's name staggered Orenil, as Radyn knew it would. He jumped into the opening like a commander sensing a weakness in the enemy lines. "I know Kaya's death changed something in the Song. We've all felt it. But I'm not a Singer, Orenil. There's nothing I can do."

Orenil's eyes turned hard, and if the young man had been a Sword or Dagger, Radyn would have prepared to draw his maniblade. He was a Singer, though, and so he attacked with his words. "You may not be one of us, but you're no mere Sword, either. I've searched your spirit with the Song, and it's louder in you than in any other Manirah I've crossed paths with, including Jyn."

Radyn sealed his lips. Arguing against Orenil when he was like this was wasted breath.

"She would have wanted you to help me find the truth," Orenil said.

Aria stood, eyes wide, ready to jump between the men if the need arose. The suddenness of her motion interrupted Radyn as he clenched his fist and gave him a moment to regain control. He breathed out through flared nostrils. "You would be wise to leave."

Orenil glared until a shudder ran through his body. His

eyes widened and he took a step back, shaking his head. "I'm sorry. I didn't mean to offend. It's only that——"

Aria glided between them. "Orenil, it's always good to see you, and you're always welcome here, but I think Radyn and I need some time alone."

Orenil stammered, then clenched his jaw shut and nodded. He shuffled to the door and pulled on his shoes. He took one last look at the Sword and his wife. His hands bunched up in his robes. Tears welled in his eyes. "I'm sorry, Radyn. I just want to know what happened to her."

The Singer turned and left before Radyn answered. Once the door shut behind him, Radyn sagged. "I could have handled that better."

Aria came up behind him and placed her hands on his shoulders, digging her thumbs into the muscles between his spine and shoulder blades, an area that was constantly tight these days. "We're all grieving. Our emotions will get the better of us at times."

Radyn stared at the door. "Do you think he's right?"

"About what? You've told me often enough you question what happened to Kaya, and your concerns seem to be borne out by the changes in the Song."

"Not that. About my being able to help."

Aria's thumbs paused. "I couldn't say. Those aspects of the Song are beyond me. You'd know better than me, so what do you think?"

"I think that any time I've explored the Song deeply, I've been guided by a hand I trust. Orenil means well, but Kaya's death has shredded his focus. He's skilled, but I don't trust him."

"Even if it means not knowing what happened to Kaya?"

His muscles bunched under her thumbs, but she continued working at the knots around his shoulders. "I don't know." A pile of words threatened to spill from him, dammed up for too long because Aria bore her own grief. She'd loved Kaya, too, maybe even more than he had. "I really don't know." He pressed his cheek against her hand, savoring its coolness.

She gave his shoulders one last squeeze, then retreated to the couch. Radyn followed. "How are you feeling?"

"I'm ready for this baby to come. I think I'd rather be carrying it on the outside instead of on the inside."

"You'll be a wonderful mother."

"I hope so. It won't be an easy world we're bringing this child into."

"It never is. There will always be darkness in the world, though, and if we give up on children, the darkness wins," he said. He guided her feet onto his lap and massaged them. Aria lay down and closed her eyes, the swell of her belly enormous.

Their child.

The snakes in Radyn's stomach tightened again. He wasn't sure about a great deal these days, but he clung to a single truth he couldn't deny. He'd give anything for the two lives sharing the couch with him.

Aria was sleeping when his silent oath was called due. A messenger knocked on the door, and when Radyn opened it, he saw a pale face staring at him with wide eyes. "The Blade demands your presence immediately. The nuddu's behavior has changed, and we have a messenger. They're targeting Skystone."

2

The hallways outside Radyn's apartment greeted him with an unnatural silence. Despite the harvest being completed, the work of survival was never done, necessitating a constant flow of men, women, and children through the halls. Underhill's labyrinthine passages served as its veins and arteries, its denizens the lifeblood that carried necessities to the people and places that needed them most. The halls being empty made Radyn think of a heart that stopped pumping, and a shudder ran down his spine.

The few people he passed hurried by, as though their apartments were somehow safer than Underhill's halls and workshops. Radyn didn't fault them, though. He longed to hold Aria, to curl up in bed beside her, but the only chance of ensuring such a future required offering Jyn his maniblade today.

Magni stood outside the door to the council room. His eyes were closed, and his giant arms were crossed over his massive chest. He shook his head as Radyn approached. "I can feel you even when I'm not connected to my shards."

Radyn ignored the comment. "Jyn's in there?"

"Everyone is. We've only been waiting for you."

Radyn's eyes narrowed. He'd come immediately following his summons. "Why invite me last?"

"Skystone sent Veylan."

Radyn's spirit reached for his shards before reason restrained the instinct. His nostrils flared and he stepped away from Magni, lest his friend become the unfortunate victim of a hastily drawn maniblade. He held himself as stiff as the beams of Makers' steel, afraid that if he moved at all, he'd leave a trail of bodies behind him.

Magni's discerning gaze didn't miss a moment of Radyn's struggle. Like an experienced commander directing a battle, he tracked the ebbs and flows of Radyn's emotions. His hand never strayed far from the maniblade at his side. Showing considerable wisdom, he made no effort to justify or explain Veylan's presence.

Through clenched teeth, Radyn said, "Not the best way to ask for help, I'd say."

The tension in Magni's shoulders relaxed a touch. "They need you in there, but Jyn said that if you refused, he'd understand."

The temptation to flee the pain that awaited was strong, but he was no child demanding comfort or the illusion of fairness. The Seer had found another shrine. Firestone and all the other cities were at risk, and he wouldn't doom them because he wanted to kill the man on the other side of the door.

Veylan didn't deserve his hatred. If anything, Radyn owed him a debt of gratitude. Veylan could and arguably should have killed him a week ago, but he'd spared Radyn even as he executed Kaya. Radyn recognized that Veylan had walked a difficult path, balancing the orders of his frightened Blade with mercy and compassion. It didn't make what was coming any easier.

He met Magni's close gaze. "I appreciate the warning."

Magni tilted his head toward the door. "Shall we?"

Radyn gestured for Magni to lead the way, and the giant opened the door. Radyn took a moment to shake out his hands, then followed.

Firestone's elders, Jyn, and the clan's leadership were gathered around a long table. Radyn froze as he caught sight of Veylan. Skystone's Senior Sword sat among Firestone's Manirah, as though being surrounded by comrades would protect him from the cut of Radyn's maniblade.

Ice spread from Radyn's veins, locking his limbs in place. The sight of Veylan threw him into memories he'd rather keep locked away. Of Kaya standing beside the Engine, of that knowing smile, as though she was right where she was supposed to be. Of a maniblade, separating head from shoulder and spirit from flesh.

Radyn's palm itched for the feel of Elora's maniblade, and every eye in the room watched as he gripped it tightly. The cords wrapped around the hilt dug into his palm, and thanks to those cords, he could imagine Elora beside him, chastising him for giving in to emotion when his skills were most needed.

Veylan sat with his hands flat on the table. Close as they were, Radyn could be across the table and cutting before Veylan reached his maniblade. The foreign Sword knew it, the softness of his gaze inviting Radyn to strike: not because he believed Jyn's warriors would protect him, but because he accepted Radyn's judgment as justified.

Radyn breathed out and let go of the maniblade. His spirit wouldn't allow him to bow, but he dipped his head in

Veylan's direction. "Senior Sword Veylan. I fear your arrival brings trouble."

Several among Jyn's council audibly released soft sighs of relief. Hands that had wandered toward maniblades fell loosely to their sides, and Veylan bowed deeply to Radyn.

"I'm afraid you are correct," Veylan said. "Skystone, like every other city we are in contact with, has been pursued by the nuddu that have broken free of their equatorial confinement. Until yesterday, that was a problem, but not a deadly one. Yesterday, the behavior of the nuddu changed. Skystone has had one following us like a dumb beast, similar to how Firestone is leading its pair in circles."

Veylan looked at Jyn, as if to check if his understanding was correct. Jyn nodded and gestured for him to proceed.

"That is no longer the case. Messengers from nearby cities have confirmed that they are no longer being pursued, and have added that the nuddu following them have set a course to Skystone's area of operations. By our best count, five nuddu are in the process of encircling us. We're attempting to evade, but our Singers aren't certain we can break free of the circle. Even if we can, there's no guarantee they won't try again."

Jyn spoke on behalf of Firestone. "I am sorry, Veylan. Yesterday, Radyn told me that he'd sensed a tremendous expression of shadow's power, but we didn't know how to interpret it."

The Blade chose his words carefully, but Veylan still winced at the implication. He turned to Radyn. "Is there anything more you can tell me? Some piece of information that might help Skystone?"

Poisoned words danced across Radyn's tongue, but he corralled them before they flayed Veylan with the judgment he so richly deserved. "I'm sorry, but I don't have anywhere near the sensitivity to the shadow song that Kaya possessed. I know nothing you wouldn't guess on your own. The Seer is still with Nightkeep, and together they've found a second shrine. I would guess he now has some level of control over the nuddu, but that's only speculation."

Veylan's face paled at the unspoken accusations Radyn heaped upon him, but he didn't object or plead for mercy. "Is there anything that can be done?" he asked.

Radyn shook his head. "I'm sorry, but I don't have her skill. As far as I know, no one does."

Veylan's face fell, but he wasn't surprised. He gathered his thoughts for a moment, then said, "I don't have the right, but if there is any help Firestone could offer, I'd request it."

"What did you have in mind?" Jyn asked.

"Manirah, if you can spare them. Dragons, too. If we can't escape or outsmart the nuddu, we are left with no choice but to fight."

Veylan's proclamation was greeted with a deafening silence. Fighting a nuddu was no more possible than turning aside a storm, at least according to the legends. Jyn sending Manirah to Skystone's aid was no different from sending them to a premature death.

Jyn wasn't so quick to dismiss Veylan's request, though. "There are many here who would call me a fool to help you, and chances are they'd be right. Still, it seems to me that we keep making the same class of mistake by putting our personal survival so high above the needs of others. It would be easy to allow Skystone to fall, but those nuddu will eventually come for us."

Though it was clear in which direction Jyn's preferences lay, not a soul in the room spoke against him.

Radyn waited, expecting a hurried objection or emotional outburst. As time stretched, he waited for a logical, reasoned argument, but none came. The silence confounded him, for it wasn't as though Jyn ruled Firestone with an unyielding fist, and it wasn't as though the decision met with unanimous agreement.

The eyes of the councilors explained the silence. Fear ruled them. Not just the fear of destruction, but the fear of making the wrong decision, of being responsible for the deaths of so many. Those voices, which were so quick to argue over meaningless matters, went silent when they knew their arguments carried disastrous consequences.

And that, more than his strength or charisma, was what separated Jyn from the others. The Blade had spent years training both body and mind to face such choices, and though Radyn thought he knew Jyn well enough to guess that he would have preferred a life free of such responsibility, he didn't shy away from what was required of him. That willingness to simply *choose* was what raised him above the other councilors. That was what made him a man worthy of leading Firestone.

Jyn allowed the silence to stretch, but when no argument came, he nodded once, the decision made. "Very well. Veylan, we'll send a contingent of warriors and dragons to assist Skystone. They'll be under Magni's command, and my directions will be for them to assist you in any way possible. We can accept some of your citizens as refugees, provided they swear an oath and bring with them enough food for half a year. Our supplies are too low to accept them without it."

It was more than Veylan could have hoped for, and he bowed deeply to Jyn.

Radyn raised a hand, and Jyn gestured for him to

proceed. "I'd like to join with Tanwen, if Veylan and Magni will have us."

Magni's approval was given without hesitation, but Veylan wasn't so easy to convince. "I'd be honored to have a Sword of your skill by my side," he began, "but I must ask why. You, more than anyone else, have ample reason to allow Skystone to suffer its fate."

"It's not too complicated. The Seer and Nightkeep, and thus the shadow song, have decided that Skystone must die. Which means I will do everything in my power to make sure you live."

Veylan flinched at Radyn's bitter criticism, but nodded. He accepted this chastisement, too, without complaint. "It's a truth I wish I would have learned earlier. I'd be honored to have your help."

If Kaya were still alive, Radyn figured she would have approved. She'd always been quick to forgive.

He didn't share that quality, but if saving Veylan gave the Seer a black eye, then it was more than worth it.

3

Radyn caught sight of the nuddu before Skystone. Veylan's floating home had been stationed approximately a hundred miles north of Firestone, which explained why the desperate city had turned to them and how he'd reached them so quickly. Two nuddu, one north and east of Radyn and one north and west, pointed in the same direction, their gazes as good as a compass for the flight of dragons. The space between the nuddu was great enough that Magni had no concern about flying between them.

Radyn extended his awareness toward the monsters as Tanwen passed between them, but physical proximity revealed no greater detail than he'd known before. He sensed the shadow within, a roiling mass of activity that defied his attempts to understand it. He retracted his senses before shadow overwhelmed him.

The nuddu advanced with relentless steps. Both had assumed vaguely human shapes, but their gait proved the appearance a lie. To move forward, the shadow of the trailing leg lifted from the ground and pulled into the creature's torso, disappearing as it was sucked in, then extended forward, planting itself hundreds of feet ahead of where the trailing foot had been. The sight sent a shudder down Radyn's spine, no matter how many times he'd seen it. Fortunately, Tanwen's flight soon put the monsters behind him.

Less than ten miles separated the advancing nuddu from Skystone, and it came into sight as a set of low-level clouds blew past. It was a taller and narrower structure than Firestone, giving it the appearance, from a distance, of a crude dagger hanging in the sky, poised to strike at the land below.

Veylan led the flight of dragons toward Skystone's Nest, a landing field barely wide enough for two dragons to land at once. Skystone's farmers were still hard at work in their fields, the routine of harvest recognizable even as Radyn and Tanwen circled high above. Young men and women labored under the bright sun, hauling bushels of grain toward the stairs and slides that would carry the precious food to the lower levels, where it would be prepared for storage in the enormous granaries. The nuddu were little more than a day away, but the work continued, as though the city's future was as good as guaranteed.

Tanwen landed, and Radyn and three other Manirah from Firestone climbed down. Veylan gathered them together, then escorted them into the heart of Skystone. They dodged around overeager youths who carried wheat, corn, and potatoes toward a nearby stairwell. Veylan chose a less active path and took the stairs two at a time, descending three levels and then leaving the stairs behind. Their path ended at a pair of doors that opened to reveal a small auditorium with a chalkboard hung on the front wall. Firestone's warriors trickled in and took seats. Radyn felt as though he'd jumped back in time and rejoined the academy.

Veylan pulled Radyn aside as he stepped through the door. "Theren would like to speak with you, I'm sure."

Radyn allowed himself to be guided down the stairs and to a door at the front of the auditorium. Veylan knocked gently twice, then opened it. "Sir, Radyn is here."

The room was too dark to peer into, but a voice escaped the gloom. "An unexpected honor. Please send him in."

Veylan stood aside and gestured for Radyn to enter. Radyn did, his eyes quickly adjusting to the darkness. An older man sat, legs crossed, near the corner of the room. The Song was strong within him, and Radyn assumed he stood before Theren, Blade of Skystone. He offered a slight bow only.

"Have you come to kill me?" Theren asked.

"No."

It was hard to tell in the deep darkness of the room, but Radyn swore Theren's face fell at his answer. "I see. You offer your skills in our service, then?"

"I do."

Theren's face twisted and his head dropped. "I am sorry, Radyn. When my Singers felt what happened to Nightkeep, the fear in their eyes was like nothing I'd seen before. There was little argument when Nightkeep proposed their ultimatum. I've never seen the Singers so quick to agree on anything."

Radyn took strength from Elora's maniblade at his side. He forced himself to observe the broken Blade, to listen to the words that poured from him like tea from a cracked pot.

He could understand, but forgiveness remained beyond his reach. "You believed Nightkeep's lies and ordered the execution of the only Singer who might have saved us. Kaya would never have hurt you."

"Then you should have told us about her! What would you think if you were in my place and you discovered another city had a Singer who could bring down our refuges on little more than a whim?"

"We should have told you? The *moment* you learned about her true strength, you ordered her dead. Is it any wonder we hid her?"

Theren shrank deeper into his dark corner, but a gentle hand on Radyn's arm focused Radyn's glare on Veylan. "We were wrong. We know. He's wanted to apologize since, which was why he sent me to Firestone. I'd beg your mercy on behalf of both of us, though."

Theren had his legs drawn up to his chest, and his long, thin arms were wrapped around them, holding them close. He'd once been an honored warrior, but all his battles were behind him. He waited to surrender his soul to the gate, too great a coward to set his own spirit free.

Radyn offered another curt bow. "I thank you for your apology, and I accept it."

He couldn't tell if Theren even heard him.

Veylan shook his head. "I'd hoped he could meet with the others, but he can't be seen like this."

Radyn agreed. "We're here for your city and your people. Not him. Lead the discussion yourself."

The two left the room and Theren, closing the door behind them. Radyn took a seat as Veylan walked to the front of the auditorium. The murmurs of the Manirah quieted as Veylan picked up a long piece of chalk. He drew a circle on the board, as well as six crossed marks evenly spaced around the circle.

"This isn't exact, of course, but it gives you a sense of what we're dealing with. Half a dozen nuddu have surrounded Skystone. They're exhibiting a level of intelligence and cooperation we haven't seen before. Our Singers have attempted to escape the ring, but not only do the nuddu close ranks in the direction of our escape, they do so while retreating, ensuring we can't squeeze through a closing gap."

Veylan's news set off another round of murmurs from around the assembled Manirah. They'd had little direct experience with nuddu until recently, but in the legends, nuddu were dangerous but dumb. They followed Engines using the shortest viable path. The tales never mentioned nuddu retreating, and Radyn certainly hadn't seen it personally.

Magni's deep voice broke through the confusion. "We know that the man who calls himself the Seer has taken control of another shrine. He's responsible for the nuddus' new behaviors."

One of Skystone's Manirah spoke up. "Does that mean we should find him, then?"

Magni shook his head. "He's traveling with Nightkeep, which fled deep into the equatorial zones once the barrier containing the nuddu fell. We can't reach him in time, and even if we could, I don't think we have the numbers to overwhelm Nightkeep. Our fight is here."

Veylan continued his presentation before the discontent erupted into something more disruptive. "Our Singers have tried almost every evasive trick they know, but we haven't come close to breaking away, so it's time for more desperate measures. I've gathered you all here because I'd like a group of volunteers to attack a nuddu directly."

The same Dagger who'd spoken last argued again. "Sir? Every legend we know tells us that's suicide."

Veylan nodded. "I don't doubt that was true generations ago. We may have lost the Makers' skill in building, but our clans have only grown stronger since the exodus. Our only other options are worse, so we try this first."

Radyn raised his hand. "Tanwen and I will try."

He was the only warrior from Firestone to volunteer, but that wasn't a surprise. Magni argued for evacuation, and none of the rest were compelled to risk their lives on so little expectation of success. For their own families, perhaps, but not here.

Magni pulled him aside after the meeting ended. "Are you sure about this?"

"Not particularly, but it's a chance to understand our enemy better. If we can hurt it, that's a fact that could change this war."

Magni shook his head. "Don't push yourself too far. If I come back without you, Jyn will beat the daylights out of me."

Radyn snorted. "Well, I wouldn't want to put you through that, would I?"

VEYLAN GAVE the volunteers just enough time to grab a quick bite at one of the community kitchens before they met outside the overcrowded Nest. Tanwen's displeasure at his lack of space echoed clearly through their connection. After years of relatively wild and spacious living, the Nest felt more like a cage than a home.

Radyn, too, had grown used to long walks across wide fields, the horizon bending away in the distance, and so he hardly blamed his old friend. Every visit to the cities cut another sliver of his soul away. Wholeness only existed below, on the surface.

Dragon and rider waited as other volunteers shuffled

their dragons to the small patch of dirt that served as the departure point. The first dragons to leave were packed so tightly together they couldn't spread their wings, and so they simply dropped off the edge and fell until they had enough speed to catch the wind.

When Tanwen's turn came, the dragon eagerly launched himself into the sky. Tanwen was young by the standards of dragons, and the flight over had done nothing to sap his tremendous strength. Before long, the gathered dragons and riders circled above the head of the nuddu, which ignored them.

The assembly gradually descended, a crown of dragons placed upon the nuddu's head. Radyn took advantage of the unparalleled proximity to extend his senses. The strength of the shadow threatened to overwhelm his spirit, the silence eager to smother the Song in his chest. Radyn kept his spirit balanced as the warring forces fought over its fate, probing deeper into the nuddu as he did.

He reached a point where he could push no further: where, if he crossed, he was certain to doom himself. From that point, he peered deeper and was rewarded only with the deafening silence of shadow.

He was about to retreat when he thought he heard a whisper. He relaxed his focus, welcoming into his awareness whatever existed within the shadow. The whisper came again, softer than an early morning summer breeze, and then another, a slightly deeper pitch. He strained his senses, and the whispers vanished like an illusion that disappeared under an intense stare. Again he relaxed, and again the whispers, so quiet he wasn't sure if they weren't a product of his imagination, returned.

Whatever secrets the shadow held, they were clutched too tightly for Radyn to discern. He returned his senses to his immediate surroundings and saw they'd grown very close to the top of the nuddu's head. The shadows shifted and twisted within, gently swirling ink in an amorphous container.

Radyn felt the signal to attack through his connection to Tanwen. He drew his maniblade, connected to the rest of his shards, and let Tanwen fly freely. Some riders preferred to keep a tight rein over their dragons, but Tanwen flew best when he flew according to his instincts. His old friend twisted and dove while Radyn held on tight with his left hand.

The nuddu's head swelled as though bruised. A wave of shadow passed through Radyn, sending a shiver up his spine. His stomach flipped, and he obeyed the dictates of his intuition. "Get us out of here!" he shouted.

The bulges across the top of the nuddu's head exploded, extending into sharpened pillars of shadow. Skystone's dragon closest to the top of the nuddu's head didn't have a moment to react. The oversized spear caught the dragon in the chest, and the shadow tore through the dragon from chest to tail, emerging bloody out the back side of the creature. Her rider, a young Sword, was flung off the dragon's back. The Sword tumbled end over end, screaming as he fell. He struck the top of the nuddu's head and disappeared within. His screams cut off the moment he made contact.

The story repeated across the surface of the nuddu. Dragons farther away had more time to evade, and a few, like Radyn, had sensed the danger a moment before it struck. Even so, five dragons fell from the sky as dark spears pierced armored hides with ease.

Tanwen was already shifting as the first spear came for his heart. Instead of sacrificing speed, he twisted and dove. The spear of shadow bent in response, but Tanwen's speed carried him away from the deadly tip before it reached him. Tanwen whipped down the nuddu's side, not just falling, but adding his own strength to the dive. Radyn held himself close to Tanwen's neck, afraid the wind alone would rip him off if he wasn't careful.

A handful of shadowy bulges grew ahead of them, and Radyn swore. Tanwen flung them off their original line as the bulges exploded and dark spears filled Radyn's vision.

Tanwen's evasions brought them even closer to the nuddu, and Radyn reached out with his maniblade. The weapon carved through the side of the nuddu with ease, peeling away shadow wherever it touched.

Tanwen warned him a moment before he spread his wings. Radyn's breath was driven from his lungs as his body was pressed against Tanwen's. Their vertical momentum became horizontal speed, and dragon and rider raced away from the nuddu. Radyn glanced back. He was sure his cut had done damage, but there was no sign of it. All he saw was another set of bulges in the nuddu's skin directly behind them. "Dive!" he shouted.

Tanwen dropped without question, and not a moment too soon. Shadow spears filled the air above Radyn's head. Tanwen fell for a heartbeat longer, then leveled off once again. Radyn twisted his head but saw no more bulges.

He looked up at the sky. Less than half the dragons they'd left with were returning, and several of those were injured.

The nuddu hadn't even missed a step as it closed in on Skystone.

4

The hallway outside Jyn's study seemed empty without Magni standing guard. Bertram, the Sword currently fulfilling the role, was a perfectly competent warrior, and attentive to his duties, but he lacked Magni's presence. Nikki couldn't imagine a would-be assassin seriously considering fighting their way past Magni. They'd take one look at the giant, shake their head, and probably right their evil ways. Far better to repent than experience the delights of Magni's massive fist pounding an otherwise sturdy skull into small bits.

She had no doubt that Bertram was dangerous. Swords always were, but there was no threat in his bearing. He even smiled when she came around the corner and he first caught sight of her. "Ma'am. How can I help you today?"

"I need to speak with the Blade. It shouldn't take long, and no, before you ask, he doesn't know I'm coming."

Fortunately, the Sword knew her well enough not to question her need. He knocked twice on the door and turned his back to her as he poked his head in to speak to the Blade. Nikki stared daggers into his back. Granted, she wasn't an assassin, but familiarity was no excuse for lax behavior. Jyn's life was too important, now more than ever.

He turned back to her, then frowned in confusion at her glare. "He said he can see you."

"Thank you." She brushed past him and shut the door behind her. "Your security is poor without Magni here," she announced.

Jyn looked exhausted, which told Nikki all she needed to know about how dire their situation was. She'd seen him go days without sleep and appear perfectly refreshed at a council meeting, so the bags under his eyes spelled their doom more clearly than any shouted warning. "That bad?"

He gestured her to the seat across the table from him. "It is, but it's nothing you need to concern yourself with. If you're here, it's for a reason."

"I am, but I am worried about your safety. Bertram's a fine Sword, but if I had meant you harm, I could have easily killed him when he turned his back."

"You think so little of my ability to defend myself?" Jyn almost looked hurt by the implication.

"That's not what I mean, and don't act the fool," Nikki snapped.

Jyn crossed his arms in front of his chest. "Your concern is noted, and I miss Magni, too, but he needs more command experience, and this is an opportunity for him to acquire it."

Nikki arched an eyebrow. "You've chosen him as your successor?"

"For now. Radyn would be a better choice, but that would be a—complicated—process."

Nikki snorted. The savior of Firestone, at least twice by Nikki's count, but also a Manirah exiled by Jyn and still held by most to be responsible for the death of Jyn's predecessor. Complicated hardly described it.

"It's good that you mentioned him, because he's the reason I'm here. He wants me to dig around in the archives looking for information on the clans we've been running into on the surface."

Jyn frowned at the idea. "That seems pointless. Those texts have been studied to death over the years."

"I told him the same, but he argued they were studied by people who didn't realize some fraction of humanity had survived upon the surface. Knowing that, he hopes the texts might shed some fresh light on our enemies."

Jyn considered for a moment, then scribbled a few lines on a piece of paper, folded it over, and sealed it. "You know Adele?"

"The senior archivist? We've crossed paths a few times."

"Take this to her. It'll give you access to everything in the archives, but I've also asked her to answer any of your questions. She's got most of the archives memorized, so it's fastest to ask her. I don't think you'll find much, but it's worth the attempt."

He handed her the orders. "Let me know if you find anything."

"I will. And Jyn?"

The Blade grunted, his attention already halfway returned to the work on his desk.

"Get some rest. You're no good to us if you collapse from exhaustion."

IT WASN'T until she left the neighborhood the clan had claimed as their own that she realized she was going to need directions. She'd officially been a resident of Underhill for months, but in those months she'd served less as a Shield and more as a laborer. Jyn hadn't needed her particular skills since Firestone had half-crashed into the hills, and the survivors needed farmers far more than investigators.

Her sun-kissed skin was darker than it had ever been, but the daily routine of wake, eat, and work in the fields meant she had never wandered the lesser-used levels and corridors of Underhill. If her destination wasn't between one of the community kitchens and her small apartment, she didn't know where it was.

She wandered down the hallways until she ran into a farmer she recognized, a younger man who'd been one of the original Soulkeeper inhabitants of Underhill. He kindly gave her directions, then offered to escort her. Pride forced her to decline, but she thanked him profusely. Armed with the necessary knowledge, Nikki found the archives with little additional difficulty.

Like Firestone's archive room, Underhill's archives were housed in a standard large apartment that had been modified for its new purpose. Firestone's had been just outside the academy, allowing both students and full-fledged Manirah easy access to the precious documents. Here, Jyn had chosen a location a few levels down that would be safe from the most likely threats. An extra set of locks had been attached to the door to prevent prying eyes from uncovering knowledge best left alone. Nikki knocked on the door. She listened to several of the locks click, and then the door opened to reveal an older woman with white hair and a wide smile.

"Archivist Adele, I'm—"

"Senior Shield Nikki, yes, I'm well familiar with who

you are. Come in, dear. I just put a fresh pot of tea on, and you look like you could use a cup or two."

"I've never been one to refuse a cup. Thank you."

Adele led her into what would have been a hallway in most apartments. Here, the walls had been demolished and rearranged, creating what amounted to a small, well-lit study. Two waist-high shelves held a few dozen books and scrolls, and a large desk took up most of the central space. Books and papers were spread across it, the edges of each article parallel with its neighbors and with the desk. The surface of the desk shone, nearly as reflective as a mirror. Dust, it seemed, didn't receive the warm welcome here that she'd been granted.

Adele measured the tea before transferring it to each cup, then wiped the teapot, the measuring cup, and the counter with a rag before handing the cup to Nikki. The Shield bowed, waited for Adele to sit, then handed her Jyn's orders. The archivist examined the seal, cut through it with a knife, and unfolded the letter. Her eyes narrowed, and Nikki couldn't help but suspect she was sitting in stern judgment of Jyn's sprawling handwriting, which wasted the precious gift of paper. She folded the note and returned it to Nikki. "How can I help?"

"I'm interested in materials that are pre-exodus or perhaps immediately post-exodus, specifically anything that might reference people who survived on the surface. We know now that there were survivors, and a good number of them. I'm hoping we might learn more about them."

Adele tapped her fingers against the side of her cup as she considered the request. "I'm afraid we have little here that's that early. As you know, most records were destroyed shortly post-exodus."

Everyone knew that, although no one knew why.

Shortly after taking to the sky, the Makers, or perhaps a small sect of them, had destroyed much of what was known about the world before, leaving their descendants desperate for answers about their origins and the creations that kept them alive. "But some survived."

"A very little, yes, but most of it is stored in Nightkeep. Did you know Firestone was the last city to take to the sky, and that it almost didn't?"

Nikki shook her head, feeling like a child disappointing their teacher in the classroom. "I'm ashamed to admit I always imagined all the cities took off at once."

Adele sipped silently at her tea. "They were actually staggered over what ended up being an entire year. Nightkeep was supposed to be the last launch, as it was designed to evacuate the Makers' capital, but unknown circumstances caused it to launch before Firestone. To protect his archives, Firestone's clan commander Aron ordered them moved to Nightkeep, which is why Nightkeep has always had the larger archive, even following the destruction of most records."

As interesting as the history lesson was, Nikki didn't see how it mattered. "Do you have anything that can help?" she asked.

Adele thought a moment longer, then nodded. "Your best bet will probably be the journals of Cole and Karolyn, a pair of siblings who lived through the exodus. It's been years since I've browsed through their pages, but they made several expeditions to the surface in the years after the exodus. I don't recall any mention of survivors, but you'll have to forgive me. My memory isn't what it once was."

"Would it be possible for me to look through them?"

"With those orders from Jyn? You could burn them if you wanted, though you'd break my heart."

Adele stood and turned to the door in the room. One large lock held it shut, but the archivist pulled a key from her pocket and opened it. Nikki put down her tea and joined Adele as they walked into the heart of the archives. "Is there anything else you know about the exodus? Anything that might lead me toward the survivors?"

The room behind the small study had once been several rooms in an apartment, but the walls had been removed and shelves crammed into every bit of available space. They stretched from floor to ceiling and covered three of the four walls. More shelves filled the middle of the space, packed so tightly together Nikki had to turn sideways to fit between the rows. Adele slid between the shelves like a wraith.

"Did you know that when the cities launched, they didn't take everyone from the surface?"

Nikki frowned. She thought she'd heard that somewhere before, but she wasn't certain. "I don't know."

"Unfortunately, there were far more humans living upon the surface than the Makers could save. My understanding is that they did what they could, but even they couldn't build enough Engines and cities to evacuate everyone. Many of those who knew they were going to be left behind formed new clans that fought against those who were assigned to the cities. The two biggest of those were called the Iron Wolves and the Order of Reconciliation."

"I didn't know that."

Adele shrugged. "Few do anymore. The clans won't really lie about it, but they don't teach it as part of their history anymore. They figure the best way to protect their future is to keep silent about their past."

The older woman stopped beside a shelf and ran her hand across a series of books. She cocked her head to the side, then ran her finger across the titles again.

"Do you need help?" Nikki asked.

Adele shot Nikki a withering look. "My dear, I know where every book, scroll, and scrap of paper in this archive is."

Nikki dipped her head in apology as Adele ran her finger along the spines one last time. She shook her head. "They're not here."

"Did someone else borrow them?"

Adele's glare turned Nikki's blood to ice and she held her hands up in surrender. "I know, I know. You're aware of the location of every scrap of paper in this place. So if you can't find these journals, what does it mean?"

"My dear, it means that someone has stolen them."

5

Skystone's Nest overflowed with people and supplies pressing against one another as they prepared their escape. Enormous cargo carriers made of Makers' steel yawned open to accept gut-busting quantities of food, seed, and people. Manirah herded frightened citizens like cattle into small, roped-off spaces to keep them out of the way while laborers hauled the life-giving supplies into the carriers. Each roped-off space represented a single carrier's worth of people, those gifted a chance of survival if the worst came to pass. If Veylan ordered it, the ropes would open, and each group would sprint for their designated carrier.

Hopefully the day wouldn't come to that. Radyn looked around and saw what they might save, but the Nest's thick walls conveniently blocked the sight of all they stood to lose, the hundreds upon hundreds of citizens whose fate rested entirely on Veylan and the Singers' daring roll of the dice.

He stood next to Tanwen and made himself small so that those with more vital duties could hurry past. He searched the faces of the laborers, quietly awed by the discipline they maintained while they worked. Those chosen to escape Skystone had been selected with care. Veylan had focused on families of Manirah with children, and he hadn't been able to save even all of those.

Farmers, builders, and merchants grumbled about Veylan's choices. They whispered of favoritism and unfairness. Few acknowledged the bitter truth of the matter: that humanity needed warriors most, and that the Manirah were best suited to the fight ahead.

Such a decision had the danger of carrying hefty repercussions, from small protests to outright chaos. Radyn had yet to witness such consequences, though. Perhaps it was only because of his limited view into Skystone, but he guessed from the looks of those who passed him by that the lack of complaint represented a darker reality.

Events had divided Skystone into two camps of people: those who still held out some small sliver of hope for the future (and it was never more than a sliver), and those who considered the first group fools, who had resigned themselves to the inevitable. Most who passed Radyn fell into the second camp, and they completed their orders without enthusiasm, hoping only to finish their tasks and return to whatever manner of diversion they preferred to pursue as the end of their city stalked ever closer.

The proposed destination of the carriers likely had some effect, too. Those in the Nest, if they were forced to flee, bought themselves what most considered a temporary reprieve. Underhill might welcome new citizens with open arms, but the surface wouldn't, and the feeling in the air was that it wouldn't be long before all humanity's cities lay in smoking ruins across the continent.

The circle of nuddu grew close now, and there was no

way to fly around them. Veylan hoped, though, that it might be possible to fly over them.

To the knowledge of everyone in Skystone, such a feat had never been tried. No legend spoke of anything similar. It was a balance of reason and madness, and no one knew which side of the coin Veylan's desperate flip would land on.

They would learn soon enough. The mad press of bodies around Tanwen eased as the laborers packed the last supplies into the waiting carriers. More could have fit within, but the dragons could only carry so much weight, and each would be near their limit for this flight. If they had to escape, the dragons would still need breaks on their way to Firestone and Underhill. All that remained was the space for the people.

The Nest cleared out as the last of the laborers finished their tasks. Once the final young man left, the gates of the Nest were closed and barred, and just in time. Radyn couldn't see the nuddu from where he stood, but he could sense them without effort. His ability to sense the shadow song had improved, but he didn't need it now to know their doom surrounded them.

Once word reached the Singers that preparations were complete, their Song changed. Almost all of Skystone's Singers served this afternoon, for the city desperately needed their strength. The few that weren't in the Engine Room huddled within small, roped-off areas throughout the Nest. The Engine answered the Singers' exhortations. Radyn wasn't connected to his shards, but he couldn't miss the incredible outpouring of energy that pushed Skystone higher into the air.

Veylan stood on the Nest's wall. He had no wife or children, and so, following his own orders, he remained behind. He bellowed for those in the roped-off areas to head to their carriers. Assigned leaders pulled out the long stakes securing the ropes and guided their charges into the carriers. Children wailed, intuitively sensing their parents' barely concealed distress. The doors of the carriers remained open, allowing Radyn to see the families huddled together, their fate firmly out of their control.

Radyn and the other riders mounted their dragons. Skystone's would transport the carriers, while Firestone's would provide whatever defense they could.

Though the small Nest was crowded, it remained a pitifully tiny fraction of Skystone's total population. Radyn's throat clenched, and he turned his mind to other matters. He connected with his shards and with Tanwen, and the Song of the Engine consumed the greater part of his attention.

Despite the efforts of the Singers, the Song of Skystone's Engine struck several discordant notes. They were loud, honoring the requests of the Singers for *more*, but they were out of tune, like a violin whose strings had relaxed.

The Singers didn't know how to respond to the Engine's weakness, and Radyn's heart bled at Kaya's absence. It had never been enough for her to manipulate the Engine. She'd bent her whole life to the purpose of understanding the Engines better, ignoring the dogma the Singers so readily embraced. Without her, Skystone's Singers wandered paths they didn't know how to navigate, and they defaulted to Singing louder, as though the simple application of more force could solve the problem.

Skystone fought for altitude, then settled at a new height only a few hundred feet higher than before. Radyn frowned. The Engine weakened as they drew away from the source at the center of the world, and that had been a worry as Veylan had outlined his plan, but it shouldn't be a problem this low.

Tanwen rumbled.

"You know something?" Radyn asked.

Tanwen responded with visions of the nuddu. In the visions, the shadow song around the nuddu extended well beyond their physical limits, embracing Skystone as it struggled for the sky.

"They're choking off the Engine?" Radyn asked.

Tanwen rumbled again, confirming Radyn's guess.

"Is there anything we can do?"

Tanwen's rumble took on a deeper tone, which Radyn interpreted as *not in time*.

Radyn clutched the dragon's scales tighter. The shadow song sat as an uninvited guest in the back of his mind, silently laughing at his inability to stand against it. Nuddu had to be within a mile of the city, and Skystone's Singers drove themselves to the brink of madness, exhorting the Engine to greater heights. The Engine's Song responded the best that it could, but like an elderly warrior preparing for battle, it lacked the strength.

A shadow rose in the distance, and Radyn leaned forward for a better look. He swore as it burst through a cloud and revealed itself to be a nuddu's hand. The arm stretched like a pliable piece of rubber, inky shadow running from the shoulder below to inflate the hand ever larger. It peaked a few hundred feet from the edge of the Nest, then plummeted to the surface of the city.

"Seal the carriers!" Veylan boomed.

Several of the carriers were locked by those who hid inside, the combat manirah keeping their heads. Doors slammed shut and bolts were thrown. Riders closed other carriers before climbing onto nearby dragons.

The young woman in charge of the carrier beside

Tanwen fumbled with the long bolt that would seal the carrier door shut. She cried out, her hands shaking so hard she couldn't grab the bolt out of the trampled grass.

Radyn glanced up at the falling hand of shadow, then leaped off Tanwen. "Get on your dragon and prepare to leave!"

She looked at him stupidly, but Radyn ignored her. He grabbed the bolt, made sure the door was tightly shut, then slammed it through the holes that locked the door closed. By the time he turned back to the woman, she was climbing up the side of her dragon. The distant look in her eyes meant she'd connected with her dragon, and the act had calmed her nerves.

Radyn turned back in time to see the enormous hand crash upon the surface of Skystone. Perhaps half of the hand landed inside the Nest, while the other half landed on the other side of the wall. Radyn spread his legs and prepared for a jolt as the nuddu dragged the city out of the sky.

Instead, the hand split into dozens upon dozens of compact figures, each of which grew into a much smaller nuddu, a horde of human-shaped shadows that spread across the Nest like a fire blown across dry grasslands by an angry wind. The Manirah closest to the dissolved hand died quickly. The shadowy figures grew familiar dark blades out of their arms, and they cut through flesh as easily as their maniblade counterparts.

The figures swarmed at the nearest dragon, a protector that had been loaned to Skystone by Firestone, and she died almost as fast as the humans around her. Blades of shadow cut through her armored scales as she roared and tried to bat them away. Dozens of the shadows turned to mist against the force of her blows, but not before they had climbed across her back and driven blade after blade into her spine.

She died with a roar that shook the air, and her death cry was picked up and echoed by the companions she'd left behind. Tanwen's spirit shattered at the loss of her life, and Radyn's soul, connected to the dragon's, was forced to mourn equally. The ground trembled as the mighty dragon's neck crashed, lifeless, across the battered grass of the Nest.

None of the dragons could take off without a little space. They were packed in too tightly, and were sitting targets for the shadows.

Magni's bright maniblade flashed among their enemies, clearing a space that none of the shadows seemed eager to challenge. "Clear the Nest!" he commanded.

Radyn pulled the maniblade from his hip and connected to all his shards. A fragment of Tanwen traveled with him, granting him an additional pool of strength he could draw from. He skipped across the grass between the dragons and crashed like a wall into the shadows.

He cut and cut again, and the shadows fell as easy as wheat. They were slow and clumsy, suffering the nuddu's same weaknesses even though they were so much smaller. Thin spears of shadow sought to slow his advance, but none were fast enough to catch him.

Radyn reached the edge of the Nest, planted a heel, then shot himself like an arrow at the darkest concentration of shadow. Once again he cut through them with ease, his maniblade turning shadow to mist wherever he wandered.

His counterattack stunned the shadow. Those that had swarmed toward the dragons now slowed, and Radyn wondered if they were like the larger nuddu in another way: that they were attracted to the most powerful expression of the Song nearby.

He called upon Tanwen's strength, and burned until his Song was almost the only one he could hear.

The shadows turned toward him, an enormous family preparing for a feast that featured him as the main course. The distraction served the other Manirah from Firestone well. Led by Magni, they fell upon the shadows with vengeance, clearing large swaths as the deadly shades focused their attention on Radyn.

His success left him with no choice but to retreat. No individual shadow posed much of a threat to a prepared warrior, but their numbers sufficed to overthrow a dragon. His maniblade kept them respectfully wary, but they drove him back towards the edge and the fall that awaited after. Radyn gave up ground as slowly as he dared, grimacing as the shadow blades scored shallow cuts across his arms and thighs. The wounds felt as though they'd been inflicted by icy daggers, his skin freezing and burning at once, but they did little to slow him.

Magni and the other Manirah cut through the rear of the horde, racing to reach Radyn before the shadows pushed him off the edge. The Blade's closest friend and most trusted protector fought like a man possessed. A nuddu hadn't killed his wife, but she'd died protecting Firestone against the threat of shadow, and for the first time he could turn his maniblade directly against the force.

Veylan seized the opportunity Firestone's Manirah bled for. "Dragons, to the sky!"

Two of the enormous creatures, guided by their riders, ran across the Nest and jumped off the edge. They rose moments later, banking sharply back at the Nest. Powerful claws closed around the dragon-sized handles at the top of the carriers. The Song that surrounded them rang like a bell as they lifted the carriers into the sky and away from Skystone.

Radyn glanced back. Perhaps a dozen paces remained between him and the edge. A moment later, he had to leap back as a new type of shadow sent two spears at his chest.

Most of the shadows maintained a vaguely humanoid shape, and their movements roughly matched those of a young swordsman. Not so with this one, which shifted and glided between shapes with ease. One moment it resembled a child, the next a wolf, the next a thin wall. Radyn stepped forward to meet it, but it flattened itself against the grass and fled between the feet of the other shadows, a nightmare that could reappear at any time.

Magni's arrival banished the worst of his fears. With the giant warrior guarding his weak side, Radyn held his ground. Firestone's other Manirah followed close behind, and another pair of dragons used the opening to launch themselves off the edge of the city.

Radyn cut through another pair of shadows and searched for the one that had given him such trouble, but if it was around, it gave no sign. He let his gaze roam across the battlefield. The dragon's loss drove needles of sorrow into his heart still, but they could have lost much more. Firestone's Manirah killed the last of the shadows as the dragons launched and grabbed their carriers.

His throat tightened at that, and his gaze traveled up to the wall. Veylan still stood upon it, his maniblade in hand and lit. He divided his attention between the fields outside the Nest and the Nest's evacuation. He granted the greater part of his attention to the other side of the wall, though, and he hadn't halted the evacuation.

"Radyn!"

He turned at Magni's call and followed the point of the giant's maniblade. More shadows flooded onto the city to reinforce the first wave. They crawled over the lip of the edge, first in ones and twos, and then in greater numbers. Magni and Radyn charged them together, striking the shadows before they could gain a defensible foothold upon the surface. Their maniblades cut through the shadows as one, and they soon stared over the edge.

Empty sky opened beneath them. Like Firestone, Skystone's edge fell away from the surface, and so Radyn leaned over further.

The sight froze his blood cold. Hundreds of shadows swarmed over the stone that formed Skystone's sides. They clung to the rock like spiders, oblivious to both the pull of gravity and the wind that whipped at Radyn's clothes. When he let his gaze travel even lower, he saw the dark shadow that connected Skystone to the nuddu. The creature had grasped onto the flying city, and the thousands of shadows that had once comprised its body worked their way up the shoulder and arm of the nuddu, emerging from what had once been the monster's wrist.

Magni saw the same. "We hold here until the last of the carriers is away."

Radyn couldn't get words past his constricted throat. He nodded, took two steps back, and braced himself. As the other Manirah finished with the last of the shadows, they joined the two friends near the edge.

The shadows struck as the line formed, but Firestone's Swords and Daggers were up to the task. The shadows possessed no greater strategy. They came over the edge when they reached it and made no effort to coordinate with their companions. The Manirah turned the shadows into mist with little difficulty.

As they held the line, dragons took off. With each launch, the Nest grew more open, allowing other dragons to take to the air with greater ease. When Radyn glanced back again, only a few Skystone dragons remained, and they would be off before long. Veylan still stood on the wall, his back completely turned.

"Do we stay?" Radyn asked.

Magni also glanced back, then shook his head. "I'm afraid there's nothing we can do."

"We could push them back," Radyn argued.

Tanwen broke in, and in his mind's eye, Radyn saw that the other nuddu had already arrived. Skystone's surface swarmed with countless shadows, and many of them poured down the now-undefended stairwells where, just the day before, the harvest had been sent for storage.

Magni's face reflected Radyn's pain. "I'm sorry, friend. There's nothing to be done."

Radyn swallowed the bitter truth with a nod and turned his frustration onto the next pair of shadows that crawled over the edge.

The last of Skystone's dragons pulled their carriers into the sky, and Magni gave Firestone's warriors the order to retreat to their dragons. Radyn lingered after the others had gone, walking up and down what had once been their line, cutting down any shadows who crawled over the edge.

"You coming?" Magni asked.

In answer, Radyn killed one last shadow, then followed the giant back to their dragons. He climbed onto Tanwen and took another look at the wall. Shadows were climbing over it, attracted to the Nest and the dragons still within. Veylan calmly walked along the wall, cutting down any shadows that came too close. Most ignored him in favor of the dragons.

"Veylan!" Radyn called.

The commander looked, and Radyn gestured for him to flee. The shadows weren't yet close enough for Tanwen to be in danger, and there was room on the dragon's back for Skystone's commander.

Veylan shook his head, then bowed deeply toward Radyn. He held the bow for a long moment, then straightened and returned to the task of clearing the wall of shadows.

It occurred to Radyn that he could order Tanwen to make a grab for Veylan as they left, but he dismissed the thought before it developed roots. Veylan's maniblade glowed on top of the wall, the lone light against a growing mass of shadow, but Radyn couldn't look at the weapon without seeing it coming down to separate Kaya's head from her shoulders.

He still might have saved Veylan if not for what he witnessed next. Despite the overwhelming force coalescing around him, Veylan strode through the shadows on the wall with one confident step after another. His sword never strayed from its intended line, nor did it hurry, but it carved an effortless path through the darkness. Radyn sensed the Song of Veylan's spirit, ringing one crystal-clear mournful note.

Tanwen asked if they should leave, but Radyn held them in place for another few moments. He would honor Veylan as a witness. The commander of Skystone continued his last patrol of the wall, and Radyn dipped his head in Veylan's direction.

Tanwen took off before the shadows reached them, taking to the air with a single beat of his powerful wings. One shadow, gliding between shapes with greater ease than the others, stretched its entire body out to spear Tanwen's belly. It pulled other shadows into it to lengthen its reach, but Tanwen was too quick. The spear fell short, and the one shadow disgorged the others as it shrank back to the size of a human.

An ear-splitting cry of tortured metal and stone pierced Radyn's ears and brought tears to his eyes. Skystone tilted, dropped, then steadied out for a moment, and Radyn was a fool, but he hoped the Singers could keep the Engine alive.

Then the Song of Skystone's Engine vanished, leaving a cavernous silence deep within the fabric of the world.

The enormous city dropped from the sky, and the last sight Radyn had of the surface of the doomed city before it fell behind the clouds was Veylan's bright maniblade cutting through a pair of shadows.

6

Armed with a list of names and a description of the missing books, Nikki strode toward the center of Underhill. As expected, Miranda wasn't in her study, but an aide helpfully directed Nikki to one of the community kitchens. There, she found Miranda in conference with a group of farmers and cooks, discussing how best to store the extra food that might soon be on its way.

Nikki waited until Miranda finished, then bowed as she approached. The Soulkeeper's eyes narrowed. "If you're here, I have to assume there's some sort of trouble."

Nikki told Miranda of Radyn's request, as well as the discovery of the journals' absence. "If they haven't been destroyed, they're somewhere in Underhill. Archivist Adele gave me a list of all the people in the city who have access to a key. I wanted to let you know I'm planning on investigating."

"This isn't Firestone. You don't have the authority to barge into people's apartments without their permission."

"All but one name on my list are from Firestone."

Miranda arched an eyebrow. "And I'm the only name from Underhill."

"I'm not looking to add to your problems. By the gate, I didn't even put that much faith in Radyn's idea until I found the books missing, but I don't have the time for you and Jyn to argue over rights and authority. I came hoping for your blessing, but if I have to proceed without it, I will."

Miranda pressed her palms against tired eyes. "I imagine you'd like a master key?"

"It would be welcome."

The older woman sighed and pulled a thin chain from around her neck. A key hung on the end, which she dangled in front of Nikki. The Shield reached for it, but Miranda pulled it back. "I'd like to see the list first, please."

Nikki debated briefly, but the truth was that she trusted Miranda. She reached into her pocket, took the piece of paper with the names and addresses, and handed it over.

Miranda looked over it quickly. "So long as you confine the use of the key to these addresses only, you have my blessing." She held out the key again.

Nikki didn't grab it. "Including your place?"

Miranda didn't bother to hide her irritation. "Of course."

Nikki took the key. "Thank you."

Miranda looked tired, the weight of a city's responsibilities weighing heavily upon her shoulders. "Just save us. That's all I've ever cared about."

NIKKI POUNDED on the door hard enough to make the wood tremble. The two Shields she'd asked to accompany her leaned against the opposite wall, eyes closed. "This is

Senior Shield Nikki. Please open the door, or we'll open it for you."

Her patience, already worn thin by the endless bickering of the preceding archivists, lasted only half the time she should have waited. An angry voice called out from the other side of the door. Nikki rolled her eyes and slammed her newly acquired master key into the lock. The door opened on squeaky hinges, and she stepped into the entryway.

"I told you I'm busy," a gravelly voice called from the living room further in.

"And I mentioned that I'm a Shield on an official visit," Nikki answered.

The walls of the narrow entryway were unadorned and painted a flat white that might have been the room's original color. The two Shields accompanying her pushed themselves off the wall and followed her in, hands close to the batons at their hips.

Their wariness, though appreciated, proved unnecessary. The owner of the voice was bent over a table filled with books and scraps of paper. A cup of water perspired at his feet so as to leave the entire table full for his study, which, for the volume of paper piled upon the desk, could have easily been the complete history of all the cities. Her gaze ran across the volumes, looking for the missing journals, but they didn't appear to be among the collection.

Since this was the last name on their list, that was something of a shame.

The man who sat at the table was shorter than Nikki and probably weighed about as much, though only if his clothes were on and they were soaking wet. His hair had gone from gray to white, and he held the paper he read almost up to his nose.

"I take it you are Archivist Renner?"

Her only answer was an impatient grunt. Nikki walked over, placed her hand on his wrist, and pushed the paper down. Eyes the color of freshly tilled soil rose to meet her gaze. "I am, and you're tremendously rude, young lady."

Nikki gestured to the other Shields, who began a thorough but careful search of the apartment.

"I'm also quite certain you don't have the right to be searching through my rooms," Renner added, more annoyed than angry.

"They'll be done quickly. Did you know that several important documents have gone missing from the archives?"

Renner's eyes narrowed, and for the first time since she'd stepped into the room, Nikki felt as though she possessed the majority of his attention. "What documents?"

"The ones first noticed missing are the collected journals of Karolyn and Cole, although Adele is currently searching through the archives to see if anything else has gone missing."

Renner grunted again. "So that's why you're here."

The hairs on the back of Nikki's neck tingled, the way they did when she thought she might finally have cracked open part of a mystery. Renner's name *had* come up in several of their previous interviews, but never in such a way that had convinced Nikki he was a person of interest. They were just going down Adele's list, and he happened to be last.

"And why are we here, sir?" she asked.

"Because if those are the documents that are missing, the other archivists almost certainly would have mentioned my name. I've probably spent more time with them than anyone else in Firestone. Or, uh, Underhill," he said, correcting himself.

They had, but most of them, in the next breath, had admitted there was little point in Renner stealing the journals, as he likely knew every word within them by heart. Nikki decided it was best not to inform Renner of his suspected innocence. "We have heard your name thrown around quite a bit, but you seem a man of honor, so I'll ask you directly: did you steal them?"

"No."

"Do you have any idea who might have?"

"No."

Nikki held back a smile. She liked the old man. His answers weren't short because of a lack of manners, but because they were complete as they were, and he refused to adorn them with speculation or excuses. "Do you have any idea why someone would want to steal them?"

Renner's gaze traveled to the ceiling and remained fixed there for a long moment. "I imagine there are those who are finally realizing the past might have some answers to our most pressing problems. Too late, it seems to me, but better late than never."

Nikki gestured to an open chair at the table. "Do you mind if I sit down?"

His expression told her the answer was yes, but he had the grace not to say so out loud. "Please be my guest."

"Why are these journals so important? Before today, I'd never heard of them."

"That says less about the importance of the journals and more about the quality of your upbringing."

The two Shields finished their exploration of the apartment. "We didn't find anything, ma'am."

"Thank you for your help today. You're dismissed, and

if you don't feel the need to report to the duty desk for the remainder of your shift, I won't say anything."

The Shields grinned and bowed. "Thank you, ma'am."

They left with more enthusiasm than she'd seen from them all day.

Nikki turned back to Renner. "You understand the intent behind my question. You seem to know why someone would want these books, and knowing that might help me find whoever took them."

Renner leaned back in his chair and crossed his arms. He tapped the fingers of his left hand against his right bicep while he weighed some judgment of her. "Very well. You know nothing of the journals?"

"You have my permission to treat me like the idiot you already think I am."

That earned a hint of a smile, and he uncrossed his arms. "Karolyn and Cole were siblings who were children when Firestone launched. Unfortunately, their journals say little about the birth of Firestone and the events that forced the Makers into the sky. The journals begin about ten years after the exodus, and they deal almost exclusively with the duo's own adventures. We can guess that their father was a Maker military commander who either died during the exodus or shortly after, but that's about all we know of the pair's biographies."

The archivist's words came faster as he warmed up to his subject. His dark brown eyes danced, and he leaned forward as he continued. "What would interest you today, and what should have interested the clan long before, was that they frequently returned to the surface, a habit that dropped them in no small amount of trouble here in Firestone. They weren't writing with an eye to the future, and so they left out a lot of details that were probably meaningless or obvious to them. My idea is that the clans were already actively discouraging people from attempting to return to the surface, but Karolyn and Cole believed humanity could still return. They completed several scouting expeditions and eventually tried to build a habitat on the surface, one I imagine was much like the one that shelters us today."

"Could they be the ancestors of the warriors our Manirah fought on the surface?"

"It's possible, but I would personally think it's unlikely. We have a record of Karolyn's death on Nightkeep a good four decades after the writing of the journals. I've never been able to track down what happened to Cole. Karolyn's final entries were very terse and cryptic, but it's hard to believe their venture was a success."

Nikki had entered Renner's room with the goal of crossing the last name off her list, but now she wondered if she hadn't stumbled upon something far more valuable. "You've heard of the shadow song by now?"

Renner nodded.

"The Blade believes it has a source. We know that those who survived on the surface are linked to the shadow song."

"And so you hope to find clues to the location of the source by learning more about the survivors of the exodus," Renner finished for her.

"Exactly. Can you help us?"

Renner cleared his throat. "It's not that I can't, but that I won't."

Nikki could offer nothing but a blank stare. "Excuse me?"

Renner shrugged and tilted his head toward the stack of papers sitting on his table. "I'd rather not prolong humanity's suffering. The shadow has broken free of its confinement, which means there's little time left for any of us. Even if there is a source, what will you do? Kaya was the only Singer with any of the old skill."

"Though that might be true, we don't give up."

Renner sighed. "It's not just that there's no point in fighting. It's that there's nothing to fight for. Look at me. I've spent my entire life teasing out the hidden histories of this world, but the clan refuses to teach even a single line of my many writings. They call upon us when they need us, but otherwise treat archivists as meaningless tools. I have no family, because I've never wanted to bring children into a world that will only make them suffer. The cities kept humanity alive, but it's hardly an existence worth fighting for. Better, I think, to end it all here. To take our rest for good."

Nikki opened her mouth to object, only she didn't know where to begin.

"There's no argument you could offer that would persuade me," Renner said gently. "I've long since resigned myself to humanity's fate, and it's freed me like nothing else has."

"Are you a disciple of shadow?" Nikki asked.

"No, though I can understand why the cult has the appeal it does. Do you know what I've learned after a lifetime of studying history?"

Nikki shook her head.

"Humanity never changes, and it never improves. There were Makers who, in the exodus, believed that humanity had been given another chance. The original purpose of the clan academies, if you can believe it, wasn't just to pass on basic facts and identify those suited to become Manirah. It was to create generations of virtuous citizens. But now they only teach a very basic, watered-down history. They spend more of their time teaching their students better ways to kill one another. We always fall back to the level of beasts. It's time to end the farce."

"If reason and duty fall short of convincing you, what of greed? I report directly to the Blade, and if it is within his power to grant, I'm sure he'd offer it in exchange for your knowledge and assistance."

"A generous offer, but there's nothing I desire."

"Nothing?"

Renner considered for a moment, then ran his eyes up and down her like a wolf hungry for a meal. "There is, perhaps, one thing."

Nikki stood and turned to leave.

Renner mocked her as she strode toward the door. "Maybe you should ask your precious Blade and see what he says. It would be done in moments, and then everything locked away in my mind would be yours for the taking."

Nikki reached the door and glared at him. "And you have the temerity to accuse humanity of failing to learn from its mistakes. You sit here and judge only because your spirit is too small and weak to strive for the changes it desires. As great as your knowledge may be, you do nothing with it."

She stormed from the room before he answered.

7

Tanwen fled from the falling city, sacrificing a considerable portion of their altitude in exchange for speed. They dropped through the clouds, the Song of Tanwen's spirit churning beneath Radyn, who gripped the dragon's scales tightly enough his knuckles turned white. He didn't understand the rush until Skystone hit.

A low sound, deeper than the boom of a thunderstorm, served as Radyn's first warning. He glanced back, and the sight stole his breath away. An enormous dust cloud rose into the sky, racing upward and outward. The low roar grew louder until it was deafening, the world itself protesting against the violent blow. The trees below trembled, weak-kneed before the approaching destruction.

Moments later, they shivered and collapsed as the ground gave out underneath them. Decades of slow growth, of digging deeper roots year after year, came to nothing as they suddenly realized they had nothing to hold on to. The entire world shook, and Tanwen's response was to push even harder for more speed, as though he was in a race he was certain he was going to lose. Destruction sped ahead of them, the ground breaking faster than Tanwen could fly.

Radyn saw the ripple in the air a moment before Tanwen twisted hard. The dragon put his massive bulk between Radyn and the destruction. He was folding his wings in when the wave hit.

Pain cut deep into Radyn's body and his spirit. The air was crushed from his lungs as his ears popped, but his suffering was nothing like what he felt from Tanwen through their connection. The blast crushed Tanwen's chest, and one of his wings, caught halfway between being stretched wide and folded in, broke against the force.

Dragon and rider spun end over end, Radyn helpless as a newborn babe. Flight was Tanwen's domain. All he could do was hold on and hope for the best. Ground and sky danced chaotically in his vision, blurring into a meaningless kaleidoscopic illusion.

Tanwen extended his good wing and used the Song of his spirit to slow their spin, then tentatively extended his other wing. Radyn cried out as the pain of it flared across his arm, which burned as though dipped in oil and lit by a torch. Tanwen held the wing out despite the searing agony.

They still fell too fast, but Tanwen had regained some control. With one last mighty flare of endurance and spirit, he slowed enough to land hard on outstretched legs. Radyn slammed hard into Tanwen's back, knocking the air from his lungs. Tanwen cut their connection. Much of Radyn's pain fell away, and he leaped off Tanwen's back. The dragon settled to the ground, and Radyn pressed his palms against the dragon's scales, but Tanwen firmly rebuffed his attempts to connect.

Radyn took a few steps back and looked around. The enormous cloud of dust that marked Skystone's grave dominated the sky, but Radyn felt certain they were distant enough to avoid the dangers the cloud posed. The ground felt loose, and there were downed trees nearby, but the worst of the destruction had passed the place where Tanwen had landed.

They were safe for the moment, though Radyn wasn't sure how long he'd trust that safety. Long enough, though, to look to his friend, who had almost certainly saved his life by taking the worst of the blow.

Radyn thought of Veylan and the thousands of souls that had been trapped upon Skystone, then shook his head.

Later. Now he needed to figure out how to get home, to return to Aria's embrace.

He ran his eyes over the horizon one more time, and then, satisfied he was as safe as the moment allowed, turned his attention to his wounded friend. Tanwen barely moved where he lay, though the Song in his spirit burned as bright as the sun. Radyn approached cautiously. "May I help you?"

Tanwen cracked open one eye, then closed it again. Unsure if that counted as consent, Radyn took another careful step and placed his hand against Tanwen's scales. The dragon didn't shake him off, and Radyn connected with his shards, extending an invitation to his old friend.

Tanwen didn't reject the connection outright, but he seemed hesitant to accept it. Given the strength of the Song pouring through him, Radyn could guess why well enough. Tanwen gave everything to heal himself. Connecting to the dragon now was almost as dangerous as connecting alone to an Engine. Radyn studied the energies as they flowed through Tanwen's wounded body.

"I can handle it," he said.

Tanwen hesitated a moment longer, then relented. Fire ran up Radyn's arm and across his body as barely controlled energies surged through him. If not for the long years he'd spent adapting to the shards in his body, he wouldn't have stood a chance against the force. As it was, he barely held on. Tanwen's strength lashed across his spirit, an untamed energy that could have shattered mountains.

Radyn planted his feet and focused the Song the way Elora had taught him so long ago, though neither of them had ever imagined he would endure this much of it coursing through his veins. A small fraction of this had knocked him out cold when his fellow students had first welcomed him into the academy.

He wouldn't lose Tanwen. Not to the shadow, and certainly not like this. His will formed unbreakable passages that channeled the Song into Tanwen's most grievous wounds. Several of the dragon's ribs had cracked, and one had broken, puncturing a massive lung. Radyn groaned as he forced the power across the broken rib, setting it straight and rebuilding it as good as new.

Once the rib was in place, he twisted the passages until the song focused its healing on the lung. Radyn held it there, as though he was attempting to hold a struggling bear in place.

When Radyn finally broke the connection between him and Tanwen, the sky was dark. He thought that night had fallen, but a sliver of light broke a crack open between the shattered land and clouds overhead, and he realized the dust cloud had spread far above them, blocking much of the sun's light. He shivered as he wondered how far the cloud would spread.

His tongue stuck to the roof of his mouth, and he searched for any sign of a stream nearby that would slake his thirst. He pressed his lips tightly together as he considered the broken land.

No water, then, and no food, either. If he hadn't stayed

behind to offer Veylan an escape, he would be with the others now, safely away from this disaster. At least, he hoped they'd been far enough away to stay safe.

He stuffed the thought with all the others surrounding Veylan and Skystone, a locked chest he didn't plan on opening until he was somewhere far away.

Radyn stumbled back toward Tanwen, connected with all his shards, and resumed the long healing process.

He lost track of time as darkness fell. He served Tanwen as long as he was able, but his body and spirit could only endure the strength of Tanwen's song for so long. When he reached his limit, he broke the connection, shuffled a few paces away, and collapsed to the ground. Tired eyes watched the horizon, but he and Tanwen were the only living things larger than a blade of grass within miles.

Twice he fell asleep, a restless experience that left him more tired upon his waking than when he'd gone to sleep. Still, he pushed himself to his feet, returned to Tanwen, and connected once again.

He woke sometime in the morning, not having remembered falling asleep. He blinked dust and grime from his eyes and sat up. A heavy haze filled the sky, and Radyn was alone in a world of gray. He twisted and saw the enormous shadow of Tanwen close. The dragon looked to be resting peacefully, and the Song within his spirit didn't burn as brightly as it had through the night before.

Radyn lifted his tunic to wipe the dirt from his face, only to find he was covered in a fine dust from crown to toe. He fought his way to his feet, tired limbs complaining about the demands his spirit placed upon them. His own spirit felt weak, a flickering ember barely reminiscent of its former glory. Blood pounded in his head, and he knew he would pay for the help he'd offered Tanwen—not that he'd ever do any differently.

He searched the haze for any sign of movement, but he caught none. The surroundings too were strangely silent. His time in Underhill had taught him that land that seemed empty rarely was. Beyond the bugs that burrowed beneath his feet, birds and critters were everywhere, and if he listened long enough, they'd make themselves known.

Not today, though. He was as alone as he'd ever been, the fall of Skystone stripping this land of life. Any who could move had surely fled by now. The only sound that reached his ears was that of Tanwen's easy breathing.

Wandering from Tanwen's side seemed the height of foolishness. He couldn't tell if any danger lurked in the murky haze, and it wasn't as though there was anything for him to explore. All that was out there was destruction on a scale he'd never considered possible. Hunger, thirst, and the hollow pain of using too much of his strength warred within his exhausted body, but Tanwen needed rest, and so Radyn sat with his suffering in silence.

Eventually the dragon stirred. He raised his head, and his eyes were clear.

Radyn breathed easier at the sight. He invited a connection, though his body protested the continued use of his shards. "How are you feeling?"

Tanwen shared his litany of aches and pains not as complaint, but as truthful answer. Despite them, he was ready to take to the sky and be gone from this place.

"Me too, old friend."

Radyn climbed onto Tanwen's back, and the dragon cautiously lifted himself to his feet. He stretched one wing and then the other, testing them before allowing his Song to flow through and across them. Tanwen reported he was ready, and Radyn held tighter as the dragon pushed himself into the air. The haze didn't fade until they were well above the surface, but the warmth of the morning sun began to beat back the icy dread that had been creeping across Radyn's spirit.

The cool wind generated by Tanwen's flight blew the dust from Radyn's body and soul, and despite the events of the past few days, he dared to hope they might yet find a way.

Tanwen banked so that they flew toward Underhill, but they didn't make it far before a sudden emptiness opened within Radyn's heart. The shadow song struck a single note, a string plucked too hard, freezing the blood in his veins. He and Tanwen turned as one toward the answering silence. Radyn saw nothing at first, but then the haze that covered the surface like a dirty pond bubbled.

Several of the small bubbles joined to form a bulge the size of a small hill. It continued to grow, the hill becoming the better part of a mountain. The small humanoid shadows that had brought down Skystone swarmed across the surface like ants over the corpse of some other small bug. Their shadows melted into the dark, rising mountain. Shapes formed, a head rising from the top of the mountain as enormous arms extended to its sides.

Radyn couldn't tear his eyes away. He swore, then looked away as the nuddu began its long hunt for another floating city to kill.

8

Nikki followed well-known hallways that her feet could walk without conscious intervention. Storming out on Renner had been the very least he deserved, and he was fortunate she hadn't gone further than that. There had been a time in her life when she would have left him broken and bleeding across his precious papers and not thought twice about the devastation she'd left behind.

The quiet monotony of Underhill's evening routines sapped the righteous anger from her heart. The day's work was done, and the few people she passed were workers returning home late after a long day of service. Despite the nuddu chasing after Firestone in an endless circle only a few miles away, they'd collapse on their couches, or play with their children, or make love with their husbands and wives. Life thrived, even in the shadow of death.

If it were possible to physically pound a lesson into someone's skull, that was what she'd etch onto the nail that would pierce Renner's thick-headed illusions. Surrender wasn't just cowardly; it was plain wrong.

She didn't deny the twinge of guilt that lurked in the shadows of her mental tirade against the archivist. If he had information that could save Underhill, wasn't what he'd asked a small price to pay? She'd long ago sworn to do all that was within her power to protect Firestone, and she slept well at night knowing she'd kept her promise. Would her dreams come as easily tonight?

Eventually her feet brought her, as she knew they would, to the large front gate of Underhill. A pair of junior Daggers standing guard stopped her. Neither recognized her, too young and self-absorbed to be bothered to learn the names and ranks of all their neighbors. The taller of the two stood in her way. "It's getting close to nightfall, ma'am. No one except clan Manirah may leave."

She fixed him with a withering stare that did approximately nothing to his composure. "I'm Senior Shield Nikki."

Her appearance might not have opened any doors, but her name certainly did. The youth bowed and stepped out of her way. "Of course, ma'am. I'm sorry I didn't recognize you. Four knocks will get you back in."

Nikki stepped through the gate and into a world of subdued browns and grays. Clouds on the horizon threatened rain, welcomed by farmers and fields alike. A chilly breeze raced ahead of the clouds and cut through the thin layers of Nikki's clothes.

Fabric was quickly becoming one of Underhill's more pressing problems. No feat of Singing would move Underhill to warmer climates, as Firestone had done when it housed almost all of them. Families that had never seen snow before now needed the boots and heavy cloaks necessary to survive it, and they didn't have nearly enough wool, leather, and fabric for everyone. Requests had been sent out to other cities and, if the rumors Nikki had heard were true, even to other Soulkeeper settlements. But now that the nuddu were loose, larger problems had taken precedence.

The thing was, though, was that just because they had larger problems, it didn't mean the small ones couldn't hurt them.

Nikki stayed close to the edges of the mound. The warning system Kaya and Aria had built meant it was most likely safe to wander farther, but she wasn't in a mood to test her luck. Her thoughts wanted space, but she didn't need any greater risk than what she was taking by merely being outdoors.

She stopped at Kaya's grave marker. She hadn't spent as much time with the Singer as Radyn or Aria, but they'd fought side-by-side, so she felt as close to Kaya as a sister. Her throat tightened at the sight of the silent stone, and as she thought about the circumstances that had brought about Kaya's death, she wondered if Renner didn't have the right of it. Any city that would condemn someone like Kaya to death deserved whatever doom befell it.

And at the end of the day, was Firestone or Underhill any different? She hated Skystone and Nightkeep and all the other cities that had demanded Kaya's head, but if she hadn't known Kaya personally, wouldn't she have called for blood, too? It was all too easy to put herself in their position.

She had no simple answers.

Nikki completed the lap around the mound, then returned to the sealed gate and knocked four times. The Daggers let her in, and she wandered the halls until she reached an intersection. Left would return her to her apartment, while a right led to Archivist Renner's.

She paused, but only for a moment, weighing her options. Then she turned left.

Her sleep that night was deep and dreamless.

***

THE NEXT MORNING, Nikki reviewed what she knew about the missing journals, which was pitifully little. Her interviews with the various archivists hadn't given her any solid leads. Renner was the only real question, but in her gut, Nikki didn't believe he'd taken the journals, which left her with…nothing. She could retrace the steps she'd already taken, see if any stories changed, but that was probably a waste of time. Years of this kind of work had given her a sense of when it was necessary to walk the same ground again and when it was better to try a new way forward, and this had the feel of the latter.

In lieu of choosing a specific direction, she delayed by visiting the small headquarters Firestone's Shields had set up after their unexpected move to Underhill. The room nestled among Underhill's lower levels, closer to where supplies were stored and where the various shops that churned out Underhill's necessities were found. It was a far cry from the more central location they'd enjoyed in Firestone, and their new location echoed the awkward territory all Shields found themselves in after the transition to surface-dwelling.

Prior to the unplanned arrival of the refugees from Firestone, Underhill hadn't had Shields, nor any Soulkeeper equivalent. Those who had lived upon the surface had been thoroughly vetted, passing through the discerning eyes of the Soulkeeper elders and granted a place in the underground city. Because of that, and because those who had lived in Underhill had enjoyed the vast benefits of shared purpose, the Soulkeeper settlement hadn't needed to wrestle with the problems Shields needed to solve in the cities. There was no real theft or disorderly behavior to speak of, and what slight problems did arise could be solved by the elders.

Not only had Underhill not needed Shields, but they'd been proud of that fact. But then they'd opened their gates to Firestone's refugees.

The vast majority of Firestone's residents caused no problems, but some did, and the Shields had offered their services. As Nikki understood it, there had been quite the debate between Jyn, Miranda, and the councils of both Underhill and Firestone.

In the end, they'd reached an uneasy compromise, represented by Firestone's Shields residing in what was obviously an old storage room in Underhill's lower levels. They still performed the duties they'd served in Firestone, only now they were no longer considered a branch of the clan. They reported directly to Underhill's council, which was why Nikki and several others had temporarily resigned their official duties and taken other roles within the city.

Nikki still wore the uniform, though, when the need arose, and still called herself a Shield. Awkward, yes, but like the location of the Shields' headquarters, it sufficed for the moment.

Most eyes in the room noted her arrival, but few paid her any special attention. The Shield at the front desk, though, greeted her warmly. "You had a visitor earlier today," she said.

"Who?"

The young woman frowned and searched through her notes. "An archivist, if I recall. Ah, here it is. Renner. He didn't say much when he found out you weren't here. He just wanted to tell you he wanted to see you again."

"Were those his exact words?"

The Shield made a face, as though dredging up recent memories was a chore she preferred to avoid. "I think so?"

Nikki would have pressed for more details, but the Shield seemed to be at the limits of her memory. No matter. She could find out the rest with a bit of legwork. "Anything else I should know about?"

The other Shield's blank stare was answer enough. Nikki grunted. "Never mind. Thanks for letting me know."

She'd suspected her day would include another visit to Renner's, and now that was as good as certain. She'd bet a week's worth of rations, though, that he only wanted to make another pass at her. As far as he was concerned, the world could burn. All that mattered were his own selfish needs.

Nikki resigned herself to the encounter, but chose to visit Adele first. The senior archivist would know Renner best and might identify an angle Nikki could take to pry the information from those journals out of him. Maybe she'd even found something else after their last visit that would help.

Adele was, as Nikki expected, sitting at the desk at the front of the archives. She looked up and nodded when Nikki stepped in. "Senior Shield. I hoped I might see you again today."

"You found something?"

"I did. The journals of Karolyn and Cole are probably the most complete works we have from the time immediately following the exodus, but they aren't the only writings from that time. After your visit yesterday, I combed the archives for all that I could think of, and I'm afraid the problem is greater than I feared. Almost all of our collection from that time period is gone."

Nikki's heart pounded faster, and she looked around the room, as though someone hid in the nonexistent shadows, waiting to pounce. She silently cursed Radyn for involving her in another mess, then doomed herself as a hypocrite by thanking him in the next breath. There was a hunt on. Her attention, too long unfocused, narrowed. Memories of the past faded into mist, and the future was barely worth considering. She turned the full force of her renewed attention to Adele. "Does the set of missing books tell us anything about what our thief was interested in?"

"Nothing we didn't know before. There's no common theme among the various works. One work is a novel. There are the journals. We have a ledger from a banker."

"A banker?"

"The Makers facilitated exchange through the medium of money. A problem of abundance we don't have."

Nikki vaguely remembered her academy lessons and nodded. "So random, except for the fact of when they were written."

"Exactly. So, it stands to reason that whoever took them was also looking for information from as close to the Exodus as possible."

"Or they were trying to keep anyone else from finding it."

Adele's eyes widened a bit, as though that idea hadn't occurred to her. "That could also be true."

Nikki's thoughts were like a beam of light piercing deep into the darkness of the mystery. "It gives us a valuable clue, though. It limits our suspects."

"How?"

"Removing one set of journals from the archives would be difficult, but not impossible, without specialized knowledge. To know all these different books, though, and to remove them without any other archivists being the wiser? I suppose it's still possible it's not an archivist, but that doesn't seem likely to me. Would you agree?"

Adele gave a curt nod. "I wouldn't have considered that, but you're right. It has to be one of us. Did you have any luck yesterday?"

"Renner's name came up often, and I'll confess he didn't impress me when we met in person."

The ghost of a smile passed over Adele's lips at that. "He rarely does."

"Perhaps you could offer me an insight into his character. He freely admitted that he could probably help me with my questions regarding the journals, but refused to do so, for he feels that it's too late for humanity. Is there a way to motivate him to help? He came to find me today, but I doubt he's had a change of heart."

Adele's eyes narrowed to slits. "He came to see you?"

Nikki nodded. "Is that surprising?"

Adele recovered and leaned back in her chair. "It is. These days, he's become as good as a recluse. He's not the only person I know who's given up hope, but few have done it as dramatically as he has. If he left his rooms to find you, it's clear you made more of an impression on him than you give yourself credit for."

"You think he might be willing to help?"

Adele shrugged. "I long ago gave up trying to understand what motivates that man. It's promising, though. If there's anyone who knows the information you're looking for, it's him. As a point of fact, he knows more about everything within the lost books than anyone else."

"If he's still not willing, do you have any advice?"

"None that you want to hear. He's a man of base passions, a problem that has only grown worse these last few years. He's come to believe that nothing matters more than his own pleasure, and he seeks as much of that as possible before his spirit travels to the gate. Still, he's an honest enough man, and you can trust what he says."

"I was hoping more for a secret I could use to extort his cooperation."

Adele snorted. "I'm afraid he's long since passed the time that extortion would have any effect. You could threaten to cut his rations, but I expect it would be several days before that convinced him to help."

Nikki bowed. "I appreciate your advice. I'll stop by again after I talk to him."

"You're going to him now?"

Nikki nodded.

"Then I might recommend trying the cafeterias first. If you got him to leave his apartment, he might be out sampling all the delights he can get his fat fingers on."

Nikki followed Adele's advice. She slipped through the busy hallways like a ghost, passing unnoticed by those consumed with their own worries and duties. The air felt thick, as though the filters and fans had stopped working, but it was only the accumulated fear of so many people.

Fortunately there were only four cafeterias currently in operation, so she didn't have many places to check. She couldn't find Renner's figure anywhere in the first, and she was on her way to the second when the earthquake hit.

Her heart leaped into her throat as the world rumbled. In the blink of an eye, she was back on Firestone in the middle of The Little Fall, as everything that was supposed to be solid became an unstable lie. She'd grown up encased in a mountain, and it had been all too easy to forget that the mountain flew hundreds, if not thousands, of feet in the air.

Underhill wasn't supposed to tremble, and it certainly wasn't supposed to feel as though it were falling. It was the one promise the surface made that Firestone never could: that no matter what happened, the ground beneath her feet would never shake. Her stomach twisted and knotted, a scared child once again looking for someone stronger to hold her close.

The force of the quake threw her off her feet and against a wall. The lights in the hallway dimmed, though they never went completely dark. Dust leaped from its hiding places in crevices and on top of ledges to rain down upon anyone caught in the halls. Makers' steel cried out in agony as the world sought to bend, twist, and crush it like a piece of clay.

The quake vanished as quickly as it had appeared; the rumbles passed through Underhill like a ripple passing through water. Nikki coughed and spat and tried to stand, but her legs trembled as though the ground still shook, and she fell back against the wall. Her heart pounded in her chest, even as the lanterns in the hallway returned to full strength and banished the fears of her past.

She sat huddled in the corner for a moment longer until the moans and cries of the injured pierced the comfortable haze that had settled over her thoughts. They stabbed her spirit, and she cursed her fears. She wasn't a child anymore.

She stood and checked herself for injuries. At worst, she might have a bruise across her back in the morning, but she was otherwise unharmed. Others nearby hadn't been so lucky. One tall young man had fallen into the bottom of a lantern and earned a deep cut across his scalp that bled worse than some stab wounds Nikki had witnessed.

Glad to have something to focus on besides her fears,

Nikki hurried over to the young man. She pulled a dagger from the sheath at her side and cut a strip of linen from his shirt that she tied around his head. "Can you move?"

He nodded, then winced as he regretted his decision.

"Good. Get yourself to a healer. Don't stop for anything, and whatever you do, don't close your eyes before you get there. Do you understand?"

She helped him to his feet, then pushed him in the appropriate direction. Then she looked around again. The hallway immediately surrounding her was filled with confused and worried men and women, but she saw no more blood. A woman cried for help down the hallway, and Nikki rushed toward the sound. She found a woman huddled close in the corner of her room, holding a baby tight to her chest. The baby wasn't crying, and the woman held it so tight Nikki couldn't see if it was capable of moving.

She introduced herself and then entered the room to see how she could help.

Nikki slumped onto a bench outside the healer's rooms. The last person she'd helped had been an older man who'd taken a nasty fall inside his apartment when the quake had hit. Despite his insistence that he'd broken his hip, she'd helped him walk to the healer, supporting most of his weight on the way. She suspected he'd bruised his hip only, but decided it was best for her fraying patience if he learned that from the healer instead of her.

She leaned her head back against the Makers' steel of the hallway and closed her eyes, hoping to take some strength from the material. The quake had shaken and squeezed the steel, but it held, the long-dead Makers still protecting their descendants. If it didn't quit, she wouldn't either.

She'd helped people across a decent slice of Underhill, and while the quake had put the fear of the gate in most, the actual damage done to Underhill seemed minimal. The structure had bent under the pressure but held its form, and the vast majority of injuries were minor. Other problems might yet arise, but those problems were Miranda's.

A long night in a quiet bed called to her, but she wouldn't be able to sleep until she spoke with Renner, so she heaved her body off the bench and navigated the hallways toward his apartment. People were already sweeping the hallways and washing the walls, returning Underhill slowly to normalcy.

They could sweep and wipe the dust away, but they couldn't so easily remove the fear that made their eyes skitter back and forth, couldn't erase the terror that kept shoulders hunched. Several she passed reminded her of prey hiding in the bushes, ready to sprint at the crack of a twig. They'd already been through too much. Most had survived The Little Fall, as well as the barely controlled descent to the surface only a few months ago. Now even the surface trembled, a visceral reminder that there was nowhere safe they could hide.

Nikki couldn't take their fear away. She could barely contain her own. She could, though, fight for a world in which that fear would eventually fade.

She knocked at Renner's door, but there was no answer. When another knock failed to stir the archivist from whatever activity distracted him on the other side of the door, Nikki tried the doorknob, which turned easily in her hand.

"Renner?" she called.

When there was no answer, she stepped inside, then swore as the thick, sweet smell of death hit her nose.

She drew her dagger out of habit, though she didn't anticipate needing it. Given the smell, the killing had happened several hours ago, at least.

She found him at the same table he'd been at the last time she had entered. He'd be glad to know, she imagined, that his death hadn't destroyed too many of his papers. He'd been stabbed half a dozen times in his torso, at least, and the blood had dripped down over the chair until it collected in a puddle around the chair's thick legs. His arms were clear of defensive wounds, and Nikki's first thought was that he'd been too lazy even to defend himself.

She thrust her dagger into its sheath and swore again. She should have sought him out as soon as she'd known he was searching for her. What she'd thought of as an annoyance took on a different feeling now.

She made an oath to his corpse. Her negligence might have served to get him killed, but she promised him she would find his killer and bring them to justice.

9

Removing his hand from the shrine was harder than letting go of a lover's arm, but the Seer resisted the temptation to reach out and caress the shrine again, to connect with the darkness and silence that waited within. He gestured for Belzrak to cover the shrine with an oversized piece of cloth, and the surface clansman carried out his wish a moment later. The shrine still called to him, but the covering dulled the longing ache in his spirit.

Belzrak was too observant not to notice the emotions that openly played across the Seer's face. "It is gaining power over you."

The Seer wiped the sweat from his brow. "It does. It is powerful and starving, and it will twist whatever it touches so that it may consume ever more of the Song."

"If its purpose so closely aligns with yours, then why resist it?"

Belzrak's question cut to the heart of the matter and forced the Seer to lie. The clansman's belief in the shadow song was simple and unshakeable. That belief made him a useful tool. Unfortunately, the blade of Belzrak's service was sharp, and the Seer had to be careful not to cut himself.

"Because it has no intelligence of its own. It is a dumb beast, and one needs to look no further than the nuddu as proof. The creatures chase cities around the world, but because they simply pursue, the cities can run. The shrines, at least for now, need my intelligence even as I need their strength. I look forward to the day I can surrender my will to that of the shadow song, but not until I'm sure its purpose will be complete."

Belzrak's gaze saw too much, the Seer's lies too thin a protection, but little choice remained. For the moment, their purposes aligned, and so long as that remained true, he needn't fear. Belzrak leaned back, his inquiry complete. "What will you do when Nightkeep discovers you have no intention of allowing them to live?"

The same thing I'll do when you realize the same is true of the shadow tribes. "We have the shrine. Through it, I hold a blade to their necks, and if that time comes, I will remind them of it."

"You play dangerous games."

"They are not games to me."

A knock at the door interrupted Belzrak's interrogation. The door opened, and one of the Daggers guarding the door poked his head in. "There's a messenger requesting your presence at a council meeting."

The Seer had no desire to leave the shrine, but Belzrak had sworn his life to its protection, and the Seer couldn't ask for better. It would be a relief to flee from those searching eyes. Belzrak was no fool, but he wasn't yet sure enough of the Seer's duplicity to take action. The Seer walked along a razor's edge, danger lurking on both sides.

Such was the life he had chosen, the dangers of a life of purpose. Belzrak hadn't drawn his blade against him yet, and now he had to ensure Nightkeep's council kept theirs sheathed, too.

"I'll be right there," he told his guard.

The number of guards standing watch outside the council chamber made the Seer wonder if the council members expected a coup. He'd witnessed battles with less Manirah, and those that clogged the hallways wore stern expressions like they were a mandatory part of the uniform. They looked down their noses at him, many scowling as he passed, not even bothering to hide their disdain. The Seer imagined running down the hall, strengthened by the shadow song, his midnight blades carving through the guards as they failed to react in time.

Soon. The farce was almost over. The day would come when they no longer looked down their noses. When they understood the true nature of the man they judged so unfairly.

The door was opened for him, and he was as good as shoved inside. The room had been nearly silent before his arrival, and as every face pivoted to fix him with a sharp stare, he surmised they'd been waiting for him. He stood on the opposite side of a battle he hadn't planned for, and his enemies had marshaled all their forces.

Semuel and Lynae sat near the center of the table, the commanders at the head of their forces. Dougan, Master of Nightkeep's Song, sat beside them with his fingers steepled.

It was no wonder they had as many guards outside as they did. If trouble were to erupt in this room, Nightkeep's leadership would be crippled.

The Seer feigned ignorance. After so many months of

practice, the act came almost as naturally as breathing. "You wished to see me?"

The weight of their combined regard was nearly suffocating. Some of the assembled council stared, as though they feared being deceived if they so much as blinked.

His expression was as blank as a snow-covered prairie, revealing nothing of the emotions hidden deep within. Semuel let the Seer's question linger as his allies searched for cracks in the facade. When none were readily apparent, he said, "We do. We've just received disturbing news."

The Seer looked at Semuel with undisguised curiosity, as though he waited in suspense for the Elder's reveal. When none came, he asked, "What news, sir?"

Again, his question was met with a wall of judgmental gazes, each weighing his perceived innocence. Sweat slicked his armpits, but he kept his expression curious. Finally, Semuel nodded to Dougan, who said, "The Singers have felt the death of Skystone's Engine. The city has fallen."

The Seer bowed his head, hoping the gesture conveyed a sense of sorrow. His reply came easily, though, for he'd suspected the purpose of this meeting. "Though I've long foreseen this day, I'm sorry to hear this fate has come to pass. My only experience with Skystone was through Veylan, and I found him to be an honorable man."

Too honorable. And it cost him his city.

Thankfully, his face was hidden by his posture, and he didn't fear whatever flicker of emotion crossed his features. He waited to rise until he was sure of his expression, the very ideal of a man in mourning.

The weight of the judgment against him hardly lessened. He stood at the crux of the battle now, and if his lines held here, his victory was as good as assured.

Dougan's gaze searched him for any sign of betrayal as he asked, "You knew nothing of this?"

"Sir, as I've said many times, I'm no Singer, so what happens to the Engines is beyond my knowledge. It is the shadow song I understand."

"And it didn't warn you of what was about to happen?" Dougan pressed.

"Does an Engine tell you when it's about to fail?" the Seer replied.

He held up a hand to stall any outbursts. "Apologies. News of Skystone's fall has shortened my temper. I do not mean to insult you, but you must understand my limitations. I have seen only a glimpse of the future, and I've told you all that I know. With the assistance of the shrine, I can hide Nightkeep from the nuddu, but nothing more. Perhaps with more shrines, I might learn more of the shadow song, but for now you know all that I know."

A heavy silence greeted his explanation as each of the elders and leaders present carefully picked apart and weighed his words.

Like Belzrak, they were no fools who simply accepted his claims. Twice now they'd witnessed the nuddu ignore Nightkeep just as he'd claimed to do. What that meant, though, they hadn't decided. That he was a weapon was beyond doubt. Who that weapon was pointed at, though, was anybody's guess. They hoped it was at anyone but them, but they couldn't be certain.

Semuel let his gaze wander around the table, inviting any of the elders to share their opinion, only to be greeted by a silence the shadow song would have been proud of. It wasn't a Singer or an elder, but Lynae who spoke against him. "We are fools to trust him. I cannot deny he has kept us safe with the shadow song, but everything in my spirit rebels against his presence within our city."

Lynae's distrust of him came as no surprise, but Semuel's silent acceptance of it did. The Seer fumbled for an answer. "The Song of the Engines stands in opposition to the shadow song. After a lifetime of welcoming the Song into your body, your distrust is understandable. All I can ask is for my actions to speak for me. I've protected Nightkeep. Let that be proof enough of my intent."

"So you say." Lynae crossed her arms. "I can't point to any one act and claim it as evidence. I have been persuaded, both by Semuel but also by my own fears, to accept your presence, to let you worm your way deeper into the heart of our city. Yet my spirit still argues against you, and for every tale you tell us that is true, there is another that is equally likely, and I cannot weigh with any evidence which one is real."

Dougan, whom the Seer counted among his allies, leaned toward Lynae. "What other story is there?"

Lynae shrugged, as if to say she had no proof other than her imagination, then said, "That he is closer to the shadow than he lets us believe. That he hasn't simply hidden Nightkeep from the nuddu's gaze, but that he has commanded them elsewhere to gain our allegiance."

He couldn't have given away much, but she'd focused on his face as she uttered the accusation, and from the way her eyes widened, it was enough. She wasn't the only one, judging by the shifting postures around the room. The accusation had been a guess, but its edge was no less deadly than evidence. His defenses had been breached, and attackers poured through the gaps.

The Seer's thoughts froze, his troops unable to respond to the unexpected assault. In the sudden silence, the shadow song used the foothold in his spirit to sneak behind his reason and fill his body with its terrible power. Compelled by a force he understood far less than he believed, the Seer formed the shadow song into the shape of an attack Belzrak and the other shadow warriors had taught him as words poured from his throat. He wasn't even sure if they were his. "Beware the power of my master!"

He released the attack, and Lynae's eyes went wide. She stood and clutched at her chest as emptiness filled her heart and lungs. The lanterns in the room darkened as shadow overwhelmed the feeble trickle of the Song these humans had twisted to such mundane purposes.

"Lynae!" Dougan called. The Master of the Song seized the light from the Engine, but too late, his surprise nearly as complete as the Seer's own.

Lynae's chest bulged outward and, with a final, strangled cry, burst, the emptiness inside her wanting to spread. Blood and viscera flew, coating the table and the Seer. He wiped his hand across his face, and it came away bloody, and when he licked his lips, his mouth filled with the coppery taste of someone else's life.

Lynae's corpse fell forward, and the Seer stared with everyone else, for he couldn't have done what had just been done. Not here and now.

The silence of the shadow song surrounded him, cocooned him even as the first shouts for aid filled the council chambers. Mouths moved and fingers pointed, but all the Seer heard was the shadow's silent, mocking laughter at the feebleness of the humans who dared oppose it. The feeling found fertile soil to take root in the Seer's heart, and a madness took him then, laughter booming from his ample stomach.

The eyes that turned toward him no longer withheld judgment, no longer weighed his assumed intentions against theirs. Condemnation poured from every expression, but he shook it off like excess rain pouring off the sides of the cities. Why had he ever cared one whit for the cooperation of such creatures?

His laughter expelled some of the sudden madness that had seized him, and reason slowly reasserted its hold over the course of his thoughts. He stared at Lynae's corpse with mounting horror.

He'd never killed anyone before. Not like this. He'd ordered the deaths of countless souls long before he'd ordered the nuddu to bring down Skystone. Not once had he tossed and turned at night because of it. Humanity was a problem he solved one death at a time. His insides turned to water, and he looked from face to face, searching for the one friend who would save him.

The door to the council room opened behind him, and guards poured in. Strong arms took his own. He fought against them, but his strength was nothing against theirs. He sought the focus to form the shadow blades that came so easily to him in his rooms, but he might as well have tried to summon a thunderstorm.

The silence around him collapsed, and noise filled his ears. Everyone was shouting, from the council to the guards. He longed for silence once again, and the shadow grew firmer within his spirit.

Dougan pointed and shouted above the rest, and something struck him in the back of the head, and his wish was granted as consciousness gave way to a syrupy darkness.

10

Nikki sorted through Renner's papers as the other Shields wrapped and removed the body. Once finished, they returned and searched the room for clues. She could have told them they wouldn't find anything, but saved her breath. They did their duty thoroughly, and she supposed she wouldn't have it any other way. She'd already told them about Renner's role in her ongoing investigation and shared her certainty that his death related to the missing journals.

"Are you taking this murder, then?" Lyndsi asked. She was an older Shield, a veteran with more years of service than Nikki had of life. She was competent, but she'd burned the last of her enthusiasm many years ago. Though she was old enough to end her service voluntarily, she stayed on. Rumor was that she'd tried to quit once before, gotten too bored, and returned.

Whatever the truth, she was happy to leave this mess on Nikki's plate. Nikki considered for a moment. The suspect pool was limited, and what mystery remained wouldn't be solved with legwork that would require Shields to be beating down doors and demanding questions. "I'll take it."

Lyndsi nodded her thanks, then returned to her search of the apartment.

Nikki flipped through the piles of paper on Renner's desk. She didn't hold out much hope. If Renner had been killed because of the journals, and the papers on his desk had been useful, a reasonable killer would have taken them. On the other hand, most murderers tended not to be thinking too clearly during the act of murder, so there was a sliver of a chance she found something useful.

Renner, it turned out, was a copious note taker whose notes defied any attempt at organization. Passages had been copied, underlined, circled, and crossed out. Lines connected ideas on different parts of the page, and sometimes, as far as Nikki could tell, on other pages as well.

The subject of most notes was the 8th Blade of Firestone, Kaitlin. Nikki recognized the name, but knew nothing else about her. After studying Renner's notes, she knew only a little more about Kaitlin, but nothing about the murder or the time immediately after the exodus.

Nikki frowned. If Renner was an avid note taker, where were his notes about the journals?

"Did you find any other notebooks or piles of paper?" Nikki asked.

"Only what was on the desk," Lyndsi said.

Nikki tapped her finger against her leg as she thought. He was an archivist and a recluse. If Adele had spoken true, he rarely left his apartment.

Thoughts tumbled one after the other, and Nikki let them fall where they would. Better to let her mind wander without putting it on a leash. Investigation was the art of connection, and those connections came most easily when she didn't focus too hard on any lone detail.

She stood up from the couch and arranged the papers on a corner of Renner's table. "Would you do me a favor, please?"

Lyndsi grimaced, but Nikki was already taking the murder off her hands, so she agreed.

"Could you make another, deeper search of this apartment? I suspect he had either a notebook or a pile of papers that he was killed for. If they're in here, I'd like to know. I'm going to investigate another lead."

Lyndsi agreed to the favor, and Nikki almost bounded from the room.

Nikki knocked on the door. "Senior Archivist Adele? It's Nikki. I was hoping to ask you a few more questions."

She pressed her ear to the door to listen for sounds on the other side, but the room was quiet. She knocked again and listened.

When she was certain no one was coming to open the door, she pulled out the master key to Underhill's doors that Miranda had given her. She looked up and down the hall to ensure no one was coming, then opened the door, stepped through, and closed it behind her. The apartment was dark, so Nikki turned on the light in the entryway.

Adele's apartment was cleaner than one of the community kitchens. No paintings or decorations hung on the walls. There was a small mat for shoes next to the door, but the mat was empty. The rooms smelled too clean, as though every floor had been doused with the strong cleaners the workshops on the lower levels used.

The only furniture of note was a large bookshelf built

to take up an entire side of the room. It was a custom piece, which meant Adele had gone to considerable effort to acquire it. The shelves were mostly full of books. Nikki tilted her head and read the spines, halfway hoping she'd find the missing titles here. None of the names were familiar, though, and Nikki continued her search.

She'd been a fool for not suspecting Adele earlier. The archivist had played her hand well, always eager to provide Nikki with all the information she could. Nikki had also given her too much leeway because she was the Senior Archivist and had so convincingly played the role of the victim.

A growl escaped the back of Nikki's throat. She'd gotten careless in her months working in the fields. She'd practically led Renner to his death when she'd told Adele of the archivist's search for her. It wasn't the only explanation, but it was the story that fit the pieces best, and if Nikki were one to gamble, she'd place a considerable number of her ration cards on the table.

Her suspicions were confirmed when she reached the small sink in the bathroom. Chunks of blackened paper were still pasted around the drain, and underneath the smell of the cleaner was the smell of smoke. She ran her fingers through the ashes, but only the smallest of fragments remained. If Karolyn and Cole had left behind any secrets in their journals, those secrets were lost to history.

Nikki let out a heavy sigh as she resigned herself to a fruitless search. Whatever Adele had hoped to hide, Nikki had arrived too late to stop her. The chances of any meaningful scrap of evidence being left behind were thin. Adele was too shrewd.

She looked to the front door and wondered if it wouldn't simply be faster to start the hunt for Adele. She'd need help from one of the Soulkeepers to pursue her quarry through the unfamiliar nooks and crannies, and it would be best to start sooner rather than later. Who knew what advantage Adele could make of the day's earlier chaos?

Still, it was best to leave no stone unturned. She was here now, and it wouldn't take long to search the place. It was clean enough that a grain of sand would stand out.

A short hallway connected to the living room, with doors for a small bedroom and an even smaller second bathroom. Nikki made for the bedroom, leaning through the door to turn on the light before she entered.

A soft whisper of fabric behind her warned her she wasn't alone. She spun as her hand instinctively reached for the dagger at her side. Adele had emerged from the second bathroom, a knife held high, dried and crusted blood coating the sides of the blade. She brought the knife down.

The archivist had the advantages of surprise and momentum, but she was an older woman whose hands were more comfortable flipping delicate pages than wielding a deadly piece of steel. Nikki retreated a step into the bedroom, and the knife stabbed through nothing but air. Adele stumbled as her momentum carried her forward, right onto the tip of Nikki's waiting dagger.

Adele's bloody knife dropped to the floor, and Nikki guided the mortally wounded archivist to a nearby chair. She saw no fear of the gate in the woman's eyes, only resignation, a mild disappointment she hadn't completed her task.

"Why?" Nikki asked.

"He needed my help, and so I gave it to him."

"Renner?" No, that couldn't be it. The last pieces fell into place. "The Seer."

Adele nodded. "Humanity poisons all that it touches. Once you see that truth, you can't unsee it. All our histories, all our stories, they all point in the same direction. We don't deserve this life we've been given."

"What about Renner? Is he one of the Seer's disciples, too?"

Adele grinned at that. "No, though our thoughts often ran in parallel. I think that's why he and I always butted heads. We were too similar. I didn't think he'd help you."

"But then I told you he came to see me."

"He told me that although he thought it was hopeless, he wasn't quite ready to give up. So I had no choice but to help him along."

Adele had answered all her questions but one. "Where can we find the source of the shadow song?"

The archivist grimaced, then took Nikki's hand in both of hers and pulled the dagger free. Blood pumped from the now-open wound, and the older woman sagged as her life flowed from her. "Even if I told you, it wouldn't matter. Humanity's days are numbered. Radyn and Jyn and all the Manirah in the world can't do a thing to stop what's coming, so they shouldn't bother. Take your last days and cherish them, and thank you. I didn't want to see the end, but I was too great a coward to do this myself."

Adele closed her eyes and enjoyed a peace she didn't deserve.

Nikki cursed, for as much as she'd learned, the only question she didn't know the answer to was the only one that mattered.

11

The Tanwen that took to the air after the long night on the surface was a different Tanwen than the one who'd flown out to do battle against the nuddu. Bones had healed, wounds closed and muscles strengthened by the Song, but Radyn's old friend was far from whole.

Radyn shared Tanwen's aches and pains, wishing that, in the sharing, he could ease a portion of his friend's suffering. Instead, he was forced to experience a share of the pain while knowing there was nothing he could do. Tanwen's flight was steady enough, but the muscles that joined wing to torso burned in unending agony, and the newly healed bones groaned every time a gust of wind gave them an unexpected lift.

The long miles crawled beneath them, but Radyn demanded no more from Tanwen except that he get them home. To return to Aria was enough.

They limped through the sky together, and when Firestone's familiar silhouette appeared over the horizon, a weary smile cracked Radyn's lips.

Wary scouts raced toward them, then raced back with the news. Dragon and rider kept plenty distant from Firestone, though Radyn asked that they approach close enough he could make out the two nuddu still pursuing Firestone in an endless circle. Assuming they were under the Seer's control, he couldn't guess why they didn't bring down Firestone like they had Skystone, but he wouldn't question their good fortune, at least for now. It couldn't last long.

Thanks to the scouts' warning, a small crowd gathered as Tanwen landed outside Underhill. Macken was one of the first to reach the pair, and his expert eye looked Tanwen over as Radyn dismounted. "You gave us a bit of a scare," he said.

Now that they were surrounded by the relative safety of Underhill's defenses and Firestone's Manirah, a wave of weariness crashed over Radyn. It threatened to pull him into a deep, dreamless sleep, and there were precious few reasons to fight it. "It was too close. The worst of Tanwen's injuries have been dealt with, but he needs more healing than I can provide."

"It'll be done. Don't you worry."

Radyn held his connection with Tanwen open a moment longer, sharing the relief of another safe return. Tanwen assured Radyn all would be well, and Radyn allowed the connection to drop.

He searched through the crowd until he found Aria, standing alone behind the rest. Her hand was on her stomach and her eyes glistened.

Jyn and Magni had both come out to greet him, and he shared a few quick words with them. He told them he'd seen the nuddu reform out of Skystone's rubble, demolishing what little joy the two clan leaders had felt celebrating Radyn's return. Jyn took the blow in stride. "It's disappointing, but not that unexpected, I suppose. Regardless, it's good to have you back."

"It's good to be back," Radyn agreed.

Jyn's eyes followed Radyn's gaze. "We won't keep you."

Radyn found a bit of a grin hiding beneath the weariness that blanketed him. "You're a remarkable leader, but you're just not that pretty."

Jyn laughed out loud, the sound shattering the gloom that had fallen over the small group. "True enough." He clapped his hand on Radyn's shoulder. "Take some rest, but see me soon. There is much to discuss."

Radyn wondered what that could be, but his curiosity wasn't sufficient to delay his reunion with Aria. He wished the two clan leaders well, then worked his way through the rest of the crowd until he reached her. "I'm sorry if I made you worry," he said.

The tears she'd been holding back fell as she shook her head. She wrapped her arms around him and held him close. Her tears dried quickly, and she soon released him. "They said you stayed to rescue Veylan."

"I tried. He refused my help." At her questioning glance, he said, "I think part of it was honor. Another part was penance."

"You would have saved him, though, if you could have?"

Radyn was surprised the answer came as easily to his lips as it did.

"I would have."

THEY WALKED hand in hand as they meandered through the twisted and dusty halls of Underhill while Aria told him of the quake. Thankfully, Aria had been in bed, and the quake had done nothing but toss her around the cushions. She'd cleaned their apartment while waiting for Radyn to come home. Magni's return had sent her spirit crashing, and though she'd never given up hope, it had been little more than a sputtering flame. She'd joined the other builders as they inspected Underhill for more serious damage, and she'd worked longer than anyone else.

Her voice was low as she spoke of the concern her fellow builders had shown. How they'd invited her to join them in the dining halls, or how one young woman had offered a place among her family as Aria waited for Radyn. Instead, Aria had worked until her vision went blurry. She'd only been awake for a couple of hours.

Radyn apologized again for the suffering he'd caused her, even while hating that he'd almost certainly have to do it again.

His steps slowed, and Aria shot him a quizzical look.

"There was a time when I thought I would have left all of this behind if it meant you and I could live in peace," he said.

"I remember. You told me we could live wherever I wanted."

"I believed it then. I'm not so sure I do anymore. When we bring our child into this world, I think maybe we need to be surrounded by others."

A ghost of a smile played upon her lips, as though he'd just discovered a fact she'd known for a long time.

"Problem is, it means we can't run away, and I can't avoid fighting to protect Underhill and Firestone. It means I'll have to leave you again."

She squeezed his hand tighter, as if to say that she would never let him go, that she would hold no matter what forces conspired to pull him away. "Then you'll have to keep coming back."

Radyn's throat tightened around the promise he wished he could utter, capturing it before it rolled off his tongue. "I'll try."

They were nearly to the door of their apartment when a shudder passed through Aria's body. Her hand clenched against Radyn's for support, and her eyes went wide.

"What's wrong?" he asked.

She pressed her free hand against the wall. "I think the child is coming."

"Now?"

Radyn feared her eyes would roll out the back of her head. "Yes, now. Help me to the apartment."

Radyn did, though her steps were strong enough on their own.

***

He sat in the living room of their apartment, forced by tradition to become less than a spectator as his child was coaxed and pushed into a fallen world by Aria and the midwives that had answered Radyn's call. The women had claimed the bedroom and the bathroom as their own, and the youngest of the midwives, still apprenticed to the others, guarded their privacy with the fervor of a Sword protecting their city's Engine. Aria's cries pulled Radyn toward the rooms, but every time a glare from the young woman turned him aside.

A knock at his door distracted him from the battle he had no part in. He found Nikki on the other side, accompanied by Jyn and Magni.

The sight of all three of them, here and now, landed like a body blow to his stomach. "What's wrong?"

Nikki frowned at the question, then grunted. "Your little favor sent me down a rabbit hole, but that's not why we're here."

"Then what are you doing here?" Radyn asked.

Jyn shook his head. "We're here to sit with you while your child is born."

Radyn blinked twice, then a flush of color ran to his cheeks. His throat tightened, and he nodded. "I'm honored. Please come on in."

He ushered his guests into his living room. Jyn and Magni settled their bulky frames onto the couch, and Nikki pulled out the chair from Aria's writing desk.

"Can I get you anything to drink?" he asked. "I'm afraid we don't keep much on hand, but I can get some water."

Jyn shared a look with Magni that Radyn couldn't decipher. "What?"

A slow grin spread across Jyn's face as he reached into a pocket and pulled out a small flask. "You know it's not the first one of these I've attended, right?"

"I—I guess I've never given it much thought."

Jyn's grin grew wider. "Clearly. It's something of a tradition for the higher-ranked Swords and Daggers to invite the Blade to the birth of their children. They would claim they consider the Blade's presence something of a blessing, but many use it as a convenient excuse to get more time with the Blade."

Now that Jyn mentioned it, Radyn remembered hearing of the practice. Had he remained a closer, more official part of the clan, he would have likely heard more in recent years. His status as an outsider, followed by his self-imposed exile to Underhill, meant little contact with the softer traditions of the clan.

Jyn continued. "Magni figured you wouldn't think to

invite us, so we invited ourselves. Today marks the first time I've attended a birth without an invitation. Of course, that meant I couldn't expect you to host us in the manner most do."

The Blade held up the flask. "So, fortunately for us all, I brought my own libation. Grab us some glasses, please."

Radyn did so, though the cries from the other rooms almost pulled him from his task. A stern look from the younger midwife kept him from following his instincts. Left with no other choice, he took the glasses back to the living room, where Jyn poured a small measure of precious brown liquor into each of the glasses.

Radyn, like most Manirah, rarely imbibed, but the tantalizing scents of vanilla rising from the glass made his mouth water. He bowed deeply to Jyn. "I'm honored."

"So am I. After the last few months, it's good to be reminded of why we fight." Jyn raised his glass in a silent toast, and the others did the same. They took their first sip together, and the liquor transported Radyn to better times, to days when there'd been plenty to celebrate. He couldn't remember ever tasting better. The liquid lacked the harsh edge most liquors from the cities possessed, allowing the rich flavors to shine.

Another cry came from the rooms, though less distressed than before. Radyn glanced back at the door, clutched tightly at his glass, then set it down before it broke in his hand.

"You know, Radyn, there are days when I'm jealous of you," Jyn said.

Radyn knew full well the Blade sought to distract him, but he couldn't resist the bait. "Why?"

"You possess all the things I lack and desire. A loving wife and family. Freedom most could only dream of. And soon, a child."

Radyn took another sip of the drink, remembering the day he'd been made a Sword and the celebration he'd had with Elora and Jelrik, when they'd celebrated much like this. The memory had sharp edges now, linked as it was to their deaths, but today he remembered only the love they'd shared. "I never took you for much of a family man."

Magni scoffed. "You should spend more time with him. He complains about it constantly."

Jyn didn't deny it. "I've always known I wanted to be the Blade of Firestone, but I didn't always realize what that would mean. It feels foolish now, but I didn't realize how profoundly it would shape people's opinions of me. There are those who would seek to marry me because I am the Blade, and there are others who would never consider marriage because I am the Blade. Few consider that I am Jyn, too."

Nikki coughed and put her glass down.

Jyn's gaze turned to her. "Too personal for you?"

She shook her head and thumped her chest with a fist. "No. Just forgot how to drink, that's all."

From the slight twist of his lips, Radyn guessed Jyn wasn't fooled. Jyn took a sip, then said, "Regardless, I'm jealous, and even more so now. I'd like to have children of my own someday, if fate allows it."

Radyn cocked his head to the side, as though studying Jyn in a new light. "I think you'd make a great father."

"Thank you. Hopefully someday I'll have the chance to find out. Otherwise, it feels like all of this is a waste."

Magni closed his eyes and leaned his head back against the wall, in the attitude of a friend forced to endure a repetitive complaint. "You think you'd still feel that way if you saved Firestone and Underhill?"

Jyn swirled the last of his drink in the bottom of his glass. "I do. Not that saving Firestone isn't important, of course, but the older I get, the more convinced I am that raising healthy families is the most important thing a man can do."

Nikki wasn't so easily swayed. "I've been talking to a fair number of people lately, and a lot of them feel like it might be time to surrender. That humanity isn't worth saving, and that we shouldn't be bringing children into a world like this one."

Jyn cursed softly. "It's a poisonous idea, and even more tempting because it puts on the mask of mercy. They'll claim they're doing future generations a favor, because better no life at all than this one. It's wicked."

"Why?" Nikki asked.

"Because it's a denial of hope. A denial that the world can get better. That we can make it better. It's surrendering a fight without even getting bloody."

"Besides," Magni added, "the strongest argument against it requires having children. It's only when we learn to live for someone besides ourselves that we're willing to fight for a future we might not see."

A new cry from the other room interrupted their discussion. Radyn stood as one of the midwives came out. She bowed to the assembly, but spoke only to Radyn. "Congratulations. Your new family is ready to meet you now."

Radyn stood frozen for a moment until Jyn laughed from behind him. "Better get going."

It was all the encouragement he needed. He hurried forward and passed through the open door. Several of the midwives were cleaning the mess that was made, but Radyn had eyes only for his wife and child. Aria glowed, and though she looked exhausted, she couldn't stop smiling. Their child, a baby girl, nestled tight against her chest.

Aria's hair was matted to the top of her head, but somehow her smile grew even wider when she saw Radyn.

"Radyn, I'd like you to meet our girl, Elora. And Elora, it's time for you to meet your father, Radyn."

She held the girl out, and Radyn took her, his heart close to bursting.

12

The Seer woke in a darkened room that cooled the heat from his flesh and rejuvenated the shadow lurking within his spirit. He ran curious hands across his body, searching for bruises, cuts, or other wounds that would prevent him from continuing his service to his master, finding nothing except for a tender spot near the back of his head, where he assumed he had been struck by the hilt of a maniblade. He grimaced as his fingers brushed against the bruise, then hissed when they came away damp.

He hadn't been unconscious long. In the darkness of his small cell, he remembered well those final moments of lucidity, of Lynae clutching at her chest, realizing all too late that she had challenged a power against which she was as helpless as a babe in a cradle. The Seer sighed at the memory, the pleasure of its recollection almost transcendent in its intensity. A shudder ran through his body as a smile spread across his face.

For as long as he had served his master, there had always remained one question unanswered. For all the gifts granted to him, and for all the orders he'd given that had doomed countless souls, never once had his master acted directly through him. Never had he taken a life with his will and hands. Though not usually given to doubt, he had often wondered that when the moment came, would he be capable, or would some deep part of his biology, some remnant of the Song of the Engines that he hadn't purged, prevent him from becoming the warrior his master needed him to be?

As he listened to the slow and steady beating of his heart in that room, he finally knew the answer.

He'd lost track of the number of times he'd imagined drawing his shadow blades against the strongest warriors the Manirah fielded. When he heard his master most clearly, it was all he could do to restrain himself from attacking those servants of the Song.

The Seer rose from the cot and groaned at the stiffness in his back. He stood, stretched, and twisted, dropped into a squat, then stood and bent over and touched his toes. The rapid movement caused his head to swim, but otherwise he felt fine. His tongue was dry against the roof of his mouth, but that hardly merited concern. He listened for his master and was pleased to find him close. He focused his thoughts on the shadow song and worked his will with his master's strength. A blade of shadow appeared in each of his hands, and he looked to the door with thoughts of cutting it down.

After another moment of consideration, he allowed the blades to return to mist and shadow. He didn't fear. With little more than a thought, he had already killed one of the strongest and most respected Manirah across all the surviving cities. He'd been unconscious and in their power, and even then they hadn't dared strike him. He was as good as untouchable, so there was no need to rush his escape.

The Seer listened more closely to the shadow song, seeking the power of the shrine. He breathed out easily when he found it right where he'd left it. He couldn't imagine Nightkeep would have been so foolish as to harm the shrine, but there was no telling what they would have done in the throes of Lynae's death.

Satisfied that both he and the shrine were safe, the Seer settled in to wait. He used the time to make a detailed observation of the room he'd been locked in. The only light in the room came from the crack underneath the solid door made of Makers' steel. A switch on the wall promised light with a touch, but he preferred the darkness. Bare walls gave him little to fix his attention on, and a small toilet in the corner served as his only distraction. He crossed his legs on the cot, closed his eyes, and fell into a trance as he meditated upon the lessons his master had blessed him with.

He didn't know how much time elapsed between his waking and the arrival of his first visitor. A tentative knock disturbed him from his meditation, and as he opened his eyes, the door opened slowly, as though the person on the other side expected a trap. As soon as his guest realized that the room was still in darkness, and the Seer likely still unconscious, the door began to close.

He called out, "I am awake, but thank you for your consideration."

The door opened, revealing Firestone's Master of the Song, Dougan. His eyes were sunken and his cheeks hollow, and even in the darkness, the Seer noticed the red-rimmed eyes.

"You are welcome to join me, although I'm afraid my hospitality is not as great as I would like."

The dry comment earned a hint of a smile from the distraught Singer. "Considering the circumstances, I would say a lack of hospitality is among the least of our concerns."

"I've just woken, and I've had no news of events. My memory of coming here is vague. Would you be willing to share what has happened? And you are welcome to turn on the light if you like."

The Singer stood at the threshold of the cell, choosing between paths that would take him in very different directions. The Seer watched him without comment, his ears attuned to his master's song like never before. Dougan was a powerful Singer. Nightkeep's Master of the Song couldn't be otherwise.

Even so, shadow had found a foothold within the man, although the Seer couldn't tell if Dougan possessed the awareness to know it lurked within his heart. The Song of the Engine battled against his master, but this close to the influence of the Seer, the fate of the battle was determined before it began. Dougan sighed heavily, then stepped inside and switched on the light.

The Seer winced against the sudden brightness, but his eyes adjusted quickly. He gestured to the cot, but Dougan shook his head and leaned against the opposing wall. The Singer studied him carefully, and the Seer sensed notes from the Song washing over him, seeking to explore the spirit that had once belonged to it. He endured the examination, but wondered what Dougan was searching for. The Song receded, but Dougan seemed no more certain than before. He crossed his arms as though he could somehow appear intimidating. "How about you tell me what happened in the council chambers."

The Seer opened his arms wide, as though the truth was apparent for anyone to see. "I never intended to hurt

Lynae. She and I rarely agreed, but I never once had reason to doubt that she wanted what she believed was best for Nightkeep. The shadow song acted through me."

Dougan's lips formed a hard line. "You have always led us to believe that you have control over the shadow song."

"Until Lynae, I would have argued the same, but it has grown stronger, and it overwhelmed the barriers that I put in place."

"If that's true, what use are you to us? How can we trust you or anything you say, knowing that at any moment you might be in thrall to this song?"

Where before the Seer might have chosen a path of timidity and pleading forgiveness, he now struck a bolder tone. He couldn't yet reveal the full extent of his plans, but he no longer had to pretend to be as weak as they wanted him to be. He barked a short, harsh laugh. "Please, let's not pretend that you have ever trusted me. Such trust would be welcomed, but I never expected it. You work with me for the same reason that I have worked with you, and that is that if we hope to survive what is coming, we need each other."

The argument failed to sway Dougan. "It seems to me you have much more need of us than we have of you, especially if at any moment you might lash out and kill us."

"Then why are we having this conversation? Why am I still alive?"

"Those are questions the clan is violently debating as we speak. Semuel and I were against rash action, but even we suspect the clan's vengeance is well deserved."

The Seer shrugged. "If you kill me, you will die. Not even Belzrak and the surface clans have learned to master shadow to the extent I have. I will not lie and claim that my help is without risk, but even you must admit it is in my best interest to keep you all alive for as long as possible. I can't stop what's coming without you. If you kill me, you are sentencing all of Nightkeep to the same fate as Skystone."

Dougan clenched his jaw tight. After a steadying breath, he asked, "And if we let you live, what next?"

"My plan hasn't changed. We collect the shrines and hurry to the source of the shadow. Only there will we be safe, and only there will I have any chance of banishing the shadow for good. I only hope that I reach it before shadow overwhelms me completely."

Dougan cursed under his breath. "I shall speak to Semuel and the others. I cannot guarantee that I can stay the clan's blades, but I will try."

The Seer leaned back against the wall behind him and nodded. "It is all I could ask of you, but please hurry. My time to influence what is happening grows short."

13

Nikki was picking through her lunch rations in one of Underhill's cafeterias when the Shields who'd helped her examine Renner's rooms found her. They walked as though they'd just been found guilty of a crime, their heads down and their gazes locked on their feet. They bowed deeply and held the bow for longer than was necessary. "Apologies, ma'am."

Nikki arched an eyebrow. "What for?"

Lyndsi answered. "Negligence, ma'am. We searched the room as you asked and found nothing. But this morning, as the keepers were preparing the body for burning, they discovered this within the archivist's clothing." She extended a piece of paper with Nikki's name scrawled across it. The writing was Renner's, but shared little with the tight, close handwriting that filled most of his notebooks.

Nikki accepted the offering and unfolded it. Three words had been hastily scribbled across the torn paper.

"An unexpected journey?" she asked the Shields.

"Sorry, ma'am, but we have no idea what it means.

After the keepers delivered the note to us, we revisited his apartment and did another search with an eye to understanding the message, but we came up empty. We requested that the cleaning of the apartment be delayed, though, if you wanted to look for yourself."

Nikki turned the paper over in her hand as her senses tingled, the case finally revealing a new opening, narrow as it might be. "Thank you. I appreciate your bringing it to me."

The Shields looked as though they'd expected to be more strongly berated, but they didn't question their good fortune. They bowed in thanks and hurried from the cafeteria.

Nikki studied the words as though they held the answer to all of life's mysteries. She rearranged the letters for hidden messages, but failed to create anything meaningful. Perhaps it was some sort of code, but she doubted it. As an archivist, nothing was more valuable to Renner than paper, and his normal handwriting made the most of every scrap. If he'd had the time to encode a message, he would have had the time to write neatly.

The delivery of the note returned hunger to her stomach, as though body and mind suddenly realized they would need the energy to pursue the next lead. She shoveled the remaining food into her mouth, returned the tray to the kitchen, and thanked the cooks for the meal.

Hurried steps brought her quickly to Renner's room, which she opened using the master key. The room was in the same order that she remembered it, and she thanked the Shields for going about their search carefully.

Nikki spent the rest of her morning combing through Renner's effects, which left her with nothing but tired eyes. Whatever "an unexpected journey" referenced, it wasn't within the room.

But that hardly meant the search was over.

———

Radyn answered the door with Elora in his arms. She was wrapped up in wool blankets, and he bounced lightly on the balls of his feet, soothing her with the gentle motion.

"Sorry to bother you," Nikki said softly, "but do you have a moment?"

Radyn stood aside and welcomed her in. "Aria is resting in the other room, but as long as we talk quietly, there's no problem."

Nikki stepped in but didn't take a seat. Radyn paced slow ovals across the living room, his eyes rarely leaving the baby's face, even when Nikki spoke. She was so used to the intensity of his undivided attention that its absence was an almost physical sensation, like she'd become a wraith that hardly merited his concern.

"The keepers discovered a note on Renner's body. It was addressed to me and had only three words written on it. 'An unexpected journey.' Do those words mean anything to you?"

Radyn considered for a moment, then said, "Not a thing. I've never heard them before."

"Me neither. I've searched Renner's apartment up and down. Any idea where I should continue the search?"

She guessed the question was a foolish one. Radyn barely spared her a fraction of his attention, but he at least gave the appearance of thinking before saying, "No, I'm sorry."

Nikki spared a glance at Elora and clenched her fist. They needed Radyn now as much as they ever had, but he'd been stolen away. She ground her teeth together and said nothing about it. "Sorry to bother you. I'll keep looking, and if I find anything, I'll let you know."

"Thank you," Radyn said.

Nikki almost said more, but Radyn had already forgotten her, his entire world wrapped up contentedly in his arms.

JYN AND MAGNI gave her a greater share of their attention, but offered little in the way of help. Quick interviews with all the remaining archivists landed her in the same place she'd been when she started. After finishing the last interview, she returned to the cafeteria to eat and think.

The message had her name on it, so Renner must have thought she could figure out what it meant. Perhaps it had been a mistake to ask others. She'd only distracted herself from solving the problem on her own.

As a phrase, it could mean anything. A trip Renner had taken when he was younger. An expedition he'd hoped to lead but never had. It could be a description of Firestone's flights around the continent. It was as good as meaningless.

So maybe it wasn't a phrase. The thought wasn't new to her, and she'd asked the young archivist on duty if there'd been any books with that title in the archives. They'd looked through the index, studiously maintained by the archivists, and found nothing.

But Renner had been an archivist. If the words weren't a phrase, they had to be a book.

Nikki ate the last bites of her food, barely tasting them. She stood and strode out of the cafeteria, inspiration guiding her steps.

There was no archivist on duty after the evening meal, but Nikki's master key gave her access to the outer study. It didn't work on the newer door the archivists had installed that separated the study from the shelves of books in the back rooms, though. Undeterred, Nikki used a set of picks to rake the lock open. The smell of old paper greeted her, and she turned on the lanterns and began her search.

Her gaze hopped from book to book as she read the titles printed on the spines. The sheer breadth of material astounded her. There were journals from farmers exploring the best ways to grow food on the floating cities, abstract books of theory penned by Singers, adventure stories written for children, and a book detailing one woman's beliefs surrounding proper courtship. More knowledge than Nikki had imagined, locked away and out of sight. The books were available for any Manirah to study, but from the dust gathered on the shelves, most hadn't moved since they were placed.

It was a shame, but a small one among many. The need to survive could motivate tremendous discoveries. It was said the Engines were only developed once the Makers realized they either had to flee the surface or perish. But it also disincentivized people from studying and learning widely, from diving deep into "frivolous" knowledge to make new connections. Here they had generations of learnings at their fingertips, and yet only a few took advantage. What future did they have if such gifts were ignored?

Nikki flipped through the first few pages of any book that looked promising, searching for any reference to "an unexpected journey," but it wasn't until she reached the final shelf, back in the deepest corner of the rooms, that she stumbled upon the hidden treasure Renner had buried. It was a thin volume, bound by hand, and without a proper cover. The paper didn't feel as old and brittle as most in the archives, and when Nikki pulled it free, she read the title printed in small, neat, familiar handwriting across the front.

She grunted, amused by Renner's unintentional irony. He'd never added the book to the index, and so as far as the other archivists were concerned, it was as though the book didn't even exist. What better place to hide a book but in a room stuffed wall to wall with them?

Renner had written a concise introduction on the book's first page. This was, he claimed, his best reconstruction of Karolyn and Cole's journeys, pieced together from their journals and supplementary resources, such as the logs the Singers had kept from those days. His claimed hope was that someday, when interest in returning to the surface grew among the clans and the people, the reconstruction would provide a list of places for the clans to investigate.

Nikki's pulse beat faster as she flipped through a handful of pages. This was what she'd been looking for. What Radyn had first sent her after. Information worth dying for and worth killing over.

A series of numbers prefaced every entry, formatted in a manner that looked familiar but escaped Nikki's recollection. Reading a few passages pulled the knowledge out of her distant memory. The numbers were coordinates, written in the fashion of the Singers, that guided them to their destinations. Numbers she'd never make sense of on her own.

She needed help, but fortunately, she knew just where to turn.

NIKKI BARELY RECOGNIZED the young man who opened the door to Orenil's apartment. For the briefest of moments, she thought he had a friend over, but no, behind the sunken, red-rimmed eyes, the matted hair, and filthy clothes, the Singer remained. "You look terrible," she said.

Orenil grunted. "What do you want?"

"Help deciphering and mapping the coordinates made by a pair of surface explorers from the years immediately following the exodus."

Orenil blinked twice, shook his head, then started to close the door on her. Nikki thrust her foot forward and jammed the door open. Orenil pushed harder, but Nikki tapped into the shard hidden under the band around her thigh and slammed the door with an open palm. The door smacked into Orenil's shoulder and sent him stumbling several paces back. He barely kept his balance.

Nikki strode into the apartment, whose appearance matched Orenil's. She wrinkled her nose at the stench.

"You don't have the right to be in here."

"Shut up. What is all this?" Nikki swept her arms across the scene like a crime had been committed. For all she knew, one had. Even a sloppy criminal could have hidden at least two bodies under the piles of dirty clothes and crumpled papers.

"I've been too busy to clean up, and what do you care? Get out of here."

Nikki put her hands on her hips. "I need a Singer, and you're the only one with time. The others told me you're on leave, and everyone else is either busy Singing to the Engine or sleeping so they can Sing to the Engine once they wake. So it needs to be you, and we need this information as quickly as we can."

Orenil wavered between fight and surrender, but he had so little strength the outcome never seemed in question. His shoulders slumped. "Fine. What do you need?"

"First, I'm going to need you to take a shower. Do you have a shovel around here?"

"A shovel?"

"For pushing all this junk into a corner."

He fixed her with a flat stare. "I don't have a shovel, and I'm not taking a shower."

"Take one on your own or I'll drag you in there. I won't be able to work with you smelling that way."

He ran his hand down his face, pulling on his cheeks. She could practically hear him debating the odds of winning a fight in his head, but when logic informed him the number was close enough to zero to be indistinguishable, he surrendered and shuffled to the bathroom without a word.

While he showered, Nikki cleaned up the mess as well as she was able, mostly by kicking piles of clothes and dumping papers into a corner. By the time Orenil emerged, hair still dripping, she'd cleared off a small space for them to work. Some of the life had returned to his cheeks.

"You're looking better," she said.

"Yeah. Hate to admit it, but you were probably right. Now, could you explain again why you're here?"

"Kaya told Radyn there was a source of the shadow song somewhere on the surface."

Orenil flinched at Kaya's name, and so Nikki soldiered on, putting the name as far behind her as she could. "Radyn asked me to search for any old books that might refer to a source, even indirectly. To make a long story short, I've found this," she held up Renner's book, "which summarizes the adventures of a pair of explorers who lived shortly post-exodus. This could be exactly what we're looking for, but all the coordinates are written using Singer's notation, so I need a Singer."

Orenil rubbed his chin. "So this is for Radyn?"

"I'd say it's for the survival of us all, but yes, Radyn was the one who got it started."

"Then I'll help you, but on one condition."

Nikki swore. "Are you going to need to sleep with me, too?"

Orenil frowned. "No. What the—no. Gross."

At a look from Nikki, Orenil's eyes widened and he held up his hands. "Sorry, that's not what I meant. It's just that I'm not attracted to you. I mean, I am. You're very attractive. But that's not—"

"Orenil." The ice in her voice froze him in place.

"Yes?"

"I understand. You should stop talking."

Orenil swallowed hard and nodded. Once he was calm, Nikki asked, "What is your condition?"

"Radyn needs to help me in exchange. He already knows what I'll ask."

"You know I can't convince Radyn to do anything he doesn't want to, but I'll try my best."

"That's good enough for me. Do you have a map?"

Nikki unfolded the other piece of paper she'd acquired from the Singers when she'd first gone to them to look for help. "I do."

Orenil grinned, and Nikki wondered how long it had been since his face had seen a smile. "Then let's get started."

NIKKI HADN'T DONE MUCH MORE BESIDES flip through a few random pages of Renner's creation since she'd found it, and so was surprised when his project pulled her into its mystery. Renner had organized his notes more carefully than the Singers maintained their logbooks. Each entry was labeled with the date, or Renner's best guess of the date, and a position, as well as a detailed recounting of what Renner believed had happened that day. The influence of sources beyond the siblings' journals was apparent, for there were entries in which detailed events were described that the siblings shouldn't have had more than a passing knowledge of.

Orenil charted the positions of the entries on Nikki's maps. Dots represented locations mentioned in the journal that seemed to have little or no bearing on the shadow tribes or the shrines. Small crosses denoted locations where Karolyn and Cole had interactions with surface survivors. Nikki and Orenil combed through every word of Renner's notes, seeking any connections with the modern surface dwellers. Orenil drew a small star over locations in which the siblings encountered anything not immediately explainable, which happened with surprising frequency.

Despite not being a person who read frequently, Nikki could hardly tear her eyes away from the passages. If she'd been asked before, she would have claimed a solid understanding of Firestone's past, but Renner's notes burned like flame, illuminating a past much darker than she'd imagined. They answered several of her most pressing questions without saying a single word that directly addressed them.

She grunted as Orenil put yet another cross on the map. It joined more than a dozen others scattered around the continent. "I'd always imagined the exodus as being— cleaner—somehow."

Orenil looked up from the map. Much of his spirit had returned, and his eyes danced with an inner light. "How so?"

Her finger traced across all the crosses on the page. "I

assumed that the exodus was a clean break, and that it was more successful. I thought there weren't more than a handful of people who didn't make it to the cities, and that those who didn't basically died immediately after the cities left. In hindsight, neither assumption makes any sense, but I'd never thought to question them. Of course not everyone would have made it to a city, and of course not everyone died right away. That's not how the dangers of the surface work, but I never connected all the pieces."

Orenil shrugged. "You never had a reason to."

Nikki leaned back in her chair and let her gaze roam over the map, seeking some pattern not immediately visible. "Before just now, I also wondered how we'd come to be so wrong about the shadow tribes, but as we're reading through these notes, I'm starting to understand."

"The few survivors Karolyn and Cole encountered weren't doing well."

The ghost of a smile played across Nikki's lips. That was an understatement. The survivors the siblings had met barely deserved the title. On average, they lived on the brink of starvation, were hunted by shadow, and were often hostile. Cole, who'd been a Senior Dagger through most of the entries thus far, had been forced to kill many, a fact that tormented him to no end. It was no wonder scholars assumed no one had survived.

For all the questions the journals answered, they raised even more. Karolyn and Cole's travels had frequently passed through the equatorial latitudes, and Firestone and Nightkeep, where they'd ended up, had followed them without question or problem. She'd asked Orenil about it, but he'd had no answer. Likewise, they were halfway through the journals and neither sibling had mentioned nuddu, though they'd extensively wandered through land known to be thick with the creatures.

Shield and Singer continued their hunt, and before long, they'd closed the last page. Nikki had halfway expected a straightforward answer written plainly in the text, the way they'd appeared to her back when she'd been a student, but Karolyn and Cole made no claims to ever coming across anything recognizable as a shrine. Nor had they met anyone Nikki could confidently point to as a distant ancestor of the modern shadow tribes.

Though if it had been easy, it wouldn't be a mystery Radyn asked her to solve.

After a moment of silent reflection, she asked Orenil, "What do you think?"

The Singer had his eyes closed, and he didn't answer for a long moment. "I'm not sure," he confessed.

Nikki stabbed her finger down at a place on the map marked with both a cross and a star. "We can't be sure, but to me, this seems like the best bet."

The location was one of the earliest detailed in the journals, a garden surrounded by shadow and inhabited by a mysterious man. It was slim evidence, but it was one of only a few places where the siblings had encountered both unusual events and survivors.

"Possibly," Orenil said as he cracked open his eyes, "but something about it doesn't feel right."

The Singer sat in silence, then pointed to another location marked with both a dot and a star, because they hadn't been able to decide if the position was unusual enough to merit the star. "My guess is that the source is here."

It hadn't even been on Nikki's list of top five most likely places. "Why?"

"A few reasons. First, we know that the shadow song seeks to destroy life, and that's the only location mentioned in which there is no life nearby."

"But that had nothing to do with the shadow song." The siblings had described an enormous crater and the dead lands surrounding it. They'd speculated that something large had crashed into the surface recently and killed everything nearby.

"Possibly, but it's the only location where there's no life, which seems to follow if it's close to the source, right? But there are also the reports from the Singers of Nightkeep to consider."

Nikki warmed up to Orenil's point. Nightkeep had suffered trouble with the Engine as they'd passed by. Karolyn, a Singer, had reported the weakness of the Engine's Song, but Renner's notes made no connection with the crater below. "Which matches what Radyn told us about the nuddu and their shadow interfering with Skystone's Engine."

Orenil nodded quickly. "And one last point, though not one you'll take as seriously as I do. Before Kaya died, she told Radyn the source is near the center of the equatorial zone."

The Singer took his pencil and sketched two parallel lines across the map. The crater sat close to equidistant between the lines. Orenil put the pencil down and stabbed the dot and star markings with his finger. "I think the source is there."

14

Aknock on the Seer's door informed him that Nightkeep had arrived over the site of the third shrine. He nodded to Belzrak, who glided across the floor and opened the door, accepting the formal invitation of the Sword delivering the message. The shadow warrior bowed and thanked the Sword profusely, but their master's force danced eagerly within him. Dougan had promised the Seer safety, but after Lynae's death at his hands, the Seer would have been a fool to trust that promise.

Belzrak agreed. Since his release from his cell, the surface warriors remained on constant guard. Two stood beside the door at all times, and his food and water were tasted before he ate and drank. None of Nightkeep's furious Manirah had attempted to kill him yet, but he didn't for a moment take that to mean that he was safe.

Today's journey to the surface was filled with both promise and peril. Never would the vengeful Swords and Daggers have a better opportunity to kill him, but if the Seer survived and acquired a second shrine, nothing upon this world would stop him from finishing the work his master had started so long ago.

Belzrak and his clansmen formed a box around him, and they stepped into the hallway, forcibly removing anyone who tried to get close.

Semuel and Dougan met them at the entrance to the Nest. A woman who stood as stiff as a piece of Makers' steel stood beside them. Her hair was halfway through the transformation from brown to gray. Dark eyes stared over a sharp nose. She was competence personified, and she gave a slight bow as the Seer approached.

"This is Vale," Semuel said. "She will serve as the interim Blade until we complete a more formal selection. She's been a Senior Sword for almost two decades, and her service has been exemplary."

The Seer returned Vale's bow. "Thank you for your service to Nightkeep."

Dougan chimed in. "Try not to kill this one. There will be no protection for you if you do."

The Seer didn't mind the insult, but losing Dougan as a staunch ally troubled him. He needed Nightkeep for a time yet, and Dougan was nearly as much a heart of the place as Semuel was. "I'll do everything in my power to keep her safe. I still lament Lynae's loss."

Dougan was far from satisfied, but he let the matter drop. The gates opened, and those descending to the surface passed through. The Seer's impression of Vale was confirmed as she hurried them onto dragons. In no time at all, they were in the sky and dropping toward the surface.

The interim Blade circled their destination before landing, studying the terrain and searching for traps and ambushes. The Seer wasn't sure what she hoped to discover, though, for the thick canopy of trees permitted little more than quick glimpses of the ground below.

Vale gave the order to descend, and the dragons landed in a clearing east of the shrine's destination. The Seer was, as always, glad to be off the dragon's back with his feet on solid ground. He stretched and admired the sights. Between the trees he spied a collection of homes, built on land but blending in so well with the giant elms that the Seer couldn't help but compare them to bird nests.

"Every shrine location is so different," he observed to Belzrak.

The stony-faced warrior grunted. "This clan has always held itself apart, so even I know little about them."

He'd said as much before, but seeing the small, graceful wooden houses gave those words a weight the Seer hadn't fully appreciated before. There was no Makers' steel to be seen, and they lived openly on the surface, their homes exposed to all the dangers of both the world and shadow. If not for living in the equatorial zone, they would have been discovered by the cities long ago. The Seer's heart beat faster. The shrine nearby called to him, and he would answer.

A collection of warriors from the small village moved through the trees like wraiths, their advance so silent the Seer wondered if they were illusions. The demands of surviving on the surface had shaped all the shadow tribes. All were dangerous, yet something about the way these warriors moved made the Seer's palms sweat.

Their hosts numbered five, and they lined up across the clearing. A broad-shouldered man stepped forward, and the Seer almost jumped backward when he spotted a maniblade hilt at his side. Yet shadow coursed through the man's veins like blood.

"My name is Caleb, and I serve as the head of this village. We welcome you in peace, so long as it is only peace you bring." The man's voice was as deep as the rumble of stone in an earthquake, and though he spoke the language of the cities, the words came slowly, like a glacier sliding downhill. Everything about him spoke of steadiness and constancy. He and Vale would get along well, so long as they weren't trying to kill each other.

The Seer and Belzrak stepped forward and introduced themselves, and Caleb's gaze settled heavily on the Seer.

"So, you are the one who has been woken by our master." It was half a question, half a statement.

"I am."

"And you've come to take our shrine from us?"

"It's time for it to return to the source from which it came."

Caleb's regard lingered on the Seer a moment longer, and then he inclined his head, his judgment passed. "Then follow me."

They did, walking the well-worn paths through the trees, sounding like drunk cows beside the silence of Caleb's stride. Caleb stopped before they reached the first of the small homes hiding between the trees, and he gestured toward Vale and the Manirah that accompanied her. "This is as far as they may go."

Hands went to maniblades, but Caleb made no move to respond in kind.

"The Seer is under our protection. He'll not advance without us," Vale said.

Caleb shrugged, indifferent to Vale's protests. "It is not a matter of choice or preference. Our home has been consecrated by the shadow song and protected by our master. He will strike fatally at any who are strong in the Song of the Engine. If you wish to test the truth of my words with your lives, it is of no concern to me."

"We'll follow," Vale announced.

The Seer allowed himself a moment to imagine Vale's

surprise as she discovered the truth of Caleb's warning, as blades of shadow tore into unsuspecting flesh and slaughtered the Manirah she'd so recently taken command of. Pleasurable as the imagining was, he couldn't ride the dragons without Swords, and besides, Semuel would never let him back onto Nightkeep if he returned alone. "I would heed his warning. The shadow song is as strong here as any place I've traveled. I will return."

"You'll forgive me if I don't take you at your word," Vale responded. "You could easily betray us."

"I won't ask for your blind trust. But I assure you, to test this boundary is to die. Have no worries. I still need the dragons, and I need Nightkeep. There shall be no betrayal. To abandon you is to doom us all, myself included."

Vale's imagination failed the same as everyone else's, for she wanted to survive. She wanted to live, wanted to create a world where her children could live in peace. She couldn't bring herself to understand that for the Seer, the act of living held no more appeal. Breath was a burden he was all too ready to surrender, and she would never understand. Thankfully, it meant that any appeal to his self-preservation won him a degree of belief he hadn't earned. Lynae, maybe, had seen through him, or at least was familiar enough with the idea that some causes were more important than a mere life, but Semuel, Dougan, and now Vale didn't. The interim Blade of Nightkeep accepted the flawed argument, and the Seer and Belzrak advanced into the village alone.

The homes they passed were small and tidy, built to blend into the forest instead of dominate it. In observing the construction, the Seer peered into a different future, one in which humanity attempted to live with nature instead of control and harness it. Would his master have risen if humanity had learned its place earlier?

One building dwarfed the others. It stood twice as tall as the next largest construction and at least three times as wide. It towered over a clearing that was otherwise devoid of life. Not even grass grew in the hard-packed dirt that surrounded it. The Seer stopped and stared at the intricate etchings carved into the wooden walls. Distorted human figures reached out to one another from the flames, their skin melting as they screamed. He couldn't guess what it represented, but the sight of it stirred his spirit.

"Do you like it?" Caleb asked.

"Very much. What is it?"

"You are here for the shrine our master left us, but it is this, here, that is our legacy. The shrine is as good as yours, but never may you dare touch those walls."

Caleb's eyes wandered over the building, filled with reverence mixed with awe. After a moment's pause, he said, "This building dates back to the founding of our village. Do you know the true story of the exodus?"

"As well as any cursed by birth to grow up within the floating cities."

"We trace our lineage here to the Order of Reconciliation, who fought against your ancestors in the years of the exodus. They were the first to recognize shadow's rightful dominion over this world, and fought on its behalf."

The story was familiar enough to the Seer, found in bits and pieces of stories scattered across the cities' archives, but still he leaned forward, having never heard this perspective.

"Not long after Firestone launched, and we knew the cities wouldn't fall, my ancestors were tested. They had given their faith to the shadow song, but humanity lived on in their floating fortresses, untouched by shadow. The Order had failed, and that failure caused a schism between two factions. One believed there was no point in continuing the fight, that they had done all they could and it would be best to die and give themselves completely to shadow. Others believed the fight hadn't been lost, only prolonged, and pledged to fight on."

A dilemma not unlike the one that faced the cities today. "What happened?"

"The Order retreated from the Makers' ruins and sought solace in nature. They settled here, and those who believed there was nothing left to be done carved out this clearing and used the wood to build a cabin a little smaller than what you see before you. They filled it with hay and oil, and on the night of the winter solstice, when the night was longest, they packed it from wall to wall. Mothers and fathers brought their children, and there was singing and rejoicing. Once all were inside, my ancestors barred the door, poured oil over the walls, and lit the flames."

The Seer closed his eyes and imagined the sight, flames rising ever higher, licking the tops of the trees. "It must have been beautiful," he said.

Caleb agreed. "It was witnessed by all those who chose to live on, and my greatest hope is that someday I may witness an act of equal beauty. My ancestors built this around the ashes of the home to honor their memory. It is the heart of our village, given to our master. No blade of grass has grown in this clearing since. Birds refuse to fly over, and even the ants build their hills on other land."

The Seer bowed. "Thank you for sharing it with me."

They stood in appreciation of the sight for a while longer, then followed Caleb as he continued his journey through the village. Their destination turned out to be a small, nondescript cabin, identical to any of the others scattered around. Designed to be hidden among the other cabins like a bug that blended into the leaves of the trees, it never would have fooled the Seer's senses. Shadow burned within, an emptiness with a presence to rival that of a dragon.

"No guards?" the Seer asked.

A smirk spread across Caleb's face. "There's no need. The shrine is guarded by forces beyond my comprehension. Anything I would add would be a waste."

"Is that why you seem to care so little for my arrival? Others have fought and tested me, but you've greeted me as an honored guest."

"We serve the same master. The decision is not mine to make. If you choose to enter, it is shadow alone that determines your fate."

The Seer cocked his head to one side. "Have you ever been within?"

"Every adult in this village has. When every boy and girl reaches the age of sixteen, he or she is given a choice. They may either enter the house and endure the test of shadow, or they may leave the village and brave the wilds with all the skills we've given them."

The answer sent a shudder down the Seer's spine. No wonder Caleb walked like a ghost. They'd submitted their bodies and souls to the shadow in a way no other shadow clan had. What strength must be hidden within the unassuming walls of the surrounding cabins! New possibilities opened themselves to the Seer's plans, and he licked his lips with anticipation.

The sentiment died almost as quickly as it was born. They were not his to command, and the pernicious idea that he was deserving of the responsibility was his human pride. It was the wish of the shadow song that spoke loudest here, not his petty desires.

Belzrak stepped forward to open the door, and the shadow song rang a low note of warning within the Seer's spirit. He explored the feeling to better understand its meaning, then said, "My friend, it might be best if I enter the room alone."

"If all who live in the village have passed the test, I have nothing to fear," Belzrak argued.

Caleb ended the disagreement before the Seer could soothe Belzrak's wounded pride. "If he has accompanied you this far, he must enter as well. Those who would serve our master must be worthy."

Belzrak snorted. "I've served our master since before you could walk."

The Seer looked into the darkness of the unassuming cabin and squashed the dread that crawled up his spine. Of his own allegiance to shadow he had no doubt, and Belzrak was loyal enough, but his daughter's death at Radyn's hands had shaken the warrior's faith in the shadow song, probably more than even he knew.

Their path had been set before them, though. Caleb's warriors surrounded them, and not even the Seer could shield Belzrak from his fate. He could do nothing more than utter a quick prayer that Belzrak's service and faith would be sufficient. He'd come to appreciate the shadow warrior and his grounded pragmatism.

Belzrak, eager to banish any doubts of his worthiness, strode through the door with his back straight and head held high. The Seer took one last glance at Caleb and followed him in.

Cool, damp air prickled his skin, reminding the Seer of the time he spent underground in the bog acquiring the very first of the shrines. He paused two steps into the room to allow his sight a chance to adjust to the darkness and gloom of the cabin, deeper than the absence of light could explain. The natural sunlight streaming in from the open door didn't penetrate as far as it should have, dying before it reached the Seer's feet. Light was no more welcome than the Song of the Engines.

The shrine sat on a plain wooden table, and though the walls of the cabin revealed the advanced age of the structure, the table looked as though its joints had been carved and fitted just the day before. The one-room cabin was otherwise empty. If Caleb's traps were physical, he could spot no sign of them.

Belzrak, so bold upon entering the cabin, froze once embraced by the darkness. Brave and proud, yes, but he was no fool to toy with the tremendous powers of shadow contained within the shrine. He looked to the Seer for guidance, and the Seer stretched out his sense of shadow. As one would expect from the home of a shrine, darkness filled the room, shifting gently, as though carried on the currents of a bucolic stream. Maddening glimpses of a deeper order hid within those shadows, too deep even for his senses to penetrate.

The Seer pressed his lips together and advanced toward the shrine. Two steps brought him face to face with an actual shadow. One moment there'd been nothing between him and the shrine; the next, the creature waited. Before the Seer could gasp in surprise, the creature formed a dark blade and stabbed it deep into his stomach.

Ice spread from the wound, the shadow song racing through his veins like a virulent disease, eradicating the last traces of the Song within his spirit. Little remained, but what held on did so desperately. Shadow song burned bits and pieces of his spirit away, and the Seer screamed, the sound ripping out the back of his throat.

He fell to his knees, and the shadow withdrew its blade. The Seer clutched at his stomach, only to find the flesh unharmed. He wasn't hurt.

Except his heart no longer beat and his lungs no longer

drew breath. The last vestiges of the Song in his body had kept him alive, and without them, his body betrayed him. He had no strength of his own to so much as blink. The darkness of death closed around him, and he knew there'd be no gate to welcome his corrupted spirit.

Better oblivion than whatever the Song promised on the other side of the gate, but his work wasn't completed. Humanity still lived, and for a time, so must he. Visions of the future danced before his eyes. Cities would fall from the skies, and the force of so much destruction would cloud the sky for years. The few surface clans that survived would be next, targeted by shadow until the last human had been destroyed. The beauty of the vision moved him to tears and solidified his desire to fight on.

Without the Song, only one force remained that could keep his spirit tethered to this world, and its messenger stood before him. The Seer could make no sound, but in the depths of his spirit, he offered everything, every scrap of who he was, to shadow.

The shadow accepted it without question, and the Seer had never tasted a sweeter breath. He filled his lungs with air blessed by the shrine and its servants, then turned as he heard a gurgle behind him.

A second shadow had its sword in Belzrak's stomach, and the older warrior was snarling even as blood bubbled up through his mouth. He stared at the Seer with a hatred that would have started a war, had he had the opportunity. "You never meant to protect us," he said.

So he'd had a similar vision too, and the Seer felt the weight of years of lies lift from his shoulders. "The sins of our ancestors apply to us as much as they do to those who took to the sky."

Belzrak formed a blade of shadow, but before he could cut at the Seer, the creature who impaled him stepped back and pulled his blade free. Belzrak's limbs lost their strength, and his arms dropped low. He fought for breath, but the Song that had kept him alive had been burned from his body and, stung by the betrayal of his master, he refused to reach for shadow.

He died proud, but he still died, and could do no more good for his clan.

Before he'd entered the cabin, the Seer might have felt a pang of regret for Belzrak's meaningless rebellion, but now he only saw another human dead, and the shadow that was now his spirit rejoiced.

He emerged into the light a few moments later, carrying the shrine. He looked at Caleb. "It seems my former ally lacked the conviction our master requires." He held the shrine up high, its power coursing through him. "I bring the end of days. Will you follow me?"

Caleb bowed. "It would be my honor."

15

The concerns of the world brushed as lightly across Radyn as a cool autumn breeze on a warm summer's night, promising the change of seasons and more challenging days to come, but such was the warmth Elora brought into their small apartment he could hardly bring himself to care. Days and nights blurred into one hazy sense of bliss. He brought food from the kitchens while Aria fed the child, then sang softly to Elora while rocking her in his arms. Already she liked to move, and they found the quickest way to get her to sleep was to hold her close against Radyn's bare chest while he paced around the room. Some nights his feet ached as though he'd walked to the next nearest Soulkeeper settlement, though he'd never left his living room.

Elora was hot and cold, Song and shadow, love and despair wrapped in a bundle small enough to fit in most air vents. Most of the day she spent content, eyes wide, and why shouldn't they be? Wasn't she seeing everything for the first time? She cooed and gurgled and tossed her arms around, then acted surprised when she realized they were attached to the rest of her body. Those moments were a delight, and they made up most of their time together.

When the storms struck, they did so without warning. One moment she'd have her little fingers wrapped tight around one of Radyn's, and the next she'd be screaming loud enough for her wails to reach her namesake on the other side of the gate. Once fed or changed or napped, the storm vanished and the skies turned clear again.

"She has your temperament," Aria said as she nursed one afternoon.

Radyn scoffed, but Aria insisted. "You're old enough to contain it better, but she holds the same depth of feeling that you do."

"You may be right, but my hope is she'll never have to carry a maniblade."

It was as close as they came to allowing the outside world to disturb their peace, and they retreated from the topic, afraid that if they continued, the world would come crashing through their door with all its attendant problems.

They slept in turns and sometimes together. Firestone's midwives visited frequently, helping Aria learn the ins and outs of becoming a new mother. Though the moments slipped through his fingers like water, Radyn tried to remember them, tried to burn them into his memory so that when shadow came again, he had these days to hold onto.

Their peace couldn't last forever, and Magni interrupted it with a knock at their door. "Everyone is gathering to decide what we do next. You should be there."

Radyn would have rather driven a nail through his foot, but Aria took Elora in her arms and cut off his complaints before he could utter them. "Go. They need you, and we'll be here when you return."

Radyn swallowed hard, but he nodded once and

followed Magni through the halls, feeling like a boat cut adrift from its anchor.

"I'm sorry to take you away," Magni said.

"It's not your fault. We knew the day would come and treasured the time we had."

"It's never enough, though, is it?"

And Radyn knew Magni thought of his wife, lost in the fight against the shadow song and the Seer's disciples. "Even if I were to live to see a hundred years—no, it wouldn't be time enough."

The face of the guard at the door was familiar, though it took Radyn several moments to recognize it. "Bragen?"

His old roommate bowed, though not in time to hide the grimace that spread across his face. "Senior Sword."

"It's good to see you. How have you been?"

Though they'd lived together for years, Bragen answered without a hint of familiarity. "Well, sir."

Radyn took Bragen's cue and didn't press further. He'd have thought that years apart would have healed the old enmity between them, but apparently not. He and Magni passed through the door together, entering the most crowded conference room he had ever set foot in. Jyn and the clan elders were there, of course, but they were joined by several senior Swords who rarely joined such discussions. Among them was another face Radyn remembered well. "Astram? You're here, too?"

His other roommate stood and bowed, with the hint of a smile on his face. "I just earned the rank of senior Sword a few days ago."

"It's good to see you. How have you been?"

Whatever pleasure had been sparked by their reunion disappeared at the question. "Well enough, considering the times we live in. We'll have to speak later, but I'm sorry, I need to speak with the other Swords."

Radyn let him go, wondering what he'd done wrong.

He was still wondering when a new delegation entered the conference room, filling it nearly to bursting. He didn't recognize a single face until his gaze landed on a tall, thin woman near the center of the pack. Their gazes met, and he blinked twice as his suspicion was confirmed.

Though both of his old roommates wished only to be done with him, she left her group behind and came to see him. "Radyn. It *has* been a long time."

Radyn bowed slightly. "Melanie. I've always wondered what happened to you after the attack."

She was the woman who'd first introduced him to the ruins on the surface, first made him wonder about the history he'd been taught in the academy. But then she'd disappeared, and he hadn't seen her since.

She arched an eyebrow. "You don't know who I am?"

Miranda joined them before Radyn could answer, throwing her arms around Melanie in a tight embrace. "It's good to see you in person again. Do you know Radyn?"

Melanie smiled. "Not well, but our paths crossed once before. He's done more than I'd dared to hope."

Miranda's eyes narrowed as she guessed at Melanie's meaning. "You tried to recruit him!"

"I did, but it seems you beat me to it."

Both women noticed the confusion written across Radyn's face, and Miranda laughed out loud. "Radyn, I'd like to introduce you to Melanie. She's the woman who started the modern Soulkeepers."

"You started all this?" he asked, gesturing to the room, meaning Underhill and the other ruins across the lands the Soulkeepers had tried to make homes within.

"I did, though before you give me more credit than I deserve, I was building upon the work of many who'd come before. The Soulkeepers have existed on and off throughout the history of the floating cities. I only learned about them and had the resources to continue the work they'd started."

Radyn glanced between Jyn and Melanie and marveled at the twists of fate that came to define their lives. "You know, there was a time when the Blade had hoped I would infiltrate the Soulkeepers and report their activities to the clan."

The observation earned a brief half-smile from Melanie. "We were never truly opposed to one another; we just had different ideas about how to best protect humanity from the shadow."

As the last of the invitees arrived at the meeting, Jyn sat down and called for silence. "Thank you all for being here, especially those of you who have come from some distance. I'll not sweeten the bitter truth. Our situation is dire. Nuddu have broken free of their equatorial confinement and started coordinating attacks against the cities. If there's a way of defeating them, we haven't found it. There is one last hope, though. Before she was killed, Singer Kaya told Senior Sword Radyn that she believed the shadow song had a source, and we think that we've found it." He gestured toward Nikki, sitting only three chairs away from him.

She picked up the thread of his argument. "Senior Sword Radyn asked me to help investigate ancient records to search for any sign of the source. In the process of the investigation, I enlisted the help of Singer Orenil, and through our efforts, I believe we've found it."

The Shield pulled a large piece of rolled-up paper from behind her chair and unrolled it across the table. It was the most detailed map of the continent Firestone possessed, the one used by the Singers to plot their course across the inhospitable lands. Orenil, sitting beside Nikki, pulled figurines from a small pack and placed them across the map.

Nikki pointed to a figurine that looked like a shrunken and overturned teacup. "Here's the position of Underhill," her finger moved to a column with Firestone's symbol carved on top, "and here's Firestone." She ran her finger south, into the equatorial zone and close to the center of the continent. Orenil removed another column from his pack, shorter than the one for Firestone. He placed it with the top down, so the symbol written upon it couldn't be seen. "And this is where we believe the source is. It's about a week of travel away at Firestone's fastest speed."

The proclamation set off a round of soft muttering around the table. Radyn stared at the short column and wondered at its nearness. A quarter of the continent separated the two columns, so it wasn't that they were close in a physical sense, but Firestone, under the careful and continual guidance of its Singers, could cover an enormous amount of ground.

Melanie spoke above the din. "How certain are you of this?"

Everyone quieted to hear the answer.

"It's hard to say," Nikki hedged. "We know that *something* is there, and from what we've been able to uncover from ancient journals, we believe it might be the source. But I'll be the first to admit the conclusion is based on guesswork."

Orenil jumped in. "There is one corroborating piece of evidence, though. This is the general direction Nightkeep has been traveling for the last week and more."

He took out several small tokens and placed them on

the map, and if Radyn connected them in his imagination, they drew something of a jagged line that drew ever closer to the supposed source. "I've been keeping an eye on Nightkeep for some time now, and these have been its approximate locations. I believe it's making for the source, too, though making some stops along the way."

"Likely to pick up more of the shrines," Radyn guessed. He hadn't sensed any surges of shadow as of late, but perhaps the Seer no longer needed to express himself in such powerful ways.

Jyn spoke before the meeting split into a dozen smaller conversations. "This is what we know. I've asked you here today to help decide what we do with the knowledge. We're battered and weak after our previous bouts with Nightkeep and the shadow, and I don't know what the Seer will do when he reaches the source, but I doubt it'll be good for us."

As Radyn cast his gaze around the room, he noticed several of Firestone's council and elders glancing in Astram's direction. Why they would care for the opinion of a newly risen senior Sword was beyond him until Astram cleared his throat and said, "I take it, then, you'd take all the Manirah we can gather, stuff them in Firestone, and send them toward the source?"

Jyn's eyes narrowed at the surprising lack of respect in Astram's tone.

Radyn clenched a fist under the table as he imagined driving it straight into Astram's nose. They'd been roommates for years and had tolerated each other well enough, but Astram came from an old clan family, proud Manirah for generations, and he'd always looked down on Radyn.

His recent ascension to the rank of senior Sword took

on new meaning in light of his comment. The rank was officially bestowed on him by the clan elders. Typically, it was only awarded to those whose service to the clan was exemplary and who could channel the energies of three shards, although sometimes the strength requirement was set aside for special circumstances.

Astram had never been a particularly sensitive Manirah, and so three shards seemed a stretch. Had the elders raised him up for the sole purpose of standing against Jyn? Most Manirah respected the Blade, so the elders would need someone with Astram's background if they hoped to gain any meaningful backing from the clan.

Jyn leaned back in his chair and tapped his fingers against the table as he weighed this new challenge. "Yes."

Astram leaped on the answer like a cat on a mouse. "And what is the plan that you offer us? That we'll somehow fight Nightkeep and defeat this source? Relative to our forces, Nightkeep has never been stronger, and even if we find this source, how do we defeat the very heart of shadow? We can't even defeat the nuddu that it commands."

Jyn answered the questions one at a time. "We send out a call for aid. We attack with all we have. And no, I don't know how we defeat the source. All I know is that we need to try."

Astram scoffed, and Magni was halfway out of his chair before Jyn grabbed his wrist and guided him back to sitting.

Astram said, "Call for aid? We don't even know if our messengers would be welcome. It was only weeks ago all the cities banded together to demand Kaya's execution. Maybe some have reconsidered, but what are the odds they have and will risk their cities on such a desperate gamble?"

"We have no choice but to try," Jyn argued.

"That's where you're wrong. I admire your bravery, Blade. Everyone at this table has nothing but respect for you. But there's a time to recognize that the fight is lost."

Radyn connected with one of his shards and stretched his awareness lightly across the spirits in the room. He felt no influence of shadow within Astram's heart, even as the Sword argued the shadow song's cause.

The meeting room had gone eerily silent in the argument's wake, as though they were nothing more than spectators watching two warriors duel in an arena. Instead of answering Astram's challenge directly, Jyn looked slowly around the room, weighing the currents of opinion that twisted and danced like leaves on the wind. Astram had revealed himself, and Jyn was the commander forced to judge the forces arrayed against him, though they hid behind expressionless faces.

The Blade responded carefully. "You'd have us surrender, then?"

Astram refused to accept the Blade's wording. "I'd simply ask if it's worth it to separate the Manirah who have already given so much from the families they love and wish to protect. You'll admit, surely, that the odds of success in this venture are so low as to be nearly nonexistent. Why not take what peace we have while we can get it? If we are doomed, as you think, then it's far better we remain here with the ones that we love."

The pull of Astram's words swayed even Radyn. His heart was here in Underhill, split between two beautiful women most likely napping in bed together. Leaving them would be little different from splitting his heart into pieces. No doubt others felt the same. Against the backdrop of almost certain death, a warrior's priorities became clear.

It was the one argument Jyn was weak against. Most

here around the table had families and loved ones, but Jyn had only the clan. None would say it out loud, but they'd all have in the back of their heads the knowledge that their Blade, in pursuing the source, wouldn't be making the same sacrifices they would. Neither would Magni, the Blade's closest friend and ally.

And so the responsibility settled on him, but did he want it? He interrogated his heart and found the answer was easier to arrive at than he'd expected.

He answered Astram's challenge.

"I can speak for no one but myself, and I'll be the first to admit Astram's words appeal to my soul. My wife gave birth to our first child only days ago, and our future weighs more heavily upon my shoulders than ever before. The idea of leaving them behind makes me sick to my stomach."

Radyn let his words sink in, then said, "But it is because of my family that I have no choice but to stand beside the Blade of Firestone. We fight to give our children not just their lives and their futures, but to return the surface to them. I'll walk into battle knowing full well the odds, because I could never settle for less for my new family."

More threatened to spill from his lips, but his point had been made. Sometimes, the less said, the better. His argument stole the momentum from Astram's offensive, but his old roommate was quick with a rejoinder. "You would leave your newborn behind to fight a hopeless battle?" he sneered.

"No battle is without hope. The Song of the Engines hasn't faded from this world yet. And yes, I would leave them behind if it's their only chance for a future. I wouldn't like it, but I wouldn't hesitate." Radyn's calm confidence left Astram without an avenue of attack.

Jyn said, "It is my intent to take Firestone south and attempt to destroy the source of the shadow song. I would ask all the remaining Manirah to join me."

Astram crossed his arms. "Is that an order from our Blade?"

Jyn's chest heaved with barely contained frustration, but he paused before answering. "No. Those who stay behind will face no punishment. Senior Sword Astram, I believe you're wrong, but I respect your argument and understand the compassion at its root. Any who wish to stay may. Miranda will serve as your Blade until I return."

An outcry arose from many of the gathered Swords, surprising both Radyn and Jyn. Astram's support in the room was stronger than Radyn had guessed, and for the first time, he worried Jyn might not have the support necessary to mount the attack against the source of the shadow song.

Astram took courage from the assembled Swords. "You'd have us report to a Soulkeeper?"

Jyn connected with the shards across his body, silencing the room with the expression of his strength. He stood to make his point. "I am the Blade of Firestone, and the clan and the city are coming with me. You may choose not to join, but while I'm gone, you are no clan."

Radyn contained a chuckle in the back of his throat. Say one thing for Jyn, but he didn't lack courage or conviction.

Astram bristled until Jyn revealed an even deeper level of strength, enough to stun even Radyn. His body burned with Song, with no fewer than six shards, and maybe more. No human, to Radyn's knowledge, had ever pushed themselves so far.

"Care to make a point of it?" Jyn asked.

Astram, unbelievably, was slow to respond. He looked

around the room as though weighing his odds, then shrugged as Jyn's display had its desired effect. He understood when a battle was lost. "No. Your wisdom, as always, is just. I fear you may be in for a lonely trip, though."

16

The Seer walked through a world both familiar and new. Caleb's village was no different from before, but his conversion transformed his sense of the place. The trees, grass, gardens, and children threw off a faint aura of golden light that was almost painful to his new sight. Except the other adults reflected none of the light of the Song, their shapes calm islands of darkness in a world drowning in light. He examined his hands and was pleased to find no poisonous glow emanating from his flesh.

Caleb noticed the attentions of his gaze. "Those who survive the trials emerge changed. There is a period of adjustment, but soon your new senses will feel as natural as your old ones."

The Seer turned his hands over, then looked up to the plants and the trees, and a shiver ran down his spine, for his master's purpose was greater than he'd imagined. "It's not just humans, is it?" he asked.

Caleb frowned in confusion before he understood. "You ever thought otherwise?"

The events of his past took on a new and unexpected

shape, and hindsight bathed the decisions in his life with a fresh light. The shadow song had misled him, but whatever betrayal he might have felt faded to awe as he better understood his master's ways. He was driven to confess, for if any understood, it would be the man who now walked by his side.

"In my life before, I was a Singer, although never the type to be spoken of in the ancient legends. I was capable of no brilliant feats and possessed no stunning insights into the nature of the Song. At best, I possessed a basic competence that allowed me to complete my daily tasks with ease. I longed for more, but now I think it was that limited competence that opened my eyes to truths more skilled Singers couldn't recognize. While they were busy pondering the endless mysteries of the Song, I did nothing but demand that the Engines change our altitude or head in such-and-such a direction. I saw that we did nothing but take and take from those beautiful stones."

He clenched his fists. "When the strongest Singers first suspected that the Engines were growing weaker, I remember thinking that it seemed the most natural thing in the world. The others had deluded themselves into believing they commanded an infinite resource, but I'd always felt that our true legacy was that of a mere consumer. While I had no great skill for the Song, I loved it dearly and didn't want to see it depleted. The solution, to my mind, seemed entirely straightforward, though too dark for most to contemplate."

Caleb nodded along, as though he'd heard similar stories many times before.

The Seer continued, "For the Song to survive, humans needed to perish. I had no great attachment to anyone, and so the idea never troubled me. I spent months using every spare moment to research all I could about the

Engines and their creation. My study revealed the true nature of the Engines and the shadow song. The more I learned, the more I became convinced that the shadows that had exiled us from the surface were not evil in the way our legends taught us. I believed they had come to return a balance to the world that had long been missing." He paused as his new understanding sank deep into his spirit. "But it was never about balance, was it? It was always about negation."

Ironic that he'd been so blind, even though his disciples called him "Seer."

Understanding came easily now. He saw how the shadow song had sensed a weakness in his spirit, a crack in his heart that allowed truth to take root. He should be furious, and yet, as he looked around with fresh eyes, with true eyes, he realized his own thinking simply hadn't gone far enough. It wasn't only humans that called upon the Song and drained it of vitality and beauty; it was all living creatures, all of whom were parasites upon this land.

Shadow had deceived him, but only in service of revealing something true. He thanked his master for the deception. He walked through the village with a spring in his step, and the aches and pains in his body melted away.

He and Caleb emerged to find Vale pacing a line near the protected border of the village. She looked up sharply when she saw them, and her eyes narrowed. "Where's Belzrak?"

The Seer forced his expression toward sorrow, like putting on a mask that didn't fit properly. "Unfortunately, he demanded that he be allowed to participate in the trials necessary to acquire the shrine. The tests upon his spirit killed him."

The news of Belzrak's passing ruffled Vale less than a

soft summer breeze. "Fine. That's one less weight our dragons need to carry."

She turned, then stopped, studied the Seer, and took a step back. "What happened to you?"

He'd wondered if the change in him would be noticed, wondered if the transformation had left its mark upon his flesh. "What do you mean?"

"Your eyes. When we flew down they were brown, but now they're gray, like his." Vale gestured to Caleb.

"A consequence of passing the trial Caleb's ancestors set for me. I'm not the same man I was before."

Vale said nothing, but her expression told of a distaste possessing such depth she likely would have lacked the words to describe it if she'd tried. She was too new to her role to act upon that distaste, though, and Semuel had ordered her to protect the Seer, so she swallowed her feelings and gestured toward the dragon. "If I had my way, I'd leave you here to rot. Let's leave before we wear out our welcome."

The Seer almost reminded her that humanity had worn out its welcome hundreds of years ago, but recognized the wisdom in silence. He allowed Vale to lead them to the clearing where the dragons waited. A low rumble like distant thunder caused the ground to tremble beneath his feet and the leaves to dance as though blown by a strong breeze that didn't reach the surface. Vale's pace increased, and then she swore as she broke into a run.

A knowing smile spread across Caleb's face, but he was in no mood to share whatever secret knowledge he possessed, so the Seer hurried after Vale in search of answers.

The rumbling increased as he grew closer to the dragons, and when he reached the clearing, he had to shield his eyes from the brightness of the Song burning within the dragon's chests. Once his vision and senses adjusted, he had to stifle a laugh, for the pair of dragons that had flown him down paced the clearing, looking for all the world like they were chasing each other's tails.

A dragon's frustration was no laughing matter, though, and the Seer killed his mirth before it escaped his lips. Strong as he might be, even he knew better than to pick a fight with a dragon less than an hour after fully committing his spirit to his master. Vale stood before the dragons, waving her arms, looking like a novice shepherd unsure of how to win her flock's attention and obedience.

"What's wrong?" the Seer shouted.

"I don't know! I've never seen them like this, and they won't speak with me!" Vale answered.

The Seer retreated until he enjoyed the protection of a pair of enormous oaks, then watched as the Blade of Nightkeep waved and shouted like a fool. Sometimes, it strained belief that humanity had held on as long as it had. Vale was among the strongest and best of them, and yet she was reduced to *this* so easily. It was disgusting.

Eventually the dragons settled, though it appeared to be through no effort of Vale's. Once they calmed, Vale's eyes took on that distant look so familiar in Swords who had connected with their dragons. They conversed briefly, and then the Blade's eyes regained their natural sharpness. She fixed her gaze on the Seer. Her hand drifted toward the maniblade clipped to her belt, but she stopped short of drawing it. "They say they won't allow you near them."

Once again, the Seer suppressed the urge to laugh out loud. The old Seer, who'd navigated his way through the labyrinthine ways of clan politics to build a following of like-minded individuals, would have been on his knees, humility perfected in human form.

Never again. "That's inconsiderate," he said.

"They say that there is nothing of the Song in you anymore, and that it would be better for you and us if you were to die."

Shadow song gathered behind the Seer. Caleb was the only villager who'd followed them along the path, but they were hardly alone. If Vale understood the danger she placed herself in, she gave no sign of it. Their presence filled his spirit with strength, for shadow was strongest when it gathered together. The nuddu were proof enough of that.

Tempting as the fight was, the second shrine was still on Nightkeep and needed, and the city remained his quickest transportation. He recited the same argument he'd given so many times before. "My ways may not be your ways, but our paths lie in the same direction. I have no wish to die, nor any wish for humanity to perish. The dragon speaks true. I have given up the last of the Song so that I may control the shadow better."

Vale wanted to believe. He saw it in her eyes, the hope of a warrior who wanted to live and foresaw precious few ways of doing so. "There's no way of living without the Song. It means you're dead."

The Seer held his arms out wide, for all the world was nothing but an illusion, and so why shouldn't everyone focus on him? "Search me with your spirit as you will, and you'll see I speak the truth. There is no Song within me, and yet I stand before you, alive and well."

Vale did. After, her eyes took on that distant look as she argued with the dragons. From the expressions that passed over her face, the Seer guessed the discussion went poorly. She looked from the dragons to the Seer, then sighed. "They won't be swayed."

The Seer silently cursed the dragons. Their lack of support tied a knot in his plans. He needed their help to reach the final shrine and the source as quickly as possible, and what argument could he make against an enemy who saw so clearly?

Caleb stepped forward, the first time he'd seen fit to interfere in what he apparently considered fine entertainment. "If the dragons will no longer take you, there are other ways."

Vale and the Seer turned toward him in unison. "Other ways?" the Seer asked.

"Of course. We have horses here, and I'd be honored to offer them to you."

The Seer scratched at his chin. He would need the shrine in his room brought down from Nightkeep, but that could be arranged. The dragons' reticence would cost him several days, at least, but what other choice did he have?

The Seer bowed to Caleb. "Then let it be horses. Flying never agreed with me, anyway."

17

Nikki approached the Blade's study without being stopped by a single Sword or Dagger. Nearly every Manirah was either already in Firestone or packing to return. Dragons flew the large carriers back and forth throughout the day, Magni's gift for keeping track of people and supplies on full display. Jyn hoped to be flying south by tomorrow morning, and from all the signs Nikki had observed, his hopes would come true.

It was the Swords and Daggers not preparing to leave she worried about. Jyn's declarations in that final meeting had shaken the clan just as the fall of Skystone had shaken Underhill's foundations. At a glance, the structure held, but who knew what damage had been done in unseen places? The Blade's acts were unprecedented, and only the speed of his action and the sheer overwhelming strength of his allies prevented his opponents from a more decisive response.

They hadn't struck yet, and Nikki hoped they never would, but surely Jyn could spare a guard outside his door?

She knocked on the door to his study, and his voice answered a moment later. "Come in, Nikki."

She did, shutting the door behind her. "How did you know it was me?"

"You've been wearing the shard I gave you, which lends your spirit an aura that's recognizable. And before you lecture me, I'll be fine. I need Magni elsewhere."

"There are other Swords."

"There are, but I can look after myself for now. We've passed the point of greatest danger."

"How do you figure?"

"Everything is already in motion and too late to stop. If they make a move, it will be against Miranda—not me."

"I fear you ascribe to humanity more reason than I do. They may make the attempt simply out of spite."

"We may not agree about the way forward, but I choose to believe that they are still my Manirah. I order no warrior to follow me. It is enough."

Nikki would have had as much luck arguing with a wall, and so she let the matter drop. It wasn't why she had come, regardless. "I'd like to come with you," she said.

Jyn leaned back and crossed his arms. "Why?"

Nikki swallowed, suddenly at a loss for words. She'd come up with half a dozen good reasons on her way here, even though the simple fact was that she knew how to fight, and fighters were what Jyn needed. She shrugged, hoping the gesture looked natural. "I can fight."

"I know that well enough. Almost all the Shields can, and I know full well you frequent Manirah training halls more than most. But almost all your fellow Shields are electing to remain behind. Why do you want to come?"

Possible reasons danced across her tongue—perfectly defensible reasons she'd thought long and hard about—but each was an untruth, and Jyn didn't deserve them.

She swore at her own hesitation. There was no point in hiding, not now. "I want to be by your side."

Jyn cocked his head slightly to one side, as though her words demanded a new perspective. Then he grunted and frowned. "Now? After all this time?"

Nikki's cheeks felt as though they'd caught on fire. "Blame Radyn. He made me realize what I probably should have realized a long time back."

The silence stretched between them, long enough for Nikki to feel as though a fire had been lit underneath her chair. Who was she to talk to the Blade, to talk to Jyn, like this? Before her sat the man who had fought tooth and nail to guide Firestone through the most difficult years of its existence.

Jyn cracked a smile, and his posture eased. "I don't think I've ever seen you this uncomfortable before."

He didn't prolong her agony. "You're more than welcome to join Firestone. We'd be——" He interrupted himself, then said, "*I'd* be honored."

Nikki hardly heard the words over the pounding of her heart, but once they penetrated, her pulse slowed and a warmth spread from her chest to the tips of her fingers. Some dreams were too distant to be recognized, for their pursuit could bring nothing but pain. To recognize and then grasp such a dream revealed a hidden well of joy that filled her spirit to bursting. All she let escape was a half-smile, though she suspected Jyn knew full well what it represented.

She stood and bowed before she lost what small amount of composure remained to her. "Then I'll leave you to the mountain of tasks before you. I look forward to seeing you on Firestone."

"And I you."

Nikki let herself out, but before she closed the door behind her, she said, "And Jyn?"

She wasn't sure she'd ever called him by his given name, and the privilege sent a shiver down her spine. He didn't even seem to notice. "Yes?"

"Be careful. You may think you're out of danger, but I'm not so convinced."

He grinned and dipped his head toward her. "It seems like I have a new reason to stay safe. You have my word. I'll be cautious."

FIRESTONE's eventual departure from Underhill was less of an event than Nikki would have guessed. The last of the supplies were loaded with great effort, but they posed no difficulty beyond the challenge of moving large amounts of goods in a short time. The Swords and Daggers left at Underhill didn't strike out at Jyn or any of the Manirah that had chosen to leave.

Nikki aided the effort as she could, mostly as muscle moving supplies from the storage spaces in Underhill to the storage rooms in Firestone. The work was made easier by another of Aria's more recent inventions, a series of carts that was connected to a rail system powered by Song. The carts ran from several doors on the surface to common destinations below, including storage rooms, workshops, and the Engine Room. All Nikki had to do was load her deliveries onto a waiting cart and press a button on a nearby panel that specified the destination. The cart would glide away, and she'd work on filling the next. If not for the invention, they never would have left as quickly as Jyn wanted.

The floating city would only carry a fraction of the

population it once had, but even that small fraction would require an enormous amount of food. Jyn and Miranda had decided a month's supply seemed suitable. It gave Firestone enough time to reach the source and return, with at least two weeks' cushion for the unexpected.

Nikki's brief time as a farmer had given her some idea of the sheer mass of food needed to feed a population, but it wasn't until she had to carry it from the dragons' carriers to the carts that she understood in her bones how much mere survival required.

She was on the surface when a familiar dragon landed not that far from her. Tanwen settled so that his passengers could climb down, and Nikki recognized Radyn, Aria, and Elora. Her heart skipped a beat.

Radyn saw her and waved. "I didn't realize you were joining us."

Nikki shrugged. "Didn't really have anything better to do, so I figured I would keep you company."

Radyn grinned, though the mirth was short-lived. Nikki knew the feeling well. It was hard to laugh when every step upon the surface of Firestone reminded them of their purpose for being here. The pair of nuddu trailing relentlessly behind the city cast a long shadow, too. "It's good to have you here, though I wish we didn't need you."

Nikki had intended to let Aria and Elora's presence pass without comment, but curiosity got the better of her. "Why did you bring them?"

She cringed as soon as the question left her lips, not just because the curiosity was impolite, but her directness was the height of rudeness. Fortunately, Radyn took no offense.

"It was a difficult decision. I wanted Aria and Elora to remain behind, but the idea of splitting our family now made both of us sick to our stomachs. Aria argued that there's a good chance we might need her, as no one in Firestone understands the Makers' works better. She also pointed out that if the mission fails, the lengths of their lives would be measured in days, not years or decades. I'm still not comfortable flying with them into the danger, but there's another part of me that's glad they're here."

It wasn't the choice Nikki would have made, but she understood the reasoning well enough. Firestone's journey south represented an end, one way or the other, and perhaps the chance to be together a few more days was worth the risk. With luck, the ending would lead to another beginning, but only time would tell. She bowed to the couple, and Aria led them down the stairs to their old apartment.

Nikki labored the rest of the day and watched as more familiar faces arrived. As the sun set, orders came to rest. The supplies had all reached Firestone, and though there was more organization to be done, the essential supplies were stored properly and the rest could wait. Magni saw little need to drive everyone to exhaustion before they left.

Nikki took the stairs to the surface the next morning, eager to watch the moment of their departure from the edge of the city. One question loomed above all others as they began their final preparations: Would the nuddu follow Firestone, as they had for weeks, or would the sudden change in direction and speed be enough to turn their attention to Underhill's Engine?

The change in direction, when it came, was so subtle Nikki wouldn't have noticed if she hadn't been paying close attention. The slight shift under her feet lasted barely a moment. She peered over the fence that edged the fields and saw the hill they'd been flying toward now passing slightly toward their left. Firestone flew south, toward the coordinates she and Orenil had uncovered.

She twisted to look behind Firestone, and her heart stopped racing. The nuddu followed, pulled, as always, by the bright Song that kept the city in the sky. She watched for a few minutes longer to ensure her first impressions held true, and soon there was no doubt of it. At this pace, they'd reach the source in about a week, and the question of the shadow song would be settled for good. She left the sight of the nuddu behind and found one of the foremen who would direct her for that day's labors.

THAT NIGHT, as she was hauling her weary body toward her apartment, she ran into Jyn, who looked as though he'd just come from attempting to visit her. "I was hoping I might run into you," he said.

Her heart beat faster. "I'm glad you found me."

"I've asked Magni and Radyn to join me on the surface for a bit. Would you like to accompany us?"

It wasn't the invitation she'd expected, but she welcomed it all the same. All three were good men, and from the glint in Jyn's eyes, he had something special in mind he hoped to share. "I'd be delighted."

"Excellent." Jyn offered his arm, but she hesitated.

"Any chance I could stop by my apartment for a shower first? I've been helping with the supplies all day."

He continued to offer his arm. "As have we, and so I assure you, you have nothing to fear."

She took his arm, sensing the strength not just of his muscles, but of the shards he kept across his body. The Song was soft within him at the moment, but the amount of energy he could call upon with a thought made her dizzy. Most of the strongest Swords stopped at three shards, yet both he and Radyn had pushed themselves to previously unheard-of levels of strength.

Nikki tried to remove her hand when they passed a Dagger in the hall, but Jyn used his free hand to hold hers in place. The Dagger dipped his head, hiding any surprise in the gesture, but Nikki felt his eyes on her back after they passed.

Jyn led her up the stairs and onto the surface, now lit by countless glittering stars. They walked through the barren fields until they came upon a large blanket that had been laid out. Radyn and Magni were already there, talking to one another. Their conversation ended as Jyn and Nikki approached. Neither of the men looked surprised to see Nikki on Jyn's arm. Magni even smiled at the sight, a rare occasion in the days since he'd lost his wife. Nikki and Jyn sat down beside them.

"You got us all out here, so what's this all about, Jyn?" Radyn asked.

"All good things, friends," Jyn assured them. "Did you bring it?" he asked Magni.

"I did, though I'm still not sure what it is I brought." Magni patted a basket beside him.

"You'll find out soon enough. Pass it here."

Magni did, and Jyn opened the basket to reveal a bottle and a set of dented metal cups.

"What do we have here?" Radyn asked.

"A bribe from Nightkeep. One of the first gifts I received from them after I ascended to the role of Blade. Semuel was worried about what shape our retaliation might take, and as part of our negotiations, offered me this. One of the finest spirits created by Nightkeep's best distilleries. I was told that even among those who know such things, this was considered a particularly fine creation. I'd like to share it with you all. As we get closer to the equatorial zone, it's an open question what we'll find, and so I wanted to relax while we could," Jyn said.

Radyn chuckled. "Aria is going to be furious when she finds out she wasn't invited."

Jyn shook his head. "I spoke to her before I found you. She was invited, but she elected not to join us."

He set the four cups out and poured healthy measures of the dark brown liquid in each. They raised their cups and toasted those they'd lost and the success of their endeavors. Conversation came easily, the four long acquainted with one another.

Three drinks in, a question spilled from her loosened lips. "What happened on the day that Nightkeep invaded Firestone? I know the official story is a lie, but I've never been able to figure out the truth. Radyn was involved, but I don't know how."

Radyn laughed at the sudden discomfort on Jyn's face. At an inquiring look from the Blade, he shook his head. "I don't have any problem with her knowing. I'd guess she's figured out a large part of it, at least."

Jyn didn't seem pleased by the answer, so turned to Magni. His trusted advisor considered the question longer than Radyn, then nodded. "If she's going to become who you want her to be, she should know. Besides, she's been waiting long enough. She deserves the truth."

Jyn looked at the cup in his hands and took a long drink before answering. "Radyn was responsible for Nuela's death, but not in the way we led people to believe. He killed her because she was a traitor who had offered Firestone as a sacrifice."

Nikki choked on the sip of liquor making its way down her throat. "Excuse me?"

Jyn continued. "Radyn discovered that Nuela and a handful of the Firestone Singers were working with a group of Singers and Swords from Nightkeep. He and Elora fought their way into the Engine Room, killing no small number of Nightkeep's best. Ultimately, Radyn killed Nuela, and Elora sacrificed her spirit to the Engine to keep it whole."

Nikki stared at Radyn. "You killed Nuela?" The woman had widely been considered one of the strongest and fastest Manirah to have ever lived, and Radyn had been a newly appointed Sword at the time.

"I did. She was better than me, but I caught her by surprise."

Nikki chewed on the revelations, fitting them into the holes she'd once had. "And Elora?"

Radyn cast his eyes down at the mention of his mentor's name. "She Sang to the Engine alone. No one has been able to tell me how she did it, but she kept our Engine healthy all by herself. It cost her everything, though."

Magni shifted uncomfortably on the blanket, for his wife, too, had given everything to save the Engine from a surprise attack from shadow's disciples.

"Why lie?" she asked Jyn.

"Nuela was a hero, and people were scared. I intended to tell the truth, but Radyn convinced me to lay the blame at his feet. There was no telling how people would react, and Firestone desperately needed unity. Too many people knew Radyn and I were close, and there would have been suspicion about my ascension. It is perhaps my greatest regret as a Blade. I've tried to always be as truthful as possible, but it hurts, knowing that it all started with a lie."

Nikki studied Jyn in light of the recent revelations. She'd known there was something more to the attack, known a lie lurked somewhere in the past, but now that she knew, did it change her thoughts about him?

"I'd make the same decision again," Radyn said. He finished his cup and set it down. "I don't like that we lied, but Jyn's leadership has made the sacrifice worth it. No one could have led Firestone better than he did."

The warrior stood, swaying slightly as he did. "And with that, I must be off. I'll need some sleep so I can help with Elora in the morning. Jyn, thank you for your generosity."

Jyn bowed in acknowledgment, and Radyn disappeared into the dark, down the stairs. Magni finished his drink, thanked Jyn, and took his leave as well.

The Blade of Firestone stretched out on the blanket and looked up at the stars, fingers interlaced behind his head. "I would have preferred you never know the truth. I'm still ashamed I treated Radyn as I did, though it was with his permission. Every time I think about that choice, I put myself back in the interrogation room and wonder if I would do differently."

"And do you?"

"Sometimes, but rarely. It seemed the best of poor choices, and it still seems that way today. I'm not proud of it, though."

Nikki lay beside him. "Radyn believes in you."

"He does, and I'm honored by that. He's probably the only warrior alive who has a chance of killing me in a fair fight, but he's never once threatened me. I don't take that lightly."

In that moment, Nikki decided she didn't care about the lie. She snuggled closer, and Jyn extended an arm so that she could lay her head on it. They lay in silence for a few minutes, until Jyn said, "I always wanted Radyn to take over as Blade if something happens to me, but I don't think he ever will. Did you know there was a time when his only goal was to become the strongest Manirah that ever lived?"

Nikki shook her head. "What changed?"

"I think it started with Elora—his master, not his girl. He looked up to her like no one else, and she and Jelrik were quite a pair. She wanted him to be the best warrior he could be, but not at the cost of the rest of his life. When she sacrificed herself and Jelrik practically disowned him, I think he questioned what mattered most. Once he found Aria, he understood why his father had given up the maniblade. I think he would do the same if he thought he could, now more so than ever."

"Do you think you'll ever convince him to accept the role?"

"No. The Blade will pass to Magni, and he'll be worthy of it."

There was a certainty in Jyn's voice that perked Nikki's ears. "You speak as though it will happen soon."

Jyn turned his gaze from the stars to look at her. "May I confess something?"

"Of course."

"I have a deep foreboding. Call it a silly superstition if you like, but I believe the Song is preparing me for the end. I don't think I'm coming back from this."

Nikki's throat tightened, and she shook her head. "No. We're all coming back from this. You'll make sure of it."

He offered a sad smile. "I'll try."

And Nikki believed he would, but she could see in his eyes that he didn't believe he would succeed.

So she ran her fingers up his arm, determined to do her best to inspire him to want to return.

18

The days following the dragon's abandonment introduced the Seer to a side of the world he'd never expected to know. Caleb's horses made good time across prairie and forest, their sure-footed walk slow enough for the Seer to make a close study of his surroundings while still fast enough to devour the miles that stood between him, the last shrine, and the source.

They traveled with most of Caleb's warriors, an unexpected accompaniment that proved fortuitous within a day of leaving the relative protection of the forest. The Seer's brief visits to inhospitable places rarely involved the dangers that had driven humanity from the surface, thanks in large part to the efforts of the shadow clans he'd visited. As a result, he'd started to take his safety for granted, which was an error in thinking the world quickly sought to correct.

They walked their horses through what the Seer would have called an empty stretch of prairie, their only companions the occasional family of deer grazing in the distance that would sprint away if any of the humans came too close. A lack of distinct scenery lulled him into a gentle trance, the swaying of the grasses and his own mount hypnotic. He didn't understand why the scout up ahead shot up his hand and called them all to a stop.

The Seer sensed no danger, but he alone failed the world's test. Every warrior sat straight on his or her horse, empty hands ready to grasp shadow weapons with little more than a thought.

The banti attacked first from the west, then again from the east once Caleb's warriors turned their attention toward the sunset. A simple ruse, though containing the potential to be devastatingly effective, and more than the Seer had thought the creatures capable of. The Seer tightened his grip on his reins and bit back the shout that threatened to escape his throat. His bowels contracted, and he feared for a moment the cleanliness of his pants.

Caleb's warriors proved his worries unnecessary. They formed spears, daggers, and swords of shadow, calling to mind whatever weapon best served their deadly purpose. They kept sure control of their mounts as they cut their way through the ambush, the horses almost as eager as the riders to spill banti blood. The latter part of the ambush posed no greater challenge than the first. Any unoccupied rider wheeled their mount around and dealt with the second wave while their friends finished the first. There were a handful of moments when the Seer's fear returned and it appeared the banti might overwhelm the clan's best efforts, but Caleb's warriors fought on, eventually winnowing the numbers enough that the Seer was assured of his safety.

The last banti whimpered and cried out for its lost brethren as it crouched low and fled from the failed ambush. The Seer couldn't see it, but he could watch the ripples in the grass as it ran without fear of giving away its location. Caleb's warriors hadn't suffered a single death, though two of the warriors bled freely from new wounds. They circled the horses and used the opportunity to eat a quick supper while healers cared for the wounded.

Caleb was flushed with victory when he found the Seer. "A worthy attempt, was it not?"

The Seer's opinion of the banti was perhaps lower than Caleb's, but there was no need to antagonize his new ally. Seeing the incredible skill of Caleb's warriors had impressed upon him their usefulness. "It was. I didn't realize the banti were capable of such organization."

"It is only in the last few years that we've seen their tactics evolve. Their attempt today contained greater numbers than we usually see, but we've seen their methods plenty of times before."

"Do they attack so often?" From what little news he heard from Underhill, the banti attacks had nearly come to a stop, much to his dismay.

Caleb interpreted the question differently than the Seer had intended, but his answer was no less interesting. "You think banti wouldn't attack those of us who serve the master?"

He hadn't thought of it until Caleb made the point, but now that the thought had occurred, it bothered him. "I wouldn't have thought us completely immune to their urges, but yes, I'm surprised they strike you as often as they do."

Caleb smiled as one might smile at a bright but naïve student. "Our master may have chosen you, but you are still such a child of the cities."

The Seer took no offense, for the statement was true. He spread his arms out wide. "Teach me, then."

"The banti don't serve our master in the same way that we do, or the nuddu do. We enjoy a direct communion with our master, whereas the banti are nothing more than simple beasts. Our legends claim shadow unleashed them, but beyond that, they obey no master. They exist only to kill all that moves and grow in number until they flood the land. They are crude tools, but effective."

And so it went, the land and Caleb teaching him about all he'd never known. The knowledge Caleb possessed was vast and new to the Seer, and he soaked it up gladly. He learned to hide the signs of his passing, practiced the art of being aware of his surroundings, and tried and fumbled at the practice of moving without a sound.

Several days of travel brought him to the outskirts of a large Maker city. They broke their fast late in the day near the edges of the ruins while a handful of Caleb's scouts wandered ahead looking for signs of danger. A mountain range ran from north to south up ahead, and even from miles away, the Seer could see the top of one mountain was missing, no doubt used by his distant ancestors to create one of the hateful cities.

"What is this place?" he asked.

Caleb shrugged. "We have a name for it that would be meaningless to you. Our legends say it is the site from which one of the last cities was launched, but we know little else. We've had only meager contact with the clan that lives here. It's been years since we last saw them."

"Is that unusual?"

"Not so much. There's little benefit in mingling with others. Like your friend Belzrak's clan, the clan here never truly surrendered to shadow. They're a disgrace, holding onto the ruins of the past, hoping someday to return to glory."

"Do you know much of their history?"

Caleb shook his head. "They're descended from the Iron Wolves who survived the final battles, as is Belzrak's clan. It's why they cling so desperately to the belief that they will live on. They never understood the purpose of the shadow song. Why our master bestowed shrines upon them is beyond me."

The scouts soon returned with news that all was quiet up ahead. Caleb and the Seer mounted their horses and picked their way through the ancient ruins. Rubble and broken lines of sight demanded a slow pace, but the Seer appreciated the opportunity to cast his gaze upon the shattered remnants of his ancestors' lives. The Makers, as they were now called, had mastered their world to a degree nearly unbelievable today. Their fallen buildings had stood taller than anything the clans could create, and they'd possessed the time and resources not just to survive, but to sculpt, paint, and write. It wasn't anymore, but once, this city had been beautiful, with sculptures, canals, and trees. All was broken, dry, and barren today, but it required little imagination to reassemble the pieces and envision the world that had once been.

Hubris, all of it. They'd reached for the stars and deserved the pain of the fall. They were parasites who'd thought themselves masters.

Here and there the party passed signs of more recent life. The remnants of gardens, hidden carefully between the ruins. A sudden explosion of green space that had once been a park, now fenced in for cows, pigs, and lambs. None revealed any signs of life beyond the wild seed that had taken root. The Seer noted Caleb's expression. "What's wrong?"

"This place is different from when I was here last. They'd been living this far from the center then and had been growing rapidly. They'd mastered the art of survival in this place." Caleb swept his hand across the fenced-in field. "This had been packed nearly full of animals, and they threw us a feast my warriors still talk about nearly a decade later. It looks like they stretched too far, and our master punished them."

The Seer sensed a hint of "I told you so" in Caleb's observation, and he wondered if that had been a point of contention between the two shadow clan leaders. Perhaps that was why Caleb hadn't returned in as long as he had.

The shadow song had brought him to Caleb, and for that, he was grateful. The man's devotion was pure as freshly fallen snow, before life trampled it down and covered it in mud. Caleb's every breath reminded the Seer of his own shortcomings and his own human weakness. The shadow clan leader tolerated the other survivors, like Belzrak, but didn't consider himself their equal. His surrender to the shadow song had elevated him to a higher level.

They stopped when they came across the tracks of a nuddu. Never as deep as one would expect, given the size of the beasts, but still strong enough to destroy everything they touched. Buildings were flattened and trees turned into toothpicks, but the impression in the ground itself wasn't more than a foot or two deep. Unmistakable, regardless.

"These weren't here the last time I visited, either," Caleb observed.

The horses picked warily through the broken streets until Caleb called for a stop at the base of a taller building, five stories high and built of Makers' steel and reflective glass. Other nearby buildings had been flattened, as though a nuddu had stopped to dance around the area.

The Seer sensed the final shrine, an emptiness near the top of the standing building.

Caleb dismounted and looked around, and his eyes twinkled with barely contained mirth. "This was the home of the clan. At one point, hundreds lived here. To stand in the square was to feel, however briefly, what it was like to live in a Maker city."

The way he said it made the Seer think Caleb wasn't sad to see those days fade into memory.

"Nuddu appear to have made short work of it," the Seer observed.

Caleb nodded as though the Seer had made a compelling argument. "Those who forget our master are doomed to such a fate. Your friend Belzrak was the same."

The Seer nodded to the top of the standing building. "The shrine awaits."

Caleb left most of his warriors with the horses, but he and four others accompanied the Seer into the building. They found the nearest stairwell and began their climb. Patterns had been painted onto the walls of the stairwell with blood, and the Seer studied them. He was well familiar with the symbols, useful for calling and gathering the shadow song's power. He'd largely moved beyond needing them, but his disciples found them a useful scaffold to help build their familiarity with their new powers.

The blood had long dried upon the walls, the symbols a plea for the safety and protection of the shadow song. They ascended the stairs slowly, allowing the Seer to read and take careful note of the writing. The more he read, the more he was convinced everything in the stairwell was the work of one writer. All the blood sacrificed by a single person, likely over the course of weeks or months.

He saw pleas for forgiveness and protection, and for revenge upon the cities for calling some great calamity down upon them. He read apologies written in blood, the writer's mood changing by the day and by the season.

Up they went, surrounded by the writings of a broken mind. The door to the fifth floor was open, emitting a powerful stench of decaying bodies and human waste. The Seer pinched his nose, but Caleb stepped through the door and extended a shadow blade from his palm. He shouted into the darkness, "Who dares defile a shrine like this!"

For an endless moment there was no answer except silence, the challenge shouted into a hall of the dead whose souls had never reached the gate. The Seer followed Caleb in, and though the smell had given him some sense of what he could expect, the sights on the other side of the door brought him to a stop.

Bodies in various states of decay lay everywhere. They'd been placed and organized, many of them in similar poses, offered as sacrifices to a master that wanted nothing to do with them. Arms had been crossed over chests, and one leg crossed over the other. They lined the hallway, toe to head, head to toe, a pattern that stretched into the gloom. Walls displayed their bloody symbols proudly, proclaiming the names of those who'd died as well as a plea for the shadow song to welcome their spirits into its embrace.

"They knew nothing," Caleb snarled.

The Seer made no comment. Caleb's spite wasn't undeserved, but the symbols of dried blood dripped with old sorrow, and he would take that pain from shadow's followers if he could. For wasn't that the promise of shadow? An end to all pain, to all suffering.

He stepped as quietly as a mouse down the narrow path between the bodies. Caleb and one of his warriors scouted the way while the others came up behind, cocooning the Seer as well as the terrain allowed. Though they protected him from any physical danger, they did little to alleviate the weight on his heart.

The hallway felt like a broken promise, and he the messenger sent to explain the failure. Instead of ending suffering, those who had pledged their spirits to shadow experienced an even greater share.

Caleb stepped through the open door at the end of the hallway and made a disgusted noise in the back of his throat. He stepped to the side to allow the Seer to enter. The shrine sat on the floor in the corner like discarded trash. The corner was the only clean part of the room, but it was hardly the honor the shrine deserved. A man was draped over it, and at first glance, the Seer thought he was dead. Then the corpse drew a thin, ragged breath, barely audible as the shrine's shadow song filled the Seer's spirit. Caleb raised a dark blade to strike, but a grunt from the Seer restrained the blow. "I'd speak with him."

Caleb spun on his heel and retreated to the entrance of the room to join his other warriors. "His name is Seren, and he led this clan," he said as he passed.

The Seer approached and squatted next to the dying man, his knees feeling young and strong despite his girth. Shadow's strength coursed through his body, and unless he missed his guess, the same was true for Seren. His teeth had rotted, and his breath stank of decay. No food or excrement was near, but there was no way this emaciated skeleton had the strength left in his withered muscles to move. Shadow alone sustained him, although poorly.

"What happened here?" the Seer asked.

Seren's ribs and lungs rattled as he pulled in enough strength from the shadow song to speak, more than he'd likely pulled in months. The Seer couldn't imagine such a will to survive, as good as trapped here, motionless, holding on, but why? Seren's eyes sparked at the question, and for the briefest of moments, the Seer glimpsed the ruler Seren had once been.

"It was the cities! One flew directly overhead, followed by a nuddu, and the nuddu's footsteps paid no heed to those who served it. Buildings crumbled and lives vanished like smoke on the wind."

The Seer thought he was finished, but Seren held himself up a moment longer.

"Find the city that did this, and bring it down for all of us," Seren croaked.

Only one city had entered the forbidden zone in the past few years. The Seer promised Seren nothing he hadn't already promised himself. "The city's name is Firestone, and I swear to you, I will have your revenge."

Seren grinned, mouth empty of teeth, and the Seer formed a shadow blade and did him the favor of separating his head from his shoulders.

Caleb grunted his approval. "He was a powerful man once."

"Now his burden is ended, while ours grows heavier. Thank you for helping me to carry it," the Seer said as he picked up the cube.

"It is an honor," Caleb said without a hint of sarcasm, "for when you bring down the last of the cities and sacrifice our bodies to shadow, all will be silent and our master's purpose fulfilled. I am only pleased I will live to see that day."

19

The danger of what lay ahead gifted Radyn a determination that had been lacking before. Firestone's flight to the center of the continent was an ending, and the idea of leaving work undone itched at his conscience and refused to leave him alone. His desire to speak with Orenil hadn't grown, but he couldn't leave the matter any longer. The Singer had been courteous enough to grant Radyn space, though any time they were in the same room, Radyn caught sight of the desperate looks cast in his direction. If nothing else, Kaya's memory demanded he reach out his hand to support the Singer. On the second day of their flight, after ensuring both Aria and Elora were sleeping contentedly through their afternoon nap, he snuck from their apartment and sought Orenil.

A brief search found the young Singer standing watch outside Firestone's Engine room, not on duty but immersed deep within the Engine's Song anyway. He was gaunter than before, his whole being dedicated to seeking a truth that might not even exist. He didn't notice Radyn's arrival, and startled when Radyn placed a hand firmly on his shoulder. His eyes were unfocused for a moment, then confused as he tried to determine whether or not Radyn was a hallucination.

"Radyn?" His voice sounded as though it was coming from a different room, distant and faint.

"I owe you an apology."

Orenil blinked and his vision cleared. "I'd hoped you would come soon. Let's hurry and connect to the Engine."

Radyn held out a hand to slow Orenil's charge. "I'm here to help, but we need to talk first. You've made a lot of claims, and I haven't made much sense of them. Start from the beginning and tell me everything."

Orenil sat up straighter in his chair and motioned for Radyn to sit next to him. He used the opportunity to collect his thoughts, then swallowed hard and said, "When Kaya was alive, she told me there was something different about Firestone's Engine. She thought Elora was responsible."

The Singer stopped and shook his head. "Sorry, I should start before that." Orenil adjusted the sleeves of his robe, then tried again. "There is a group of Singers who have long been concerned about the focus the shadow song has had on Firestone. Although messages pass slowly between the cities, Firestone has borne the brunt of the shadow's attacks. Kaya had some guesses why that might be, but she ran out of time to prove any of them."

The corner of Radyn's mouth turned up in a sad smile. Of course she'd had guesses. He'd rarely met anyone so fearlessly curious about the world, so willing to guess and try and fail, only to try again the following day. Her gift had been what most remembered, but others with such a gift wouldn't have accomplished half as much. She'd been special because she'd coupled her gift with a relentless desire for answers.

"Thanks to the ease with which she could reach out to other Engines, she investigated a question none of the rest of us could. She could ask what, if anything, made Firestone different, and it was a question she continued to explore until she was killed. She claimed our Song was different from the others."

"How?"

"She couldn't say exactly. The best description she ever gave me was that Firestone always felt closer to Nightkeep than she expected."

Radyn frowned at the comparison.

"She grew up around not just one Engine, but three working in unison. She compared it to that. With most Engines, like Underhill's, Singing felt like a duet, but with Nightkeep and Firestone, she claimed it was more like leading a chorus of voices. She never found out why, but I think I might have stumbled upon something important when helping Nikki find the location of the source."

Orenil pulled a small notebook out of his pocket. "Here. I copied the passage so I wouldn't forget a detail. This was from the Unexpected Journey notebook."

He passed it over to Radyn, who dutifully read the passage indicated.

Passing over this ground feels like walking through a dream, these streets I still remember from my childhood crushed by the corpses of falling dragons, undisturbed since that fateful day we fled from the surface. What were our lives to them, that they would give their spirits to power our Song?

Radyn read the passage twice and still failed to understand. He shook his head as he passed the notebook back.

"Renner told Nikki before he died that Firestone wasn't supposed to be the last city that escaped the surface. He believed there had been some sort of trouble with the

Engine, and with this passage, I think the dragons did *something* to save us. Whatever that was, I believe our Song still echoes with that sacrifice. Or, put another way, some fragments of their spirits have been given to the Engine."

Orenil grew more excited as he spoke, his words coming faster, though Radyn couldn't yet see the destination.

The Singer continued. "But that's not all. I believe that since then, Firestone's Engine has echoed with other spirits, people who have sacrificed everything to protect it."

The claim hit Radyn in the chest with the force of a falling sledgehammer, and he suddenly found it difficult to breathe. His last memory of Kaya as she reached for the Engine, Veylan's maniblade falling toward her neck. He'd always suspected, but did he dare believe? He wanted it so badly to be true, which meant it required the greatest degree of doubt.

Words refused to escape his throat, and he cleared it before trying again. "What proof?"

"None I could show you here. You would need to follow me into the Song. The other Singers think me mad."

"They don't sense this?" Radyn asked.

Orenil grimaced. "None are sensitive enough."

"But you are?"

The grimace grew more severe, and he shook his head. "No. When I dive deep into the Song, I swear I hear something, a soft chorus at the very limit of my senses, but I've not heard it clearly, which is why I need your help."

Radyn slumped in his chair, the thrill of Orenil's earlier claim bitter upon his spirit. By the gate, he'd wanted so badly to believe, he'd almost fallen into the same trap Orenil had. He started to stand, but Orenil's hand snapped out and grabbed his wrist. The desperation in his eyes bordered on madness. "Radyn, please. I know how it sounds. I do. But I think this explains why the shadow song is so focused on Firestone. Somehow, back then, the dragons gave our Engine a strength the others lack. It's why it wants us destroyed. Give me a chance to show you."

Radyn didn't pull away, torn by the desire to believe and the brutal truth that Orenil's claims were a product of a mind and spirit shredded by grief. What if Orenil was right?

The question wormed deep into his heart, and he found he couldn't risk the possibility of not knowing. Kaya had known *something* in her final moments, and he had to know. "Very well. I'll help you, but I'm not a Singer. I can't go as deep into the Song as you can."

Orenil's eyes lit up, and Radyn doubted the Singer had even heard his caution. He allowed Orenil to pull him down into his seat.

"You'll want to connect with all your shards," Orenil said.

Radyn did so, grateful the Song stripped so much of the exhaustion from his body and mind. He loved Elora more than life itself, but raising an infant was a battle against his sleep like none he'd fought before. Nighttime training drills at the academy had been less intense.

This close to the Engine, the Song's sheer intensity threatened to overwhelm him, and Radyn fought to keep his balance, poised delicately between giving in to the Song's strength and losing himself, and pulling too far away to be of help to Orenil.

Radyn straddled the edge of power with the ease that came from a lifetime of practice, remaining perfectly still until Orenil's spirit met with his own. The spirit had little in common with the body that housed it, bright and vibrant while the flesh tired and weakened. They dove into the Song of the Engine, allowing the power to draw them to itself.

It had long been a source of wonder and curiosity for Radyn why it was that the Engines pulled so strongly on their spirits. It felt as though Song and spirit were parts of a whole, sundered long ago and yearning for reunion. With a start, he remembered he had felt this pull before, in a very different place.

Today marked the first time he'd allowed himself to explore the Song since the nuddu had escaped the equatorial zones. The first time since he'd almost died in his efforts to rescue Kaya from the shadow warriors. The pull of the Song was no different from the pull of the gate.

Orenil guided them, his spirit in the lead, preparing the way for Radyn. The power didn't tear at him as strongly as he expected, a gift from Orenil that allowed them to proceed deeper within the Song until its harmonies surrounded them. For a good while, Radyn did nothing but listen.

When he'd first heard the Song, all those years ago, he'd sworn it was the most beautiful sound he'd ever heard. It had competition now. Aria's laugh. Elora's cooing. Yet its beauty still possessed the power to bring him to tears, if he let it. He'd tried to describe why to Aria once and fallen woefully short. It wasn't just the complex harmonies of the notes or the patterns they created, but it was the meaning behind the notes, the unspoken mystery the music wrapped around. No human word came close to describing the majesty of that mystery too vast for a mere human mind to comprehend. And yet it was a part of him, too, woven into spirit and flesh and the greatest source of his strength.

Orenil's spirit, sensing his own reticence, urged him to push deeper, and after listening to the Song from his position a few moments longer, Radyn followed. He stopped soon again, for Orenil's protection of him had faded, and the pull of the Song became dangerous. To go further was to risk not returning. Orenil tugged, but Radyn remained rooted. He opened his body fully to the shards of the Engine embedded within his flesh, and the boundaries between him and the Song grew fuzzy. He held on and listened. When Orenil realized he'd go no further, he did the same, disappointment bleeding through their connection.

For the longest time, the Song was nothing but the Song, the same Radyn had heard from his very first days as a student with the clan. The longer he listened, though, the more the Song seeped into him, the more it became a part of him. As it became part of him, he heard the chorus of notes Orenil had described. Faint, yes, but unmistakable. The Song of Firestone's Engine wasn't one, but many.

Radyn's throat tightened as the Song resolved into spirits he'd never thought he'd sense again. Elora was there, and Jelrik, too, joined with the Song as long as the Engine existed. There were other, deeper voices that reminded Radyn of Tanwen, ancient and calm.

And Kaya, her Song jubilant as it twirled around Radyn and Orenil. Radyn couldn't breathe, couldn't focus. Her spirit wrapped around them, then flittered off, seeming to skip between the notes of the Engine's Song.

Radyn pulled back, unable to bear any more. Orenil had no choice but to follow, his ability to protect them dependent upon Radyn's strength. Spirits returned to flesh, and Radyn opened his eyes and blinked away the tears. Orenil ran the back of his hand across his face, but Radyn let his sorrow fall. The well eventually ran dry, and he bowed his head deeply to Orenil. "You're right, and I'm sorry that I doubted you for so long."

Orenil, unable to speak, simply nodded.

Radyn sat a moment longer, then stood and faced the young Singer. "You've convinced me it's true, but what does it mean? Does this give us a new weapon against the Seer?"

Orenil looked like a man who'd just found shelter from an approaching storm, only to realize he had no way of reaching it. "I don't know. That our Engine is special, I have no doubt. What it means for us in our war against the shadow song, I couldn't say, but I'll find out before it's too late. You have my word. Will you speak with the other Singers with me? I'll need their help, and your word might sway them."

Radyn extended his hand and helped Orenil up. Instinctively, he pulled the Singer into an embrace. "Of course. You've given me our first real hope since the shrines were discovered. We'll do all we can to turn that hope into opportunity."

20

The Seer and Caleb mounted their horses, the shrine safely secured and carried by one of Caleb's most trusted warriors. Caleb had wrapped the shrines in silks and then in canvas, ensuring no harm would come to the precious objects.

The small war party continued their journey through the city that had birthed Firestone, angling further south toward the source. The tallest of the Makers' buildings were behind them when they came upon a massive set of bones, belonging, no doubt, to a dragon.

Time, predation, and weather had stripped the bones clean and bleached them white enough to blind the unwary when the sun hit them directly. The Seer reined his horse to a stop so that he could gloat at the sight. They were fearsome beings when they were alive, but they were nothing but bone underneath, same as him. Once the shadow song devoured the core of the Song on this world, the dragons would die alongside humanity.

Caleb took a slightly different lesson from the bones. He tilted his head toward the sky, toward the three cities of

Nightkeep, which followed a few miles behind their war party. "It doesn't matter how high they fly. Eventually, everything falls down."

The Seer nodded. Yes, indeed. It wouldn't be long now before they all fell down.

<hr>

THEIR DAYS BLED TOGETHER after they left the city. Banti occasionally attacked, and at night the sound of wolves howling in the distance reminded the Seer that they were never as alone as it seemed, but no danger touched him. Caleb and his warriors didn't know this land, but they had learned to live in the nuddu's shadow. Now that the monsters were gone, mere survival posed little challenge. To escape the mundanity of the ride, the Seer embraced the shadow song, practicing calling upon the power of the two shrines that were never far from his side.

He had no teachers, no masters to show him the way, but his training as a Singer had given him the mental focus and the techniques to learn the shadow song. Ironically, many of the Singers' methods were more useful in commanding shadow than the Engines. Once he'd established basic competence, curiosity, intuition, and the sense of being guided by shadow itself took him the rest of the way.

He didn't know what would be required of him when they reached the origin of the shadow song. He sensed it would be a working far more powerful than any he'd attempted before, but the shape of it remained beyond his understanding. Fear remained distant, though, for his master had always shown him the way before, and would again.

Several days after leaving the ruins of the Makers' city,

all life came to an end. Their journey had taken them through small forests and prairies, across rolling hills and gentle rivers, all long untouched and unscarred by human hands. Then, without warning, nothing. Bare dirt lay ahead, without so much as an ambitious weed poking through. They brought their horses to a stop and marveled at the sight.

From their perspective, the line appeared straight, though if the records he'd read were correct, it was actually an enormous circle stretching miles in diameter. And at the center, the origin of the shadow song. The home of his master.

They would enter in time, but other tasks demanded their attention first. He dismounted and looked back at the three cities of Nightkeep, following behind like well-behaved dogs on leashes.

Where he and Caleb were going, Nightkeep couldn't follow. The warriors didn't make camp, but they started a fire with what fuel they could find and settled in to wait.

It didn't take long for dragons to detach from Nightkeep and descend toward the fire. The Seer watched, intrigued, as they remained carefully distant from the edge of the dividing line. The dragons landed perhaps a hundred paces away, clearly reticent to approach any closer.

A collection of Manirah jumped off the dragons, led by Vale. Semuel followed behind, and after that Parnell, carrying the lockbox that held the last surviving shrine. A pair of Swords kept Parnell from advancing, though, keeping him close to the dragons. The rest spread out, ready to fight. Many of Nightkeep's most powerful Swords stood before them, but even with the dragons, Caleb didn't seem concerned. The Seer adopted the same attitude for himself as he stepped forward to meet Semuel and Vale.

Their postures spoke of a long, unresolved enmity, but if they planned to kill him, there was no point in their being here. They might hate him, but they hadn't decided what to do with him yet.

The Seer didn't bother bowing. A sharp wind rose from the dead lands behind him, blowing dust between them.

The Seer spoke first. "It is time. Give me the third shrine, and it shall be done."

The pair stood in silence for a long time before answering, and when the answer came, it came from Vale. "You would be capable of great evil, should you wish it."

"I've been capable of great evil since we first met. With the amount of shadow at my command, I could reach out with a thought and bring Nightkeep to the ground. Would you like me to demonstrate?"

Vale's face turned as white as the bleached bones of the dragons, and it was Semuel who spoke. "There is no need for threats. We seek reassurance before entrusting you with this even greater power."

"What assurance can I give that I haven't already? You have my word that I seek to protect Nightkeep, to establish your cities as the sole survivors of the disaster to come. I could kill you all right now, as I did Lynae, though I've made no move to do so. How much more must I do to prove myself to you?"

Vale's lips were set in a thin line. "Lack of aggression alone can't earn trust. There must be something more."

The Seer stretched his arms out wide. He could kill them all now, the shadow song within his body easy to command. He longed for the opportunity, yet still he waited, for Nightkeep hadn't yet fulfilled the extent of its purpose. "If it is within my ability to give, all you have to do is ask."

Semuel spoke, and it became immediately clear this

exchange had been planned between the two. "It is a troublesome question, for you have nothing beyond your own life to pledge, and you've offered that to us several times already. You have no children, no family, no connections we can draw upon to ensure your word. We have come to the moment of decision, and we cannot trust you to do what is best for Nightkeep. Teach us how to control the shrines and the nuddu."

The Swords stepped forward, hands held menacingly close to their maniblade hilts.

The Seer didn't flinch away. What did he have to fear from mere Swords? Let them bluster all they wanted; they carried less threat to his person than a stiff breeze. He called to Semuel. "And what will you do? As we stand here arguing, the nuddu bring down city after city. It may be days from now or perhaps in a week, but eventually only one city's Song will remain, and without me disguising it, they will come. Capture me, question me, torture me. It makes no difference. If you stand in my way, I'll drop the protections I've cast over Nightkeep, and you will perish."

"I don't believe you," Vale said.

The Seer fixed her with a haughty stare. "You've stood on the edge of your city and watched a nuddu pass you by, a scene that by your own admission should have been impossible. I have shown you miracles, and still you doubt. The only reason you can stand here and threaten me is because I allowed you to live!"

Even Vale paused at that. Like a boulder rolling downhill, though, she could not alter her course. Her pride committed her. She took another step forward and reached for her maniblade.

The Seer never let her reach it. In her hesitation, she'd given him the time he needed to shape the shadow song to his whims. She coughed and held her hand to her chest.

Her face paled, and she stared at him, wide-eyed. The Song within her fought his control, but she only possessed three shards, and she'd only been connected with one when he attacked. She was his, and in her gaze, he saw she knew it.

He spoke softly, allowing a sorrow he didn't feel to creep into his voice. "We've all fought for too long. I understand your doubts well enough, but there is nothing I can do in the time we have to earn more of your trust. Vale, I wish no harm upon you. Too many have died already. But if you persist, you leave me no choice. This is the only way I can save even a fragment of humanity."

"Stop!" Semuel shouted. "We were afraid and acted rashly. Let her go, and we shall retreat."

"I don't need you to retreat. I need the third shrine, and I need Nightkeep to protect me from any who would stop me."

"We'll do it!" Semuel cried.

The Seer didn't let go of his hold. Vale struggled on, but there was no chance of her breaking his grip. "I know you're a reasonable man, Semuel, and a wise leader. It is Vale I fear to trust, for her mistakes might doom us all. I must hear it from her."

Vale's eyes burned with cold hate, the gray of her eyes glinting like a well-used and trusty knife catching the light of the sun, and for a moment the Seer feared she saw through his lies and would force him to kill her.

Fortunately, her spirit broke before her body. She sagged in the grip of shadow, then said, "You have my word."

The Seer let her go, and she slumped to her knees. Her chest heaved as she battled for the breath she'd so recently taken for granted. He held his command of shadow in readiness, more than halfway expecting her to break her word as soon as she regained the strength to fight.

If she had known what was coming, she would have.

The hope he dangled before them was too tempting, the consequences of failure too terrible to contemplate. He didn't know to what extent they believed him, but it didn't matter. Being their only hope gave him absolute power over their choices. If he insisted, they would fall to their knees and grovel before him. They would lick the dirt off his boots.

Tempting as the idea was, he denied himself the pleasure of it. Perhaps he was close enough to his goal to abandon Nightkeep for good, but why risk it?

He called out to the fallen Singer huddling in the back. "Parnell, come over here, please."

The Singer glanced at Semuel, who nodded, then scampered over like a frightened bunny looking for cover. The last weeks hadn't been kind to him. Sagging skin hung from loose muscles, and he looked as though he and sleep hadn't met in several nights. Not that it mattered. His usefulness had ended the moment Kaya's head and torso had traveled in different directions. The Seer jerked his head toward Caleb and the waiting warriors, and Parnell went to them.

Three shrines belonged to him now. Hopefully, enough for what his master demanded.

He bowed to Semuel and Vale. "Thank you for your protection." He rose and turned his back to them, as good as done with Nightkeep.

He barely heard Semuel's desperate plea. "Just find a way for us to survive what's coming."

21

Two nuddu trailed behind the city, and who knew what dangers lay ahead, but in this moment, the only moment that mattered, Radyn knew a joy deeper than he'd thought possible. He cleaned Elora's fresh vomit off his tunic while he listened to Aria softly sing her to sleep. Caring for Elora was a messy and exhausting task, a never-ending labor that he sometimes wished was easier, but what he suffered was rewarded tenfold when she looked at him, wide-eyed and curious, and gripped onto his fingers as though they were all that kept her from falling into an abyss.

With little else to do, their apartment became most of his life. Orenil occasionally visited, mostly to update Radyn on their exploration of Firestone's Song. Radyn's confession to the other Singers had served as impetus enough to take Orenil's claims seriously, and they'd worked together night and day since. They'd developed some techniques to eke more power from the Engine, but so far had failed to make the breakthroughs Orenil hoped would soon result.

Radyn scraped the last of Elora's vomit off, considered changing, then rejected the notion. Their daughter, young as she was, possessed a remarkable ability to dirty clothes, and there was no need to provide her fresh targets.

He sensed the subtle shift in Firestone's travel under his feet a few moments before the sound of alarms echoed down the hallways. He dashed into the bedroom, where Aria cupped her hands over Elora's ears. A quick kiss goodbye wasn't enough to express himself, but it was all the time he allowed himself. Any longer, and he might never convince his body to leave. He held his family for a moment, pressing the sensation of their presence deep into his spirit. He squeezed them tight, then turned and left, joining the flow of warriors running for the surface.

Macken met them at the entrance to the Nest, whose main gates hung open for this flight. The senior Sword waited until most had gathered, then said, "Scouts just returned after spotting dragons on the horizon. They didn't get close enough to identify who they belonged to, but we can be reasonably sure they belong to Nightkeep. There's no one else nearby."

Jyn's voice came from behind the crowd, and all eyes turned toward him. "We're putting almost all our dragons in the air, prepared for air-to-air combat. There's no point in assaulting Nightkeep's surface."

No one argued outright, but one senior Dagger raised his hand. "Sir, with all due respect, what's our plan? Nightkeep has at least three times our dragons."

Jyn accepted the question calmly. "Our plan is to demonstrate our strength and gather more information. Odds are we can't beat Nightkeep in a straight fight, but we can remind them how much it will hurt to have to fight us. Meanwhile, if we can get a sense of their determination and numbers, it'll help us decide what comes next. I'd rather not fight on this flight, but if we have to, we'll be ready for it."

The answer didn't inspire, but everyone on Firestone had stepped on board with their eyes open to the risks.

Jyn continued, "I'm flying out with you today. Magni has agreed to serve as the interim Blade in my absence."

The announcement calmed nerves, and Radyn could do nothing but shake his head. Jyn was a natural-born leader, possessing a skill he would never understand.

Swords made their way to their dragons, forming connections and preparing for battle. Jyn fell into step beside Radyn as he walked toward Tanwen's shelter. "Whatever happens out there, it can't last long. The Singers slowed our advance to give us more time before we meet Nightkeep, but it means the nuddu are gaining. By the end of the day, if nothing is done, we're going to be stuck between two very immovable and dangerous forces."

There was a suggestion there, but Radyn was either too exhausted or too dense to understand it. "You're going to have to spell out what you mean."

Jyn grinned, recognizing the exhaustion behind Radyn's eyes. "We've been in this situation before, you know. Exploring the forbidden zone while chased by nuddu. You left us then, and I was furious, but you ended up saving the city. If you see something, I want you to know you have my blessing."

Radyn grunted. "Hopefully I'm not doing anything like that today, but I appreciate it."

Jyn went to Magni's dragon while Radyn went to Tanwen. The dragon was already up and alert, watching as the Swords climbed upon their powerful allies. Radyn ran his hand along Tanwen's scales as he connected. "You ready for this?"

A powerful assent washed over Radyn, surprising him

with its strength. Tanwen wasn't just ready; he was eager. Radyn's frown only lasted a moment; then he climbed onto Tanwen's back. They joined the line of dragons and riders and before long were in the air, flying south. He took strength from Tanwen and fought to keep his thoughts off the battle that loomed ahead.

They hadn't been flying long when they spotted the first signs of a warm welcome. Nightkeep's dragons appeared as distant birds at first, but their altitude and speed betrayed their true nature. What first appeared to be five or six doubled as the distance closed, then doubled again, and still the numbers grew. Radyn's heart sank. Though no plan stood much of a chance, their greatest hope had been to pick off Nightkeep's greater numbers. The force of Nightkeep's response cut any such plan into pieces.

Still, Jyn flew on, projecting a confidence that had to be an illusion. Even if every Firestone Sword brought down three dragons, they wouldn't come close to victory.

Up and down the line, riders looked to one another, silently asking for guidance. They would fight if Jyn asked them to, but everyone with eyes to see recognized the futility of the act. Their deaths would be little more than the Song's dying gasp as the shadow song choked off its light.

Finally, Jyn shifted his weight and gave the sign to retreat. Radyn couldn't possibly hear the breaths of the other riders, but he imagined he could hear the collective exhale of relief. What other choice did they have besides pointless suicide?

Dragons dipped and banked sharply, setting a course that would return them to Firestone. Radyn shared the order with Tanwen, who continued to fly straight and level.

Radyn repeated the command more insistently, but to no avail. "Tanwen?"

A feeling passed between them, deeper than language, of warmth, companionship, and loyalty. Images of other dragons pressed upon his thoughts, making Tanwen's meaning easy enough to interpret. "You think they're allies?"

An affirmation, loud and clear.

Radyn sat up straighter and considered. He wouldn't hesitate to call Tanwen a friend, despite the vast differences between dragon and rider. Tanwen had also never lied to him, and it wasn't as though there were better plans waiting. He sent his own agreement through their connection. "I trust you, old friend."

Nightkeep's dragons descended upon them like scavengers spotting a fresh carcass. The dragons closed in from above and below, from the left and the right, converging with such speed a mid-air collision of leathery wing and tender human flesh seemed inevitable. A shard-enhanced shout from Jyn called after him as Firestone's Blade turned around to witness Radyn's fresh foolishness.

Radyn could do nothing but hold on, carried by Tanwen and the ever-shifting currents of fate. The presence of so many dragons in such a small area surrounded him with the Song, as though he flew through the center of a bonfire whose flames couldn't quite reach his skin. Ambient energy buzzed through his veins.

Nightkeep's dragons twisted away before they came within a hundred paces of him, sudden movements so coordinated they felt like the action of a unified being. Shouts of dismay rose from the dragons' riders as they were denied their prey. Several flew close enough that Radyn could see the shock and confusion written across their faces. Others gripped their dragons with distant, focused expressions as they tried to bend the dragons to their will. Fortunately, even the strongest human will paled in comparison to the ancient power of the dragons.

The sudden breaking of the threat tore a hearty laugh from Radyn's chest. Through no effort of his own, he flew through a swirling cloud of tooth and claw, of maniblades drawn and lit but too distant to be dangerous. He and Tanwen were untouchable.

Which begged an important question: What did he do with this newfound gift? It didn't feel like his to answer, though. He was but a passenger, carried to places he barely understood. He posed the question to Tanwen, who returned a vision of Nightkeep. Radyn would have laughed again if the idea weren't so likely to lead to his death. Here in the sky, he was safe, but there was no stopping the flood of Swords and Daggers that would seek his life if he attempted to land, uninvited, upon Nightkeep's surface. Tanwen, though, didn't seem to treat the ask as a jest.

"You're serious?" Radyn asked.

Tanwen was, and Radyn considered again. He gripped the dragon's scales tighter. "Very well. Take us there."

Nightkeep's riders shouted curses at Radyn and at their dragons, who swooped and twirled through the sky, too busy playing with one another to get on with the serious business of war. Jyn and Firestone's other riders had halted their retreat and now circled at a reasonably safe distance away. The Blade would want to try his luck, but Radyn hoped he possessed the reason to wait.

Nightkeep's three cities grew steadily larger, and it wasn't long at all before Tanwen circled the main city's fields, scouting out a place to land. Several of Nightkeep's dragons came closer too, as though they also planned to land. The dragons' riders shouted invectives at their allies, though, revealing their continued lack of control. Swords and Daggers gathered in the field to greet the invader, maniblades in hand, many of them lit and eager for blood.

Tanwen settled in the field as though they were here to welcome him instead of kill him. The crowd waited for no order, but charged Tanwen with murder on their minds. He lowered his head and roared loud enough to loosen Radyn's bowels. Alone, Tanwen wouldn't have broken the charge, no matter his fierceness, but the other dragons coming in to land beside him joined him, clearing a space around the Firestone dragon the Nightkeep warriors didn't dare attempt to penetrate.

Long minutes of confusion followed. Nightkeep riders swore and shouted at their dragons while the Swords and Daggers in the field swore and shouted at the riders. The charge broke into pieces, and no one person seemed to possess the authority to organize the chaos. Tanwen stood in the center, proud and regal, and Radyn followed his dragon's lead. He didn't dare dismount, for it seemed more than likely he'd need to take off soon.

The furor died down as a pair of individuals worked their way through the crowd. Radyn didn't recognize either of them. One wore the insignia of a Blade, and the other was an older man. He'd be Semuel, then. Though the Blade had a maniblade at her side, Semuel was unarmed. The Blade spoke with one of the dragons protecting Tanwen, and she stood aside to let the leaders of Nightkeep pass.

Assuming the dragons meant to protect him, the two came intending to speak. Tanwen reinforced the guess as he settled into the field so that Radyn could easily climb down. Radyn looked around for potential ambushes, then joined the two leaders in the field. He bowed to them, daring to hope that diplomacy might work after years of antagonism had led them here.

The woman who was the Blade spoke first. "You must be Radyn. Stronger than anyone I've ever met, but you don't fit Blade Jyn's description."

"I am, but I'm afraid I don't know you, ma'am."

"Blade Vale, and this is Semuel, who serves as our Elder."

More bows were exchanged, the moment surreal. Then Semuel drove straight to the point. "Nightkeep will not let Firestone pass. The Seer must reach the origin of the shadow song."

Radyn breathed deeply and held his master Elora's training close to his heart. His instinct was to argue and fight. Semuel and Vale were tense, expecting no less. Instead of fulfilling their expectations, he asked, "Why?"

They shared a glance, but honored his curiosity with an answer that couldn't be anything but honest. Semuel said, "We have learned the shadow song intends to destroy most of humanity. The Seer has given us his word Nightkeep will be spared. We will become the ancestors of all tomorrow's children."

The straightforward confession put into a new perspective all that Nightkeep had done. Reprehensible, of course, but Radyn found it difficult to blame them. Though he'd never say as much out loud, if he were given the choice between Elora and Aria and watching the three cities of Nightkeep fall from the sky, he'd probably choose his family. Not noble, but true. There was an obvious flaw in their thinking, though. "And you believe him?" Radyn asked.

Semuel shrugged, a gesture that held years' worth of weariness. "Does it matter? We've seen the power of shadow. Our Singers have felt the death of Skystone and know that other cities are soon to follow. We've seen the nuddu pass us by, though our Engines burned with their combined Song. He is our only hope of survival."

"What if he wasn't?"

The elder looked more amused than impressed. "You think you have a way to defeat this power that has haunted us since before the cities took to the skies?"

"I think we have no choice but to try," Radyn said.

Semuel shook his head. "*You* have no choice but to try. We have another option, terrible as it is."

"You'd stand by and watch the rest of humanity die, merely because one man has convinced you that he *might* keep you safe?"

Semuel nodded. "And unless I miss my guess, you'd do the same in my place. What anger you feel isn't directed at me. It's anger at the fact that it's not you who has the choice."

His words carved out Radyn's heart and bared its wickedness for all to see, a selfishness he didn't deny and couldn't convince himself was evil.

He couldn't surrender, not yet. "If we fought together, perhaps we would have a chance."

Semuel bowed. "You seem a pragmatic man, Senior Sword Radyn. You'll understand, then, when I tell you I put more faith in the Seer's promises than in your desperation. Our dragons may not help us, but I will use these cities to stand in your way, and you will not pass. Farewell, Senior Sword. I'm sorry we didn't meet under better circumstances."

He turned and left, leaving Vale and Radyn standing across from one another.

Radyn cursed his failure. There had to be something more for him to do. Tanwen had brought him here for a reason, but now sat maddeningly silent.

"Do you feel the same?" he asked Vale.

"I do not trust the Seer, but I cannot fault Semuel's reasoning. It is a slim hope, and perhaps a foolish one, but there is none better, I'm afraid."

There would be no argument, then, no alliance. Radyn bowed and turned to leave.

"Tell me, of you and Blade Jyn, who would win in a fight?"

Radyn cocked his head to the side, but Vale seemed sincerely curious. He grunted. "It would be a close fight, but I suspect that most days, Jyn would win."

"Impressive. With the two of you together, I'm almost tempted to believe you have a chance. I'll wish you well."

"Thank you."

He climbed back on Tanwen, and the dragon took off without being asked, leaving Nightkeep and their chance for an alliance behind. The dragons continued to refuse to attack, and Radyn hurried to join the protection of the others.

The nuddu approached from behind, and Nightkeep barred their way, and Radyn didn't have a guess how they would survive. He leaned close to Tanwen and said, "I'm sorry, old friend."

Tanwen roared in response, and together they flew to inform Jyn of their failure.

22

The Seer, Parnell, and Caleb and his warriors wandered deeper into the broken land. Not a single ant crawled along the ground, the bugs wiser in the ways of the world than the humans tracking boot prints across the dusty soil. A soft breeze blew from the south, slowly erasing their tracks as they plodded on. Before long, there would be no evidence they'd ever passed this way.

The Seer's master held complete and utter dominion here. Any seed unfortunate enough to be blown across the dividing line would wither and die unsprouted. Any creature foolish enough to wander within would feel the Song stripped from them, overwhelmed by the shadow song's deafening silence.

The emptiness comforted him, and his spirits soared. Parnell, who embraced the Song in his heart while proclaiming his loyalty to the Seer out loud, withered as the broken land leeched his vitality away. The Seer, in contrast, couldn't remember feeling stronger.

The ground sloped downward so gently the Seer didn't

notice until they'd descended several feet, the horizon noticeably higher than it had been before. They were close.

A building shimmered ahead of them. He thought it an illusion at first, but it solidified as they neared. Made of thick Makers' steel, it was a boxy design that looked like it had been constructed with nothing more than efficiency in mind. His stomach turned as they came closer, and he frowned. "There's a small amount of Song surviving within that building," he said.

"Shall we search it?" Caleb asked.

He wanted only to reach the origin and begin the ceremony, but nothing in his years of study had said anything about the Makers building anything here. They were nothing but a nuisance, even from the other side of the gate. "I suppose we must," he said.

Just before they reached the building, a hole in the land appeared on the other side, previously hidden by the monotonous colors of the land surrounding it. Once past the building, the ground started sloping more steeply away. Somewhere down near the bottom was the source of the shadow song. The heart of his master. The Seer tore himself away from that meeting and turned his attention to the building.

Layers of dust had built up on top of the exposed surfaces, and though there was a hint of the Song within, it was weak compared to the shadow song that surrounded it. What had the Makers intended with this building? He'd find no answers staring at its blank walls, and so he gestured for Caleb to lead the way in.

The door was unlocked and long abandoned as Caleb brushed off years' worth of dust from the handle before turning it. Lights flickered on as the door opened and Caleb poked his head in. "There's nothing inside," he announced. He held the door open so that the Seer could step in.

Two waist-high tables dominated the center of the room. Unlike the exterior, the inside was free of dust, as though a servant had just finished coming through and wiping every surface, nook, and corner clean. The tables were the source of the Song, though what use they made of the power was beyond him. He pressed his hand against one table and sensed the channels of Song within.

He grunted and pulled his hand away as though the table burned. The Song of the Engine could be directed through the tables in myriad ways. If he still had any connection with the Song, he would have explored the tables' possibilities, but the tables didn't respond to the shadow song, rendering them no more useful than any plain wooden surface.

The same story was repeated throughout the small building. Every wall and surface accepted Song as both power source and command. There was nothing about this technology in any of the reading the Seer had ever done. No hint in any of the cities that such technology existed.

Caleb waited impatiently at the door, arms crossed, making it known by his frequent glances and grunts that he had no interest in the room and that the Seer was wasting his time.

The Seer couldn't tear himself away. How long had it been since anything related to the Song of the Engines had made him feel this way? It had been common once, especially when he'd first encountered the beauty of the Song. He brushed his hand across the table and wondered what memories it held. It was a fusion of human will and the Song's sublime majesty, but why did it stand here, empty and unknown?

The only answer that came to mind was that it had to

have been built after the exodus. If the Makers had possessed this technology when building the cities, they would have used it.

Or would they?

He ground his teeth together, cursing the Makers, for they'd destroyed so much of their history and left their descendants with too many questions. They'd created works like this and then cast them away as though they were nothing.

"Parnell!" he called.

The Singer shuffled to the door, a husk of the man he'd once been.

"These require the Song to operate. Can you use them?"

Parnell turned sideways and slipped past Caleb, who didn't move for the Singer. He waddled into the center of the room and placed his hand on a table. He closed his eyes, but after a moment shook his head. "You're right that they require Song, but they aren't responding to my efforts. The controls are…more subtle than what I'm used to."

The Seer snarled and turned on his heel. He cursed the Makers and their mysteries and cursed Parnell for his uselessness. None of it mattered. He strode out of the building, his purpose as clear as it had ever been.

"Let's go," he said.

***

It hadn't been that long ago the Seer had cursed the necessity of walking across a single city, but this close to the origin of the shadow song, his legs ate up the miles remaining without a whisper of complaint. His body became that of a youth, filled with boundless strength and the itching, never-ending desire to use it. Perversely, in serving the shadow song, he felt alive in ways he never had. Before, he'd been nothing more than a Singer with no real power. Now he would shape the world.

They came to what looked at first glance like a ledge. When they reached the edge, they discovered a crater at least a mile across and several hundred feet deep. At the very center, far below them, lay a black stone similar in appearance to the shrines, except that instead of being a cube, it was spherical. It appeared small from their vantage point, but it must have been greater than the size of a man for them to see it so clearly from where they stood.

He reached out with the shadow song, sensing the unfathomable latent power still held within the sphere. Enough to roll across the plains, mountains, and forests, stripping the Song from the world and leaving it at last at peace. There was a silence inside that would forever mute the Song of the Engines. All it needed was a push.

The origin of the shadow song possessed the strength to change the world and yet was strangely inert. The Seer and Caleb stepped over the ridge and began their descent.

Unwelcome questions settled in the Seer's thoughts. Given the strength of the sphere, why hadn't it pierced the protective layer of Song that prevented it from burrowing deeper? His master's intent couldn't be clearer, and now that he saw the sphere, he understood the role he'd been born to play. But why was he needed at all?

The question chipped the smallest flakes of stone from the edifice of his belief. Like a sculptor knowing he'd carved a bit too deep, he threw the chisel of inquiry away, certain his faith was strong enough.

Their descent into the crater brought them closer to the war for the fate of the world that had been silently waged for generations. The Song of the Engines remained, buried under the silence of the sphere, but a whisper against senses the Seer had abandoned when he surrendered himself wholly to his master. It held the sphere at bay, an uneasy equilibrium that the Seer and the shrines meant to disrupt.

Caleb and his warriors stared at the walls of the crater as they picked their way downslope. The otherwise unperturbed leader couldn't make sense of the sight, and questions danced behind his eyes, but for the moment, he was too proud to ask them.

His restraint lasted until the slope was no longer so steep. He descended at the Seer's side and asked, "Do you know what happened here?"

The Seer briefly reveled in their change of positions, of his knowledge being greater than the warrior's.

"I have guesses, though none of them are certain. Did you know humans aren't from this world? That we came from the sky?"

Caleb looked up and squinted, then cast a suspicious glance toward the Seer, as though certain he was being mocked.

"I believe it's true, though I don't think even the Makers knew. Or if they did, it wasn't common knowledge. But we came from the sky, and eventually, we were followed by this," the Seer said as he pointed down at the sphere, now less than a half mile away. "It crashed into the world, creating the crater we're in. It was aimed, I think, at the core of the Song, which lives in the center of the world, but the Song was strong enough to hold it back. Our master has made progress over the years. Our own feet have proven that truthfully enough. It is why we've descended, ever so slightly, since we passed the line after which nothing grows. The land gives way against our master's relentless pressure."

"What purpose, then, do we serve?" Caleb asked. "It is right for me to be here, but I cannot say why."

"Our master's war against the Song has waged for many generations, and in that time, it has attempted different strategies. One of its first was to spread across the land, to wipe out life and weaken the Song. The shrines, I believe, were part of that effort. Unfortunately, the shrines represent a considerable fraction of our master's strength, and without them, our master was unable to reach the source of the Song. Our purpose—the one I was born for—is to reunite our master with the shrines and provide it with the strength to finish its mission."

"And us?" Caleb asked.

"The Song will fight to protect itself. Once I begin the work of reuniting the shrines with that sphere, I will be of no further use in this realm. It will fall to you to keep me safe, to ensure the work is completed."

Caleb looked again to the sky. "So this is the last day I will be forced to look upon the sun."

"It is. Once our work here is done, all suffering will be ended."

"Then let us make haste."

THE SPHERE at the center of the crater wanted to consume everything, from attention to soil. Almost close enough to touch it, the Seer finally sensed clearly the shape of the battle between shadow and Song, focused around the bottom of the sphere, which pressed with the weight of a city against the land and the Song, and the land and the Song pushed back. The war was mirrored in his stomach, his spirit caught in the edges of the maelstrom.

He caught one of Caleb's warriors drifting slowly

toward the sphere, her eyes locked on the inky shadows moving within. He grabbed her wrist and tugged, once and then again when his first effort wasn't successful. She was slow to come out of her trance, blinking and staring at him as though he were some sort of mysterious creature out of a children's legend.

"Don't look too long within it," he cautioned. "It devours, and it doesn't care much what it consumes. Stare too long, and it will take all of you, and you're needed yet."

The woman offered a small bow, then turned her back to the sphere so she could face the enemies the Seer suspected would soon surround them. The others noted his warning and moved cautiously, wary gazes wandering in every direction but toward the sphere.

He instructed the warriors carrying the shrines in their placement, three points of an equilateral triangle with the sphere at their center. The shape wouldn't focus the shadow song's energy as well as a square, but it would do. He shifted one shrine a few inches and admired his handiwork. They were as ready as they would be.

His last instructions were to Caleb. "I don't know what nature of trials awaits me, but whatever comes to pass, make no effort to save me from the effects of shadow."

Caleb's expression told the Seer he didn't have to worry himself on that point.

"All you have to do is make sure the ceremony isn't interrupted. You'll know when it's finished."

"May your efforts prove successful," Caleb said. "My ancestors and I put our trust in you now."

The Seer wouldn't bear the burden lightly. He sat down next to one shrine and stripped his sweat-drenched tunic off. He leaned back so the cube pressed against the lower half of his back, as close to his core as he could get it. One last time he looked around, allowing himself his final glance at the world.

He wouldn't miss it much.

He closed his eyes and connected the shadow that was his spirit with the tremendous energies within the shrine. What little fatigue that remained in his body was washed away like footprints carried away by the crash of sea waves across a sandy beach. Shadow embraced him tight, the borders between his spirit and his master's command thin as worn gauze. His will remained, though, and he stretched his sense of shadow as far as it would go.

Pitiful, desperate Nightkeep stood between Firestone and the shadow's origin. They formed a wall Firestone would never fly around, and two nuddu trailed closely behind the cursed city. Jyn and Radyn and their ilk would die before coming close to stopping him.

Reassured, the Seer set his sights next on connecting the three remaining shrines: the first of two dangerous feats, for it was more shadow than he'd ever channeled at once.

His master pulled at his spirit, though, and the idea of stretching out his shadow and connecting to the other shrines felt deeply right, the single deed he'd been born to complete. Even Caleb, for all the strength their master had granted him, knew the task was beyond him.

And of course it was. Only the Seer possessed the will to grapple with this power. Only he, among all the Manirah who thought they understood the Song, truly grasped the nature of reality. The future was his to shape.

He reached shadow first toward one, connecting it with a gentle touch. The shrines joined with deceptive ease, the vast majority of the strength flowing only between the two cubes. No additional strength flooded through his body, lending him the confidence to attempt the third shrine. He willed the shadow toward the last point of the triangle, stretching it from the other two points equally. The connection snapped into place effortlessly.

The Seer shifted and frowned. With such power at his command, shouldn't there be more effort on his part? He sensed the tremendous flow of strength, but in the same way a visitor might look down upon a roaring river crashing through a narrow cavern of stone below. The energy was undeniable, but it barely brushed across him.

He set his shoulders and focused on the rising and falling of his chest, centering himself for the task to come. The shadow flowing between the shrines still answered to his will, and so he bent the flow of shadow until it brushed, ever so gently, across the sphere.

A cavern opened inside him, a hole no amount of dirt and stone could fill. He became no more than a sack of flesh draped over the memory of a skeleton. He'd told Caleb's warriors the sphere consumed, but even he'd underestimated the depths of its hunger. Whole worlds wouldn't fill the maw that yawned inside him, and his spirit stood face to face with the vast silence that awaited. He stretched his arms out wide, the silence a visitor he'd longed to meet.

The silence stared at him, then turned its back and thrust the shadow that was his spirit away. The forces his master had protected him from snapped around him, and even his mighty will wasn't enough to keep him safe from the blow.

Unconsciousness rushed to greet him, but it wasn't silent. In the moment before his world went dark, he realized the screams were his own.

23

Flight made conversation next to impossible, the sound of the wind too loud in their ears to pass complex messages back and forth. Through facial expressions and hand signs, Radyn informed Jyn of his failure. Jyn kept a close eye on Nightkeep and its dragons, dividing his attention between the enemy, Radyn, and a silent conversation with the dragon he rode.

The three cities of Nightkeep were spreading out, their strategy obvious to anyone who'd played a childhood game of tag. By extending the line of the cities, it made it nearly impossible for Firestone to advance. The cities were too large to turn quickly, so Nightkeep didn't have as much airspace to cover as they would have against a more nimble opponent.

Jyn ordered his Manirah to return to Firestone. He didn't land in the Nest, but in the empty fields, implying it might not be long before they took off again. Riders dismounted and conversed. Jyn made a straight line for Radyn. "If you have any ideas, now would be the time to share them."

Radyn spun in a slow circle, estimating the distance still separating Firestone from Nightkeep, then judging the advance of the nuddu. Firestone had slowed below the nuddu's speed to allow Jyn and the others an opportunity to find a way forward, but their time ran low. The nuddu were less than a mile away and eating steadily at the gap. At Firestone's current speed, they had less than an hour before the nuddu caught them. But if they went much faster, it wouldn't be any longer before Nightkeep stopped them.

They'd flown themselves into a deadly corner, and he didn't have a clue how they'd escape it.

Jyn pondered out loud. "We could just aim Firestone straight ahead and increase our speed. They don't have enough time to evacuate a city, and Semuel wouldn't risk the lives of an entire city to stop us."

Radyn thought back to his brief conversation with Nightkeep's elder. "I'm not so sure. His decisions are reasoned enough, but he believes they're all doomed unless he does all he can to protect the shadow song. He very well might sacrifice a single city."

Magni left the Nest at a run and joined them. "What news?"

Jyn allowed Radyn to share recent events while he sought a way out of the rapidly tightening noose. Magni listened closely, then scratched his chin. "You say Nightkeep is spreading out in a line?"

Radyn nodded.

"Then the answer is easy enough. Veylan showed us the way."

Radyn frowned while Jyn grunted. "If you have a plan, let's hear it."

Magni shrugged. "We jump over them."

Radyn stared at Magni, openmouthed. Why hadn't he

thought of that? It was such a simple idea, yet he'd let his thinking become too locked in specific patterns. If Elora had still been around to chastise him, she would have.

Even when it was full of people and supplies, Firestone was lighter than Nightkeep, and the difference was more pronounced now. In addition, the increased output Orenil was pulling from the Engine gave Firestone a significant edge in maneuverability. Not enough to dance around the line of cities, but if they caught Nightkeep by surprise, they could absolutely adjust their altitude faster.

His blood froze as he followed the line of thought, though. The nuddu were trailing them. Their behavior was no longer as certain, thanks to the Seer's influence, but odds were they'd crash right into Nightkeep. It would be Skystone all over again.

He could tell himself that Nightkeep had made their alliances and deserved whatever consequences resulted, but he wasn't so cold-hearted as to believe that. True as it may be, the vast majority who lived within those cities were innocent. They had just as much claim to life as Radyn or anyone else.

He watched the calculations and arguments dancing behind Jyn's cold eyes, and Radyn said a silent thanks, once again, that this responsibility wasn't his. He couldn't imagine the weight that would settle upon Jyn's spirit if they lived to see another sunrise. With the fate of the Song and all life hanging in the balance, there could only be one decision, no matter how terrible it was.

Jyn, as always, wasted no time in pointless debate or recriminations. "So be it. Pass the word down to Orenil and the Singers."

Magni and Radyn spread the word quickly, and Magni delivered the orders to the Singers. There was little else to do. What supplies they had were already stored and packed securely, and the city was as ready as it would ever be. The Manirah and dragons sat down in the fields, ready to fly at a moment's notice. The rest was left in the hands of the Singers.

Firestone picked up speed, a process that pulled like a gentle pull on Radyn's core. He connected with a single shard to listen to the Song. Firestone's Engine burned bright, its Song ringing loud and clear as a bell on a quiet day. The Song tugged at his spirit, and he let himself be carried along by the soft but powerful melodies.

Orenil's voice was first among the Singers, the soloist all others followed. His notes were filled with conviction, an enviable certainty Radyn had lost somewhere between his youth and adulthood. He sniffed as tears gathered in the corners of his eyes. Kaya had loved Orenil, but if she could see what he'd become, her pride would have rivaled what Radyn felt for his daughter.

Perhaps some part of her could. Such questions were beyond his ability to answer, but he took comfort in believing it so.

Nightkeep grew close enough he could pick out the Song of their Engines in the distance. The three Engines neared one another in response to Firestone's additional speed, closing the gaps they suspected Firestone would try for. The nuddu fell farther behind, though they were still close enough to send shivers down the back of his spine if he considered them for too long.

The cities rushed together, a seemingly inevitable collision stretched out over minutes. Radyn could now make out the details of Nightkeep. Their dragons still circled in a lazy patrol, but there was nothing they could do. Radyn dug his fingers deeper into the soil, for they were close enough now, and the cities moving quickly enough, that he wondered if Orenil had misjudged, had waited too long to spring their surprise upon the other city.

Orenil's voice shifted, carrying a note of command that the other Singers soon echoed. The resulting eruption of Song from Firestone's Engine crashed over Radyn and momentarily blinded his senses. He disconnected from his shard and blinked away the tears as his stomach was pushed deeper into his core.

The mountain that was Firestone groaned as the Makers' steel that reinforced the city cried for mercy. Fields quaked, and Radyn nearly ran for the stairs to save his family, convinced the stone that had so long been his home was about to split apart. The trembling eased as Firestone settled onto a new vector, gaining altitude nearly as fast as a dragon. Nightkeep dropped out of view. Radyn held tight to the soil, sensitive to any further changes in speed or direction.

None came. They'd either surprised Nightkeep to such a degree that the cities hadn't responded, or they'd tried to match Firestone's change and failed. Radyn breathed a deep sigh of relief, noting the air had grown considerably thinner in the space of a few minutes. He spared a thought for Aria and Elora and hoped the air was thicker down below, trapped behind several locked doors.

Their altitude peaked as the Singers eased up on their demands of the Engine. With no need for surprise, the Singers let the city descend gently. Radyn stood and walked to the trailing edge of the city, peering over the fence to the scene below.

Nightkeep's three cities appeared to be charging suicidally at the nuddu. Slowing the massive constructions of stone and steel was no easy feat, and harder yet if the Singers catered to the needs of more tender flesh, but considering the fatal consequences of failing to stop in time, the Singers weren't pushing their cities hard enough. Radyn's fingers tightened against the fence, silently urging the Nightkeep Singers to do more, to unleash the full power of their Engines and stop, no matter the price in broken bone and shattered lives.

They never heard his silent pleas. Nightkeep's smallest city, the one furthest to the west, won the misfortune of meeting the nuddu first. Both attacked it at once, their shadowy arms stretching out to block the light of the sun before they descended upon the surface. From his safe vantage point, it looked as though the nuddu arms simply broke apart, like a glob of ink dropped onto paper that spread as it stained.

Memories of Skystone remained too fresh, the scars of that battle ripped open, and again Radyn was helpless, forced into the role of mere spectator as the city died. The fence groaned under the strength of his grip, but he didn't turn away. Though he hated Semuel's cowardly choices, they weren't hard to understand. People needed hope as much as they needed food and water. Without it, the spirit died and, denied hope, they would search and scramble for it the way a starving man might look for nuts, berries, and carrion on the surface.

Semuel had lost his hope, and in so doing had lost his city.

Nightkeep's death required witness, for it was the fate of them all if they, too, surrendered to fear. Radyn's spirit also demanded that he watch, for he'd played a role in the city's end. He deserved to bear the burden of the consequences.

Shadows swarmed over the surface, spreading quickly as the two nuddu combined their efforts. Maniblades fought off the invaders, little lines of light that combatted the darkness. The lights winked out quickly, though, until the surface was shadow only. Before long, the city began to tilt and lose altitude, and then finally, it fell.

The drop wasn't nearly as high as the heights Skystone had fallen from, but the destruction was barely less impressive. The ground rippled as though it were water, uprooting trees and tossing them through the air like toothpicks. Air bent as the force of the impact ripped across the sky. Nightkeep's remaining two cities rocked and shook as the wave hammered at their stone, but both remained in the air.

Firestone rumbled as the wave reached it, stone and steel grumbling like an old man forced from his bed. Somewhere beneath Radyn's feet, stone cracked. His stomach sank for a moment as he cursed his helplessness, but Firestone absorbed the damage without further complaint as it continued its journey south.

Dust and ash billowed from the massive pile of stone and steel that represented Nightkeep's gravestone, hiding the deadly shadows that crawled and seeped through the cracks. Radyn refused to turn away as the ruin fell into the distance.

Nightkeep's other two cities had come to a stop and now hovered, motionless, above the ruin of their sister city. Radyn silently urged their Singers to retreat, to flee while they still had a chance. Losing a city was terrible, but if the other cities fled, the dead would at least have the right to claim their deaths as a sacrifice. Whether because of confusion, a lack of orders, or a misplaced desire to help the fallen, the cities remained in place.

Radyn sensed the nuddu recovering before his eyes caught any sign. Shadow strengthened and deepened, like a hole that had suddenly tripled in size. He sensed no command over the creatures. Their hunger for the Song served as their sole guiding purpose. The dust cloud obscuring their growth bubbled as the shadows merged into the larger nuddu, then broke as it stood up straight, like an old man rising from a squat.

Nightkeep's remaining two cities shifted south, chasing after Firestone like a pair of younger children who decided they wanted to play after all. Radyn grunted as Jyn came to stand beside him. "I'd hoped they would at least flee in different directions and pull the nuddu away."

Jyn didn't answer immediately, his eyes unfocused as he stared at nothing in particular. Then his gaze hardened. "Semuel just lost the last thread of hope he's been hanging onto for a very long time, and there's no telling what a man without hope will do."

The Blade turned the matter to other subjects. "How close are we?"

Radyn tore his thoughts and his gaze away from the fallen city. He couldn't afford to give the emotions building in his chest free rein, not yet. He sealed them away. "Close now."

Jyn tilted his head towards the field where the dragons and Manirah awaited. "Then let us not waste a moment. It's time for us to finish this for good."

24

The Seer awoke to a world gone mad. Consciousness returned well before vision, leaving him groping along the shattered and uneven ground with only his hands to guide him. Caleb shouted in his native tongue, too long divorced from the language of those who had fled the surface for the Seer to understand. He didn't need to know the words to guess what was being said, though. Caleb gathered his warriors to him, and from the barely concealed panic in the voices that answered, the Seer surmised he wasn't the only one afflicted with blindness.

The knowledge cushioned his pride from an otherwise devastating blow, for if the affliction was shared there was no failure on his part. His spirit and efforts still pleased his master, even if his master had no time for him.

The shadow song struck mighty blows against the land and the Song that protected it. Every few moments, the ground beneath the Seer would reverberate like an enormous gong struck with an iron mallet, shaking hard enough to throw him from his feet. After two failed attempts, the Seer decided that crawling on hands and knees would serve as an adequate form of transportation. He reached out with one hand, clawing the air as he searched for the shrine he'd been standing beside. His hand struck flesh first, and one of Caleb's warriors cursed at him.

A rumble struck as he extended his arm and caused him to lose his balance. He fell to his side and lay there, breathing hard. He didn't even know in which direction he crawled. For all he knew, he'd been crawling away from the shrine, away from his life's work, driven by panic like a mere Manirah.

The Seer sought the echoes of his master, calming his spirit so he could sense his surroundings more clearly. His connection to his master wasn't as strong as before. Such was the strength of the powers surrounding him, though, that the muddied connection mattered little. The sphere housed the greater part of the shadow song, and it rose and fell, accelerating so fast it seemed as though it had disappeared from the sky and suddenly reappeared upon the surface. If not for the wake of shadow that trailed behind the sphere, he wouldn't have recognized its movement.

His master's power swirled around him, a twisting tornado of shadow that grated across his flesh like sand and dust blown before an angry wind. Caught within the maelstrom, he couldn't sense the shrines he'd carried so far across the continent. He extended his senses farther, pushing deeper into the shadow, but found nothing. The shadow controlled by his senses picked up speed and suddenly changed direction, rushing toward the sphere like water swirling around a drain.

Light returned to the Seer's eyes, and he blinked away his tears as the sun beat down on him from above. The cloud of shadow continued to twist and writhe, moving faster and faster. Anyone still caught in the cloud was as good as dead, the force too great for even the strongest Manirah to endure.

He wasn't the only one stumbling around under the sudden light and peace. Caleb and his warriors were bigger and stronger mirrors of the Seer's disorientation, their hands held over their eyes to shield their gazes from the sun. Parnell was on hands and knees, emptying the contents of his stomach. Beyond the Singer's sickness, though, exposure to the shadow had done no harm. The Seer squinted against the glare of the sun and looked for the shrines.

They were gone. The marks in the soil where they'd been placed remained, but he could find no other trace.

His gaze and senses traveled to the twisting cloud of shadow, now spinning so rapidly it looked nearly as solid as a wall of dark Makers' steel. It shrank further, pouring itself into the sphere, and the Seer finally understood.

The shrines had been part of his master, and by bringing them here, he'd returned his master to its full strength. Or at least, close enough. Kaya had destroyed one shrine, and he couldn't guess how deeply that loss would be felt.

The last of the shadow cloud swirled into the ball, the last bit triggering a wave of force that once again knocked down all who stood too close. The Seer coughed and struggled back to his feet. All the strength he'd felt abandoned him, leaving him an aging and weak man who'd surrendered his body and spirit to a master he still didn't fully understand.

His doubt passed as quickly as a dragon flying overhead. He was the one who'd helped his master reach this stage of wholeness. He was the one who'd fought against the Song for most of his life, sabotaging it in ways both obvious and subtle. And he was the one who had unraveled the Song's plans, the one who ensured that Kaya, the Song's greatest hope, died. Without him, the Song would have triumphed eventually.

He stood tall and faced the sphere, which no longer pounded against the surface like a drunk trying to gain access to their apartment. It hovered above the ground, and the Seer could hardly sense the shadow within. He stared, seeking the understanding he was certain eluded him.

His senses brushed against the sphere, and he jumped back as though he'd unexpectedly found himself too close to a raging fire. The amount of shadow within the sphere defied explanation. His spirit could fall forever and never plumb its depths.

There was movement inside the sphere, the darkness within spinning, swirling, and twisting in a pattern just beyond the Seer's understanding. The chaos subsided, and a crack louder than thunder split the air. Sunlight slipped through the center of the sphere, revealing parts of it that had been encased in darkness for generations. Something shifted within, expanding and contracting like a pair of lungs desperate to take a full breath. The sphere split and twisted, its surface transforming from the inky swirl of the shrines to something harder, something alive. Limbs stretched and extended like a nuddu taking a step. Shadows took on familiar curves and shapes, and the Seer swore under his breath. He blinked, and a woman floated in the air before him.

Her skin was a pale white he'd never seen on the living, and her hair was perfectly dark, absorbing all the light that touched it and reflecting nothing back. Brilliant green pupils took in her surroundings as her hands ran down her body. She wore clothing unlike any he'd seen before, a single piece of fabric that clung tight to her flesh but moved with it.

Despite what his eyes told him, his other senses noted the woman as nothing more than shadow. Shaped into an exquisite form far beyond what he would have guessed possible, perhaps, but fundamentally no different from a shadow blade or spear.

That awareness fled as she set her mouth in a grim line and fixed him with a hard stare. She couldn't be just an expression of the shadow song. She was something more that his crude senses couldn't pierce.

The woman descended gently until she was standing across from him, but the Seer noted that her feet never touched the ground. Her voice sank its claws into his spirit, freezing him in place with nothing more than a statement. "You failed to protect me."

The Seer fell to his knees, unsure if he'd meant to or if she'd forced him down. He stammered, then chastised himself for behaving thus in front of his master. "What do you mean?"

"I am not whole."

The fourth shrine. "It wasn't my fault. Belzrak's clan failed to protect it."

The woman took one gliding step toward him and leaned close to his ear, her voice barely more than a whisper and still containing enough strength to shiver his bones. "But you are the one I called. You were the one I trusted."

The Seer couldn't respond. His spirit rose to a realm of pure bliss as she confirmed he was her chosen one, only to be shredded by the knowledge that he'd failed her. Any explanation was an excuse, and there was no point. She knew all already.

"What would you have of me?" he asked.

She reached out with her left hand and grabbed him by the throat. Flesh as cold and unforgiving as ice cut off his breath, and he thanked her for it. Life was, and always had been, a burden, but he was too great a coward to end it himself, too attached to the greatness within him to leave without accomplishing some legendary purpose.

She was his purpose. Every breath, every plan, every murder had been to bring her here, to restore her. He hadn't understood before, but as hands that had never known the warmth of a pulse stopped the air from reaching his lungs, it all became clear.

She dropped him, and the Seer fell to his knees. He coughed as he sucked in cold air. Once he could speak, he said, "Tell me how I may serve. If it is within my power, it shall be yours."

That cold, weighing gaze once again fell upon him, measuring some aspect of his spirit and flesh. A satisfied smile crawled across her face, baring teeth that looked more at home tearing flesh from bone than reassuring a weary soul. "You know not what you offer, but as it is freely given, I thank you. I still have some need of you, but a fragment should suffice."

She gave him no opportunity to question her cryptic answer. She raised her arm, calling to mind a Blade summoning their clan to war. Tendrils of the shadow song wrapped around his chest and arms, holding his body in place while his dark spirit trembled under the force of her focus. His spirit, whole since the moment he'd been born, rang like a struck bell and threatened to crack.

He gasped and tried to claw at his chest, though his bonds allowed him no movement. Around him, Caleb's warriors suffered the same tribulations, bound as he was by the thin but impossibly strong strands of shadow. Some struggled against the theft of their mobility, while others accepted their master's use without complaint or argument.

The Seer's spirit rang out once more, shivering beneath his master's violent efforts. He quenched his body's natural urge to fight. There was no greater good than to serve his master. She alone understood the truth of the world. She alone understood him.

He would become her greatest commander and general, an irreplaceable servant. He would lead her shadows across the land, killing those small pockets of humanity that always seemed to survive. And then when he was done, he would present himself to her, the last human left on this wretched world, and she would kill him. His death would complete her purpose, and she would remember him always.

The vision of the future was repeating itself when his spirit fractured within him. His body felt no pain, and yet he screamed in mortal agony. He would have collapsed to his knees if the shadow had allowed it, but he remained upright, forced to watch as some part of his spirit crawled out through his open mouth. Darker than ink, it flowed from his lips like cursed vomit, only to take shape.

The shadowy form solidified and took on a humanoid appearance. It turned its back on him and marched away. Caleb's warriors expelled shadow warriors, too, and before long Caleb's small fighting force had become an army, hundreds strong. The Seer vomited again and again, each time surrendering another sliver of his darkened spirit.

His master's knife was sharp, precise, and cruel, each fragment of his soul as small as she could work with, so that she could create as many shadows as her raw material allowed. Tears sprang unbidden as he vomited up yet another shadow that joined its newly birthed fellows, for that was all he was to her. No hero of her cause. No champion fighting the battles beneath her. Only a means to an end and the raw material to make other tools. She had a clear view into the very center of his spirit, which he'd offered wholly and without reservation, but neither his efforts nor his sacrifices mattered.

Would she take it all? Divide him into pieces until nothing remained beyond the shadows carved from his spirit? It was an ignoble and cruel end for the years of service he'd delivered.

The knife cut once more, leaving only the very core of his spirit. He bent over and ejected one last shadow as the tendrils wrapped around his body bled away into mist. He fell to his knees before the remnants of his spirit, now fully under shadow's command.

He remained embodied but weak, and he looked around at the army summoned from the help he'd brought. Even Caleb's warriors, as tough as anyone he'd ever met, were on their knees, their faces pale from the loss. They slowly came to their feet, a final row of opponents behind the hundreds of shadows.

As one, every shadow turned north as Firestone's dragons appeared on the horizon, flying quickly toward them.

25

Tanwen sagged underneath Radyn as they crossed over the razor-sharp boundary between life and death. From the air, the land looked like an enormous pillow someone had driven a fist into, an impact of a scale that even the falling of a city paled in comparison to. The ancient impact didn't explain the lack of life within the perfect circle, though.

As a farmer, Radyn understood better than most how persistent life was. Weeds sprang into existence whenever he turned his eye away, and only unrelenting vigilance allowed the precious food to grow without having to compete against the invaders. Even on Firestone, high in the sky, weeds were a constant nuisance. Sometimes the other farmers liked to joke that the weeds were the other true descendants of the Makers, having also evolved from the seeds brought up in the soil so long ago.

Which made the complete lack of life within the circle even more worrisome. It meant that not only had something once killed all that had lived within, but an active force prevented life from regaining its natural foothold. He gripped Tanwen's scales tighter and asked why he'd been so suddenly weakened.

The answer was, of course, the influence of the shadow song. Radyn felt it around him, not as strong as when a nuddu was nearby, but more like a smoke in the air that wouldn't quite fade. It sapped his strength and Tanwen's, too.

The dragon uttered no complaint, though, and they continued their flight. One building made of Makers' steel stood out from the crater, but with no activity nearby, Jyn decided it wasn't worth their attention. On the backs of the dragons, it didn't take them long to find their enemies.

Here there was no doubt of the shadow's strength, and Tanwen and the others circled warily a distance away. A small army of shadowy figures stood guard against the Manirah, and Tanwen wasn't certain the dragons could fly close enough to lend support.

The shadows guarded a woman Radyn had never seen before, but the amount of shadow song emanating from her made his stomach turn from a mile away. She was their enemy. The Seer meant little compared to her. She took one glance at the dragons, then turned her back and strode toward the hole that marked the very center of the circle. His gaze caught sight of another figure, bent in half, behind the lines of enemies.

Parnell.

The last time they'd crossed paths, it had been while he'd observed the execution of his own daughter. Radyn's hand drifted to the maniblade at his hip as he imagined his revenge. He hadn't cut at a human since the day Kaya died, but he didn't think he'd have a problem killing the Singer.

Jyn ordered the dragons as close as they could get. The dragons gathered Song within their mighty bones and dropped toward the surface, their flight growing more erratic the closer they came to the hole. Tanwen wobbled, dropped, then caught himself on spread wings a few moments before crashing into the broken ground.

He landed hard, but Tanwen reported he was uninjured, though it would take a bit before he could gather enough Song to take to the air again. Radyn wished him a speedy recovery, then leaped off his friend's back. The shadows were already shifting forward, eating up the distance between them with unnatural strides.

Radyn lit his maniblade and was soon joined by other Swords and Daggers. A quick estimate had the Manirah outnumbered perhaps four to one, but Radyn figured the battle was still theirs to lose. The number of shadows posed a problem, but even a junior Dagger was stronger.

He revised his estimate as the shadows ran faster, their walk developing into a shambling run.

Magni's shadow fell over him, and Radyn said, "I think these are stronger than the ones we faced on Skystone."

Magni grunted his agreement. "It stands to reason. They're closer to the source of the shadow song, and the strength of our Song is weaker here." He raised his voice. "They'll still be no match."

The giant lit his maniblade and held it high above his head, prompting the nearby Manirah to do the same. His weapon fell until it pointed at the charging mass of shadow, and the Manirah leaped forward like hungry wolves spotting lame prey.

Radyn joined the others. Jyn had landed after most of the rest, but his battle cry carried to every ear in the crater.

The lines crashed upon the barren wasteland, and the sounds of charging feet transformed into the grunts and cries of the Manirah as they connected with their shards and cut with their maniblades. Glowing blades *thunked* hollowly against hardened shadow, but in almost all cases the Manirah's trained reactions were faster than the shadows' response. One of the junior Daggers near Radyn fell as he pushed too far, too fast into the crowd of shadows. He found himself alone and outnumbered, and he died without a sound.

Radyn had just met him earlier, one of the new recruits Jyn and Magni had graduated a bit early. Skill to spare, but no experience. His first battle was his last. His spirit fled through the gate, granted its final reprieve.

He could spare no more thought for the youth. Dark blades pressed on all sides, and the momentum of the Manirah's charge had been spent. They fought with all their strength simply to hold, but as the shadows pressed ever closer, it became clear they couldn't hold for long.

Jyn gave no orders. There was no need. The Manirah fought to stay together, to keep their friends and families closer than the shadow that sought to tear them apart. Once doing so demanded they retreat, they retreated. The ground itself meant nothing to them, and better to surrender it than spend their lives needlessly.

Too many Manirah fell, despite Jyn and Magni's unrelenting efforts to be everywhere at once. Every time Radyn saw a weakness in the line and made his way to it, one of the two was already there, maniblade flashing against the darkness. As the Manirah thinned the number of shadows, their retreat slowed, and Radyn sensed the tide beginning to turn.

The shock of the surface clan's warriors joining the fight reverberated up and down the line. Their movements reminded him of the clan warriors he'd fought when he and Kaya had destroyed the shrine in Nightkeep. He froze. He was back in that tiny room with a young girl attacking him, her different bladed weapons coming at him from all directions.

The cut of a shadow sword freed him from the memory and restored movement to his limbs. He scrambled backward into the waiting protection of the other Manirah.

The nearest of the surface clan warriors was less than a dozen feet to his right, pushing so hard into the Manirah lines they seemed likely to crack in the next few moments. Jyn and Magni were too busy with clan members of their own to lend their aid.

Radyn was the stronger warrior. He could see it in the shadow warrior's technique and in the speed of his cuts. Yet he couldn't bring himself to strike. He ordered his body to move, yelled at his limbs to act, but buried memories lay too close to the surface, binding him in place.

The delay cost the Firestone warriors a precious life. One young Manirah, a woman who'd been a Dagger for less than a year, fell to a blade of shadow. She cried out in agony as the blade passed through an eye but didn't cut deep enough to kill her. A second cut sent one of her arms flying into the distance, and a third ripped organs out of her stomach. The shadows and the clansmen did nothing to finish their brutal work, for she was no longer a threat. Instead, they moved on to the next group of Manirah. Radyn cut down another shadow and then met the young lady's one good eye as she pleaded with him to save her.

He couldn't, not anymore, but he refused to let his cowardice doom more allies to terrible deaths. Anger gave him what courage could not, and he leaped into the battle, striking at the knot of shadows and surface clansman from the side. His maniblade carved a quick and easy path through the shadows, who were focused on other opponents. The death of the shadows did, however, provide enough warning for the warrior from the surface to turn and meet Radyn's attack. Maniblade met shadow, but Radyn's second cut was faster. He stabbed deep into the man's throat and swiped his maniblade across, granting the warrior a quicker death than he'd offered the Manirah.

The violence of his assault had cleared a temporary space around him, and he used the moment to look around and judge the progress of the battle. Pandemonium reigned, with chaos in every direction. The assault from the surface dwellers had finally broken the Manirah lines, and the battle had become less a push-and-shove contest and more a collection of smaller engagements. Some looked to turn in favor of the Manirah, while others spelled eventual doom. But over it all, Radyn saw that the mysterious woman he'd seen from above was standing at the lip of the hole, gathering an amount of shadow to her that chilled him to the bone.

He couldn't reach her to stop it. Too many warriors of both shadow and flesh stood in his way. A dark mist like a cloud seeped from the pores in the woman's skin, spinning in a slow circle around the center of the crater. The mist thickened and spun faster, rising high into the sky.

Shadowy forms converged on Radyn, cutting off his view of the woman and her efforts. He cut them down with little difficulty, but their numbers were great enough that he couldn't advance. He and the Manirah bled for nothing as the destruction of their world was worked directly before them. Frustration and anger bubbled up from his chest, but all his shouting and cursing did nothing to cow the enemies blocking his way. Another of the surface clan sought Radyn out, grinning viciously at the Manirah's helplessness.

Another shadow crossed the sky, briefly cutting off the sun's light and sending a shiver down Radyn's arms. It grew larger as it fell, and then Tanwen was among the shadows, tail, tooth, and claws clearing the path Radyn's maniblade couldn't.

"Go!" Magni shouted, and Radyn needed no further encouragement. He sprinted toward Tanwen, ducking under the dragon's twisting neck as he snapped at one of the surface warriors. Two shadows sought to bar his way, but they vanished as Tanwen's talons raked through them.

The dragon's efforts weren't without cost. Blades of shadow worked their way between armored scales, a terrifying reenactment of the elder's death in the bogs far to the north. Tanwen roared as the blades sought his vital organs, but he fought on, shouting encouragement through their connection.

Another figure broke from the battle, his maniblade glowing bright. Jyn glanced at Radyn, nodded, then sprinted toward the woman. Radyn joined him, forcing the battle behind out of mind for the moment.

The woman showed no concern about their approach. She raised a hand that misted into shadow and joined the rest of the darkness that swirled faster behind her. A sudden burst of the shadow song caught all the mist and whipped it into a frenzy. It expanded, swallowing the woman and hiding her from sight.

Jyn lowered his shoulder as he reached the mist, but an instant of contact was enough to lift him from his feet and send him spinning and twirling through the air like a doll thrown in a tantrum. He landed hard but had the presence of mind to allow his body to collapse and roll. He came to his feet, thankfully uninjured.

Warned by his Blade's failure, Radyn didn't try pushing his way through the mist. He jabbed at it with his maniblade, and the force of impact was almost enough to rip the hilt from his hands. He gripped the blade tighter and tried to push, but it was like trying to push a piece of paper through stone. It simply wouldn't move.

Behind them, other dragons joined Tanwen, their flights erratic but sufficient to deliver them to the battlefield. They attacked the shadows and surface warriors who fought past Tanwen, giving Jyn and Radyn the time they needed to find their way past the impenetrable defense.

Not that there were many options left to them. The dragons were doing all they could, and the Singers were busy keeping Firestone in the air, too far away to help in time. Radyn glanced at the maniblade in his hand and saw that Jyn was doing the same. Their eyes met, and Radyn nodded once. "Don't die."

Jyn snorted. "You're the one who finds himself at the precipice of the gate time and time again."

He had a point.

In answer, Radyn connected with every shard in his body, the familiar surge of the Song washing the exhaustion and aches from him. The wounds that burned faded to nothing, and even now, surrounded by shadow and death, the Song raised his spirit and reminded him that there was beauty in life, even in the sorrow. He kept close to the Song, accepting the comfort it offered as it filled his limbs with light and strength. When it felt as though he could take no more, he dove deeper, connecting as deeply as he ever had.

Underneath the soaring melodies, voices whispered to him, some familiar, some not, but all united in purpose. His maniblade glowed such that the pale blue turned to a soft white, too bright to look at directly. Beside him, Jyn's maniblade reflected a similar embrace of power, most likely more than two lone Manirah had ever wielded.

Radyn's nerves burned raw with the power coursing

through them, and when his mind could pull no more, he stabbed his maniblade into the dark maelstrom. Like a heated blade quenched in the cold water from the stream, the power rushed from Radyn as it struggled against the shadow song. Another white-hot blade joined his own, close enough that the powers could link with one another, and together they stabbed deeper into the shield. They fought for every inch of progress, but the shadow slowly gave way.

Jyn groaned as he redoubled his efforts. Through gritted teeth he said, "Why does it feel like you're making me do all the work?"

Goaded on by the sting to his pride, Radyn's weary spirit sought yet a closer communion with the Song. His maniblade slipped deeper into the whirling shadow, no longer quite so solid where the two Manirah assaulted it.

Jyn grunted and grinned, then said, "That's more like it."

They took one step, then another, and then the woman was before them, her missing arm and hand whole again, the whirling wall of darkness solid behind her. She held dark blades in her hands and lashed out at the Manirah, her cuts fast enough to make a Senior Sword jealous.

The assault forced Radyn and Jyn to retreat. Their maniblades turned aside the dark blades, and Jyn was fast enough to press his own attack. She twirled away from the maniblade, her form shifting and bending to avoid the cut. Jyn's weapon sliced nothing but air, but the woman's haphazard movement left Radyn an opening.

The woman's form continued to shift, shrinking in size and reforming, flesh made malleable and shaped to the cold will of a malevolent spirit. Radyn cut where he thought the neck should be, but a dark blade turned his cut aside as the transformation completed.

He and Jyn pressed their attack. For all the woman's command of shadow, enough to silence an Engine with a thought, she was no warrior, and their blades, which burned as bright as their spirits, grew ever closer. Dark hair hid the woman's face from Radyn, but after hastily parrying one of Jyn's attempts on her life, she spun and faced Radyn with a wicked grin on her face.

Radyn's heart skipped a beat as his eyes widened. His mind, trained and sharpened to a killing edge by Elora and hard experience, shouted that he saw nothing but an illusion, one mask of many that could have been pulled over the evil spirit's essence. He *knew* it was the same woman, but it mattered not, for his spirit was bleeding freely, holding dominion over rationality's truths.

The surface girl from Nightkeep stood before him, hands empty and neck bared. "Do you remember me?" she asked.

How could he not? She'd haunted his nightmares since, and the guilt pointed inward had only grown deeper after Elora's birth. He'd wanted nothing more than to put it behind him, to force himself to forget, but his conscience couldn't so easily be put aside. He saw glimpses of her every time he tucked little Elora into bed, heard her death cry every time Elora wailed.

His daughter was the greatest joy of his life, and he'd taken that same joy from another father.

He froze, rooted to the spot, and the girl was no longer unarmed. She held two dark swords. One blocked Jyn's next attack, while the other slid deep into Radyn's gut.

Fire erupted in his stomach, but it was no more than he deserved, and he hoped that the fire would cleanse him and release him from this paralyzing guilt.

The girl pulled her sword out, laughed, and took a step back. The wall of darkness expanded to swallow her once again. Jyn pounded on the wall with his maniblade, but alone, even his unbelievable strength was insufficient. He looked to Radyn for help, but Radyn's thoughts were elsewhere. He held his hands over his stomach as he dropped to his knees, then fell onto his back.

In the darkness of the wall that grew ever closer, Radyn heard his wife and daughter crying out for help, but he lacked the strength to save them.

26

Nikki stood at the fence that surrounded Firestone's perimeter. She leaned against the upper rail, tapping a half-remembered beat against the wooden beam as she stared at the column of darkness that rose into the sky ahead. It had appeared less than an hour ago, and though there were no Singers on the surface to see it, they must have sensed it, because Firestone had been slowing down since it appeared.

The column rose to a point in the sky high overhead, far beyond what any dragon or city could reach. She couldn't guess what it represented, but she suspected she wouldn't like the answer. Some mysteries were better left unsolved.

She finished her drumming and stood up straight as familiar shapes appeared in the sky. Dragons returned to Firestone, although not without difficulty. Some lost altitude so quickly she was certain they were about to drop completely from the sky. Others weaved back and forth, like a laborer three or four drinks too deep in their cups.

She clenched her fists as a low growl escaped the back

of her throat. Never had she been so helpless to do anything meaningful. All her training meant nothing against this threat, and there were no mysteries left to solve. Survival alone remained, and that would be determined by the strength of the clan and the Song, not of her mind.

She made her way toward the Nest. There would be wounded, and though she was no doctor, she knew enough to help.

The dragons' flights evened out as they grew closer to Firestone, to the point that Nikki questioned her earlier observation. They landed smoothly in and around the Nest and began disgorging their passengers.

Fewer returned than had gone.

Far fewer.

Firestone's clan, once a source of pride, now numbered fewer than two dozen, and many of those whose hearts still beat needed care before they could hold a maniblade again. Her heart skipped when Jyn climbed down off his dragon, then sank as he gingerly helped untie a body from the back of the dragon.

Nikki rushed forward, her concerns about the others forgotten. As she pushed her way through the crowd, she saw Radyn still had a flush of color splashed across his cheeks. "What happened?"

"Explanations later. Healer first. He doesn't have long."

Nikki diverted a nearby stretcher with the intention that she would help carry it, but Jyn and Magni grabbed the poles on each end and hurried off, running faster than she would have been able to with the weight. Down the stairs they went, so quickly Nikki feared they would miss a step and fall. Thankfully, the two sure-footed warriors reached the healing quarters in what had to be record time.

Only after they'd delivered their patient and been politely but firmly booted from the room did Jyn fill her in. They sat together on a bench outside the healer's while Magni searched for Aria. His bloody hands intertwined with hers. "I think the shadow took on the appearance of the girl he killed in Nightkeep. He froze at the moment we needed him most."

His fingers tightened around hers; then he stood and paced the small hallway, swearing loudly enough to shake the walls. "We were right there!"

Jyn dropped back onto the bench and held his head in his hands.

She'd never seen him this vulnerable before, this upset. She glanced back at the healing quarters. He and Radyn had always shared a bond she couldn't quite explain, a mutual respect that had held even through their fiercest disagreements. He mourned not just the potential loss of his friend, but the loss of a man he'd considered an equal.

"Can you forgive him?" she asked.

Jyn started and shot her a questioning look.

"Killing that girl will always stain his soul. You can argue with reason and logic all you want, and you'd be right enough, but you're well familiar with the weight of having to act against your conscience, and some wrongs can't be made right. We can only figure out how to move on. He needs you, and I think you need him. Which means you need to forgive him."

She remained by his side as he wrestled with her advice. He pushed himself harder than anyone she knew, but he possessed the wisdom to know when he traveled in the wrong direction. Finally, he bowed his head. "I'll try."

They sat together in silence. He leaned the back of his

head against the wall and closed his eyes. Some of the tension had left his body, replaced by the bone-deep weariness that followed battle.

Their brief respite ended when Aria came tearing around the corner, little Elora held tight in her arms. She stopped at the sight of the Blade waiting outside her husband's healing room, and her eyes welled with tears. "Is he…"

Jyn slowly shook his head. "Not when I left. Healer kicked me out, though I'm sure if you only want to peek in, he wouldn't mind."

Aria handed Elora to Nikki. "Just for a moment. I don't want her to see." Without waiting for a proper answer, she dropped the child in Nikki's arms. "Thanks."

Then she was gone, and Nikki was holding a child at arm's length, afraid that at any moment it might spring a leak. Jyn's chuckle was low and throaty. "Not around children much?"

"I had no siblings to give me any nieces or nephews, and thankfully the nature of my work usually surrounds me with adults."

Elora sniffled, and Nikki panicked.

Jyn placed his hand, caked with Radyn's dried blood, on Elora's back and gently pushed her toward Nikki. "Nothing to it. Just hold her close and keep her safe."

Nikki followed Jyn's guidance, and as she did, Jyn wrapped his arms more tightly around her. Elora sniffed Nikki, considered the scent with the care of a bloodhound, then snuggled into her chest. Warmth blossomed in Nikki's heart.

"You look good with a child in your arms. Like it belongs."

Nikki snorted, but there was no smile on Jyn's lips. She

took another look at Elora. The baby had Aria's face, but her eyes, even this early, seemed to miss nothing. She was her father's child, too. "Maybe," she admitted.

Aria emerged before long. Nikki offered Elora back, but Aria waved her away and sat beside the couple. "The healer says he'll survive so long as we stop bothering him." She looked straight at Jyn. "He says that you saved Radyn's life."

Jyn shrugged, as though he'd been complimented for merely waking up in the morning. "Tanwen and I together, plus Radyn's will to live. He was hurt badly, though. I'm glad to hear he'll survive."

Aria forced Jyn to explain once again what had happened. Jyn did, and he'd just explained Radyn's fall when another unexpected guest joined them.

Orenil looked as though he'd run a daylong race. Sweat poured down his cheeks, and his face was flushed. He wheezed as he put his hands on his knees. "Been...looking...for...you," he gasped.

The three on the bench glanced at each other, not sure who he meant.

"The Blade," he clarified.

Jyn rose. "What's wrong?"

"The shadow song is fighting..." Orenil trailed off and grimaced, then said, "Something, although we don't know what."

Jyn stared blankly at the Singer. "I'm sorry, but I have no idea what you're talking about."

Orenil grumbled something to himself, then tried again. "None of us senses the shadow song well, but we're close enough and it's strong enough that we have a vague idea of what it's doing. It's been growing stronger since the battle, and now it's trying to dig deeper under the surface."

Orenil checked to see if Jyn had followed. At the Blade's nod, he continued. "Most of us believe it's digging toward the core of the Song to destroy it. But it's having trouble."

"What's stopping it?" Jyn asked.

"That's the problem. We don't know. The Song is involved, but it lacks the strength to accomplish what we're sensing. There's something else at play, but we can't sense it."

The Blade glanced at Aria and Nikki as if they might have answers, then turned back to Orenil. "What *can* you tell me?"

"It feels like there's some sort of barrier beneath the crater. We can't tell you what the barrier is made of or how it works, but it has five focal points where it's strongest. We're close to the nearest one."

Jyn frowned. "We saw a building as we were flying in. Could it have been that?"

Orenil shrugged. "Could be. Was there anything else you noticed?"

"The place was a barren wasteland otherwise."

"Then it's worth investigating. I'd like to go." In answer to Jyn's inevitable question, he said, "There's nothing I'm needed for here at the moment. Singing is harder here, but we have it well in hand. The Engine has made it easy for us."

Nikki stood. "If you're sending Orenil, send me as well. I'm useless up here, and I can keep him in line."

The corner of Jyn's mouth turned up. "Can't resist another mystery, can you?"

"No, sir."

"Aria?" Jyn asked.

Radyn's wife looked up, the mention of her name

drawing her into a conversation she'd paid little attention to. "Yes?"

"I think you should go with Orenil and Nikki."

She shook her head adamantly. "I'm needed here."

"There's nothing you can do by sitting on this bench. If the healers say he'll recover, he'll recover. The building below wasn't made anytime recently. I could use you down there to figure out what's happening. It might be one of our only chances to stop this shadow song for good."

Aria didn't budge. "I'm not leaving his side."

"He would want you to go. If Orenil's senses are correct, whatever is happening within that building might be the only chance we have at stopping the shadow song from reaching the core. You know what that would mean."

Aria looked once more at the closed door where her husband was being healed. She wavered for a moment, then said, "So long as we take Tanwen down. He'll tell me if something happens and I need to return."

"Of course," Jyn said.

Aria hesitated a moment longer, rightfully loath to leave but more than aware of the stakes and necessity. Jyn wouldn't have asked, and he certainly wouldn't have pressed, if he hadn't thought it was important.

Nikki gestured at the infant. "What about Elora?"

"There's no one here to take her, so I guess she's coming with me," Aria said. "So it's good that you'll be there to protect us."

Nikki swore under her breath. She'd been eager to solve a mystery, not act as the only protection for a Singer and the two women in the world who meant the most to Radyn. Still, it was a way she could help, and the shadows were closer to the crater. She turned to Jyn. "Would it be possible to get a maniblade? I'd feel better down there if I had one."

It wouldn't be much, but if the shadows advanced, it was the only weapon that killed them.

She only hoped she wouldn't have to find out if she was skilled enough to do so.

27

Nikki and Aria met Jyn and a handful of Swords shortly after at the Nest. The Swords were bloody, covered in dust, and had a tendency to stare off into the distance when their attention wandered. After a lifetime of seeing Firestone's most dangerous warriors in clean attire, their attention sharpened to a razor's edge, their general dishevelment twisted her stomach into knots.

Even so, she preferred them like this. It was too easy to consider them pompous and superior, but these trials revealed the potential and limits of their strength. Every Sword and Dagger on Firestone had chosen to be here, and these were returning to the surface mere hours after suffering a crushing defeat. Assuming they survived the coming hours, she swore to herself she'd memorize the names of every one who had joined them to honor their sacrifice.

Jyn pulled her aside as Aria and the Swords finished their final preparations. He led her toward Tanwen, who looked as rough as the Swords. Dust coated his scales, and blood dripped from several open cuts. "Will he be able to fly?"

"He insisted when he heard Aria was going, and he claims that he's fine," Jyn said.

Nikki remained unconvinced, but she wasn't one to argue against a dragon.

"One of the other Swords will connect with Tanwen for the flight back to the surface, but I want you to see if you can connect."

She stared at him as though he'd asked her to push her hand into a roaring fire. "That will kill me."

"Tanwen has agreed to restrain his spirit as much as he's able to. It won't be easy for him, and he probably won't be able to for long, but it should allow you to connect with him for a bit."

Nikki felt as though Jyn was handing her a knife and telling her to pierce her own throat, assuring her it would be fine. "Why would I risk it?"

"Because I don't have many warriors left, and there's no telling what the next few hours will hold. I might need the Swords for something else, or all the Swords may die, leaving you and Aria alone on the surface. Tanwen thinks he can connect with you for a while without hurting you, and it would be foolish not to test the ability first."

"It's foolish for a Shield who only has rough control over a single shard to connect with a dragon!"

"Will you try, please?"

She wasn't sure if Jyn had ever said "please" to her before. Her heart thumped in her chest loud enough for the shadows on the surface to hear, but she nodded. Jyn held his emotions close, but his true reason for asking was clear enough. He wasn't sure who, if any, would survive, and he wanted Nikki and Aria to have every chance he could give them. "Fine. How?"

"Tanwen will make it easy. Connect to your shard, then reach out with the Song toward Tanwen. He'll take care of the rest."

Nikki steeled herself with a deep breath, then did as Jyn asked. She connected with Tanwen moments later and gasped. Song tore through her body, just barely less than what she could control. If Jyn had asked her to run ten miles, she was sure she could have.

Jyn grinned and placed a hand on her shoulder. A small fraction of the Song flowed between them, easing a bit of the pain of sensitive nerves and inflamed muscles.

"Is this what it's like for you?" she gasped between heaving breaths.

Tanwen broke the connection, and at the moment before he did, Nikki sensed the dragon's satisfaction.

"Probably something similar. Hard to say," Jyn admitted. "Your body gets used to it."

There was still too much strength of the Song in her body, but as it faded, she caught her breath.

"The more important thing is that you connected with Tanwen. You'll have options now, if it comes to it. Please, do everything you can to come back to me."

Nikki leaned into his chest, taking comfort in the strength of his arms and the sturdiness of his stance. "I will, so long as you promise the same."

He lifted her chin gently until their noses were almost touching. "It's agreed."

NIKKI DIDN'T FLY on dragons often, but the experience of riding on Tanwen was different after they'd connected. She wasn't actively joined to him, but some remnant of their connection lingered like a ghost in her thoughts, and she swore she could feel the force of the wind against her nonexistent wings.

The sensation provided a welcome relief from the dreary sight below. She'd always considered the fields after harvest to be depressing places, acres of land once rich with a never-ending variety of plants suddenly stripped barren. Those gardens were a rich tapestry of life compared to the scene below. She squinted at the surface but couldn't see so much as a speck of green, nor even the slightest hint of movement as some small rodent scampered away from the shadow of the dragons' passing.

It was a dead land, leeched of all life by the shadow song, and if they were to fail, it was easy to imagine that it would be the fate of the entire world.

The building was easy enough to find, the only feature on a featureless surface. The dragons circled once to ensure the area was safe, then came in for a landing. Swords spread out into a rough perimeter while Aria, Orenil, and Nikki went into the building. Aria carried Elora wrapped tight to her chest.

Orenil opened the door and stepped in first, the others right behind.

Nikki had spent the short flight over debating what wonders she might stumble upon. If this building had the power to control the shadow song, it must be a wonder.

She blew out an exasperated breath when it turned out to be nothing but four blank walls and a pair of tables.

"You were expecting something more?" Aria asked.

Nikki nodded.

"It's bare, even for the work of the Makers," Aria admitted, "but I think there's more to this building than appearances would suggest."

"Can you feel it?" Orenil asked.

Aria shook her head. "What do you feel?"

"There's a Song here. Actually, it feels as though there are many Songs, each one faint."

It didn't take long for the group to focus their attention on the tables. They came a little higher than waist high. Orenil placed his hands on them and closed his eyes. "They have a feel similar to the security pillars you made for Firestone's Engine Room. May I?"

Aria nodded. She'd pulled Elora free of her wrap and walked around the room, studying the blank walls as though they'd reveal some long-lost secret if she stared hard enough.

Orenil Sang to the tables. A low hum near the edge of hearing came from the tables and the floor. A kaleidoscopic display of colors burst above one wall, following no pattern that Nikki could discern. The lights died, flickered back to life, flared bright enough to blind the unsuspecting, and finally died for good as Orenil removed his hands. The humming from the tables and the floor lasted a few moments longer, then faded to silence.

Orenil looked at his hands as though they'd betrayed him. "I rescind my statement. They're nothing like what you built. It seems like there's something I should be able to do, but it rejects my efforts. It's connected to an incredible energy, though."

"Mind if I try?" Aria asked.

Orenil stepped away from the tables. "Please."

Aria handed Elora to Nikki for the second time that day. "Sorry, but I'll need both hands, and I don't want her spirit interfering."

Nikki took the infant without complaint. It wasn't glorious, but what did that matter? She bounced the child gently while she walked a slow loop around the room. There was little to look at, but the absence of material was sometimes just as much a clue as its presence. There was no bed, no kitchen, no windows, no sign that the building had housed someone. The walls and doors were Makers' steel, but the welds that held the building together lacked the care and precision the Makers usually employed.

Someone who wasn't a professional had built this quickly. And when they'd built it, they'd not intended to live here. If it contained the shadow song, as Orenil seemed to think, the builder must have thought it didn't need continual attention.

It didn't add up to much, but it didn't have to. Mysteries were rarely solved by a single revelation, but by the slow weight of gathering evidence. Nikki noted what she could without pushing it to mean anything specific.

Elora made happy gurgling sounds, which tore Nikki's attention away from the building. The child rarely cried, and when Nikki looked down, she saw a pair of dark eyes staring back at her. She had the same penetrating gaze both her parents shared, like she saw everything with perfect clarity. A low chuckle escaped the back of Nikki's throat, and she leaned close to the child's face. "You're going to be quite the child when you grow up, aren't you?"

Elora reached out and Nikki gave her a finger, which she wrapped her small hand around and grasped with the might of a much stronger child.

Aria spread her feet and placed her hands on the table. She closed her eyes, and the hum began again.

Nikki sidled over to Orenil. "How can she use them if she isn't a Singer?"

"The Song is in all of us. Her body doesn't handle the Song well, though, so she could never reach the ability with the shards a Dagger would require, much less a Singer. Her answer, whether or not she realized it, was to develop a remarkable sensitivity to the Song as it runs through materials. She can't handle much, but what she can, she handles more deftly than anyone else I've met."

Aria overheard. "And that's why I can use the Makers' creations. They were designed for people with a control that matches mine much closer than Orenil's or Radyn's."

To punctuate her statement, all four walls exploded with color. Images danced across the blank walls, revealing maps and graphs that Nikki couldn't understand. Everything was labeled in the language of the Makers, and she knew nothing more than a few basic symbols, none of which appeared on any of the displays.

"What is this?" Orenil whispered.

"You were right. The Makers built something to contain the source of the shadow song. It's connected to the Song, but manipulates it in a way I've not seen before. There's another force here, but I don't understand it."

Orenil studied one display, then the next. Nikki followed behind him and tried to decipher what they meant. Several of the displays flashed red messages she assumed weren't promising. Orenil translated quickly. "The shadow song is close to breaking through. The shield can't handle the amount of power it's facing."

He ran his finger across the letters. "Where is it drawing power from?"

Aria searched, then said, "Everywhere. Both of you should come close to the tables."

They stepped closer, and Aria said, "Orenil, brace yourself. I think this will be a lot."

The floor opened up along seams Nikki hadn't seen before, revealing shards placed at regular intervals under the entire floor. Each was connected like a miniature Engine to several wires that pulled power from them. Orenil fell to his knees, his face pale, and Aria reversed the command, sealing the floor shut once again.

Nikki said a silent thanks. She was no Singer, but she was connected to a shard, too, and the power made her head spin and her stomach want to eject the last few meals she'd eaten. Once the floor closed, the Song as good as disappeared to her senses, though she was standing on a collection of shards whose strength easily overwhelmed Firestone's Engine.

Orenil needed several moments to recover. "They figured out a way to contain the Song completely. I can barely feel it, even now that I know what's beneath my feet."

"It's a brilliant design. What you sense as the Song is, in a way, wasted energy. Here it's collected and focused toward its ultimate purpose," Aria explained, awe in her voice.

Orenil nodded. "And the strength! Those looked like normal shards, but each was incredibly powerful."

Aria agreed. "Each shard is outputting what I'd expect from a small Engine."

Orenil's face remained pale. "Figuring out what they did would change—everything. Can you imagine what uses we could put the power to?"

"It won't mean anything if the shadow song breaks through," Nikki reminded them.

Aria looked around the room at the displays. They responded to her, changing and shifting as her gaze landed on them. "I'm not sure how much more I can do. The shards are connected to the core and are already pulling about as much as they can handle. I could risk pulling a bit more, but I don't understand this system well enough to know what would happen. We could overwhelm it completely, and the shield would be gone for good."

"Do it," Orenil said.

"Sure?"

"No, but if the shadow song is about to break through anyway, what difference does it make? It's all or nothing."

Aria looked to Nikki, but for what reason, Nikki couldn't imagine. "It seems sensible to me, but I'm hardly the one you should be asking."

Aria nodded once. She hadn't been working long when there was a knock on the door and one of the Swords poked his head in. "Sorry to bother you, but there's news you should know. We've spotted warriors from the surface clan we fought before coming this way. They'll be here in a bit, and given the numbers, I don't think we'll hold them for long."

Nikki clutched Elora tighter to her chest. There was more the Sword hadn't said. That much was obvious from his posture. He confirmed it for her a moment later. "And we've just heard word through the dragons from Firestone. They've spotted two nuddu who are coming this way, moving as quickly as we've ever seen."

Orenil cursed.

Aria stared levelly at the Sword. "How long do we have?"

"Ten minutes before the surface clan arrives, and maybe another ten after that until the nuddu arrive. If you've got something you're trying to do, you better get it done quick."

28

Radyn's spirit floated untethered, exiled from his body the way he'd once been exiled from Firestone. Like then, the exile was self-imposed, the product of spiritual weariness and physical exhaustion. He longed for slow summer days by the creek that ran to the east of Underhill, shaded by tall oaks that had loomed large long before his father had been born.

Instead he drifted, caught up in currents of the Song he barely understood. There'd been the darkness and silent bliss of unconsciousness following his fight with the woman of shadow, but it hadn't lasted long. Other spirits crowded his own, extending notes of their Song toward him, inviting his spirit to join theirs in harmony. Barely conscious, he accepted Tanwen's connection and allowed the Song to flow through him once again, guided not by him but by his old friend who'd carried him for countless miles, who'd remained beside him from Firestone to Underhill and back again.

Other voices joined Tanwen, familiar and yet changed, the way a child's voice evolved as they moved from childhood to adulthood. Friends lost long ago to the call of the gate and yet, in some very real sense, present. They clustered around him, and he rested, content simply to be in their presence. Threads of Song wrapped his spirit in gentle but firm bonds, and he surrendered to its ministrations.

Now the voices and Song had faded. His body was healed, a feat of strength and artistry few were fortunate enough to experience.

The knowledge of it added an extra layer of guilt on top of an already unbearable burden. Whose lives had been sacrificed while so much effort had been given on his behalf? He'd failed. The shadow song had triumphed, and friends had granted him a healing he didn't deserve while those who'd fought for him died untended.

Spirit and body remained rent asunder, and all that kept Radyn from seeking the permanent silence of the gate was that haunting premonition he'd heard as he came in contact with the shadow. Aria and Elora needed him, and so the burden was his to carry for longer yet.

Except spirit and body refused to reunite. In times before, when Radyn's spirit had traveled tremendous distances, the return had always been a matter of course. Unity was nature's default state, and the effort was in remaining separated.

The challenge reversed now, and he lacked the skills and knowledge to overcome it. He searched the Song, certain unification was close, but he could find no sign of it.

A gentle spirit brushed up against his own.

He had no knees to fall to, but his spirit humbled itself before Kaya's all the same. Of all his failures, his inability to protect her weighed the heaviest.

"You hold yourself to an impossible standard," Kaya said.

Her mercy was kind, but unnecessary. "Keeping a young woman safe and alive is hardly an impossible standard. So long as I was by your side, you should have been able to trust in my protection."

"I did then, and I still do. I chose this path, but I'm afraid you're the one who has had to pay the steeper price. It should be me apologizing to you."

It took a moment for the meaning of her confession to sink through his dense skull. "You chose?"

"Shadow and Song don't experience time the same way humans do. They... see more, although that's a poor way of describing it. When I came into contact with the shadow within the shrine, I caught glimpses of potential futures, each shaped by the choices we made. I chose the one that gave us the best chance against the shadow song."

She'd known.

He'd suspected, but hadn't allowed himself to believe. Too easy, then, to shirk the blame that was rightfully his. It was still too easy an absolution, too convenient. "There had to be a better way."

"I searched for one. Any future in which I lived would have caused the fear of the cities to escalate. Catastrophe inevitably followed."

Realization hit suddenly. "Wait!"

Kaya did, and Radyn said, "You said it was contact with shadow that granted you insight. When I was stabbed, I thought I heard a premonition. Aria and Elora are in danger."

"All living beings are in danger, but yes, Aria and Elora face the direct action of the shadow."

"I need to get back to them." His spirit dashed back and forth, but no matter how he searched, he found no sign of his body, no sign of his way back. When there was nowhere else to turn, he stopped searching and found Kaya's spirit still next to his. "How do I get back?"

"We need to talk about the girl."

"No, we don't." He looked around, but his environment provided him no further clues. "Is there no other way?"

"Guilt veils your body from your spirit."

Radyn searched a moment longer, then surrendered to Kaya's demands. "Fine. What is there to talk about?"

His sense of Kaya's spirit never wavered. Bright and gentle, it exuded a warmth that no ice could touch. "It's your spirit that's burdened. What do you need?"

"Nothing! I shouldn't have killed her, and yet no matter how many times I imagine that fight, there is no other way. I shouldn't have, but I had to. What else is there?"

"You've killed men and women before. She was an enemy who would have killed us. Why is your guilt surrounding her death so much greater?"

He swore. "She was a child!"

"You can't forgive yourself." It was more of a statement than a question.

"Nor should I! The cities need us to forgive one another, because we're locked inside a mountain and if we don't, it wouldn't be long before we're killing each other over long-remembered insults. But there should be no forgiveness for the murder of a child, whether or not she was out to kill me. Forgiving myself only makes me another kind of monster."

The warmth of Kaya's spirit never dimmed, even as he confessed. There was a lightness to her spirit he didn't comprehend, not after all that she had suffered. Her voice was light and playful, as though she was teasing him for his convictions. "Sometimes I can't help but think that the clan buried its claws too deep in you," she said.

"What do you mean by that?"

"Honor and justice, mercy and forgiveness. The clan's teachings have shaped the way you view the world, and I think there is little I could say that would change your mind."

Sorrow welled up from within Radyn's spirit. "I know no other way."

Kaya's spirit still held him close, still wrapped him in the warmth he so desperately needed, but the tone of her voice remained playful. "And are you some old man, too decrepit to change your mind, to learn a new way of being?"

"But I don't know what to do."

Kaya laughed. "Neither do I, but it's not moping around here."

Her voice turned serious. "I think you are right about a great many things. It sounds cruel, but I am glad you suffer for that girl's death, because it means that your heart and spirit are still kind. And though this sounds even worse, I am glad that you killed her, because had you not, all hope would have been lost. It's too much to ask you to bear these burdens alone, but I would remind you that you've never had to. You've had Elora, Magni, Jyn, Aria, little Elora, and me. You don't have to carry your sins alone."

Her spirit brushed against his, and in that moment, an overwhelming joy flooded his soul. The same joy he'd once experienced when diving deep into the Song. It was a joy shaped by the sorrows Kaya had endured, but those sorrows no longer stung the way they once had.

Her voice was soft. "Stop thinking in terms of your clan concepts of justice, forgiveness, and retribution. You are right not to forgive yourself, and you were right to kill her. Paradoxes surround us, but it is up to us to act, regardless. So tell me, what do you want?"

It wasn't her words, but his brief contact with her joy that forced a new perspective. She had given her life and gone voluntarily to the gate, and she lived with a joy beyond his comprehension. He didn't know how he would find his way forward. He resolved only that he would.

As soon as will and spirit aligned, the veil that surrounded him vanished, and he snapped back into his body without even having the chance to say goodbye to the spirit that had once again guided him to safety.

When he opened his eyes, he was in the healing room. His body was fresh, as if he had rested for two days straight. Movement in the corner of the room caught his eye as Jyn leaned forward.

"Took you long enough. Get up. We have a world to save."

***

The Seer cursed as broken shale and sharp-edged granite buried themselves in his hands. He pushed against the broken stone and looked around, disappointed that once again he had not yet found the oblivion he sought. The battle that had raged around him was gone. The shadows carved from his soul and from the souls of Caleb and his warriors were reduced, but those that remained stood in a loose circle, as still as statues, their vigilance greater than any mere human's.

"You're awake," came the deep voice of the shadow tribe's leader. "There were bets among the men about whether or not you would succumb to exhaustion."

Truth be told, the Seer wasn't sure why he hadn't. Every muscle and bone in his body ached, and his lack of strength went far beyond muscular endurance. His spirit had next to nothing left to give, leaving him a shell of the man he'd once been. His master had taken everything from him, from his strength to his spirit, but worst of all, his purpose. He was nothing to her, nothing more than a tool that she used at her convenience and discarded when he grew chipped and rusty.

He took small comfort in the wall of swirling darkness that lay no more than a few paces away from him. He'd seen the way it repelled those cursed Manirah, but he was nearly within it and didn't feel so much as the stir of a breeze. What his body couldn't feel, though, his spirit experienced in its full glory. His master had grown in strength, surpassing his wildest dreams. She swirled and cut at the rock below, her destination obvious. He may not lead her armies or enjoy the fruits of his labor, but it was his hands and his work that had allowed her this opportunity to right an ancient wrong. In that, at least, he had shown the Manirah what he was capable of.

"Why are we still alive?" His voice cracked as it worked its way past split lips. "Did we defeat them?"

"In a manner of speaking. Once our master killed one of the Manirah that attacked her, the rest realized their cause was without hope. They retreated to the dragons, taking what few survivors remained."

A few survivors indeed. The Seer let his eyes drift across the battlefield. There were no remains of shadows, given that they dissolved into dust and smoke when destroyed, but only a handful of Caleb's warriors littered the ground. The rest of the bodies were Manirah, and the sight brought a vicious smile to his lips. Firestone had thrown its full might into the attack and tasted nothing but the ash of defeat.

He looked over the work that was the culmination of his efforts and nodded once. It was good.

"Then our work is done," he proclaimed.

"Not quite."

The Seer snapped around. Where only the wall of darkness had been before, his master now stood. The wall swirled behind her, but diminished. He and Caleb both bowed deeply. "What remains?" Caleb asked.

"Your distant ancestors built an apparatus to contain my strength. It has weakened over the ages as the Song of the Engines has faltered, but it still impedes my progress and puts the project at risk. Firestone's Singers have likely sensed it, because they've sent a pair of dragons to one of the places where it is controlled. Left alone, I will be past the barrier shortly, but if they reinvigorate the defenses, it may delay me long enough for the cities to mount a larger counterattack."

The Seer raised his eyes. The words were not those of the master he'd always imagined he served. They were the words of a beleaguered general or a tired commander, of a leader who looked over the shifting lines of the battle and had no confidence their victory was assured.

The shadow song was supposed to be stronger. It was supposed to be truer. What should it matter if Firestone's pathetic survivors attempted to strengthen some defenses built hundreds of years ago? His master was *here*, their moment of triumph at hand.

If Caleb shared any of the Seer's doubts, he hid them well. "Where are these defenses controlled?"

"There are five buildings that surround this crater. Any of them may be used to control the defenses. Firestone's dragons fly to the one north of here."

Caleb bowed deeper. "We know it. We passed it on our journey here."

"Good. Then make haste. They will beat you to the buildings, but the technology is of a different age. I doubt they will understand it, much less control it, but there is no reason to take any unnecessary risks."

There should be no unnecessary risks! the Seer wanted to shout, but he kept his lips sealed and his tongue still. He couldn't die until the ultimate success of his efforts was certain, and there was still much he didn't understand. After all, his master wasn't whole, some portion of her strength destroyed when Kaya and Radyn had destroyed the shrine that was in his care. He was in no position to judge.

"It will be done," Caleb said.

"Good. I have called for the nuddu, too, and they will arrive shortly." Their master's body dissolved into black smoke that was pulled into the swirling wall, strengthening it as they watched.

Caleb's mouth was set in a firm line as he called the last of his warriors to him, and to the Seer's eye, they seemed a pathetic force. Fewer than a dozen of Caleb's warriors remained, and fewer yet that were unharmed after crossing Firestone's Manirah.

They followed their own tracks away from the crater, away from their master's final work, to once again fight against Firestone's stubbornness.

The only relief the Seer held onto was that soon their victory would be complete.

29

Radyn took the stairs to Firestone's surface three at a time. His breath came easily and his body was light, almost floating from one stair to the next. When he reached the top, he waited for Jyn to catch up, the accomplished warrior having fallen almost two full levels below him. The sun struck his exposed skin and warmed him to the bone, driving away the last lingering chills from his battle with the master of the shadow song.

Jyn reached the surface and grunted. "The healing served you well, it seems."

"Firestone's Song embraced me," Radyn said, as though that alone explained everything. He didn't want to discuss the lightness within his spirit, afraid that if he focused too hard on understanding the feeling, it would be ground out like a flickering flame beneath the heel of a boot.

Jyn didn't press. Not because he wasn't curious, but because other needs demanded their attention. Radyn sensed them before he saw them, the dark silence of the nuddu approaching from the north. He walked until the trees blocking his sight were out of the way and took a measure of their distance and speed.

Firestone could still outrun them, and easily with the power currently surging through their Engine, but their decision wasn't so simple.

Jyn expected Radyn's question. "We approached while you were still unconscious. Tried to draw them away, the same way we kept them away from Underhill. We pulled one, but the other ignored us like we were spoiled food."

"So the Seer or his master aimed at least one of them at the building?"

"Looks that way."

Radyn stared at the nuddu. They were dangerous, of course, but when he looked at them, he didn't see the threat that they posed.

"She's still scared."

Jyn grunted.

"Even after defeating us. Even after being reunited with most of the shrines. She still thinks we can beat her. These aren't the actions of a being that's certain they'll win."

The Blade wasn't so easily convinced. "But what else can we do? You and I could attack her again, but she has too many defenders for the warriors we have left. It would take everything just to get back to her, and that's saying nothing about actually defeating her."

Macken jogged up to the pair. "We heard word from the dragons on the surface. They sent shadow figures and surface warriors to the building. More than the Swords can handle, and Aria's work won't be done by the time the battle starts. They're asking for orders."

Jyn turned to Radyn. "Any ideas?"

What was the master of shadow frightened of? There

were three possible answers. The combination of Radyn and Jyn, which had almost overwhelmed her before. Firestone and its Engine, which had been the target of shadow's efforts since the beginning. Or the building below and whatever technology it represented.

Radyn didn't think it was him and Jyn. Strong as they were, their odds against the master of shadow seemed impossibly slim. Which left Firestone and the building, and Jyn's attempts to draw the nuddu away revealed what the master of shadow thought about that.

"If the nuddu's behavior represents her strategy, she fears both Firestone and the building. We need to keep both safe if we can."

Jyn's face hardened. "We don't have the strength to protect both. In truth, we don't have the strength to protect either. There aren't enough Manirah, and there's no help coming."

"We'll find a way. I don't know how, but we'll find a way."

A bitter smile turned the corners of Jyn's lips. "I wish I shared your hope."

Radyn turned to face Jyn directly. "I'd like to return to the surface and protect Aria."

Jyn had expected nothing else. "Of course."

Radyn reached out for Tanwen and asked if there was time for him to return to Firestone and make the journey back before the surface clan arrived. The distance between them was as nothing, and Tanwen replied instantly, saying there was and he was on his way.

Jyn must have sensed something of it. "You connected to Tanwen from here?"

"I did."

Jyn grunted. "You know, I've always wondered who would win between us in a fight."

"Magni seems to believe that it would be you. He was quite adamant the last time we spoke."

"He's been my chief aide and protector for years. I don't think his opinion is the most objective."

"I trust him."

Jyn nodded. "So do I." He sighed and turned his back to the approaching nuddu. "We'll do whatever we can to hold them off, but I fear I waited too long to challenge you to a sparring match."

Radyn watched him go. He spoke softly, so his words wouldn't carry to Jyn's ears. "I think you would have won too."

He turned back to the fence and climbed over the top. Tanwen was close. The dragon flashed past Radyn as he dropped to the grass on the outside edge of the fence. Tanwen peaked, casting a shadow over Jyn, who turned around to see the dragon twirl in midair and fall into a smooth dive. Radyn waved at Jyn, then jumped off the edge of Firestone, Tanwen in close pursuit.

TANWEN MATCHED Radyn's speed as he fell, and Radyn reached out, grabbed the dragon's back and pulled himself closer. Tanwen gently angled up, providing the force necessary for Radyn to position himself properly on the dragon's back. The dragon's spirit burned as bright as Radyn's, filled with the delight of a difficult feat accomplished well.

Their flight toward the building took barely any time at all, giving Radyn only a brief opportunity to survey the battlefield. As before, there was little about the terrain that sparked interest. The building was the only feature, and it hadn't been built with defense in mind. Makers' steel would fall easily against maniblades and the dark blades the surface clans used, so the sturdy walls meant little in terms of protection. Better than nothing, perhaps, but not by much.

The farther they flew from Firestone, the weaker Tanwen became. By the time they reached the building, it was about all the dragon could do to remain in the air. His landing was none too gentle, knocking some of the air from Radyn's lungs. The shadow song had grown stronger.

He'd hoped to use Tanwen and the other dragons as weapons against the surface clan warriors who approached, but Tanwen's distress made him reconsider. If the dragons were that disconnected from the Song, they were vulnerable to the surface clan's blades. He was still tempted to treat them as he would any other Manirah, but the dragons were their only retreat if the battle didn't go their way.

Aria and Elora were in that building. He wouldn't leave them without a way out.

"Don't push yourself so hard," he told the dragon. "You'll need to be ready to fly."

Tanwen offered to fight, but Radyn asked him not to. If nothing else, and Radyn fell, Tanwen and the other dragon could provide a last line of defense before helping Aria escape.

The surface clan looked to be about a mile away yet, and so Radyn risked poking his head into the building. Aria stood with her hands on a table, deep in concentration. Nikki carried Elora around in circles, but stopped when she noticed Radyn.

"It's good to see you awake," the Shield said.

"Thanks for helping with Elora."

Aria glanced at him and smiled. He gave a quick bow,

and then she returned to whatever task consumed her attention.

His resolve renewed by the sight of his family in the building, he closed the door and ensured it shut tightly. He joined the other Swords on the south side of the building.

Bragen commanded them. Radyn hadn't spoken to him since the meeting. He'd been surprised when Bragen didn't follow Astram and the other Swords who remained at Underhill, but he was glad to see his old roommate again. He was a capable warrior.

"I'm glad you're here," Radyn said. "Thank you."

Bragen nodded. "Figured there wouldn't be much left if you failed, so I'd help how I could. We're outnumbered three to one, though, and if our last skirmish is any indication, they know how to fight."

Radyn breathed in deep, feeling the Song pulsing in his body in time with his heart and lungs. The shards embedded underneath his skin seemed a part of him. "So do we."

He lit his maniblade. The blade glowed so brightly that it was more white than blue. Bragen and the others followed suit.

"I don't suppose you'd mind letting me lead, and then giving me some space once the battle begins?"

Bragen chuckled. "I'm not quite the fool I was when we were younger. I watched you and Jyn against the master of shadow. You do whatever you want, and we'll support you."

Radyn bowed deeply, took one last breath to center himself, then sprinted toward the approaching surface clan. He practically skipped across the uneven ground, covering the remaining space between them in moments. Dark swords rose to greet him.

He split through two defenders like an arrow, then

spent the last of his speed lowering his shoulder and slamming it into one of the larger clan warriors. The force of the hit threw the surface warrior back into his companions, clearing a space for Radyn to call his own.

He raised the maniblade and cut and cut again. Song burned deep in his spirit, echoed in the shards scattered throughout his body. Strength built upon strength like voices joining in harmony. Thought receded, replaced by the sheer exhilaration of instinct and training.

His maniblade slid inside the slow parry of one surface clansman, and with the flick of his wrists, he cut up, opening his enemy from bowel to chest. Organs fled their cage, spilling out onto the hungry stone and dust at their feet. He'd cut one, for the smell that followed the wound was as rank as a day-old murder scene.

He head-butted one warrior who tried to lock their blades, then spun and stomped at the knee of another. The knee bent the wrong way, then shattered as it twisted beyond its breaking point. The surface warrior groaned in pain but didn't scream as he fell, stomped on by friend and foe alike.

One dark blade cut through the upper part of Radyn's left arm, drawing a fiery line that burned as they fought. Another carved a shallow valley across his back, and another poked into his thigh. Such was the force of the Song flowing through him that they barely slowed his movements, but against so many even he couldn't last for long.

Bragen and the others arrived in time to save Radyn from his folly. The press that tightened around him lessened as Firestone's best crashed into the line.

Radyn cut through the spine of one woman who'd turned to face Bragen, then jumped backward as a dark blade cut through the space where he'd been standing a moment before. His foot landed on something soft. He caught his balance after a moment, but the moment was all his opponent needed to redouble his efforts.

Radyn remembered him from the skirmish before. He carried himself with the air of a commander, his competence beyond question. His skill as a warrior was considerable, but he also possessed an innate knowledge of where he needed to be on a battlefield to inflict the worst damage on his enemy. The warrior's assault forced Radyn away from the heart of the battle, away from the places where he could do the most good.

Despite the ferocity and success of Radyn's charge, numbers were still against the Manirah, and the commander pushed Radyn away and forced him to fight a duel. The remaining surface warriors offered no assistance, taking full advantage of Radyn's absence to redouble their efforts against Bragen and the last Swords.

Pushed aside from the heart of the battle, Radyn also caught sight of another enemy. The Seer stood behind the line of the surface warriors, twin blades of darkness gripped in hands that were white from squeezing so hard. Parnell, Kaya's father, cowered behind. The Seer looked threatening enough, standing there with his blades, but he made no move to involve himself in the battle.

Radyn parried a dark blade and twisted away. The enemy commander retreated a handful of paces, keeping himself firmly between Radyn and the rest of the battle. The Sword behind Bragen fell as too many enemies overwhelmed her, shifting the burden onto the surrounding Swords.

Radyn stepped forward and flicked his sword at the commander, who parried it half a heartbeat later than he should have.

Another Manirah fell under the mass of dark blades.

The Song burned within Radyn, and he made no effort to control it. The force pulled him back toward the enemy commander, and they passed, light and shadow blurring as they met, broke apart, and met again. Three times they passed, and on the fourth, the commander fell without a sound.

Radyn had no time to pause and savor his victory. Bragen and another Sword were all that stood between the surface warriors and the building, and they surrendered ground quickly. Radyn rejoined the battle, the dark blades always a hair too slow to stop him. The Sword beside Bragen fell as Radyn killed the last of the warriors and shadow figures.

Bragen stumbled a few steps back, then collapsed onto his rear. The front of his uniform was covered in blood, and the stain spread quickly. Blood trickled out of the corner of his mouth, but he smiled at his old roommate. "We did it."

Radyn squatted beside him. "We did. Thank you. On behalf of my family, thank you."

Bragen chuckled. "You always were too serious. Tell Astram when you see him that he's become a boring coward."

Radyn laughed. "I will."

Bragen reached out and grabbed Radyn's wrist. "I have one last favor to ask."

"Name it."

"Don't follow me through the gate too soon. Life is more peaceful when you're not around, and I could use some rest."

Radyn gripped Bragen's wrist tighter, wishing there was a way he could hold on. "You drive a hard bargain, but I'll try."

Bragen nodded, then lay down, still holding onto

Radyn's wrist. A few moments later, his grip slackened, and Radyn could no longer sense the Song within. He closed his old roommate's eyes. "Rest well."

He squatted a moment longer, then stood and turned to face the Seer and Parnell, who had remained frozen in place since the battle began.

The Seer stared at the battlefield that should have been an easy victory. They'd outnumbered the Manirah and fought with the strongest warriors shadow could field. Sure, the slivering of their spirits had sapped some of their vitality, but nothing he saw before him made sense. Was it a vision that tormented him, or reality?

Radyn alone had survived, because of course he had. He'd fallen among Caleb's clan like a reaper, and even Caleb, first among their master's servants, hadn't stood against him for more than a few moments. Not even here, close to the heart of their master's power.

It fell to him, the Seer, to fulfill his master's wishes. He spread his feet wide and embraced the hollow shadow within his spirit, forcing more of the darkness into the blades in his hand. Obedient to his will, they extended until they were twice the size of a man. They trembled, the weight almost too much for him to carry.

He twisted shadow at Radyn, hoping to explode his chest the way he had Lynae's, but the Sword from

Firestone burned with Song, and the Seer's efforts couldn't touch him.

So be it. Radyn had lived by the sword and deserved to die by one.

Radyn advanced with unwarranted confidence, and the Seer snarled at the sight of him. This, this was why his master hadn't granted him the peace of oblivion yet. This was the task left to him, to kill the greatest of the shadow song's remaining enemies.

It was his orders and manipulations that had ended in Kaya's death, eliminating the one Singer who stood in their way. Now, only this Sword remained.

Shadow swirled deep within his core, filling his every pore. Nightkeep's Blade had already fallen to his strength. What chance did Radyn have? He swung, putting every bit of strength within his body into the blow.

Darkness carved a line through land and sky, throwing up a cloud of dust that obscured the Seer's vision. He coughed as it coated the back of his throat and he took a step back, waiting for the dust to settle so he could gaze upon the body of his enemy.

A fist buried itself in his kidney, sending an explosion of pain up his side as terrible as anything he'd ever felt. The strength in his legs failed, and he collapsed like a cloth doll. His vision swam as vomit raced up his throat. When his world steadied, a vicious kick caught him in the stomach, hitting him hard enough to lift him off the ground before he went tumbling across the loose stone. He skidded to a stop at Parnell's feet, who whimpered and cowered and did nothing to help.

The Seer coughed up blood and saw Radyn walking slowly toward him.

It couldn't be. He'd cut the Sword into pieces with his attack!

Radyn stopped a few paces away, too clever to get close and risk one of the Seer's dark swords finding his heart. "What's your master's plan?"

The Seer made the mistake of looking into Radyn's eyes. They were glowing a pale blue, as if there was an Engine inside him. He scrambled away as fast as his injuries allowed. Radyn didn't follow, allowing him an opportunity to return to his feet. "You're a fool if you think I'll tell you!"

Radyn may have avoided his last attack, but he'd gotten lucky. This close, there was no way he could defend against the Seer's blades. He formed them, one in each hand. He coughed up more blood and ignored it.

Radyn tilted his head to one side, as though the Seer were a mystery he didn't understand. "What's your master's plan?" he asked again.

The Seer answered with violence, rushing forward and cutting at Radyn. Somehow, he missed, and this time, Radyn delivered a series of two powerful punches followed by a kick that sent the Seer's body skipping across the stone before once again sliding to a stop. He gasped for air that refused to enter his lungs.

Why? Radyn was supposed to be dead at his hands, the last and greatest gift he could offer his master.

He groaned and tried to push himself to his feet, and failed. Tried again and got no further, his mind and body split apart like two lovers who no longer spoke.

Radyn advanced until all the Seer could see of him was his dirty, well-worn boots. "You're not going to talk, are you?"

The sound of his voice lit a fire within the Seer, and he found the strength to stand. He staggered back and forth, swaying as though drunk. He sought the silence of the shadow song and embraced it, forming his twin swords once again.

Radyn would die, even if it was the last act the Seer completed.

This time, Radyn didn't bother keeping his distance. He moved before the Seer could react, delivering blow after blow. Ribs cracked as the Seer lost the focus necessary to form his weapons. His nose shattered when Radyn jabbed at it. The Seer's body trembled under the assault until finally he collapsed. Blood poured across his open mouth, and he spat and blubbered.

His master wouldn't let Radyn win. The Seer reached out his hand and tried to form a long dark sword, stabbing through Radyn as he stood too close. No sword formed, and when he blinked and looked again, his hand was gone.

The Seer cried then, not because of the pain, but because Radyn revealed truth, and he'd never encountered an idea so terrifying.

He was nothing. A weak-souled man whom the shadow song had taken advantage of, no different from any of the disciples who'd believed the lies he'd peddled.

Radyn gave him one last moment to confess. When he shared nothing, the Sword cut one last time. The Seer's spirit, long ago consumed by shadow, went not to the gate, but dissipated into dust, his wish for oblivion granted at long last.

Radyn stared down at the Seer's body, his heart as empty as the Seer's spirit had been. Their lives had twirled around one another for years now, but this was the first time they'd fought against one another. He'd expected more, both from the battle and from his opponent.

The Seer had been blind all along. He could hide behind lies and the weak-minded disciples who believed him, but combat laid bare the truth of a person.

The Seer had believed himself Radyn's equal upon the battlefield. He'd proclaimed as much with his expressions and actions. Every time he cut, it was with the expectation that his dark swords would split Radyn's body in two. It didn't matter that the cuts were slower than a student's, or that his body betrayed his intent long before the blades fell.

Say one thing for the Seer, he'd believed in his lies.

A growl gathered in the back of Radyn's throat. That this man's manipulations had killed Kaya tore a hole in his heart. She'd deserved for her death to be at the hands of a much greater enemy.

He spun on his heel.

Parnell held up his hands to ward off a blow that never came.

Radyn glared, and the man started running away, back toward the column of shadow. He ran his thumb across the hilt of his maniblade and weighed his options. Finally, he sighed. His maniblade fell asleep, and he clipped it to his belt. Hurried steps brought him to the building. He knocked on the door and looked north. The head of a nuddu could be seen just over the top of the horizon, heading straight toward them.

Nikki opened the door, Elora in one arm and a steel dagger in the other. "Is it over?"

"The surface clan is dead, but at the cost of the last Swords. We're all that remains down here."

She opened the door wider to let him in, and her eyes traveled up to the nuddu. "That's not very far away."

"No, it's not. We have less than an hour before it arrives."

Radyn stopped just inside the door. Aria remained at

the table, where he'd left her when he'd gone out to do battle. Orenil, though, paced along the west side of the building. It wasn't very wide, and so he had to turn every four or five paces, lending his walk an air of madness. His eyes had the same look Kaya's had when she'd been deep in the Song, and he muttered almost silently to himself.

"Orenil?" Radyn asked. There was no response from the Singer.

"He fell into this sort of trance not long after Aria began pulling additional power into the shield. He acts as though he's deaf and mute, though I don't know the truth of it."

Radyn turned to his wife. "And you?"

Aria's answer was strong. "Doing as well as expected. Controlling the shield isn't physically demanding, but I have to keep overriding the safety controls put in place by the Makers. They didn't want the mesh of shards to pull as much strength from the core as it is, but I'm not sure why. As far as I can tell, everything is running normally. It won't be enough for long, though. The shadow is pushing hard now, and I don't think it will be long before the shield is overpowered."

"Once that happens, how long until the shadow song reaches the core?"

"Not long. A minute or two, maybe?"

Radyn clenched his fists. Failure had always been likely, but only now did it feel inevitable.

But Tanwen was still outside, and they were still connected. If Radyn asked, he was sure the dragon would carry them away. Who knew for sure what would happen if the shadow song overwhelmed the core? Perhaps the land would still have a few good months. Maybe even a few good years.

One look at Elora silenced that line of thought.

Tempting as any additional time would be, it could only be seized if all other hope was lost. Otherwise, he was surrendering the future she deserved. Not just so she could have a few extra months, but so she could grow into an adult, get married, and have children of her own. Accepting anything less was cowardice.

Orenil stopped pacing and came out of his trance. "Radyn, you're here. That's good. Where are the other Swords?"

"Dead."

Orenil paled. "I'm sorry." He blinked, then shook his head. "There's still hope."

"I'd love to hear it," Radyn answered.

"It's Firestone. It's always been Firestone. I need to leave." He looked at the table where Aria stood. "I'm afraid I'm no good down here."

"There's a nuddu heading for Firestone, too."

The Singer's eyes flashed. "I'm not fleeing!"

Radyn regretted he'd made the accusation. Orenil deserved better than that. "I'm sorry. What's your plan?"

"No plan. There is no plan. Just... voices, and half-formed ideas. But it requires Firestone. Of that, I'm sure. I need to leave." He made for the door, but Radyn stood in his way.

"Should we all go?" Radyn asked.

"Anyone who wants to can come with me, except for her." Orenil pointed at Aria. "She needs to stay to hold the shadow for long enough for Firestone to matter."

Nikki handed Elora to Radyn. "I'd like to go with. I want to be with him."

Radyn didn't have to ask who she meant. He took Elora, who'd been watching the exchange with the same curious eyes she used to watch everything.

"Maybe you should go, too," Aria said.

Radyn shifted so he could see her better. There were tears in her eyes, but she stood tall at the table, a general silently mustering her army for a battle she was doomed to lose.

"It might be safer on Firestone," Aria argued.

The other option was to send Elora back with Nikki, but Radyn couldn't bring himself to let her go.

"Whatever happens, we're staying together," he decided.

His statement made it final. "Head back to Firestone on the other dragon. Nikki, protect him if you can. And Orenil, find a way to save us. If anybody can, it's you. I'm sorry I doubted you in the past."

The young Singer gave the Sword a crooked smile. "Can't blame you. I've been making quite a few wild claims as of late."

"Well, you've just made one more, and I hope you're as right about it as all the rest. If there's anything more we can do, just let us know."

"Hold the shadow from the core for as long as you can. That will be sacrifice enough, I think."

A flurry of quick embraces and farewells followed, each carrying the weight of the certainty that they weren't likely to see one another again. Orenil connected with the dragon Bragen and the other Swords had flown down, and the dragon launched into the sky with Nikki and Orenil, leaving Radyn and his family alone on the surface to stand against the shadow.

31

Nikki mourned what she hadn't yet lost. Ahead of them, Firestone hung in the air like a delicate toy ahead of the monstrous nuddu that grew ever closer.

This would be her last flight on a dragon, her last steps upon the surface of Firestone. Everything she looked at or did was a last, and that certainty squeezed her heart in a vise.

Orenil drifted in and out of lucidity. If not for Nikki's arms on either side of him, she feared he would have fallen off the dragon. When he stiffened and straightened, returning to awareness, Nikki asked him what was happening, hoping that discussing his trials would focus his attention and keep him with her.

He shook his head to clear it, then said, "Something happened to me when I tried to connect with the web of shards in that building." He gestured, searching for the words to describe his experience. "You know how the Song of the Engine calls to our spirits? You've felt it, at least to a degree?"

"I have."

"That's the closest comparison I can draw. That pull opens a longing in us we have to learn to resist to Sing to the Engines. We have to keep our spirits separate so that our wills can shape the output of the Engines. That net below doesn't work the same way. It holds me close, no matter how I push away. It demands surrender, and I wonder if it isn't right to do so."

"But we need you here!"

Orenil shook his head again, but Nikki couldn't tell if it was to clear his head or because he disagreed. His body trembled, and she feared she had lost him again, but he straightened and kept himself present. "I—I'm not so sure, Nikki. There's a wisdom within this Song, and the more I surrender, the more I see."

A fire burned in his gaze that Nikki couldn't bear to watch. Her sense of reality, battered by the revelations of the past month, couldn't guide her through these unfamiliar waters. Orenil might be lost in the grips of madness or on the verge of a revelatory breakthrough. She had no way of knowing, but hoped that Jyn or the other Singers might. All she knew for certain was that his body was burning up, consumed by a Song that had no need of his flesh and bone. The Song emanating from him was stronger than that coming from the dragon, and he carried no shards.

They passed over the boundary that marked the edge of the shadow song's encroachment, and the dragon picked up speed. Her own breath came easier as life surrounded her again.

She wished only that she could do more to protect it. Her contributions had brought Firestone here, to a place where they'd at least had a chance, but it hadn't been enough.

They landed at Firestone's Nest, where Macken waited

for them. Orenil had slipped again into one of his dazes, and Nikki explained the situation. Macken took the news with a straight face, even though the Swords who hadn't returned were ones he'd served with for years. "So, it's just Radyn and his family down there now?"

It felt like an accusation. "They chose to remain, yes."

Macken grunted. "He would. Of course, Tanwen's down there, too. He puts that poor dragon in more danger than any rider should." The keeper of the dragons shook his head, took one look at Orenil, then said, "I suppose you'll be wanting to see Jyn. He and the others are down by the Engine discussing matters with the Singers. I expect they'll still be arguing when you get there."

"You weren't invited?" Nikki asked.

"Oh, no, I was, but such places aren't for me. I trust him well enough, and I'd rather be here with the dragons. Some days, it's easier to obey a good man than figure out what to do on my own."

"Would you at least help me get Orenil down to the Engine Room?"

Macken grinned. "I can do one better. Here, let me show you."

Working together, they lowered Orenil off the dragon. Macken slung the limp Singer over his shoulder and carried him to the nearest stairway. One of Aria's carts waited on the surface, and Macken placed Orenil gently within. "Might as well climb on, too. It'll be faster."

Nikki silently thanked Aria as she climbed in. This cart had waist-high sides and had been designed to carry large loads of food and supplies. She and Orenil fit with room to spare. Once she was situated, Macken pressed a button on a nearby panel. The cart slid toward the stairwell and began the descent toward the heart of the city. The Song running through the track maintained an even speed, and

Nikki used the moments she had to close her eyes and relax. Who knew when the opportunity would arise again?

The cart slowed to a stop in the hallway outside the Engine Room. She found Magni, Jyn, and the Singers deeply involved with a set of maps. Nikki frowned at the sight, for shouldn't the Singers be in the Engine Room? The nuddu would strike soon, and moving Firestone wasn't a task lightly performed.

Her arrival silenced the debate, and the Singers and Swords listened to her account of the battle below, including Orenil's proclamation that Firestone still mattered. The Blade would have questioned the Singer further, but Orenil sat in a chair in the room's corner, eyes distant, mouth hanging open. He didn't respond to questions or to being prodded and slapped.

"He comes around occasionally. Hopefully he can answer your questions then," Nikki said.

Jyn and the others returned their attention to the map. "He'd better, because we don't have long to decide our course. If Orenil hasn't gone mad, it's another argument in favor of staying here."

Nikki started. "You're thinking of leaving?"

Jyn's answering look revealed a glimpse of the torture his spirit endured. "What else can we gain by staying? The battle is lost. Nearly all our warriors have died, and we couldn't defeat the nuddu even if we had them."

"Radyn and Aria are throwing away their lives because they still believe there's hope!"

The argument didn't shake Jyn as much as she thought it would. "And if we left, I'd have a dragon send a message to Tanwen. Hopefully, they'd get it and be able to flee before the shadow song overwhelms them."

"If we leave, it won't be long before the entire world dies."

Jyn stared that truth in the face and didn't flinch. "Probably. But if our presence doesn't make a difference, why waste our lives and our city? We can live for a time, and that's worth something, don't you think?"

His gaze was haunted, and she realized he was waiting for her to give him her blessing, to tell him there was no shame in being a coward, no dishonor in running when there was nothing left to fight for.

She wished she could give him that, but the words turned to sand on her tongue. Perhaps she was nothing more than a naïve idealist, but as long as there was even a sliver of hope, she would fight.

Magni came to his friend's rescue. "Perhaps it would be best if we took a quick break. We have a brief window before we need to make our final decision, and the Singers could use some rest."

He spoke the truth there. The Singers were worn down. Beards were unkempt, hair tangled. Most looked like they were ready to lie down and sleep. With Magni's permission, they stumbled into chairs and collapsed on benches.

Jyn came close to Nikki and gestured down a hallway. "May we?"

She took his offered arm and gripped it tight, an anchor in the chaos. They walked slowly, but it wasn't until they were well out of sight and range of hearing that he spoke. "I feel like a coward for abandoning the crater, but I genuinely don't see what good we can do. Why sacrifice the city and our lives when the battle is clearly hopeless?"

Nikki squeezed his arm. "I don't believe that hope has fled. Radyn and Aria fight on the surface, and *something* is happening to Orenil. Perhaps I'm grasping at dreams and mist, but I can't give up."

Jyn slowed to a stop. "Even if it means sacrificing everything?"

He included the city and their lives, of course, but the way he looked at her reminded her that he referred to something more, too. Her throat tightened at the thought that her presence might cloud his otherwise clear-eyed resolution.

She also couldn't deny that she felt the same. Retreat wouldn't buy much time, but any time was better than none.

The only warning Nikki received was slight pressure against her senses. She was no full-fledged Manirah, but she'd spent enough time with a shard that she wasn't completely immune to dramatic changes in the Engine. Her heart pounded in response to the Song, beating out a quick, staccato pulse. Her body grew heavy, and then a moment later, she stumbled as the hallway shifted around her.

It reminded her uncomfortably of the fight against the Seer's disciples years ago, when they'd brought Firestone down. Her insides turned to water at the sudden unexpected motion. Jyn swore. "What was that?"

They sprinted through the hallways, but didn't make it far before they ran into the Singers running the other way. Their faces were pale, and three held their stomachs as though they feared they might soon lose their last meals. "It's Orenil!" one of them cried.

"What is he doing?" Jyn asked.

"He's Singing to the Engine by himself!"

"What?"

"We don't know how, and none of us can get close. You'll have to stop him."

Jyn nodded, then pushed his way past the Singers. He walked down the hallway as though he were trudging up the heights of a tall mountain, even though the city remained level. Nikki followed easily. The Song twisted her stomach a bit, but compared to what Jyn appeared to endure, it was nothing but a trifle.

They weren't even to the lobby outside the Engine Room when Jyn came to a stop. He put his hands on his knees. His breath didn't come easily, and sweat dripped down his shaved head to pool on the decking below. "I don't think I can go any farther," he admitted.

They were still a good thirty to forty paces from the door to the Engine Room, but everything was bathed in pale blue light so bright it was almost white. Had the Engine ever put out power like this?

"I'll go," she said.

Jyn grunted, "Thanks."

Nikki walked the rest of the hallway, ignoring the increasingly unpleasant sensations in her stomach. She reached the Engine Room and peered in through the window. It was hard to see against the glare of the light, but if she squinted, she could just make out the outline of Orenil's form, standing on the platform that came closest to the Engine.

She ground her teeth together and opened the door.

Despite not being connected to any shards, the strength of the Engine still caused her to stumble backward. It was energy made matter, the air so thick she swore she walked through water. She pushed herself forward and held her hand in front of her eyes, squinting to see.

Orenil's arms were stretched out wide, as though she'd caught him a moment before he embraced the enormous Engine. He slowly brought his arms together, their muscles trembling against whatever forces resisted him. As his arms closed, the light from the Engine dimmed. Not weaker, but more contained. The force pressing against her lightened a bit, though every step forward she took was harder than the last.

"What are you doing?" she called.

"What needed to be done from the very beginning. Firestone was always the key; I just didn't recognize it until now."

She searched his eyes for any sign of madness, but he seemed the same Singer who'd always endeared himself to her. By every account she understood, he should be dead, overwhelmed by the sheer might of the Engine, but he stood easily.

He must have seen the question on her face, because he smiled. There was a knowing in the expression, the weight of an awareness of forces beyond human comprehension. "I don't Sing *to* the Engine anymore, Nikki. I Sing *with* it."

"I don't know what that means!"

He raised a hand and gestured, and the two of them were no longer alone in the room. Other figures, carved from the pale blue light of the Song, stood on the platform, shoulder to shoulder. Nikki stiffened as she recognized Elora and Jelrik standing hand in hand. Kaya was there too, a smile on her face as she stood directly behind Orenil, her hands on his shoulders.

Above them flew dragons, more than Nikki could count. They'd shrunk to a size appropriate for the upper reaches of the sphere that was the Engine Room, but the force of their presence almost drove Nikki to her knees. Tears streamed down her face unbidden. Orenil stood in their midst, and it seemed to Nikki there was no place else in the world he'd rather be.

He faced her with a confidence she'd never seen on his face before. "The shadow song will try to stop me, and it might now have the power to do so. We need your protection."

With the visions he revealed, choice was stripped from her. She bowed. "We'll do what we can."

She took one last look at Orenil, surrounded by spirits, and retreated from the room, every step easier than the one before. She found Jyn and related what she'd seen and heard.

He closed his eyes and exhaled. The burden fell from his shoulders as Orenil stole the choice from him. "Then it will be what it is."

They gathered the last of the Singers, Swords, and Daggers. Magni emptied a clan armory of the last of its weapons, and the Singers who weren't familiar with the use of a maniblade received quick instructions. The weapons were easy enough for the Singers to light, but whether they'd be any use against the shadows remained to be seen.

The group climbed the stairs to the surface. One of the two nuddu was close enough Nikki could watch the inky darkness swirling within the creature. It stretched toward them, only minutes away. Jyn and Magni took quick stock of the situation.

"We don't have enough warriors to protect the surface," Jyn said.

Magni nodded. "Once the nuddu makes contact, shadows will swarm across the city and push through every entrance."

"Then that's where we'll make our stand," Jyn said.

Macken joined them from the Nest. "The dragons say they're willing to help in whatever way they can."

"We're going to need them," Jyn answered. He cast his eyes across the surface. "I want a dragon, a Sword or Dagger, and a Singer at each entrance. Protect them as long as you can. Once you're in danger of being overwhelmed, shut the doors and retreat to the Engine Room. The dragons can choose as they will. Fight or flee, they have my blessing. Use the carts for retreat. There's no point in defending anything else. Once they're in, there are too many directions for them to go."

Magni broke the warriors and the Singers into pairs and sent them running across the surface. He was the last to go, and he and Jyn shared a long look. Magni bowed deeply, and Jyn matched it. When they rose, Jyn embraced the giant warrior tightly. "Thank you."

Magni nodded once, then hurried off to his doorway. Nikki, Jyn, and the dragon that had flown Nikki up from the surface were all that remained.

"You could leave," Jyn said.

She glared at him, and that was answer enough. Whatever happened, they'd face it together.

The city shook a few moments later as the nuddu ran into Firestone. Shadows climbed over the fence and into the fields and raced toward the last defenders, a wave of darkness threatening to swallow the last Engine that stood in its way.

32

Radyn stood at the door of the building, leaning against the frame as he watched the nuddu come closer. The second one had attached itself to Firestone like a leech, and if Skystone was a prophecy, it wouldn't be long before the city fell to the surface. It was close enough that if it did, the Makers' building they were in would be destroyed. Not even their distant ancestors had built to survive such forces.

Firestone wasn't home anymore, but it had been the city he grew up in, the city that had shaped him into the man he'd become. Jyn and Magni weren't just good men; they were friends who deserved better than what the shadow had delivered to their door.

As soon as the nuddu came into contact with the city, their last hope died. With the number of defenders on hand, the shadow figures would sweep through Firestone as good as unopposed, and the silence of their shadow would send the city to the ground for the last time. He swallowed hard and turned away from the sight.

"One of the nuddu caught Firestone. The other one will be here shortly."

Aria's face paled, but she continued her work at the table. "Does that mean it's over?"

"As good as, I think."

He came in and squatted next to Elora, who studied the dancing images along the walls. Though it was impossible that any of it meant anything to her, her attentiveness made it appear she was mining the information for the key to their eventual victory. His heart filled to bursting at the sight, his young daughter so relentlessly curious about the world even though she could barely crawl.

The sight made his next decision an easy one. "We should leave."

Aria glanced down at Elora, then at the Makers' language scrolling across the walls. She bit her lower lip. "There's really no hope for Firestone?"

Radyn stood. "I don't know if there's none, but you weren't at Skystone. The shadow will overwhelm the city in almost no time."

"How long until the nuddu arrives here?"

Radyn glanced out the door. "Three minutes? Maybe a bit more."

"Let's stay for another minute or two. Push it as far as we can and give Firestone a real chance to do something."

"If Firestone falls, we won't be able to escape the destruction."

"And if we leave now, *she* has no chance at a full life."

Aria's words pierced his heart like a spear.

"Trust them," Aria said. "They've put their trust in you often enough. Offer them the same."

Radyn gripped the hilt of his maniblade tightly, then relaxed. If all their choices were poor, he couldn't fault her much for this one. "Fine. Another minute, and then we leave."

He leaned forward to kiss her. After their lips separated, he pressed his forehead against hers. "Love you."

"Love you, too," she replied.

He returned to the door and kept watch. The nuddu grew closer, and Firestone grew smaller. Radyn squinted, doubting his senses. The city had been coming closer, and fast, when Radyn had last looked.

It wasn't retreating, though. It was rising.

"What are you planning?" Radyn asked out loud.

Aria's muttering tore his attention away from the developing scene. Confusion was written across her face as she leaned forward to read the flowing script on the wall. "I...I think Orenil is trying to connect Firestone's Engine to the web of shards here."

Radyn looked back up at the city. "Is that possible?"

"That's a Singer's domain and far beyond me. I think I can make it available to him, though."

She closed her eyes, and a moment later even more script flowed across the walls.

"Success?" Radyn guessed.

"Maybe, but it will take a bit for the connections to complete. It's an incredibly complex task, and I can't guess how he's doing it." She looked at him. "If he's still trying, we have to stay."

Radyn couldn't breathe. He feared his voice would crack when he said, "You're sure?"

She nodded.

Radyn swallowed the lump in his throat. "Very well."

He went over to Elora, squatted, and kissed her on the top of her head. "I love you so much, girl. So much."

She babbled contentedly, eyes fixed on the Makers'

wall dancing with light. Her joyful expression wrung a wretched cry from him as he turned away. Two steps carried him to Aria, and he held her close. A single kiss served as farewell, and he went to the door, took a last look at his family, and shut it behind him.

His heart broke as he went to Tanwen. He ran his hand along the dragon's side as they watched the nuddu grow ever closer. "One more ride, old friend?"

Tanwen assented, and Radyn climbed on.

"Any ideas about how we kill a nuddu?"

Tanwen had none, but took to the sky anyway, racing toward the approaching monster. They covered the remaining distance in no time at all, and the nuddu projected large spears of shadow to keep them away. Tanwen twisted and dipped, or snapped at the columns if they came within range of his jaws. Radyn extended his maniblade as far as it would go, carving away at any shadow that came close enough to reach.

Twice the nuddu almost impaled Tanwen, but the bulges along its surface gave dragon and rider just enough warning to avoid the danger. They bit and cut at the shadow, and wherever tooth, claw, or pale blade touched, the shadow wilted away.

All to no effect. The wounds closed instantly, less meaningful to the nuddu than a scratch, and didn't weaken it in the least. After a few more passes, Radyn asked Tanwen to break away. They circled far enough overhead to observe the nuddu without attracting its ire.

Radyn closed his eyes and reached out for the nuddu with Song. There had to be some weakness in the creature, some vital point he could strike at. He dove headfirst into the darkness, ignoring the danger to his own spirit. He rummaged around in the darkness like a child banging around a room at night searching for a favorite toy, but everywhere he turned, the darkness was too similar.

Thousands of silent voices assaulted him, but none of them were louder than the others. None controlled or guided. None, if killed, would matter to any of the others.

Radyn retreated as they clawed at his spirit. "I'm not sure they can be killed." He swore. "Bring us back down to the building. I'd rather be there."

Tanwen sped ahead and landed hard. The nuddu was only a few of its enormous steps away.

Radyn went to open the door, then stopped at the vision Tanwen pushed through their connection. He turned and saw it for himself. The nuddu was less than a step away, but its leading leg, set to crush the building and all those within, was frozen in midair. Darkness swirled around the bottom of the foot, but it grew no closer.

The nuddu pulled its leg back into its torso and extended it straight downward. Bulges grew over its legs and torso, and nearly a dozen enormous spears, each large enough to impale an elder dragon, shot from the body. Radyn flinched away as one came straight for him.

When he cracked open his eyes, he wasn't standing before the gate. He remained outside the building, and none of the nuddu's spears had gotten closer than twenty paces away. Like the foot, all seemed frozen in midair.

Radyn laughed out loud. He glanced back at the building. It made sense now that he thought about it. These buildings had been in the heart of the forbidden zone for hundreds of years. It stood to reason the Makers had imbued them with some sort of defense.

They had time. He searched for Firestone, but the towering height of the nuddu hid it from his gaze.

Before he could formulate a new plan, the nuddu broke apart. Shadows streamed from it like water running off a mountainside after a storm. Some stepped away from the nuddu's legs. Others fell from its arm and torso, crashing into the ground with a thud Radyn could feel through his feet. They spread out. Arms elongated and sharpened until they were swords of darkness. Small groups wandered along the invisible wall, striking out at it as they walked. Their swords never penetrated, but they were patient and many, and they kept spreading farther.

Radyn retreated until his back was against the wall. Tanwen stood only a few paces ahead.

Did they flee now? The nuddu was already halfway dissolved, and he could have his family on Tanwen's back before the barrier fell. They could be in the air in moments.

He never got the chance to ask.

There was a *thump* that sounded like it had come from deep within the world, and Radyn's legs gave out under him. It felt as though every shard in his body cracked at once, flaying flesh from his skin and leaving him exposed to the shadow.

He didn't need to open the door to ask. The master of shadow had finally broken through the barrier created by the Makers, and she'd pierced the core.

Radyn's vision swam. He remained connected with his shards, but it was like holding onto a dragon that no longer wanted a rider. Strength surged and faded, beyond conscious control. He lit his maniblade, but it flickered, ready to die at any moment.

The barrier keeping them safe faltered, too. It didn't fall, but the swords, knives, and spears of the shadow started poking holes through it. They had no faces, but their cuts spoke of their joy, of a dream long lost finally realized.

Tanwen fell to the ground, body trembling. His pain

and weakness was much the same as Radyn's, though wrought on a much larger scale. He tried to raise his long and powerful neck, but without the aid of the Song, it remained glued to the ground.

The shadow swords hacked through the barrier, growing ever closer to breaking through, and Radyn couldn't even find the strength to stand. For too long he'd grown used to the Song moving through his body, and now there was none.

The Song of Firestone's Engine called from above, and Aria connected the net of shards in the building to it. Strength returned to Radyn's limbs as both he and Tanwen stood. It was too late, though, to save the barrier. Shadows shredded the last of the force that had held them back and charged the building from all directions.

Tanwen roared and spun, using his tail as a massive whip that cleared enormous swaths of space. Any shadow that the tail came in contact with vanished, but there were too many coming from too many directions. Radyn embraced as much of the Song as he dared and joined the fray, carving a path through the shadow figures.

His sword was a blur none of the shadows could match, but they weren't trying. They poured forward, and not even the inhuman speed of his sword could stand against the tide for long. The wave pushed him back, and there were plenty that simply flowed around him, driving their shadow blades against the building.

It remained protected, but not for long. The Song was bleeding out, dealt a fatal blow by the shadow. Radyn didn't have to search with his spirit to feel it. The land and all that lived called out in pain. If any cities had survived the last few weeks, they were likely falling now, their Engines stripped of their connection to the core.

Firestone still hung somewhere high in the air above

them, a jewel floating above the darkness, but even it wouldn't last for long.

Tanwen roared in pain as the shadows pierced him with spears.

"Get out of here!" Radyn yelled.

There was nothing left to fight for. Nothing more to die for, and he couldn't fight his family free of this overwhelming shadow. There was no need to lose another friend. He'd lost too many already.

Tanwen refused, continuing to sweep his tail across the waves of shadow and clawing and biting at all he could.

Go! Radyn shouted at the dragon through his connection, putting every bit of feeling he possessed into the order.

Tanwen mourned, then spun rapidly and whipped his tail through the space between Radyn and the building's door. Shadows vanished under his attack, and Radyn offered a silent thanks. He cut through the shadows trying to hold him back, then sprinted for the door.

He reached it, opened it, and stepped through. The shadows didn't even give him enough time to take a last look at Tanwen, but he felt the dragon taking slowly, laboriously to the air, weighed down by the burden of his wounds. Radyn slammed the door shut, sweat and blood pouring from him in equal measure. He hadn't noticed the wounds as he fought, but they were deep and numerous.

He shuffled over to Elora, who still studied the script scrolling along the walls, but now with a divided attention. The walls muffled the attacks of the shadows, but some thumps and thuds could be heard growing louder, and she was getting nervous.

Radyn slumped down beside her, the hilt of his maniblade clattering to the floor next to him. He was losing strength quickly. Behind him, he heard Aria crying, but she kept control of the Makers' system, no matter how hopeless the fight had become.

He reached out with his left arm, which had more strength than the other. Elora snuggled in close to his side, and he held her tight, and together they watched the Makers' script scroll by, announcing the end of the world in a language neither of them could read.

33

Ever since Nikki had been old enough to leave their apartment without supervision, she'd trained. Her memories of childhood were of study and long days of physical conditioning, followed by as much combat instruction as she could find. There was always a Sword or Dagger eager to pass on their knowledge to the next generation, and she'd hounded many of them. She wasn't a large woman, but her hands were quick as lightning, and with the shard pressed against her thigh, she figured she was strong enough to fight anyone short of a Manirah.

The first shadows that reached them hardly qualified. Their movements were slow and obvious, and they vanished by the dozens as her borrowed maniblade cut them into mist. Despite the shadows' overwhelming numerical advantage, she dared to hope. She fought beside Jyn and a dragon, two of the most fearsome fighters ever to serve Firestone. They could defend this city long enough for Orenil to complete whatever madness he planned.

They'd started gaining altitude, and quickly. Nikki couldn't guess what the Singer intended to do with that altitude, but she didn't have time to spare a thought to the question. She and Jyn fought side by side, protecting what little fragments of light that remained in a world growing increasingly darker.

Despite their efforts, the number of shadow figures proved to be an obstacle they never could have hoped to overcome. The trickle of enemies quickly became a stream, then a flood, and even with the dragons, the few remaining Manirah simply couldn't hold out.

Still, they fought and held longer than Nikki would have thought possible. They held until the shadow song reminded them once again of its overwhelming strength. Firestone trembled beneath Nikki's feet, shaking hard enough that she almost lost her balance. The shadows seemed to double in the blink of an eye. They multiplied, then moved faster and hit harder than before.

Firestone tilted. Not quite as dramatically as when the Seer's disciples had attacked, but enough that Nikki feared for her balance.

Weak in the Song as she was, she still felt the light from the Engine diminishing, could hear the Song fading, threatening to become nothing more than a distant memory. Manirah and Singers reached for the Song, desperate to clutch it and keep it close.

The Song was beyond them, though. It flickered and faded like a candle near the end of its wick, and Nikki was certain Firestone would finally fall from the sky.

Any other Engine would have died under the force of the assault, but Firestone held on long enough for Orenil to reignite the fire within the Engine. Firestone gained more altitude, climbing high into the sky as though the city sought to escape into a sky full of limitless possibilities.

Even Nikki could tell, though, that something had changed. That their world had shattered irrevocably, and it might never return. Their engine, bright as it was, was alone. No longer was it one star among many. It was the sun, burning so bright that even if other Songs remained, only it could be seen.

Jyn called to her as he fought the shadow, his voice cracking with despair. "It's too late. The master of the shadow song reached the core."

Still, he fought. He stood against the relentless assault of the enemy, tireless, even as shadows broke through their defenses, getting ever closer to the door and the Engine below.

The dragon roared in pain as shadow figures pierced its armored scales with their dark blades and spears. It fought on, its tail whipping back and forth, but the shadows swarmed from all directions.

Nikki sensed, rather than saw, the fall of other dragons across the battlefield, for they died with shouts that split the air and her spirit. Each time a dragon died, it felt as though she was watching a magnificent piece of art being burned in front of her. What they lost today, even if they won, would never be replaced. Never be healed.

As the other doors fell to the overwhelming force of the shadow figures, Jyn decided that they had done enough. He shouted at the dragon to flee, then ordered Nikki to retreat to the door. The dragon swept its tail across the surface of the field one last time, turning a dozen shadows into mist, even as a dozen more scrambled to take their place.

With a roar, the dragon launched itself into the sky, though it didn't make it far before it lost its grip on the power of flight. Wings alone had never been the secret to the dragon's abilities. They needed the Song to fly. Now, at the end of all things, they would be bound to the land, just like the humans they had so long called allies.

Nikki wished the dragon well, swept her sword around in one last arc, then retreated to the door. She backed down two stairs and yelled at Jyn to follow. He fought on for a moment longer, because fighting against the darkness with the last of his strength was the only statement left for him to make. He fought until the dark swords scored several cuts across his skin, and only then did he leap back, landing on a stair behind Nikki and shouting at her to shut the door. She slammed it shut, but didn't bother locking it as half a dozen shadow swords pierced through the Makers' steel. It would buy them seconds and nothing more.

They sprinted down the stairs, and Nikki was reminded of being a child, of running down the stairs four or five steps at a time, racing her friends to see who could reach the lowest levels the fastest. Never would she have imagined that her childhood game would prepare her so well for the last fight of her life.

They slammed shut whatever doors they passed, knowing even as they did they were only buying themselves moments of time to continue their fight. But every moment seemed precious, and so they fought for them without question. They reached the floor that held the Engine Room and sprinted toward the very heart of the city.

"Make way!" someone shouted.

Nikki glanced back in time to see one of Aria's carts speeding toward them. She pressed herself against the wall, and Jyn did the same. The cart passed them by in a silent blur. Nikki caught a brief glimpse of a wounded Manirah with a missing arm and deep cuts across his chest and torso, being cared for by a man in the bloody robes of a Singer. The warrior would be at the gate soon, but Nikki thanked the Singer for the care he showed. They chased after the cart and arrived at the Engine Room soon after. They helped the Singer lift the wounded Manirah out of the cart and toward a corner of the lobby, where he could complete his journey to the gate in peace.

Jyn squatted beside the wounded Manirah. He took the warrior's hand in his own, and the two of them spoke. The conversation was hushed, and Nikki let them be, knowing it was a scene where she wasn't needed. A moment later, the Manirah closed his eyes and breathed his last. Jyn squatted beside him a while longer, and when he stood, his eyes were rimmed with red.

Nikki's throat tightened. What kind of man was he? Jyn had endured so much suffering and so much loss, and still kept his heart open enough to mourn the loss of a single warrior at the end of it all.

The sight sparked a fire in her chest, a determination to seize whatever moments remained, and she cursed the fates that she'd waited so long to admit a truth obvious to people who barely knew her. Jyn was a mystery she wanted to spend the rest of her life solving.

But she wouldn't get that chance.

Jyn called the survivors together. He directed his first order at Nikki. "Go to the Engine Room. Ask Orenil what he needs."

He hadn't yet given up.

She hurried into the Engine Room, fighting the nausea that came from approaching such an incredible force. She opened the door and witnessed again the flying spirits of dragons and those who had died while connected to the Engine. The spherical room danced with light and strength, and she marveled at the sight for a moment before remembering she had no time. She shouted to Orenil, "We only have a few moments before the shadows overrun us."

Orenil seemed only half aware of his surroundings. She was about to repeat herself when he said, "Keep them away. For as long as you can, keep them away. We're close."

Nikki wanted so desperately to believe him. But considering all that she had seen and all that she had sensed, what hope remained? And yet, this room made her doubts feel small.

She bowed, for what else could she do but fight for as long as time remained to her, however little that might be?

As if in response to her fears, the spirits surrounding Orenil danced around her and escaped out the open door of the Engine Room. There were shouts and cries from the surprised Manirah and Singers, followed by a sound Nikki hadn't thought she would ever hear again: laughter and awe as those who remained witnessed a working beyond their understanding.

When her eyes met Orenil's again, she witnessed in his gaze an age and a wisdom she'd not seen in him before. He tilted his head slightly, and she couldn't help but notice that Kaya's arms were wrapped around him.

"Leave the door open on your way out, so that the strength of the Engine will bleed through and give our warriors every chance they can to succeed," he said.

Nikki bowed one last time and smiled as she took what she was certain would be her last look at him. He'd come into the fullness of his ability, and she could sense the strength of his spirit reverberating with a clear and certain purpose. Few were lucky enough to experience such a gift, and she was glad for him.

She left the Engine Room behind for the last time.

She returned to a hallway filled with activity. Manirah and Singers alike grabbed whatever furniture they could find and tossed it into a haphazard barricade that would do little to stop the shadows, but would again perhaps provide the defenders a few moments of respite.

Nikki was surprised the shadow figures waited as long as they did. Full minutes passed before they appeared, giving the defenders time to catch their breath and bask in the visions of the spirits dancing behind them. Magni stood with the spirit of his wife, a distant look in his eyes that made Nikki worry he would never draw a maniblade again.

When the shadows finally appeared, it was not as a horde, but as a disciplined unit led by three figures unlike any Nikki had yet fought. They walked like miniature nuddu, their shape constantly shifting.

Magni came to stand beside Jyn. The spirit of his wife remained behind, closer to the Engine she'd become a part of. He said, "Pay special attention to those three. We fought them at Skystone, and they were formidable opponents. They'll shift around your maniblade like water dancing around a rock, and they strike from angles that would be impossible for a human."

"Will you fight beside me, then, this one last time?" Jyn asked.

Magni's grin reminded Nikki of a child who had never known the concerns or worries of the world. "You know you don't have to ask. If we can kill those three, we'll hold off the rest of the shadows for quite a while, I think."

Jyn told Nikki, "Stay back. It will be better if the two of us fight this battle alone."

Nikki's pride flared, but she bit her tongue. Jyn and Magni were the strongest Manirah in Firestone, and in a close-quarters fight, she was more likely to get in their way than help. "Save some for me," she said.

Jyn chuckled bitterly. "Oh, I think there will be plenty for us all before this day is done."

The three shadows leading the march didn't bother cutting through the barricade. They melted and reformed, slipping through the cracks like an aggressive mist, billowing out on the other side as though the barricade didn't exist. The shadow figures behind slowed as they climbed over the barricade, but if the three shadow leaders were concerned they had lost many of their followers, they didn't show it.

Magni and Jyn lit their maniblades and strode forward.

Nikki followed as well as she could, but within a moment she knew Jyn had been right to have her sit this battle out. The pale blue of maniblade met the dark encroachment of shadow, which poked and pierced at the two warriors from a dozen angles at once. She couldn't comprehend how the two warriors stayed ahead of the razor-sharp shadows that sought their lives, but their maniblades were always where they needed to be.

Against the incredible strength of the assault, they were pushed back, forced to retreat against an enemy that attacked from everywhere at once. When blood started dripping onto the decking and splattering the walls, Nikki couldn't tell which of the two was injured, nor how badly. They fought on, their blades and reactions as quick as when the fight had started, determined in a way that only the truly desperate can be.

One of the three shadow figures vanished into mist, and such was the speed of the Swords, Nikki wasn't even sure who had killed it. A shadow sword snuck through Magni's defense and cut deep across his right shoulder. He grunted, but returned the blow with one of his own, finally connecting with a creature that melted away from every attack. The creature died, vanishing into silence.

In that moment of victory, Magni lost his focus, and the third shadow struck out with deadly precision.

There was a blur of motion, and Jyn froze in front of Magni, a dark blade embedded deep within his core. He grasped at the shadow with his hand, locking it in place. Magni recovered his wits and struck a killing blow to the last of the shadow leaders. The creature evaporated, leaving only the countless shadows marching behind to deal with.

Jyn stumbled backward, his face pale. Magni caught his friend and dragged him back, then ordered those who remained to fight. The surviving Singers and Manirah rushed forward and pushed their way to the barricade, where they held the line against the waves of invaders.

Nikki and Magni attended to Jyn. His wound was deep, far beyond Nikki's ability to treat.

Jyn forced himself to stand straight and hold tight to his maniblade, though he looked like he was about to vomit and collapse. The tip of his maniblade bobbed wildly, though he tried to hold it still. Through gritted teeth he said, "It doesn't matter, we stand here."

Magni nodded, and it seemed to Nikki that he had come to a decision. "You're right, old friend. We will stand here, and we will win. You have my word."

Jyn looked up at the giant, confused, but he was too slow to react to the heavy blow that landed across the back of his neck. The Blade crumpled to the floor like a small child being dealt a devastating blow.

"Magni!" Nikki cried.

Magni bent down and picked the Blade up as though Jyn's bulk was as light as a plate of food. He carried the Blade's unconscious form to a cart and laid him gently inside. "You two should escape. You have a future together, and that's worth fighting for."

"It won't matter if we all die!"

Magni shrugged his giant shoulders. "Truth be told, it

doesn't matter much if you're here. Jyn's wound makes him worthless in a fight, and I have nothing but respect for you, but you're only a Shield. Leave the rest to me and the few Manirah that remain."

"We can't just leave you!"

"You can, and you will. The Manirah swore an oath to protect Firestone with their lives. Let us fulfill that oath."

"I took an oath, too! As did Jyn."

"You aren't Manirah, and Jyn has fulfilled his duty and can do no more. As soon as they finish cutting through the barricade, I expect you to launch that cart forward. Get to the surface and call for a dragon. Build something together, because that's all that matters."

He glanced back at the spirit of his wife, standing tall with a smile on her face.

Nikki shook her head. "I won't do it. We won't abandon you."

She expected anger, but Magni just smiled at her. "You two deserve each other. You're a worthy match for him."

Nikki didn't see the blow that knocked her into a world of darkness.

***

WHEN SHE CAME TO, she and Jyn were hurtling up a set of stairs in one of the high-walled carts. She blinked and groaned. Her head felt as though a dragon had sat on it.

"Glad to see you're not hurt." The voice was so weak, it took her several moments to realize it was Jyn. His face was pale, sweat beaded down and dripped off his chin, and a trickle of blood leaked from the corner of his mouth. He had his hands pressed tight against his wound, but it wouldn't do much to save him.

Nikki risked the briefest of glances above the rim of the

cart and immediately regretted it. Shadows filled the hallways, pouring from the surface like water racing for the Engine Room. They ignored her as she passed, the combined Song of her and Jyn so weak they didn't notice their passage. They had senses only for Firestone's Engine, which filled the dying city with its beautiful Song.

"Magni?" Jyn asked.

Nikki nodded. "He wanted us to live."

Jyn said nothing to this, barely hiding the war of emotions that played across his face. She cursed Magni, because what hope did they have? The surface of Firestone would be crawling with shadow figures, and unless Firestone somehow overcame the master of shadow, whatever reprieve Magni thought they'd won would be short-lived.

The cart reached the top of the stairs and blasted into the bright light of the surface of the city. Nikki drew her maniblade as the cart slowed, then stood up. A handful of shadows lingered on the surface, but those that did made their way to the doors that led to the levels below.

She hopped out of the cart and looked at the panel that controlled it. She pressed the buttons that were supposed to make the cart move, but it remained locked in place. If they wanted to return, they would have to fight their way through an army of shadow figures.

"He shut it off, didn't he?" Jyn said, his understanding of his old friend complete.

"He did."

Jyn ground his teeth together, then looked at the sky. "We're high."

In the rush of events, she hadn't noticed, but now that Jyn drew her attention to the fact, she did. The air here was noticeably thinner.

"Call a dragon," Jyn said.

Nikki stared at him, giving him the opportunity to change his mind, but he seemed resolute.

She closed her eyes and reached out. Fortunately, she didn't have to search far. A pair of dragons were close, and one connected with her. The force of it made her cry out as she dropped to a knee, but she held the connection open long enough to make her request. The dragon agreed and broke the connection first, easing the pain that ripped through her head.

It landed, wings spread, blood leaking from the wounds it had taken, but it bent down and allowed them to climb. Nikki needed to push and pull Jyn onto the dragon's back, and none too soon, for the dragon's strength had attracted a handful of the straggling shadows.

Once Jyn was as secure as she could make him, Nikki said, "We're ready."

The dragon stood and beat its wings. At first, nothing happened, but on the third try, wings and Song worked in unison, and the dragon lifted into the air. Nikki saw for the first time just how high Firestone had risen.

She'd never been so high. She'd probably never been half as high. The dragon struggled to keep aloft, then began surrendering altitude, holding his wings open so that he glided more than flew.

Nikki turned back one last time. Firestone flew, but couldn't for much longer. They'd already held on longer than she believed possible.

As though answering her fears, Firestone tipped, the groan of bending metal and the crack of shattering stone so sharp it felt as though her ears had been cut.

She watched, then, as the city she'd always thought of as home fell from the sky.

34

The small building trembled as hundreds of shadow figures rained blows upon its protected surface. Makers' steel thundered under a storm it had never been designed to endure. Radyn held Elora tight, pressing the side of her head gently to his chest and covering her other ear with his hand to protect her from the worst of the noise. She clung to his bloody tunic, her muscles tense, but she refused to cry, defiant against the darkness.

Aria couldn't spare a glance at her husband and daughter. She stared at the scripts flowing across the walls like silent streams without blinking.

It wasn't right. She should be here with them, especially now. He also felt the call of distraction, burned with the desire to be outside fighting, mind empty, his attention consumed by anything except what was coming.

"Aria..."

He meant to call her back, to remind her that this here was all that mattered.

Not even the sound of her name could capture her attention, though. She was lost to them.

His heart broke at her absence.

A dark sword cut through the barrier protecting the building and sawed through part of the door before vanishing. Another followed a few moments later. All was failing as the master of shadow bled the core dry. Their last layer of protection wouldn't last much longer.

"He's going to attack," Aria said.

Her eyes remained fixed on the flowing scripts, but they were sharper now, the gaze of a hunter searching for prey. They fixed on a section of the wall and then turned finally to Radyn, filled with a silent plea. "He needs the strength of this net of shards. He needs me here a little longer to keep him connected."

Radyn needed a moment to understand she spoke of Orenil. "What do you need?"

"Time. As much of it as you can offer me."

Another black sword pierced the door, cutting a long gash across the steel. It too vanished, but the door groaned under the assault. Aria flinched, as though the blade had cut through her, and he wondered how deeply she was connected to the shards. How deeply the assault upon the building wounded her spirit.

"Then you'll need to carry her," he said.

"Gladly."

Radyn slipped Elora into the carrier wrapped around Aria's torso, then kissed her on the top of her head. "Don't be scared, little one. I'll be back soon."

He stole a brief kiss from Aria, then pressed his forehead against hers. She burned as though with a fever. She was no Manirah, to bear this burden, and yet there was no one else. "You're incredible," he said.

"I know. Now keep us safe, please."

A dark sword cut again through the door, and the tortured metal finally surrendered. Makers' steel fell inward against the force of yet another mighty blow, and Radyn connected with all the shards in his body as he stepped around his family and strode to the open door.

Shadow figures crawled over one another to be the first in, eager to silence one of the last Songs in the world, but Radyn and his maniblade greeted them before they made themselves at home. His weapon burned white, and even the hardened swords of darkness the shadow figures preferred couldn't resist his cuts. Shadow vanished as he advanced, quickly regaining control of the open doorway.

One of the shape-shifting shadows pushed its way to the front, stabbing at Radyn with a spear, then cutting at his face with a sword. Radyn slapped the attacks away with the side of his maniblade. Smoke drifted through the air where maniblade met shadow, and the amorphous creature hid among the other figures.

The retreat offered Radyn a moment of respite, but only so that the figures, under the leadership of the shape-shifter, could all push together at once, a wall of spears and swords looking to cut him into pieces.

He could do nothing but give ground, forced to surrender two precious paces that almost lost him control of the door. He cut shadows down as fast as they entered, but their numbers were too great, and his maniblade couldn't be everywhere at once. The shadows forced him to retreat another step, and he reached deep, burning every scrap of strength he possessed to stay between the shadows and his family.

His arms burned, and sweat dripped from his brow. His breath came in great, heaving gasps, but his maniblade slowed.

The Song of Firestone's Engine reached his ears, barely loud enough to hear and yet insistent, determined to be heard. It was the Song he'd first fallen in love with, the one he'd pursued since his father had died defending his home and his family from invaders.

Radyn swore he'd give everything before letting Elora suffer the same fate he had, forced to watch and hide as a father died protecting his family.

Firestone's Song crescendoed, suddenly deafening in its power. To Radyn's senses, it felt as if he stood inside the Engine Room. The shadow figures broke off their assault, looked to the sky, then fled from the building. Radyn stood alone, burning with strength but lacking an enemy to fight. He strode out through the open door and looked up, and not a single shadow figure came for him. Firestone was barely a speck in the sky, higher than he'd ever seen it before.

All around him, the shadows sprinted toward the center of the crater, toward the hole the master of shadow had made. They paid no attention to Radyn or the building, no matter how brightly he burned with Song.

A burst of Song pulsed from the building, and Radyn detected notes of Aria's spirit linked in delicate harmony. The power washed over him, gently pushing him back a step. Firestone answered soon after, and the focus of the Song narrowed. The shards in Radyn's body responded, pulling him toward the locus of power. He stumbled several steps forward before bracing himself.

Radyn looked up again. Though it was too small to be certain, Firestone appeared to be growing larger. He kept his eyes fixed on the sky, and soon he was sure.

Firestone was falling.

Another pulse of Song reached to the sky from the building, and once again the link between the Makers' net of shards and Firestone tightened, pulling Radyn forward with even more force.

He'd been wrong.

Firestone wasn't just falling. It was being flown straight down, accelerated and guided by the net of shards beneath Aria's feet.

He put his maniblade to sleep and clipped it back onto his belt. There was nothing more for him to do but watch as his first home, the place where he'd met almost all his friends and fallen in love with Aria, plunged from the sky like a spear thrown by an angry giant.

A pale blue glow surrounded the city as it fell. He reached his senses skyward, to listen to Firestone's Song one last time.

It was no longer the voice of a single Engine. It was a choir that joined in perfect harmony. Orenil had successfully coaxed it from its hiding place, aided, perversely, by the shadow song ripping and tearing at the Engine over the years. Radyn recognized several of the voices. Orenil was there, unique because his spirit remained bound to a physical body. His Song no longer reminded Radyn of all the other Singers, who were so often harsh and grating in their conversations with the Engine. He Sang beautifully. The voice of his spirit matched perfectly with the will of the Engine and the host of spirits it contained. Kaya would have been proud.

Elora and Jelrik were there too, joined again after their violent separation. A lone tear trickled from the corner of Radyn's eye as he listened to their voices again. They sounded as though they were coming from over his shoulder, guiding him and encouraging him like when he'd been so lost and angry. They reassured him that all was well, regardless of what the future held.

And Kaya. Beautiful, precious Kaya, who had taught him that the world and the Song were even more wonderful than he'd imagined before. Her voice was first among many, orchestrating the rest.

By the time Firestone was large enough to be easily recognizable, it glowed like a second sun, and Radyn had to look away. He caught his last glimpse of it as it dropped into the crater, a blur of speed and power. The force of its passing dislodged stone around the crater and dropped it down the hole, pursuing the falling city like hungry hounds.

Once it had dropped from sight, the spell it had cast over him was broken. He'd seen the damage a falling Skystone had caused, and that had fallen with only a fraction of the speed Firestone had reached. He sprinted toward the building, where Aria was finally stepping away from the tables, her role in the attack over.

Radyn swept her and Elora up in his arms and pressed them into a corner of the building. He connected with all the shards in his body and braced for Firestone's impact.

Nothing happened, and Radyn looked up, still holding tight to his family. After another minute, he stood. The air on his tongue had the taste of iron.

Tanwen called to him, and Radyn connected and answered. His friend was as weak as he'd ever sensed, but he was flying toward them. Radyn strode to the door and watched as Tanwen swooped down, landed hard, then bent down for the family to climb on. The dragon demanded haste.

He pulled Aria to her feet and hurried her toward Tanwen. Halfway to the dragon, Radyn's bones vibrated, as though struck with a gong. Radyn urged Aria up first, Elora still on her back.

A tremendous rumble ran through the ground, almost knocking Radyn off his feet. He looked down, cursed, and scrambled up Tanwen's back. He offered what little strength he still possessed to the dragon.

Tanwen flapped his giant wings once, but nothing

happened. He tried again, and they took off, their flight low and unsteady, but far faster than they could have traveled without the dragon's help.

The ground erupted in activity less than a minute after Tanwen took off. It split and rumbled, and Makers' steel whined as it bent and cracked open. The building that had sheltered them crumpled and fell apart.

Radyn's stomach twisted, not at the destruction below, but in response to a wave of shadow song that swept over him. Tanwen felt it too, the silence dampening his Song and sending them plummeting to the ground.

It passed a moment later, though, and there was only Song. Tanwen's Song burned like a bonfire, and the dragon spread his wings, arresting their fall a few dozen feet from the surface. He climbed effortlessly.

Radyn looked back. The destruction still spread below as the surface shook.

"He did it, didn't he?" Radyn asked.

Tanwen's answer was clear, and Radyn looked back at his daughter, grinning as she watched the world pass beneath her.

Perhaps they'd won her a chance for a future after all.

EPILOGUE

The fields surrounding Underhill stretched nearly all the way to the foothills that stood silent guard over the refuge. Hundreds of farmers raced the chill winds blowing down from the north, a constant reminder that the first killing frost would come even earlier this year than the year before. Carts ran to and from the mound, pushed by hand, following ruts carved deep by repetition.

Radyn and his team had made quick work of their field, though through no special ability of their own. Despite frequent rains, the field had only produced a third of the amount of wheat Radyn would have expected from this much land, and his team had spent countless hours coaxing the land to produce what it had. There just wasn't enough sunlight reaching the ground. Too many days were cloudy, and the growing season was shorter than anyone alive remembered it.

The flickering uncertainty surrounding the Song played a role, too. Once it had spread reasonably equally, carried on by the myriad forms of life that stretched across the continent, but no longer. Some fields now seemed to collect Song, but then surrender it. If a pattern existed, no one could discern it. Not even the Singers could predict in the spring which fields would prosper and which would struggle.

Hence the dramatic expansion. The only answer to a wounded world was to work harder, to build more. Every spring new land was tilled and prepared for the growing season, and every year they'd kept just ahead of Underhill's needs, which grew as the city did.

As the sun reached its zenith for the day, Aria and Elora emerged from Underhill with a small cart filled with simple meals. They stopped at other fields along the way, dropping off carefully measured portions of food. Eventually they reached Radyn's, where he called for a brief break.

Elora handed him a small sack that contained a slice of bread and cured meat. He bowed in thanks, then tossed his daughter high into the air. She laughed as her long hair flew everywhere, and he caught her and spun her around before setting her down. "And what have you learned this morning?" he asked.

"It was mostly stories about how we used to live, and there was a lot of reading. We also visited the field where they keep the sheep. Soon they're going to show us how to cut the wool."

"That sounds like a full morning."

Elora nodded. "Is it true that we used to live in cities that floated in the sky?"

Radyn stopped himself from shaking his head. Firestone, Nightkeep, and all the rest were only five years in the past, but to Elora, what had once been daily life for so many sounded like a myth made up to impress her. She couldn't even imagine the cities.

"It's true. Both your mom and I were born in cities in

the sky. Someday, if you like, I can ask Tanwen to take us to one."

Elora's eyes widened. "They're still in the sky? Teacher said they weren't anymore."

He mussed her hair. "No, your teacher is right. But one survived long enough to reach us. It landed safely, but I don't know that it will ever fly again."

"Because of the Engines?"

Radyn nodded. "There was a big attack once, and the shadow that wanted to destroy us all wounded our world badly. You were actually really close when it happened, but you were too young to remember."

Elora considered these additional facts with an expression that reminded Radyn of Jyn's face when he was carefully considering a problem. "Do *you* think the cities will ever fly again?"

He looked out into the distance. "I don't know. I hope they do, because the Song of the Engines was beautiful, and the world is a poorer place for there being so little of it now, but I can't say for sure. The hurt our world suffered is deep."

As if to punctuate his statement, the ground rumbled beneath their feet. Not strong enough to worry about, but enough to feel. No one in the fields reacted, long used to the tremors that still echoed as a result of Orenil's decision to drop a mountain of Song upon the master of shadow.

Elora turned her father's ideas over in her head for a bit longer and then decided, "I hope for that, too!"

"I'm glad to hear it. We can work together to make something better for all of us. What do you say?"

Her grin stretched from ear to ear. There was little that Elora liked more than a new project. Aria interrupted the exchange before Elora could launch into a long-winded plan. "Don't forget, we still have meals to deliver. You can talk to father tonight about your ideas."

Elora huffed, but when Aria dumped a handful of small sacks in her hands, she went from farmer to farmer, handing them out as she greeted each of Radyn's team by name. They grinned and joked with her, for she was well loved among them.

"How's the harvest?" Aria asked.

"We're making good time, but it's never enough." Radyn took a few bites of his bread, then handed the rest of the sack to Aria to eat. No doubt she'd already eaten her ration, and there was no doubt she remained hungry. She rested the sack on her stomach, now extended with their second child. Their rations weren't enough to feed both her and the growing child. "We need to make more food, otherwise we're not going to keep growing for much longer."

"We will," Aria assured him.

He nodded but couldn't meet her eyes.

She took his chin and lifted it. "*We will.* The fields closest to Underhill are wildly productive. It's working."

Radyn acknowledged her point. "It should work faster."

"There's no 'should' about it. The world will work as it will, and the healing will happen in its own time. As you just said, this world is deeply wounded. But we're still here, and we're slowly healing the land. The Song remains strong around Underhill. You know it will be the work of generations, though."

He glanced back at Elora, still busy with the farmers, who were now distracting her so he and Aria could have a moment to themselves. "I only want her to have something more than this."

"She will. But don't forget that she doesn't live in fear

of the shadow, and she doesn't know the fear of worrying that someday her home will fall from the sky without warning. She has shelter, food, friends in her class, and us. It's all a girl needs."

His depression stood no chance against Aria's relentless optimism—an optimism that might have saved them all. He still wondered in the darkness of night if he would have, on his own, stayed in the building long enough to let her guide Firestone into the crater. He wanted the answer to be yes, but he didn't think it was. "You're right. Thank you."

He kissed her, then retreated as Elora returned, beaming from all the attention and accolades her father's team had bestowed upon her.

She and Aria returned to the cart and worked their way farther across the fields. All around Underhill, food was brought to the farmers from the families helping in the kitchens. Once the light meal was complete, the farmers returned to their work. Radyn kept half an eye on his wife and child. The fields were safer now than they'd ever been. Some banti still roamed the area, but they rarely approached when so many humans were out.

It was a hard life, but Aria was right. It was a good one, too.

THAT NIGHT, after he'd successfully tucked Elora into bed, Radyn let himself out of their apartment. Aria was otherwise occupied, designing a new irrigation system for Underhill, and so there was little for him to do around the apartment. He wandered through the halls until he found the door he was looking for. He knocked and the door soon opened.

Jyn grinned when he saw who it was. "Did you come to visit, or for something more intense?"

"I wanted to see if you were getting soft."

Jyn snorted as Nikki came to the door. She gave Radyn a wary eye. "I know that look."

Radyn pointed at her stomach, which wasn't as full as Aria's, but wasn't that far behind, either. Elora was excited to have a sibling and a cousin to take care of soon. "It won't be long before he won't be able to get away."

Nikki rolled her eyes. "So long as you don't give him as many bruises as last time. He complained for a week."

"I'm afraid he didn't treat me much better."

She waved them away. "Go and have your fun."

Jyn planted a kiss on his wife's forehead before leaving. Once the door was closed and they were well down the hallway, the former Blade said, "To tell you the truth, I was thinking of coming to find you tonight. I've been in the mood to hit something."

"Rough day?"

"No more than usual. There's never enough food, and people always want more than we have. Balancing everyone's needs and wants takes everything, and Astram's a constant pain in my side. There are days when I wish I had the authority of the Blade and could just tell them what to do. This council is a nightmare."

At Radyn's look, he added. "And yes, I know it's the only way any of this works, but that doesn't mean I can't gripe about it to an old friend."

They came to a larger room with dozens of wooden weapons hanging on racks. Both Radyn and Jyn took swords and walked to the center.

"You think you're going to beat me this time?" Jyn asked.

"I beat you last time. This is your opportunity to redeem yourself."

Jyn chuckled, then attacked. Radyn noticed the shift in his weight a moment before the sword came racing for the side of his head, and his sword was there to parry. The wooden weapons clacked against one another, and Jyn's cut passed over Radyn's head.

He used the opening to cut back, but Jyn danced away as soon as his blow missed. They circled and struck, and Radyn was reminded that although Jyn spent too much of his day locked within Underhill's narrow halls and small rooms, the former Blade hadn't let any of his former training go to waste. Though he couldn't rely on shards for strength and speed, he was in as good a condition as anyone in Underhill.

What differences existed between them were slight. Radyn scored his fair share of blows, but each was answered in kind. When they reached the point that their exhaustion threatened their control of the weapons, they collapsed onto a bench. Jyn groaned as he rested the back of his head against the cool wall. "Nikki's going to be furious at you."

"Probably, but getting to train against you like this is worth the suffering she'll make me endure."

They sat in silence for a bit, each nursing their injuries.

Jyn's next question surprised Radyn. "With Nikki being pregnant, I'm thinking about the future a lot more. I hate to ask this, but do you think we're going to make it?"

The question landed harder than the blows Radyn had just endured at the end of Jyn's sword. To nurse his own private doubts was one thing, but to hear Jyn, who never gave up, ask the same, was almost more than Radyn could bear.

Aria's words from that afternoon, though, stuck with

him. Their work was never-ending, and there were days when hope was awfully hard to find.

He stood up and offered Jyn his hand. "That's up to us. Our future is anything but easy. Anything but guaranteed. The only way we'll survive is if we build something better. It's up to us to make that happen. It always has been."

Jyn looked at the extended hand, nodded once, then grasped it. Radyn pulled him to his feet, and the two stumbled out of the training hall, supporting one another as they found their way home.

THE ADVENTURES CONTINUE!

Top of the morning!

I hope that wherever you are in the world, this finds you doing well. Thanks for reading, and I hope you enjoyed the story. In an age of endless entertainment options, the choice to spend your time in these pages means the world to me.

Elegy of the Fallen Swords was an absolute pleasure to write. Radyn's story has come to a close, and I hope you've enjoyed your time among the floating cities.

Before you go, I'd encourage you to sign up for my newsletter. In a world where everybody seems to be spamming people every 20 minutes to make a dime, I'm trying to do something different. I email every two to three weeks, usually on a Friday, and I do everything I can to make the newsletter something you'll look forward to reading. Free short stories that expand the worlds. Special offers. Fun conversations with fans. It would mean the world to me if you came over and took a look. You can sign up here:

https://ryankirkauthor.com/pages/newsletter-sign-up

And once again, thank you for being here. You're awesome.

Ryan

December 2025

ACKNOWLEDGMENTS

No author works alone, and I'm reminded of that every time I go through the process of releasing a new book. From the team of editors that helps clean up my words to the graphic designers who turn my scribbles into cover art, what you hold in your hands is the work of a team of dedicated professionals. To all of you, thank you.

As always, a tremendous thanks to my family. None of this would be possible without them, and all of this is for them.

And finally, a very special thanks to those readers who are part of my ARC team - picking through these books for errors and being willing to leave reviews to bring new readers in. If I miss anyone, I'm sorry - the fault is my own.

Thanks in this book, especially to:

Terry

Neil

Chris

And one final, very special thank you to all of you reading. I couldn't do this without you.

Sincerely,

Ryan

ALSO BY RYAN KIRK
FIND THEM ALL AT RYANKIRKAUTHOR.COM

Saga of the Broken Gods

Band of Broken Gods

Fall of Forgotten Gods

Rise of the Resurrected God

Last Sword in the West

Last Sword in the West

Eyes of the Hidden World

A Sword Named Vengeance

Wraith's Revenge

Frontier's End

Song of the Sagani

Legend of the Last Sword in the West

Song of the Fallen Swords

These Fallen Swords

Night of Sword and Shield

The Song of Rising Shadow

The Silence Between the Songs

Elegy of the Fallen Swords

Oblivion's Gate

The Gate Beyond Oblivion

The Gates of Memory

The Gate to Redemption

Relentless

Relentless Souls

Heart of Defiance

Their Spirit Unbroken

The Nightblade Series

Nightblade

World's Edge

The Wind and the Void

Blades of the Fallen

Nightblade's Vengeance

Nightblade's Honor

Nightblade's End

Standalone Novels

Blades of Shadow

The Last Fang of God

Of Blood and Broken Dreams

The Primal Series

Primal Dawn

Primal Darkness

Primal Destiny

ABOUT THE AUTHOR

Ryan Kirk is the award-winning and internationally bestselling author of over forty fantasy novels spanning nearly a dozen worlds. He lives in Minnesota with his family, where he enjoys long, meandering walks outside even when the snow is high enough to cover his legs. When he isn't glued to his keyboard, he's usually in the woods, either on foot or on a bike.

RyanKirkAuthor.com
contact@waterstonemedia.net

facebook.com/waterstonemedia
x.com/waterstonebooks
instagram.com/waterstonebooks

9 781953 692573